PRAISE FOR CAT SCULLY

"Cat Scully's invited us all to a party you won't want to miss. *Below the Grand Hotel* is a bloody labyrinth filled with demons and desperation, sorrow and sacrifice. The real horror in these pages is how often we have to choose between suffering for our own sake, and suffering for the sake of others. Follow the author down into a glamorous hell, where damnation comes in every delicious flavor!"

— CHRISTOPHER GOLDEN, NEW YORK TIMES BESTSELLING AUTHOR OF *THE NIGHT BIRDS* AND *THE HOUSE OF LAST RESORT*

"Cat Scully has created an art deco inferno. *Below the Grand Hotel* is a gorgeous, sumptuous perdition gilded in blood and excess that would make F. Scott Fitzgerald sell his soul to spend just a night in one of its accursed chambers."

— CLAY MCLEOD CHAPMAN, AUTHOR OF *WAKE UP* AND *OPEN YOUR EYES*

"A starry-eyed nightmare, delicious and dark. Cat Scully's *Below the Grand Hotel* gives us gilded-aged horror at its finest. Do check in, darling. You may not want to leave."

— ROBERT P. OTTONE, AUTHOR OF *THE VILE THING WE CREATED* AND THE BRAM STOKER AWARD-WINNING NOVEL *THE TRIANGLE*

"Cat Scully's latest delivers the opulence of Fitzgerald's roaring twenties drenched in gallons of blood, but it's not all glitz, glamor, and gore. *Below the Grand Hotel* is an allegorical examination of the artist's plight, torn between craft and survival in a difficult world, with hordes of demons and a biblically-accurate angel. It's the bee's knees."

—TODD KEISLING, BRAM STOKER AWARD-NOMINATED AUTHOR OF *THE SUNDOWNER'S DANCE* AND *DEVIL'S CREEK*

"Like the vaudevillians who haunt these pages, Cat Scully is herself a multihyphenate entertainer, both a gifted visual artist and agile prose stylist. In *Below the Grand Hotel*, she puts her fierce imagination on full display, guiding readers through a hell as upsetting as it is beautiful, and wrestling with one big, uncomfortable question: What would you trade, to see your dreams come true?"

—SHAUN HAMILL, AUTHOR OF *THE DISSONANCE* AND *A COSMOLOGY OF MONSTERS*

BELOW THE GRAND HOTEL

Cover by Matthew Revert

ISBN: 9781960988584

CLASH Books

clashbooks.com

To every artist who has ever toiled away
making art in obscurity, wishing to be known.

Your work matters.
Your dreams matter.
You matter.

"I was within and without, simultaneously enchanted and repelled by the inexhaustible variety of life."

— *THE GREAT GATSBY,* F. SCOTT FITZGERALD

BELOW THE GRAND HOTEL

A NOVEL BY

CAT SCULLY

CHAPTER ONE

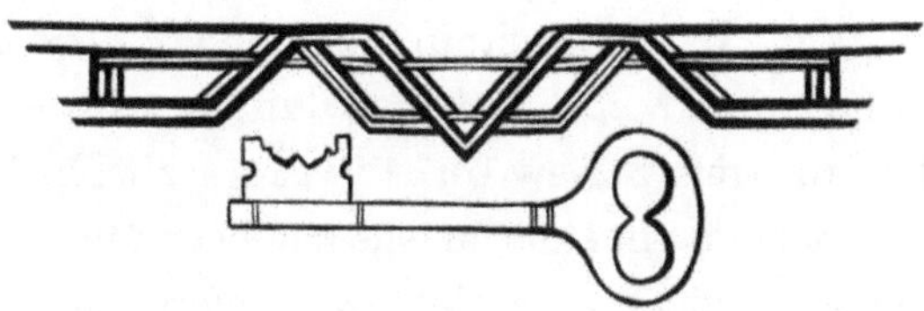

On the first night of April on the Upper East Side, a taxi rolled to a stop in front of the golden steps of the Grand Hotel. The bellhop rushed to open the taxi door as a tall wisp of a woman unfurled herself from the plush interior, stretching like a cat woken from its afternoon nap. A curl of her dark bob loosened from beneath her green cloche hat, a perfect match for her emerald silk dress that swished above heels so bright they reflected the city lights. The emerald woman lit a cigarette as the Grand's parade of uniformed porters unloaded suitcase after suitcase onto the curb. Her beau climbed from the taxi with a hand on his fedora to keep from losing it as he took in the impressive heights of New York City. He sported a tailored, navy-blue suit with thin pinstripes, an outfit that screamed new money more than the stars in his eyes as he dreamily lost himself in the city lights. The tall woman had to yank her man out of traffic to keep a Bentley from mowing him down.

As the emerald lady escorted the starry-eyed man into the glittering safety of the city's oldest and hottest hotel, the diamond around her neck winked at a girl who had watched the couple from across the street. The necklace was thick with pearls that met in a square yellow diamond at the center, a shape and color Mabel Rose Dixon had never seen before in her whole life.

They're perfect, Mabel thought.

She took a swig from her flask, careful to conceal the bathtub gin behind her menu before slipping the silver bottle back into her garter. Mabel had watched the couple from her view in the window box seat of the Café La Rose across the street. Hotel entrances were her favorite place to prowl on a Friday night. She could be invisible in such a busy scene, pick out the rubes—tourists with money burning a hole in their pockets. If she was careful, if she was clever, Mabel could make their money hers and be home within the hour. Luck had been harder to come by in 1925 than Mabel anticipated in the six weeks since she first stepped off the train in New York City. So, Mabel had resolved to make some luck of her own. Thus far, she had been pretty lucky. Seven wallets, six purses, and some family jewels swiped from the nightstand of a rich old lady had paid for a month of food and a small cot in the Richardson Boardinghouse for Women on the Upper West Side. She would take her spoils and then barter with the boy who worked the kitchen, trading her latest finds for cash and enough bathtub liquor to keep her senses sharp and line her skirts with crisp dollar bills. It wasn't the best hooch, but it was something until she could break into the big time.

Mabel checked her handbag. Two dollars left, and Ziegfeld wasn't holding auditions for his next show until the end of the following week. Mabel had heard a rumor that a Follie had bought her way in. Ziegfeld was always looking for the most dazzling jewelry and costumes for his shows. If Mabel had the right piece to offer, there were apparently ways a girl could coax a yes out of Ziegfeld after a scathing rejection.

She watched the couple disappear inside the double doors of the Grand. Mabel told herself those people wouldn't miss that necklace. Every person who had donated a lifted wallet, a stolen diamond, or a missing purse was a patron of an undiscovered Follie who just needed her big break. There wasn't a worthier cause than that. Besides, Mabel refused to give up, turn tail, and buy a one-way train ticket back home to Atlanta. She wasn't going to become a name that nobody remembered and a face everyone forgot. She was going to be the biggest thing to ever hit the stage, an "it girl," a goddamn regular Rosamund Pinchot. This couple was going to be just another addition to her roster of patrons, a list that grew longer by the week.

Mabel set down her menu. The motion caught the attention of a nearby waiter, who had hovered for the better part of an hour waiting for Mabel to order something besides a single cup of tea with lemon.

"Can I get you something to eat, miss?"

"Sorry, Charlie. My date's just gone in the wrong door with another girl. I've got to scram if I want to catch that lousy sob. You understand."

Mabel left her chair in such a rush that her paper menu fell to the floor with a clack. In three steps, she was back out on the street and in the midst of the kaleidoscope of amusements that New York had to offer. She breathed in the floral perfume of the fashionable ladies, passed beneath a blinking sign that advertised the Ziegfeld Follies' latest show at the New Amsterdam, and got a whistle from a group of dapper men in neat suits. She held onto her little red cloche hat as she scurried across the road. Her heels clicked as she weaved between motorcars. A horn honked at her, followed by a couple of whoops. She blew one of the drivers a kiss as she crossed traffic. Mabel could spare a moment for the little people.

In the weeks she had spent becoming a successful thief, Mabel had made a particular study of the hotel clientele. Guests were always in a hurry but so unsure of where they were, making them easy to distract. They were her favorite patrons, though she was hesitant to enter the hotel for fear of getting caught. Catching people as they came or went was preferable. Still, that couple had just walked away with the biggest diamond Mabel had ever seen. She could finally catch her big break with Ziegfeld and never have to wander the streets at night stealing her way to stardom again. She could break her "no entering hotels" rule just this once. After tonight, if she was successful, she'd never have to steal again.

Mabel went through her mental catalog of roles and picked the part of an heiress meeting her friends for a late room party. As she strode up the marble steps into the Grand, Mabel carried herself as if she wore diamonds and furs, not a red party dress stolen from Ziegfeld's costume department. She passed a doorman around her age who fit the cut of the Grand's black and gold uniform real swell, but he had deep circles around his baby blues as if he hadn't slept in weeks. His dark hair was swept back beneath his black and gold cap, which he tipped as she approached. The gesture made a small blush color her cheeks. If she wasn't in such a hurry, she would have considered sparing a moment to flirt.

"Good evening, miss." The bellhop gave her a little smirk as he leaned in to open the glass door for her.

"Don't know if it's good yet," she said and winked at him. "It's just getting started."

"Be careful, miss," he said, dropping his voice low so only she could hear. "Don't stay long or you will never leave."

She was so taken aback by his comment that Mabel faltered in the doorway. She collected herself and sniffed at the doorman.

"Try a new pickup line," she said, eyes fluttering. "This one ain't working."

He grinned at her as she passed and tilted his cap. "Sorry to have been a bother, miss. Watch yourself."

She ignored him as she descended into the lobby. Mabel's stomach fluttered as she entered the Grand for the first time. She had dreamed of passing through its golden doors many times, and she likely wouldn't be able to return once the grift was complete. She had to concentrate hard to keep in character and not gawk at the lobby. Her heels clacked over ornate, spiraling patterns of tiny black and white tiles. She slipped by statues of angels in flight blowing great trumpets, mermaids rising above crashing waves on the sea, men with swords of fire, and women with vines in their hair and leaves on their breasts. Together, these elemental statues held up the arched white ceiling and the enormous glass chandelier at the lobby's center.

Mabel felt more than one set of eyes on her as she drifted through the crowd. It was part of the reason she had never been inside the Grand. Mabel had made a rule to never enter hotels on the off chance the staff might remember a thief. Already, various eyes were questioning why Mabel was there. She would enjoy it while it lasted—a quick trip to the ritziest place she had ever seen, and then back to the streets. The necklace was worth the risk. It was just what she needed to get a place in the Follies and ensure she didn't need to worry about where her dough was coming from. The Grand was so lovely Mabel didn't know if she could trust herself to stay away after the job was done.

A trio of ladies dressed in matching black Patou coats gave Mabel a cursory glance as she passed. They peered at her bright red dress up and down with a sneer, as if the color was far too gaudy to be seen in public. Let them ogle, the old birds. She had a necklace to find.

Mabel scanned the lobby for the lucky couple. She passed an old man in a button-down shirt and suspenders with a ruddy face. He fanned the sweat beading on his forehead with his boater hat. His clothes and demeanor were so painfully Southern, Mabel wondered for a split second if she had somehow wandered all the way home to Atlanta.

"It's powerful warm in here," he said to Mabel as she passed. "I know I asked to never feel the touch of cold weather again, but this is ridiculous."

Mabel didn't have the foggiest what he was talking about. It was April 1st, not the middle of August when all of New York baked in the hot summer sun. Mabel refused to be sidetracked and made to feel awkward while she was adopting the persona of an heiress. She raised her nose. "You don't say. I find the lobby a bit chilly."

He chuckled at her comment. "I fear this heat has nothing to do with the temperature indoors. I brought this curse upon myself. This heat will plague me endlessly unless I can strike a new bargain with the powers that be. If I cannot, the coming of May will surely be my demise. Be careful what you wish for, young lady."

She was so distracted by him that Mabel didn't see the old woman in a great feathered hat and Victorian dress until the woman bumbled directly into Mabel's back.

"I beg your pardon," Mabel said, her Southern manners instinctively getting the better of her. She straightened her posture and threw herself back into the character of an heiress. "What business do you have running into me like that?"

"Please, miss. Forgive me. I did not see you there." The unfashionable old woman dug in her purse, tearful as she apologized. Mabel was about to tell the old lady to beat it, suppressing the pity that twisted in her stomach for the woman who clearly was still stuck in the past. "I need but a moment of your time."

The old woman pulled out a small packet wrapped in white paper, bound together with simple twine. The contents seeped red liquid all over her gloved hands.

"Please, dear." The old woman's voice tore like a piece of paper as she pleaded with her sunken eyes. She thrust the leaking package at Mabel. "Please. Take my heart. I have to give it to someone."

Mabel backed away, unsure what she meant. "No, thank you. I'm sorry, but I'm in a hurry—"

The old woman grabbed Mabel by the wrist. Even with her gloved hands, Mabel could tell the woman was colder than she should be. "I gave my heart to Frank, but he wouldn't return my affections. I begged him to end my agony. Let me love someone, anyone else. Let me give my heart to anyone else. I didn't know he'd take my words literally."

Mabel twisted her wrist until it came free from the woman's bony grip. The package dripped bright red onto the floor and immediately started to congeal. She had seen red like that before when her father slaughtered a pig for the holidays. Mabel couldn't look at the bleeding red package. Her imagination was running away with her.

The old woman thrust the package at her again. "Won't you help an old woman? See? I even wrapped it for you. Please. Take it. No one else will. Have a heart?"

Blood or no blood, Mabel couldn't stop to care what the old doll was going on about. It wasn't her concern. She wasn't going to blow her one chance at a score in the Grand on a crazy dame. She turned on her heel and trotted off to the other side of the lobby, acting as if she hadn't heard the woman at all. Her mother would have taken a switch to her for such bad manners, but it couldn't be helped. Surely it couldn't be a real heart—could it?

A shadow fell across Mabel's back. She turned to face a man who blotted out the chandelier's brilliant light, like the moon eclipsing the sun. His square jaw and high cheekbones were handsome, but unconventional, as if his face had been carved by chisel put to stone. His form was also all hard angles, brought out more sharply by his black and graying hair. He sported the typical Grand uniform colors, but his suit was a custom dinner cut rather than a standard cut to accommodate his wide shoulders and narrow hips. His fingers were long and well-manicured, but beneath his tailored suit were a pair of muscular arms that could rival Ziegfeld's first star, former strongman Eugene Sandow. The fabric was inlaid with gold accents, leaves chasing birds in mid-flight. There were six small stars on each of his lapels.

His name tag read: Raymond Black.

"Welcome to the Grand Hotel. I'm Raymond, the Concierge. What do you desire?"

The man's voice was so soft and hypnotic that Mabel's head swam. His narrow hazel eyes held a hint of gold in their center that seemed to wink at Mabel like a facet in a diamond. She shook it off, collected herself, and deepened her voice so it would mask her drawl and drip with money instead. "Thank you, but I'm terribly late meeting some dear, old friends."

Something flickered behind his honey-brown eyes. "I keep a very detailed record of everyone staying in this hotel. Might I help you locate them?"

At the other end of the lobby, the emerald lady entered the dining hall with her absent-minded beau. Mabel smiled and forced her body to relax into her lie. "I wouldn't want to be a bother. In fact, I believe that's my party entering the dining hall now. If you will excuse me."

She gave a curt bow and left before Raymond could ask her another question. Mabel didn't stop or make eye contact with anyone, debating if she should turn back and abandon the plan altogether, until she reached the dining hall.

The curtained hall was the loveliest dining room Mabel had ever seen, filled to the brim with a variety of bright, tropical plants she couldn't even begin to name. The vast room was decorated with stone water fountains and various statues, all of them depicting horned Dionysus standing in various poses with similar coy expressions. Mabel passed circular tables packed with people in their best dining jackets and dresses. At the back of the room, a waterfall churned behind an extravagant buffet laid with every dish imaginable. Mabel had to press her lips together hard to keep her mouth from watering. She didn't want to think about when the last time she had eaten a full meal was. The answer was far too long ago.

Mabel took a step to pass through the latticework entrance and was stopped by the maître d', a short black man with a thin mustache in a white suit. His name tag read Samuel Lewis, and he was the first staff member who seemed happy she was there. No, not happy. Bemused.

"Can I help you?" he offered in a warm voice that dripped like honey.

She leaned closer to the door as if searching for someone. "I'm here to meet my party in the dining hall. I'm quite late."

Samuel grinned at her, confused. "Miss, I'm sorry, but you need a room to have a table tonight. You and I both know you do not have a room."

She lifted her chin. "Not even friends of guests? What kind of place doesn't let people eat?"

Her Southern accent slipped back in, and Mabel closed her mouth so fast her teeth clacked. Samuel's brow knit together in a thin crease. He gave a nearby bellhop the slightest of nods and turned back to her, grinning wide. "I'm very sorry for your trouble. Perhaps we can come to some arrangement, find a suitable room at a suitable price?"

Mabel started to cry. It was one of her most readily available emotions, a real crowd pleaser, but she pulled back before the tears became too much. She didn't want to drown her adoring audience as she planned her escape. She would excuse herself to the ladies and slip out the front. Losing the necklace would sting, but there were other pockets she could pick in the city tonight—less complicated ones.

She felt a hand on her shoulder. The woman draped in emerald was so much taller up close and she towered over Mabel. Her cigarette smoked at the end of her gloved fingers, and her perfume lingered around her in a spicy musk that reminded Mabel of church incense. The yellow diamond sparkled like fire around her neck. Mabel found it difficult not to stare at the array of pale, gold lights twinkling inside the gorgeous princess cut. The yellow diamond held more facets than she had ever seen.

"I believe the lady is with us."

"Of course, Ms. Greene," Samuel said with a bow. "Friends of the house are always welcome. Shall I make a setting?"

Ms. Greene slid a small, velvet bag across the podium into

Samuel's hands. "We'll be dining upstairs tonight. Can you send up an ice bucket?"

Samuel's mustache twitched. Mabel could have sworn he was suppressing a laugh. "Very good, Ms. Greene."

"Glad you could make our meeting." She turned her smoky eyes to Mabel. "You need not call me Ms. Greene. The name's Evelyn."

Evelyn held out her hand to Mabel. Her long nails were painted with nail lacquer in a moon manicure. *How in vogue*, Mabel thought as she accepted the handshake.

"I'm Mabel. Mabel Rose Dixon."

Evelyn raised a flawless eyebrow. "A perfect name for a stage darling."

A bead of cold sweat gathered at the base of Mabel's spine. When Evelyn let go of her hand, Mabel gawked and quickly collected herself. How could she know Mabel's hopes and dreams?

"We're leaving, Martin," Evelyn called to her man, not bothering to introduce him.

Martin rose, abandoning their table and striding across the hall to meet them. "Change of plans, Evie darling?"

"We will be dining upstairs tonight," Evelyn said. "Our friend Mabel looks like she hasn't had a proper meal in weeks."

"Excellent idea." When he turned to Mabel, he smiled at her as if she were the sunrise. Mabel's toes curled involuntarily as Martin bowed and kissed the back of her hand. "Shall we, miss...? I didn't catch your name."

"Mabel." She had planned to use one of her typical character names—Betty or Theta—but Evelyn had ruined all of that. "Mabel Rose Dixon."

"Well, Mabel." Martin tucked his hat under his arm and held out his elbow to escort her. "I can guarantee if you will do us the pleasure of dining together tonight, you're going to have a grand old time. Why, it might even be the most fortuitous meeting of your whole life."

"Sounds jake," she said. As Mabel followed the couple to the elevator, she found herself wondering what she had gotten herself into. She was a great thief, had made a dozen successful getaways in a matter of weeks. Why was she so nervous? Was she the one still in control?

CHAPTER TWO

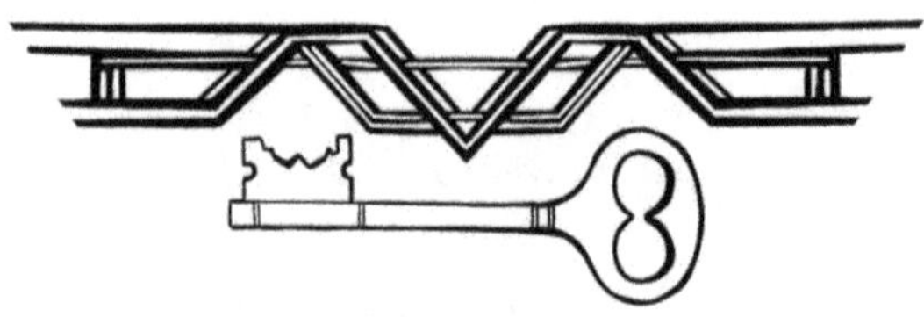

Evelyn pressed the call button and leaned on the wall beside the elevator cage door, slowly expelling another drag on her cigarette as she watched Mabel.

"So, you two in town for business or pleasure?" Mabel offered to get the conversation rolling again.

Evelyn held the smoke in for a moment before puffing out a long, trailing cloud. "Business, and pleasure. We're guests of Frank West."

Mabel tried her damnedest not to let her eyes go wide. Frank West was not only the sole heir to the Grand Hotel, but a series of hotels around the country. She had only been in town a couple weeks, but Mabel had already heard of the infamous West family and their annual lavish party. All the papers could talk about for the past month was the reclusive nineteen-year-old and the hotel empire left to his name, even though he had slunk away from the limelight the moment his parents had disappeared. The girls at Richardson Boardinghouse for Women on the Upper West Side were abuzz with the recent disappearance of Henry and Lillian West, who had vanished under mysterious circumstances and left everything to their son Frank. Likely, a bad deal with the mob on their bootleg liquor, Mabel thought. Everyone at the boarding house was scouring the papers daily for news if Frank would still carry on his parents' tradition of hosting the

Grand's annual May's Eve Ball later this month, which had always been open invitation.

Despite his recent seclusion, Frank was still one of the most sought-after bachelors in all of New York City. No one had been invited to the Grand as his personal guest, at least, not to Mabel's limited knowledge. For some reason though, he had invited Evelyn and Martin Greene. Mabel did not need to find out Frank's plans. She needed to steal the diamond and be on her merry way, but still, it had piqued her curiosity.

"His personal guest? Are you here for the May's Eve Ball?" Mabel pried.

Evelyn's eyebrows raised as she drew close to Mabel's ear and whispered a husky "yes."

The wolfish look on Evelyn's face made the hairs on the back of Mabel's neck stand on end. "What about you, little mouse? Are you here to help prepare for the May's Eve Ball? Or does Frank have you running some other errand? What crack did you scurry through to find your way into this opulent den of sin?"

Mabel backed away, but Martin quickly scooped her arm into his and held fast. There wasn't anywhere to go. "My business is my own."

Evelyn draped her long form against the wall. "Not for long, stage darling."

Mabel flushed, partly from anger, partly from mortification. Who did this dame think she was? She didn't know how Evelyn found out about her dreams, but Mabel wasn't going to let Evelyn rattle her. Mabel was grateful the elevator bell rang and announced its arrival to the ground floor, or she might have popped Evelyn on the jaw.

The cage doors clacked open, revealing an operator no older than fourteen. The sleeves on his uniform hung a little too big and a little too long. He was the same age as her little sister, Maryanne. Her heart clenched with the unexpected, violent reminder of how quickly she had fled home without a goodbye. Mabel hoped the city wouldn't chew him up and spit his good heart out the way it had done to her.

The kid placed his hand on the round crank as Evelyn and Martin led Mabel inside. "Which floor are we going to, folks?"

"Fifteen. Honeymoon suite," Evelyn said, and couldn't have possibly been more bored. She apparently found Mabel far more interesting. The way Evelyn stared hungrily at Mabel gave her the heebie-jeebies.

Mabel turned her attention entirely to Martin. “So, where are you two from?”

“Down South,” he said.

Mabel beamed. “I’m Southern too. From Atlanta, originally. What part of the South are you from?”

Martin started to open his mouth, but Evelyn shot him a look so scathing, he clammed up. The rickety iron clicked through every level as they rose in awkward silence, which was fine with Mabel because it gave her time to think of how she was going to swipe that necklace. In a crowd, there were so many more distractions that could cause one to find a piece of jewelry suddenly missing. In an elevator, there was only so much she could do. Mabel was going to have to swipe the yellow diamond using only herself as a distraction once they got to the hotel room.

There was only one reason a couple would invite an innocent-looking girl such as herself up to their suite. Mabel wasn’t interested in a petting party or whatever freaky thing they were into. She would get them talking, let them think she was into having a fling with both of them, and then swiping the necklace should be duck soup.

When they reached the top, the young operator glanced back at Mabel with sorry eyes. It gave her the briefest sensation that she should run, but Mabel shook the feeling off like a dirty old coat. Mabel had nothing to worry about. She had charmed her “patrons” before and, she could do it again. She just needed to stay sharp, stay smart. Mabel couldn’t let the bellhop’s doubts get the best of her. She kept her focus on the diamond as the bellhop opened the door.

Evelyn glided out first. Each of her wide, perfect strides were easily three of Mabel’s steps.

Evelyn, already halfway down the hall, pivoted on her heel. “Do keep up, will you? At this rate, the ice will melt before we reach the room.”

“Absolutely, darling.” Martin slipped his arm through Mabel’s and led her out of the elevator. He strode with Mabel arm-in-arm down the hall at a clip that she struggled to keep up with. Mabel didn’t know why they were in such a rush. Evelyn had just ordered the ice before they left. How could it already be waiting upstairs before they arrived? Unless the words "ice bucket" were code for something else.

"I'm thirsty," Evelyn pouted as they joined her. "And you know how I like my drinks *cold*."

Martin tightened his grip on Mabel's arm as he quickened his pace. "Patience, dear."

Ice bucket was pos-o-tutely code for something else.

Evelyn produced a hotel key seemingly out of thin air and unlocked the suite door. As she trotted inside, Martin wasted no time pulling Mabel in tow. He released her the moment they were in the room, planting her in a plush chair as if she were an unruly child.

The room was as posh as Mabel had come to expect from the Grand. Pink peonies and tiger lilies adorned the round dining table and each of the side tables in the large sitting room.

Reaching deco arches and statues of more Greek gods led to the bedroom beyond. Mabel peered in. The plush bed was decorated with dozens of black and gold pillows, embroidered smartly with a prominent letter "G."

"No need to be shy," Evelyn said.

Mabel didn't have to be told twice. She wandered deeper into the bedroom, ran her hand along the velvet chaise lounge, let her eyes fall across the painting of Aphrodite and Cupid in secret conversation, and was not shy about inspecting the excellent craftsmanship it took to build the armoire. Her brother would have gone goofy to see how beautiful the carvings of angels were in its wood face, but she didn't want to think about Avery and his furniture business right now. In the bathroom, a porcelain tub with gold clawed feet sat atop black marble. It was so big Mabel wondered if two people could swim in it.

Evelyn approached the bar cart, already fully stocked with bootlegged liquor. "Drink, Mabel?"

"That would be swell," Mabel said.

Evelyn took a glass decanter filled with dark caramel-colored liquor and poured it into two delicate glass tumblers. Because of the size of the room and the ample supply of booze, Frank was treating the couple as his most prized guests. Evelyn and Martin Greene must either be members of the wealthy elite, or some kind of celebrity.

Evelyn handed a glass to Mabel. She accepted the drink and

sipped it, but not too eagerly. Mabel needed to play coy. She decided to throw a stone into the waters of their intentions and see what rippled below the surface.

"So," Mabel said. "Ain't we having a petting party, or are we going to stare longingly at each other all night?"

Evelyn laughed and it was like a distant church bell on a hill, sweet and loud. "You're right. Martin? Keep her company. I need to slip into something more comfortable."

She unhooked the necklace and laid it on the bedside table with a thud. Evelyn vanished into the bathroom without so much as a backward glance. Mabel couldn't believe her luck. The necklace was right there, alone, defenseless—but why? Why would Evelyn leave something so precious just sitting there? Didn't matter. She edged closer to it.

Martin set his fedora down on a small side table. "So, Mabel, tell me more about yourself."

"I want to be a Ziegfeld girl," Mabel said. She stopped, surprised at herself for blurting out such a personal truth. She knew better than to break character, but Mabel couldn't seem to lie to him. Mabel tried to open her mouth and tell him something a wealthy heiress would say, but her words turned to taffy in her mouth every time she tried. It must be the liquor getting to her head. She decided to play coy instead. "There's not much to tell."

Martin took off his jacket, one sleeve at a time. "Well, that's not true at all. In fact, I find you fascinating. A Ziegfeld girl, eh? Who are you?"

He reached for her hand and drew it up to his mouth. She expected him to kiss the back of her hand, so she let her wrist go limp in his grip. Martin took Mabel's fingers and pressed them against his lips. He let his tongue play over the tips of her fingers.

Mabel didn't like where this was going. She had implied a petting party, but that had been all a part of the act. There had been men in her life, ones who had tried to take advantage ever since she landed starry-eyed in New York by herself. She was a smart girl and learned quickly. She knew what predatory signs to look for after surviving Gotham's worst. Mabel had kept herself safe by being clever, staying out of situations that could easily turn foul, but she felt herself pulled helplessly into Martin's gravity. She needed to keep him talking, edge her way around the room, grab the necklace, and run before things turned hot and heavy.

"I'm not anyone of consequence."

He grinned. "That's not true. You're holding back. Let me help you... open up."

Mabel withdrew her hand, but Martin held fast. He bit down hard on the tip of one of her fingers. She yelped as she withdrew. There was a little bead of blood where one of his teeth punctured the flesh of her pointer finger.

"You bit me!" Mabel kept her tone naive, not wanting Martin to know she was afraid. "Why did you do that?"

"Because you're delectable." Martin unraveled his tie and tossed it over the back of a chair. He smoothed back a bit of hair that had fallen out of place. "And because you're not telling me the truth. I want to know who you are. A girl with a hunger for the lights of the stage? What could be more interesting? You have a gift for the sleight of hand. I see you playing cards. You're a card shark—no, the image is clear. You're a magician! Yes, that's right. You even played the starring act in your local county fair. Mabel the Magnificent, a genuine female magician."

Mabel froze. She stared at him with wide eyes, couldn't help it. No one knew the secret she kept locked inside her heart. "I'm... not a magician anymore."

"And why is that? I thought being the greatest female magician on the New York stage was your dream? Or did you come here and find out there was no way for a girl from Atlanta to stand out? That the market was saturated with players. You discovered vaudeville was a dying art. Your dream was dead, and yet, you found a new dream."

A cold sweat beaded between Mabel's shoulder blades. "I'm auditioning with Ziegfeld next week. I'm going to be a chorus girl." Her tone was almost defensive as the unwilling truth spilled out of her like water leaking out of a cracked vase. She couldn't help but tell him.

"Only a chorus girl?" Martin took his time strolling to the bar cart and Mabel kept herself as far away from him as possible. How was he pulling words from her lips, ones she had never told anyone? She told herself not to panic as he poured himself a glass. "No, you came to

New York to be a genuine star. A headliner. You tried Ziegfeld and got turned away. You went for the lead a few weeks back, and Ziegfeld turned you down cold."

There was no way he could know any of this. Something was definitely wrong. He had watched her, staked her out, something. He had tasted her blood. This wasn't a petting party. This was something much worse. Mabel needed an out, and fast. She edged a little closer to the diamond.

"Ziegfeld is a close friend of ours," Martin said. "We could convince him to set you up with something better, a lead audition. Be the star instead of the chorus girl. We can say we knew you when."

"Sounds jake," Mabel said. She was almost to the table with the diamond now. The door was only a few steps beyond that. All she had to do was leap and it would be hers. "I can't thank you enough, but why would you do that for someone you just met?"

"Because your talent goes unrecognized, my dear." Martin's grin spread too far up his face, pulling back into too many lines around his teeth. "Aren't you tired of people not seeing you? The real you? Your parents never understood you were a star, and now neither does Ziegfeld. He will never see how you stand out from the crowd. I can change all of that... if you let me."

She didn't know what to make of Martin. How did he see right into her heart, into her past where she was the eldest daughter of twelve children? Easily forgotten and ignored as it came time for her to assume the path her parents had set out for her at fourteen. She didn't want to marry a neighboring farm boy, clean his house, bear his children. That wasn't Mabel's future, and it never had been. It was so tempting to be seen, to actually be heard and understood, but she needed to keep focused and resist. No one could give her everything she ever dreamed of with a snap of their fingers, no matter how big they talked.

"Of course, it will cost you." He unbuttoned the top button on his collar.

"I'm a modern girl," Mabel said, setting her bourbon down next to the diamond. "But not that modern."

Martin laughed, but it didn't sound natural. It was more like a violin missing a note, a horrible sound and inhuman. "Then why are you here? You don't need to pick pockets anymore. If you want to be a stage darling, I can give you your dream. All it will cost is the thing you value most."

"I'm no virgin, buster," she said. "And I'm nobody's fool, but you're right. You can give me everything I ever wanted." Mabel grabbed the diamond.

"Stop!" Martin screeched.

"Thanks for the dough!" She booked it for the door

"Thief! Give it back!" His voice had turned into nails scraping across glass. Were his eyes still the same shade of blue, or were they now a pale red?

Mabel jimmied the doorknob, but it wouldn't open. She put her weight into it, but the door remained stubbornly jammed.

She wheeled back to Martin, expecting him to be on top of her already, but he wasn't. He was taking his time lumbering toward her as if he knew she couldn't leave, and he was still unbuttoning. Something moved beneath his buttoned shirt, thick as a coiled snake. He kept unbuttoning his shirt, faster and faster, until his whole chest was laid bare before her.

There was a mouth where his stomach should be, wide as a shark, and filled with rows of every size of jagged, yellow teeth. The snake beneath his shirt had been a fat, red tongue. It rolled around, licking curled lips with gray saliva as the mouth bit at the air, jaws snapping.

At the sight of him, Mabel felt as if she had been pushed off a cliff into an icy lake and couldn't find her way back up for air. She couldn't find her breath, couldn't scream, couldn't react at all. He was a living nightmare.

The bathroom door flew open, startling Mabel so much she let out the scream she had been holding in.

Evelyn emerged from the bathroom dressed only in a sheer robe, revealing what had been hidden beneath her high-collared dress. Her second mouth was wider than Martin's and split the skin just below her neck bone, shoulder-to-shoulder. Teeth littered the space above her breasts like pearls in a shoulder epaulet. Her nails were long, exquisite blades at the end of her elongated fingers.

"Martin," she simpered. "How dare you start the fun without me?"

The purple tongue inside Evelyn's second mouth lolled as Mabel's scream reached new heights. Evelyn laughed uproariously at Mabel's fear until she caught sight of what she clutched in her hand.

"My necklace," Evelyn screamed. "Give it back."

Mabel had nearly forgotten she was still holding the diamond. She slammed her hand on the doorknob, twisting and pleading for the lock to open up. There was a sudden, sharp pain in her abdomen. Mabel glanced down at the black, thin blades poking out of her stomach. Her blood bloomed into a dark, crimson stain in the middle of her dress. Evelyn's long nails had pierced through her back and emerged out the other side just below her ribcage. The violence was so swift, Mabel's brain didn't register what had happened, but only for a moment. Her knees gave, and she collapsed.

"You stole from the wrong woman." Evelyn towered over her with bloody claws. "Give me back my diamond."

Mabel coughed hard and blood sputtered down her chin. "Take it."

Anger flashed in Evelyn's green eyes. "No. You must *give* it to me!"

There came a knock at the door, interrupting Evelyn's rage. *A guest? At this hour?* Mabel thought absurdly. The door swung open to reveal Raymond Black. He stood in the doorway beside a statuesque young man in a gray suit. Mabel's vision swam, but she recognized the other man even though she had only seen him in photographs splashed across newspaper headlines.

Frank West's brunette hair was slicked back against his head with pomade. His fair eyes were the same winter-storm gray as his pinstripe suit, but his pocket square and matching tie offset his pale attire with a dangerous red shade that reminded Mabel of fresh blood. Her hands instinctively clutched her stomach, though she did not know what good it would do.

"My dear, Evelyn." Frank's voice was filled with unexpected warmth as he kneeled and placed a gentle hand on Mabel's shoulder. "You were about to lose the necklace."

"Hardly," Evelyn scoffed as she licked Mabel's blood from her nails. "I had things well in hand."

"And once taken, you could only get the diamond back if the girl offered it freely."

Frank turned his attention back to Mabel. He took her hand in his and drew Mabel close to him. He smelled so good, like warm tobacco and just a bite of whiskey. Mabel's face flushed in spite of herself. "I hate to be the bearer of bad news. You're dying. Imminently."

"I'm dying?" she asked, ridiculously. She couldn't die. Mabel was far too young to pass through the pearly gates. She had so much left to live for, so much left to do. This couldn't be how she met her maker, but the pain in her stomach had taken over her every thought. She found it hard to think of anything else.

"May I?" Frank said. He drew her hand up to his lips, as Martin had done. Mabel flinched. "A quick taste and I shall be able to help you. Do I have your permission?"

Mabel blinked at him through the pain. "What?"

"If I sample your blood, I will know what you require, and I can save your life. May I?"

Mabel did not know what he meant, but her head was swimming too much to care. What did she have to lose? "Yes. You have my permission."

Frank licked blood off the back of her hand. Mabel wasn't sure how it had gotten there. Her other hand clutched her stomach as if it could keep all the blood inside, but the carpet around her back had grown warm, and her body was starting to feel so very, very cold.

Frank closed his eyes for a moment, savoring. "So, your name is Mabel Rose Dixon. You fled Atlanta, Georgia. Ziegfeld turned you down cold. Stage performance truly is a dying art. You know all too well what I mean. It's just like what happened to you with your magic routine, isn't it? You're too talented to waste on death. I would like to help."

Everyone seemed to know what was inside her heart. Frank, Martin, Evelyn—they all knew too much about Mabel and her past. Was she that easy to read? No. They were something else, something otherworldly. Martin, Evelyn, and now Frank had all drank her blood. She knew what they were. She had seen vampires played in enough films and read about them in her brother's dime *Weird Tales* magazine.

"You're vampires." Mabel coughed, sputtering a bit of blood Frank immediately wiped away with a flick of his handkerchief from his breast pocket.

Evelyn and Martin laughed uproariously, but Frank's eyes never left Mabel. He did not so much as crack a smile.

"I'm afraid not, dear Mabel," Frank said. "This is not how I generally like to offer my deals. Stardom is easy enough to provide, but you're also dying. It will not be easy to bring you back. I will require something of equal weight in exchange. I must ask for you to come work for the Grand Hotel, and I must ask for... your soul."

Mabel's breath hitched with pain. He had to be joking. There was no way he had just asked her for what she thought he had asked her. No one could take souls except...

Mabel swallowed hard as her stomach sank. No, they weren't vampires. She knew the truth, and it was far worse than any fiction she could conjure. Mabel knew their name from every Sunday she had been dragged to church, from every time her mother crossed herself before she warned Mabel that the devil made liquor to turn good men's hearts evil.

"You're demons." Mabel's mouth had gone too dry to say another word.

Frank's bemused smile in confirmation was almost worse than the laughter Evelyn and Martin had given in response.

"Think of us more as... simple patrons of the arts," Frank's perfect grin was a little too wide. "Not the kind you know from your bible studies back on that dusty farm you called home. I want to cut you a deal, and it's better than any you're going to get outside of these doors. I will offer you fame. I will offer you the starring role at the Grand's theater. Headliner every night. I will offer you a life, and your dream."

Mabel's head swam from the blood loss. She had to admit it to herself. She was dying. There was no way out. She was going to have to make a choice. She didn't care much for faith or the messaging of fire-and-brimstone preachers, but faced with the new reality, Mabel had to admit to herself that she hadn't stopped believing in some kind of higher power. She hadn't stopped believing she had a soul and that it went somewhere after she died. And she was dying now. Frank's form was but a fuzzy outline of gray shapes.

"I would take his generous offer if I were you," Evelyn said. She and Martin exchanged a knowing grin. "If you refuse, you will make the most delectable feast."

"Refuse him, and we will make a meal of your flesh," Martin said. His second mouth in the pit of his stomach salivated. Drool splattered on the carpet between his legs. "Then your soul, piece by piece."

"Not so fast, Martin. Her will is so delectable. We should savor the taste of her soul."

Mabel was damned. Either she must choose to give her soul willingly to a demon, or these demons would eat her, body and soul. She closed her eyes, unable to keep them open.

"Stay with me, Mabel," Frank said. "Choose. You have but moments. Do you accept the deal? Do you give me your soul, freely?"

She wasn't meant to die right here, right now, but it was her immortal soul they were talking about. If these *beings* were truly demons, that would mean hell was real, and her soul really would be damned to everlasting torment if she took Frank's deal. Once her soul was gone, there was no getting it back. At least, that's what her preacher thundered across the pulpit every Sunday morning. But if she died, there was no future to look forward to. No stage lights. No fame. No fortune. No more Mabel the Magnificent. She really would be a face no one remembered and a name everyone forgot. She couldn't give up this life. Not now. Not when she had come all this way so far from home and given everything to be the next It Girl. At least if she was alive, she still had a chance.

Mabel opened her eyes. "Yes. I give you my soul."

Frank held out his hand. "First, the necklace."

Mabel placed the heavy yellow diamond in his solid hand.

"Now offer me your soul, and we will have an accord."

"I offer you my soul, freely."

Frank's fingers wrapped around the massive necklace. He placed Mabel's hand over his until their hands were entwined around the yellow diamond. "Done."

Frank let go of Mabel's hands and the diamond to address his concierge. "Heal her."

Raymond, who had been a silent witness to their conversation, came to kneel beside Mabel. He placed a very cold hand on Mabel's chest. Something warm swelled in Mabel's stomach and rushed up inside of her. She breathed out and choked when the breath came without pain. Mabel's hands traveled over where the dark red stain had once been smeared across her stomach. The wound and blood were gone. Her dress and skin were repaired as if nothing had happened.

Raymond pressed down on Mabel's chest. Wind picked up around her hair and fluttered around her dress. As Raymond pressed his thin fingers against her ribcage, something warm swelled inside her bones. Mabel took a deep breath in as the pressure beneath Raymond's hand turned so hot Mabel thought she was going to cry out in pain. Just as she was about to beg Raymond to stop, a ball of light the size of a golf ball left the center of her. The orb floated into Raymond's hands. He took the ball and pressed it into his open hand, morphing the pliable light as if it were clay.

Mabel watched in horror as Raymond opened his palm and produced the largest silver coin she had ever seen. There was an image of something on its surface, but Raymond slipped the coin inside a purple velvet pouch and tucked it inside his breast pocket so fast Mabel couldn't make it out.

"You turned my soul into a coin," Mabel said. She felt downright vigorous, as if she had slept a whole week. She pushed herself up, refusing a hand from both Frank and Raymond. She came to stand on her own. It was only then Mabel realized she was still holding the heavy diamond necklace.

Frank frowned. "Souls are made of silver. He merely cooled it."

"Raymond," Frank said. "Make a note of the deal."

"Of course." With a flick of his wrist, Raymond whipped out a scroll of paper, unveiling a parchment several feet long. He scribbled down something fast with a quill pen and stuffed everything back inside his jacket. "Thirty days. One hundred souls."

"A hundred souls?" Mabel said. "That wasn't part of the deal."

"I told you. I require your assistance. I need more than just your soul. Equivalent exchange. It took a great deal of effort to bring you back to life." Frank nodded at the yellow diamond between her fingers. "Besides, the diamond chose you, Mabel. No one else. No one could have stolen it so successfully from two of the highest-ranking demons in this hotel. It has a mind of its own, and it's clear you were meant to be the Canary's caretaker. What it requires are fresh, willing souls. You must feed the Canary diamond one hundred souls by the May's Eve Ball, or your contract is broken, and I will personally see that you are fed to Evelyn and Martin Greene."

"You can't be serious," Evelyn said. "You're not giving her so precious a responsibility, are you?"

"I don't know the first thing about feeding a diamond souls," Mabel pleaded in spite of her disbelief at agreeing with Evelyn for once. "How am I supposed to find a hundred people willing to be fed to a diamond?"

"Ladies. Decorum," Frank said. "I think we can all get what we want here. The Grand needs a star, Mabel needs a job, and the Canary needs a caretaker that will provide it souls. She's a bright, young thing. Mabel should have no trouble completing the task in the allotted time."

"She complicates things," Evelyn said. "I thought you were going to make Lucky the caretaker?"

Frank studied Mabel. "I was, but I like making deals with thieves. Especially ones with dreams, and aren't we in the business of dreams?"

Mabel couldn't believe what she was hearing. How was she going to feed souls to a diamond? It was impossible. What had she gotten herself into?

"What about us?" Evelyn clicked her long nails against the wall. "I went through hell to bring you the Canary diamond. I'm starving."

Frank nodded at Raymond, who shoved the elevator operator out into the hall as he took Mabel by the arm and brought her inside. It all happened so fast that it took a minute for Mabel to register what they meant.

"No!" Mabel said. "Please! Don't eat him!"

Evelyn and Martin let out hungry shrieks as a scream tore from the elevator operator's throat. The couple grabbed the kid by either arm and pulled and yanked at his clothes until the bellhop's uniform tore like paper. Frank stepped through the elevator doors, indifferent to the kid's cries for help. She didn't know what to do, how to help him. Raymond guided Mabel into the elevator, steering her shoulders until she was fully inside. The double doors shut as a wet sound silenced the kid's desperate crying. The quiet pounded in Mabel's ears as she stared down at her heels. The carpet beneath her shoes turned red and squishy with blood.

Mabel froze. "How could you?"

"You've wandered into the wolf's den, I'm afraid," Frank said. "Here it is survival of the fittest. Only the best of the best survives—the best artists, the best writers, and the best performers. Be grateful I've made sure that you're among them."

She closed her eyes as Raymond set the elevator handle to return to the ground floor, whistling some horrible tune that was far too happy for the amount of blood soaking the carpet beneath Mabel's feet. These demons were going to kill her the first chance they got. Mabel ab-so-tute-ly had to get her soul back and escape, no matter what it took. If Mabel could successfully steal from New York's elite night after night, she could steal her soul back from Frank West. It would be her biggest heist yet, but as she opened her eyes and met Frank's steel gaze, Mabel knew she had no other choice. He wasn't going to let her go.

CHAPTER THREE

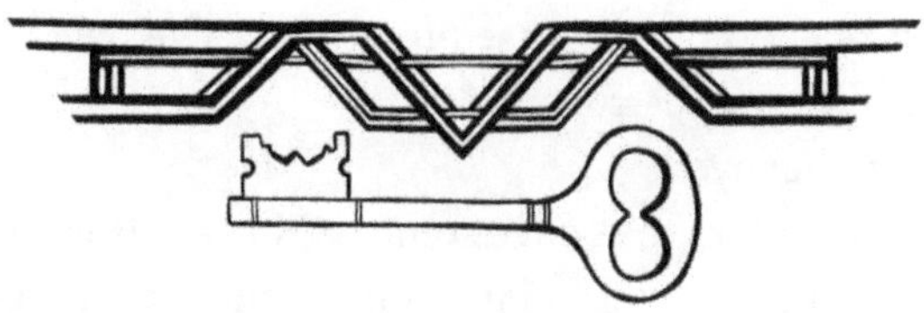

As the elevator descended floor after floor, Mabel struggled to hide how much she was shaking. She had thought she was being so smart, so clever, when she followed Evelyn and Martin into the Grand Hotel. Mabel had bitten off way more than she would ever be able to chew, and she knew it.

"I'm sure you had no idea you walked into a hotel run by the damned," Frank said, breaking the silence. "I know what a shock all this must be."

She let out a weak little laugh. "Shock? 'Shock' is the biggest understatement of my life. How could you do that to him? He was just a kid."

Frank looked a little forlorn before he replied. "I pray you don't have a weak stomach. You're going to see far more blood before the month is out than that."

"You didn't mention I had to hurt anyone. Just how much more blood am I going to see?"

"Demons have a job to do," Frank said, his tone detached from her rising emotions. "Same as everyone else. You've committed many successful thefts from, what is it you call them again? Your patrons? Very clever."

She crossed her arms. "Flattery does nothing for me. Information does. How exactly am I supposed to feed a diamond a hundred souls?"

"It's quite simple," he said, "Perform as a star and people will practically throw themselves at your feet. When they do, feed them to the Canary. You get to be a star, and my diamond gets fed—we both get what we want. And I don't need to flatter you. You know your own talent. You've survived weeks on the streets of New York. You suffered rejection after rejection and refused to give up. I've never seen a prettier thief, or a more successful one."

Mabel rolled her eyes.

"All I need is for you to seduce some willing souls with your talent and offer them to the Canary diamond. It's their own fault for being seduced. You can set that guilty heart to rest."

She couldn't look at Frank. There were splotches of blood on her dress that she needed to wipe off, but she couldn't get her body to move. Frank made it all sound so simple, but it wasn't. How was she supposed to seduce a hundred souls and feed them to a diamond? How could she look people in the eye and perform, knowing her audience was going to die?

She glanced at Raymond, hoping for answers, but he was staring straight ahead like he was not of the stature to be part of the conversation.

"Which reminds me." Frank took a step behind her and slipped the necklace around her neck so fast Mabel hadn't noticed he had clasped it as well in one fluid motion. "Best you wore this rather than keeping it in your pocket. Keep the Canary diamond safe for me, won't you?"

The Canary lay against her collarbone, heavy as lead. It was no bigger than an acorn, but the weight of it was like a second heart in her chest. The yellow reflected so brilliantly up close that Mabel had to fight to look away. She searched Frank's bemused expression for answers, but she found none.

"Why are you giving this to me? You know I'm a thief. I could walk out that front door with it."

Frank's smile stretched into his eyes, but there was nothing behind them. "Because you *can't* walk out the front door with it. I wouldn't try if I were you. It hurts to leave the Grand without your soul."

She huffed at him. More cryptic nonsense Mabel didn't understand.

The elevator reached the lobby level and dinged, interrupting their conversation. Raymond opened the elevator door and Frank stepped out first, holding his arm out for Mabel. She followed him on jelly legs out into the lobby, hating that she needed to take his arm for support. These demons were seeing all too much of her deepest thoughts and darkest fears for one evening. Mabel was beginning to feel like a butterfly pinned on a board.

"I still don't understand. How am I supposed to feed the Canary souls? How does it physically happen?"

"You'll see. People can't resist a star," Frank said with a wink as Raymond closed the elevator cage door. "I look forward to seeing your first performance. Until then."

He let her go and gave her a respectful bow of his head. Frank West glided away from her, back into the entrance of his gilded palace. A bellhop approached Frank with a letter on a gold plate and ran swiftly away. Frank took the letter and frowned deeply as he read the contents. He tucked the letter into his breast pocket and disappeared into the throngs of the evening crowd; all dressed their best and on their way to the dining hall.

"Come," Raymond said. "I've prepared a suite I'm sure you will find most comfortable."

Mabel's legs shook as she trailed him in silence through the lobby and round a corner down a series of halls on the first level. She didn't know when the shock of seeing the kid ripped to pieces would wear off, and Mabel imagined it probably never would. She didn't have the stomach to feed souls to the diamond. She couldn't imagine one soul dying at her expense, but a hundred in thirty days? She couldn't condemn more people to die like that poor kid. Mabel would have to steal her soul back before she was expected to perform. Raymond still had her soul coin in his breast pocket. If there was one thing Mabel was sure of, she was smart enough to find a way to slip the coin out of Raymond's jacket.

All a good thief had to do was wait for the right moment.

"Do keep up," Raymond said. "You're going to have to move quicker if you're going to survive Frank. He isn't as patient as I am."

Mabel stumbled after him in her kitten heels, but his legs were so long she struggled to keep up. As she did her best to trail Raymond down a labyrinth of corridors, she wondered if all demons were naturally statuesque, or if it was just the demons in charge of running things who were monstrously tall.

They rounded a sharp corner and left the familiar luxurious gold and marble decor behind to enter a dimly lit hall that gently sloped into the lower levels. Peeling damask wallpaper, the color of green bile, ran along the labyrinthine corridors Raymond led her down, reminding Mabel of her older sister's secret collection of Gothic penny dreadfuls. The beautiful white columns and marble statues were replaced by red statues of sinister gods with great horns. Their dark mouths were open in mid-snarl to bare gold teeth at Mabel as she passed, but she had been afraid enough for one day. Her resolve to escape had replaced her fear in a kind of desperate fog. She only cared about memorizing the path they were taking and checking each door's label obsessively for signs of an exit. When she stole the coin from Raymond, she would need to find her way back to the entrance.

Mabel had been afraid when Martin and Evelyn had shown their true faces, so afraid it had robbed her of her most valuable asset—her mind. Fear had cost Mabel her soul through a hasty decision to save her own skin. She would not let herself succumb to it again, not until she was free.

Down the hall, a woman with tight, fluffy, reddish-blond curls stood in the doorway. She wore a robe of fine silk, but her lingerie and garters were on display for anyone passing by to see a great deal of her form. Her smoky eyeshadow expertly enhanced the brown-green shade of her eyes, and the rouge on her lips was a perfect rose red. From her beauty, she could have easily been one of Ziegfeld's leading ladies, but she was shorter than Mabel by a head at least, and curvy in build. From the irritated look in her eyes, Mabel could tell New York had already done its dirty work of chewing up a dreamy-eyed girl and spitting her back out.

"Evening, Mr. Black," the girl said, glancing at the Canary diamond around Mabel's neck. "Is she for me?"

"No, Lucky," Raymond said. "This is Frank's new star, Mabel Rose Dixon."

Mabel's attention peaked. Lucky was the girl Evelyn mentioned earlier, the one originally meant to caretake the Canary diamond. But now that it was Mabel's, would Lucky be her friend, or her enemy?

Lucky's eyes rested on the diamond as she clucked her tongue. "So, you're the new star, huh? Frank was quick to break his promises to me."

So, enemy then. Mabel stiffened as she returned Lucky's comment with a curt nod. "You're looking at her. Sorry you didn't make the cut."

Lucky's smoky eyes narrowed. "You only get so long in the limelight, kid. Make sure the fall from the spotlight doesn't break you on the way down."

"Come, Mabel," Raymond said. "We're running late."

They left Lucky to stand in her doorway without another word. She wanted to ask Raymond who Lucky was, and more about how she had faded from stardom, but doubted she would get an answer.

Raymond made a sharp left into the wall, disappearing while Mabel debated. She hesitated, unsure if she should follow him straight into the damask. She took a few steps closer and found the illusion of a mirror wall within the wallpaper, the opening visible only from a certain angle. Mabel slid herself inside the narrow cavern, pushing her body away from the gloom and out into an open space that glittered like the inside of a jewelry box. The mirror walls ran from floor to ceiling, and the frames were crusted over with gold and inlaid with red and blue sapphires. Mabel had seen Versailles from pictures in a travel magazine, and this reminded her of the long hall of mirrors where Parisian kings and queens walked.

"Welcome to the Augment," Raymond said. "This place will give you anything and everything you could ever desire to enhance your appearance. You only need to think of how you wish to look, and the features you desire will be yours. Gaze into your reflection and choose your face."

She didn't understand what he meant, but Mabel would play his game for the time being. She regarded herself in one of the mirrors, a line of infinitely retreating Mabel's framing her. She felt so silly just standing there. Was she supposed to look any different? She wore the same red dress and matching cloche hat she had stolen from Zeigfeld's theater, but the blood was gone, and her clothes appeared freshly laundered. The Canary glittered around her neck. She reached a finger to touch it and hesitated. The diamond was so alluring, but the idea of touching it felt... sacrilegious.

"Are you keeping your face?" Raymond said. "That's barely a change. Decide quickly. I have other appointments to keep."

There *was* something different about her face. She didn't remember putting on so much makeup before she left, or so expertly. The dark shade of eyeshadow brought out the blue-gray in her eyes. She took in her body, all the things she liked, the things she didn't. The familiar imperfections had been smoothed over like clay shaped with a little water—just a push here and there.

Mabel could hardly believe how good she could look until she stepped back from the mirror and glanced down at her T-Strap heels. The blood splatter was still there. The bellhop's blood.

"It's not real?" Mabel said. "The mirror creates... an illusion?"

"The mirror reflects the version of yourself you wish you could see, the face you truly want to show to the world." Raymond's voice was cool and soft, but there were daggers of irritation laced underneath his explanation. "How do you wish to be seen?"

Ziegfeld had said Mabel was more of a Gibson girl, with full curves she desperately tried to hide by banding back her chest and hips. She thought of slender Louise Brooks, her favorite Ziegfeld girl, and her latest photo in *Vogue*. Oh, how Mabel longed to look like her, with her hair bobbed straight brunette instead of curly blond, her chic blue velvet dress and long pearls, and her boyish figure. If only beauty came to Mabel as effortlessly as Louise, maybe then Ziegfeld would have chosen her and spared her the hassle of losing her soul.

Mabel turned back to the mirror. She was wearing a blue dress, just as she had imagined. It whispered luxury against her skin, the fabric was so rich. Over the dress, she wore a coat with white fox fur sewn around her collar, just like Evelyn Greene's coat. Her blond curls were gone, replaced by a sleek brunette bob. A loud gasp escaped Mabel's throat, which she immediately tried to stifle with her hand. She looked how she always dreamed, how she always wanted, but the Canary diamond was still there, burning like a yellow star in the night sky of her dress.

She turned her attention to her new golden heels, spinning on them to inspect the embroidery on the back of the coat. It was stitched with patterns that reminded her of the arches in the lobby in black and gold. She looked like a star, and Mabel feared to even glance away from the mirror in case her dream would shatter, but the illusion was complete. When she turned back to Raymond, her outfit was still there. She patted the dress, crushed the delicate velvet between her thumb and forefinger.

It was real. It was all real. If only Flo Ziegfeld could see her now.

"As within," Raymond said. "So, without. Come. I have many things yet to do on my agenda and you are wasting both our evenings. Your room is this way."

He led her out of the Augment. When Mabel slid out of the narrow exit, the room folded in on itself like a paper fortune and became one with the macabre wallpaper again. With her new look and beautiful clothes, Mabel was feeling like a shiny new penny. She could steal the soul coin. All it would take was a simple press against Raymond's chest, a bit of flattery, and she would have her soul back. She would waltz right out of the Grand with her new look and dazzle her way into Ziegfeld's heart.

Raymond rounded a tight corner and Mabel found herself standing in front of a black door marked "Auditorium." Music drifted from the other side, joyous and followed by sweet peals of laughter. She had expected Raymond to lead her back to her rooms where she could enact her plans. This put a wrench in her works. The corner of Raymond's mouth curled into a smile as he twisted the knob and swung open the door.

"Go on. Take a gander at your new home."

The theater was enormous, twice as big as the New Amsterdam, and packed to the gills with people in their dinner finest. Mabel's head filled with the sounds of a big band, whose brass section swelled as the laughter of the boisterous crowd bounced off the walls. Mabel and Raymond drew closer until they stood in the wings of the red curtains, watching the floor show. Dancers performed a hilarious chain of comedic aerobatics involving mops and buckets to the uproarious laughter of the audience.

She had seen vaudeville routines like these when she first came to New York, but the theater had been barely full each time she went. Even coming from a little town in north Georgia, Mabel had heard that vaudeville was a dying art, less glamorous than the talkies or theatrical acts. She had never seen so many people turn up for a variety act like this.

Mabel peeked out of the side curtains and her eyes filled with stars. The black and gold theme decorated the plush seating. Diamond stars twinkled across the ceiling with a celestial moon and star chandelier at the center. It was like standing in the middle of the night sky. On either side of the auditorium, golden statues of Greek gods held the ceiling up with their great hands. Demons really seemed fascinated with the Greeks, or at least Frank and his family were when they designed the Grand.

The music faded and the troupe of vaudeville performers landed on their feet with a great flourish. The trio of boys and their red-headed female leader gave deep bows to their adoring audience. They waved at the uproarious applause, blowing kisses to their adoring fans as they exited the stage.

Fine shoes clapped across the wooden stage. Frank West appeared out of the opposite wings. Somehow he had gotten downstairs ahead of them. Part of being a demon, Mabel guessed.

He grabbed the microphone. "And now, I would love to introduce you to someone very dear to me. She's come all the way from Atlanta and the mean streets of New York City to be here tonight. Please welcome my close, personal friend, and your next stage darling, Mabel Rose Dixon."

The audience erupted, cheering Mabel's name, begging for her to appear in the lights before them. Her breath caught and became a lump in her throat. This was what she wanted, what she had seen in her dreams every night. Now that she had it, right in front of her, her mind reeled against such a thing being possible. She had never been in front of so many people before, every one of them screaming with excitement to see her. For the first time in her life, Mabel froze.

Frank held out a hand to her, the second time he had that night. "It's all right."

Mabel felt the pull of the spider's web tighten on her wings. Raymond helped her remove her fuzzy coat. She recoiled, hating herself for taking Frank's hand, but only for a moment. The call of the spotlight was too tempting. Frank pulled her gently into the light and her reservations melted off her like snow in the warm sun of spring. The second the stage lights fell on her face and played off the beadwork of her dress, Mabel was home.

Frank's smile was dazzling as he twirled her, showing her off to the crowd.

"Isn't she lovely, ladies and gentlemen? And you'll be able to meet Mabel Rose tomorrow night on her stage debut. I want to see a packed house for this little lady."

The audience cried her name, again and again. They cheered, falling over themselves to say how much they adored her. She had never known devotion like this, but she knew how to work up a crowd.

"Thank you, folks, for that warmest of welcomes! I hope you all will get your glad rags on and get goofy with me tomorrow night. Don't forget your giggle water."

She put a finger to her lips and pulled up the slit on her leg to reveal her hip flask. Mabel forgot to check if it was still there, but the Augment had whisked it away during her transformation. The hip flask was gone. Her cheeks turned the color of tomatoes as she smoothed her dress back down, and the sight of her gams made the crowd go silly. She had never shown so much leg before, and in front of so many people. It was like the Ziegfeld audition all over again.

Mabel stumbled back into Frank as a kid in the front row, a year or so younger than her, climbed up the stage to get closer. The kid was pushed back into his chair by a burly usher in a Grand uniform. Every lovely feeling Mabel had in that moment shattered like a China teacup. As Mabel saw the kid's desperate face, all she saw was the face of the poor bellhop.

"See?" Frank's breath was hot against her ear. "People can't resist a star. Something tells me you're going to meet your quota faster than you think."

Mabel paled as the red curtains closed, plunging them into darkness. Cries for Mabel to return rang out, muffled by the curtain as Frank led her off to the opposite side of the stage where Raymond was waiting.

As Raymond took Mabel by the arm and guided her back out into the hall, Mabel couldn't take her eyes off of Frank. He was smiling at her. No, not at her. At her diamond necklace.

The door clicked shut, but Mabel could still hear all those desperate people screaming her name. The sound made her shiver, but not as much as Frank's expression had unsettled her. There was something about the diamond around her neck that pleased him, something about him giving it to her on the same night that she stole it that wasn't right.

Mabel sought the clasp at the back of her neck but found only pearls. She twisted the necklace around, but there was no chain, no clasp, no way out of removing the Canary diamond. Mabel yanked the pearls so hard she thought the inner string would snap. Nothing happened, nothing at all, and the weight of the Canary grew heavier around her neck.

"What is this? Why won't it come off?"

She turned to look at Raymond, afraid his expression might confirm her situation was hopeless. He watched her with tired eyes, as if he were a parent exhausted with telling her not to touch a hot stove and she had gone and burned herself anyway.

"It's as I said, Miss Dixon. You're not leaving the Grand. At least, not until Frank gets what he wants, and Frank always gets what he wants."

CHAPTER FOUR

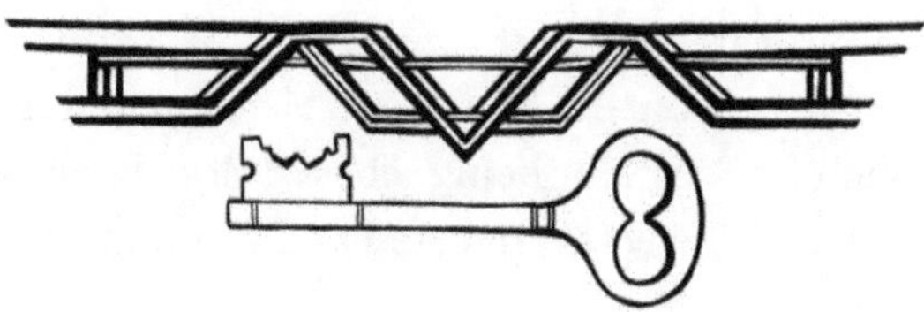

Raymond led Mabel away from the darkened Auditorium out into a brighter hallway lined with blood red damask wallpaper, a welcome change from the acrid green halls they had traveled so far. The hall was short with a dead end and six black and gold doors, each bearing a large gold star. Mabel passed the names of presumably the vaudeville group—Gisela, Karl, Stefan, and Friedrich Van Doren. As Mabel followed Raymond by their doors, she heard glass chinking and a peal of female laughter beyond Gisela's door. She couldn't understand how anyone could feel happy in this place, could possibly laugh at anything when they were all trapped.

Raymond stopped in front of the last door at the end of the hall. Mabel's name was already carved into the plaque face with a lovely, cursive type. The Grand staff worked fast, but Mabel was no longer amused by the constant decadence. She felt like a little dog being paraded around who wasn't allowed off her leash. Little did Frank know; he had trapped a fox. Even if she had to chew her own foot off, Mabel was getting out of this place.

Raymond leaned down to open the door for her. "Your suite, madam. I hope it's to your liking."

Mabel glared at him as she entered the enormous dressing room. There were several open wardrobes filled to the brim with costumes, feathers, pearls, and show dresses. There were hats and shoes, beaded headpieces, cloche hats in every color, and shoes that glittered like diamonds laid out in a row. She had never seen such a room, with floor-length mirrors for admiring her many outfits, or a vanity fully stocked with rouge, pots of powder, and lipsticks.

"If any detail is unsatisfactory, don't hesitate to ring the bell and ask for what you require," Raymond said, hanging her fur coat in the closet. "Will you be eating dinner this evening?"

Mabel had not eaten since the crust of bread at lunch or drank anything since the cafe outside the Grand. The hot water with lemon was not enough to sustain being chased by demons and then performing on stage. She was exhausted and starving, but she refused to admit she was hungry.

"I'm all set." Her stomach growled and gave her away.

"I'll have something sent down," Raymond said before she could protest and turned to leave.

"Wait," Mabel said, trying to think fast. She still needed her soul coin.

"So, how did you come to work for the Grand anyway?"

Raymond clasped his hands behind his back. "I entered a deal. Same as everyone else here."

He was the strong and silent type, Mabel could tell. She would need a character that could crack his hard exterior and make him turn to putty in her hands. Mabel glided over to him with all of her dazzling new beauty, eyes downcast like she had seen the ladies do in their picture shows. She casually let one of her sleeves fall off one shoulder as she pressed her hands against his chest. "What deal did you make?"

A flush came across Raymond's stoic face. "What does it matter? I'm no one of consequence."

"That's not true." Mabel gripped his arm muscles around his rather large biceps. "Well, aren't you a fine specimen. I bet you wished to be a strong man, or a prized fighter."

She slid her hand into his breast pocket as her lips drew near to his face. Raymond took her by both hands and gently pushed her away. "You won't find your soul coin in my pocket."

Mabel paled.

"Go ahead and try to find it."

She frowned at Raymond and dug her hand inside his breast pocket. It was empty. "Hey, what gives? Where is it?"

"Your soul has gone to join the others. It's well protected. I can assure you your soul is safe."

When Mabel didn't respond, Raymond continued. "I'll have your dinner sent up."

Without waiting to see her reaction, Raymond turned and exited the room. He shut the door behind him with a quiet click, leaving Mabel alone in her thoughts.

What had just happened? He had read right through her motives somehow. Now she was going to have to find where they were keeping all of the soul coins. Not only did she not have her coin, but she was also expected to perform again tomorrow night. She would have to find where the coin was located and steal it back in less than twenty-four hours. If she couldn't seduce Raymond, there was no way she could seduce souls into being fed to the Canary diamond.

Twenty-four hours to find her soul. She told herself that was plenty of time. She could go back and ask Lucky, or the Van Doren's. Someone in this place knew where her soul coin was. It had to be under lock and key somewhere where Frank kept his valuables. Mabel betted that the coin would either be stored in the front office or in his personal suite.

It was fine. It was all going to be fine.

Mabel was also exhausted, and starving, which was probably contributing to her feelings of self-doubt and her terrible performance seducing Raymond. She couldn't perform a heist on an empty tank. Raymond was having dinner sent up. She could spare a moment to eat before she started looking. Mabel decided to explore her suite. Perhaps there would be some clues within her set of rooms.

She had seen the dressing rooms of Ziegfeld's leading ladies, and this first room was even lovelier and more well-stocked than three of those suites combined. Mabel couldn't help herself. She rushed to touch all of the fabric. Mabel gushed over the rabbit furs, the silks, the satins, the crepes, the chiffons, and the organza party dresses. She pulled out every pair of sparkling shoes. Everything was her size, her shape. She tried on several different cloche hats and feathery headpieces, admiring herself in the mirror. Mabel still wasn't used to her dark hair, but she looked exactly like Louise Brooks save for her eyes, which were still the same dull blue-gray as a cold winter morning.

She could still see them, Ziegfeld and Louise half naked in his arms, laughing when Mabel opened his office door.

"You have a pretty face, you're a talented dancer, but do you have what it takes to go all the way and be a star? I don't think so, kid."

The memory of Ziegfeld's words made her uncomfortable, but so did her night with Ziegfeld afterward. She shook off the memory. Who wanted to think about unpleasantness when all this decadence was waiting in her honor? Mabel approached the floor-length mirror and regarded her dark bob, blue velvet dress, and the yellow diamond around her neck. She reached to tug the necklace off, but the Canary diamond stubbornly remained, and Mabel was too tired for another game of break her doggy collar. It seemed that no matter what path she took to fame; the cost was too high. She might not be able to take the necklace off, but isn't that what she wanted? To walk out of the Grand with the very thing that could buy her a spot as a Ziegfeld leading lady?

After what had happened with him, was that something she still wanted? It had to be, didn't it? She'd traded her soul for it.

Laughter carried down the hall again. Gisela's voice was muffled, but the joy rang out like morning birdsong. The Van Doren's were trapped in the Grand, locked into some deal, same as Mabel. She didn't blame them. As much as Mabel hated to admit Frank was right. The vaudeville scene was on its way out. Mabel knew that fact all too well, but hated that Frank knew that about her as well. She didn't want anyone else to know about her past. Mabel was going to have to make sure no one else drank her blood while she was still a guest of the Grand, which was such a strange thought to have to worry about.

She was going to have a new life as a Ziegfeld girl when she got out of here. That was the goal she truly needed to focus on.

She gave her best smile in the mirror and forced it to reach into her tired eyes until they sparkled. Why shouldn't she enjoy herself? It would make a good cover. He might know her past, but he could not read her thoughts. Mabel could let Frank think she was enamored with her new life and all the riches the Grand had to offer while she slipped out the front door with his diamond. After picking dozens of pockets, Mabel knew acting happy or bored deflected suspicion.

There came a knock at the door. When Mabel opened it, Samuel Lewis from the dining hall was standing in her doorway accompanied by a bellhop with a cart of silver dishes.

"Evening, Miss Dixon," he said. "I wanted to personally welcome you to the Grand and take a note of Mademoiselle's dietary preferences. We wish to serve only the best meals, custom fit to your palette."

The bellhop opened the silver dishes one by one. There were plates of roast chicken and sides of vegetables, bread rolls twisted in different styles of knots, and a silver cup of chocolate mousse for dessert. On the side, the bellhop opened a side of a brown, savory sauce for the chicken. Mabel couldn't believe it. They knew her favorite meal, but with the way things had gone she since had arrived at the Grand, she was starting to believe.

"Does everything look to your liking? Let us know if anything is unsatisfactory." Samuel handed her his card with his number at the top. "Just give me a ring anytime. My kitchen is always open."

The way Samuel looked at her was softer, more human. She needed to keep track of who was and was not a demon in this place.

"Thanks, Samuel," Mabel said, sticking her finger into the sauce. "I'll let you know, but this tastes pretty perfect to me. How did you know it was my favorite dish?"

"The Grand has its ways," Samuel said. "But you'll find that out before too long. The longer you're here, the more the hotel learns about what you like and don't like. The easier it provides exactly what you want."

Mabel blinked at him. "It can read my mind?"

"Not exactly," the bellhop added. "The hotel watches and... learns."

Samuel cleared his throat and the bellhop faltered. He had clearly said too much.

"Anyway," Samuel said. "I hope you enjoy your dinner. The bellhop will pick it up when he returns for your trays. Have a restful sleep, Mabel Rose."

"I surely will," Mabel said.

Samuel gave her a bow and his bellhop followed without any fanfare.

Mabel poured gravy over her chicken, unable to stop herself from diving into the meal. She vaguely remembered the story of Persephone, but she'd already lost her soul, she doubted fried chicken could get her into more trouble. She savored every bite. It had been hours since she had eaten that piece of bread the kitchen boy had found for her, but she was used to going without food for long stretches at a time. It had been years since she had seen her mother's cooking, and yet here it was, every flavor of her favorite holiday dinner recreated perfectly.

Something about the hotel was off. Mabel had known that from the moment she entered the Grand, but she was glad the bellhop had slipped up. She didn't know the hotel itself was watching her, learning more about her preferences the longer she was here. All the more reason to leave as soon as possible. Until then, Mabel could assume the hotel was always watching. She could use that to her advantage. Let her audience see what they wanted to see.

She grabbed a roll and pulled it apart, feeling more tired than ever. There was no bed in her dressing room, no place to bathe, or even a toilet. Mabel took her bread roll for a turnabout the room, peering behind the furniture until she found a door she had not seen before and threw it open.

The next room was more extravagant than the last. The bedroom was a palace—fit for a queen, not a stage actress. It was a mirror image of the lobby, all white marble columns beside floor-to-ceiling black velvet curtains. The ceiling was painted over like the night and star clusters danced around a small chandelier with planets and moons. Twin white and gold statues of Persephone, carrying baskets of pomegranates, and Artemis, with her bow and arrow with small animals around her feet, stood in opposite corners facing the four-post bed.

The bed was the most gorgeous detail of all. A mastery in craftsmanship, the carved posts were laid over in stars and moons like the theater. Comets trailed the starry ceiling overhead as winged Hermes chased Apollo and his chariot across the night sky. The sheets were a deep night blue and each embroidered star twinkled with interior light.

Mabel had never seen anything like this room in her life. She had imagined rooms like this when she read about Greek gods as a young girl in her library books. Its serenity and luxury were something she had deeply longed for that she hadn't even known she needed. Whatever the Grand was doing to lure her in, it was working. She was going to have to resist hard in order to not fall head-over-heels in love with this place.

Thick, Oxford blue velvet curtains covered one of the walls. Mabel pulled back one of the heavy curtains by its golden tassel until she found the entrance to the bathroom. There was Neptune again, riding a great dolphin over a wide bathtub. Water cascaded down from his trident and fed into the bath, where golden knobs waited to be twisted and pulled to fill the rest of the tub with hot or cold water. There was a toilet, a table with various colors and shapes of bars of soap, and dishes of solid shampoo. Mabel had never seen such extravagance, and it was so opulent it was beginning to get ridiculous. Was this how Frank treated his star? By showering her with decadence until Mabel would do anything to keep her life like this, even if it meant collecting a hundred poor souls?

There was a girl at her boarding house who had some sorry Charlie calling after her at least once a day. He would wait on the doorstep of the boarding house, begging her to come out and marry him with a new gift. Each gift was more gorgeous than the last. She never did say yes. When Mabel asked her why, she said it was because she had come to New York for bigger dreams than to be put away as someone's wife. She had told Mabel, "Anyone who buys you fancy things wants something of equal value in return, but not in gold or jewels. They want to buy your freedom."

Mabel wanted to be a stage star more than anything, but she wasn't going to lose her freedom to a man like Frank West, no matter how fancy his gifts. And she wasn't going to forget that poor bellhop either. But that didn't mean she couldn't enjoy herself while it lasted.

She raced over to the bed and jumped on top. Mabel sank into deep sheets. She shouldn't have jumped into the bed. Now she didn't want to leave. Her body felt so heavy, and the bed was so comfortable, like nothing she had ever slept on before. Mabel needed to stay awake. She needed to find her soul. She needed to...

She yawned so loudly it surprised her. Mabel didn't know if it was the heavy dinner or the bed of her dreams, but she could hardly keep her eyes open. She hadn't realized how much all of the running around the Grand had worn her out. Some rest, and she could slip out in the early morning.

Besides, one night's stay in the Grand Hotel couldn't hurt.

CHAPTER FIVE

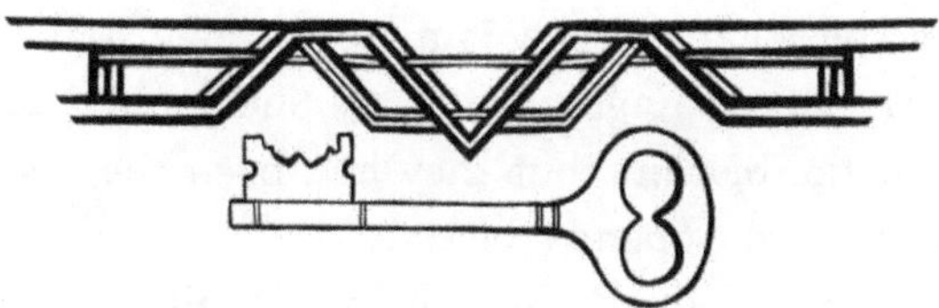

The door opened and the wheels of a food cart rattled into her bedroom, waking Mabel from a dream filled with dark figures dancing in an endless ballroom. She blinked to adjust her eyes to the low light of an unfamiliar room, forgetting where she was until the bellhop in his smart Grand uniform steered the trays of food next to her bed.

"Hello," she said, unfurling herself from the starry sheets. "What's this? I don't remember placing an order."

"Breakfast." The young bellhop handed her a large white envelope with a gold wax seal on a golden plate. "Sam sent me down with everything."

"I remember you." She took the creme-colored envelope from him. "What am I supposed to do next?"

He gave her a little bow and made a swift exit without answering her question.

Rude. He could have at least given her the courtesy of answering her. The smell of bacon and eggs wafted over from the cart. The letter could wait. Mabel had to crawl on her hands and knees in order to escape her massive bed. She had collapsed without changing and now her blue velvet dress clung to her body like kudzu on a tree.

She opened the silver trays and found more breakfast food than she could possibly eat. Every dish was piled high with bacon, blocks of cheese, boiled eggs, cups of fruit, tiny quiches, and different types of jam for the biscuits. The hotel did not know exactly which jam she liked, so they had delivered everything on the menu. So, the Grand didn't know everything about her yet. Mabel felt reassured as she picked up a biscuit, turned it over in her hands, and the texture brought her back to her mother's kitchen. Her mother had a certain recipe, one that had won many state fairs. The biscuits were always paired with a special strawberry jam. To this day, Mabel still didn't know what the secret ingredient was. She hadn't actively been thinking about the biscuits, but they had been the first thing that came to mind when she opened the tray.

Her hands trembled as she pulled the biscuit apart, took a spoonful of the red-colored jam, and smeared it across the fluffy center. Mabel was almost too scared to take a bite, but the nostalgic familiarity of the warm biscuit under her nose was a memory too powerful to ignore. She took a bite, and her mother's strawberry jam filled her mouth. Mabel devoured every bite of the crumbly biscuit, started in for a second, and stopped.

She hadn't written a single letter or even called her mother after their last argument. When Mabel had boarded the train to New York, things had gotten... nasty. Mabel hadn't eaten a single biscuit since leaving the South, but they were her favorite memories of her mother. The biscuits had smoothed over an ache Mabel didn't even know she had. Somehow, the Grand had cracked open her memories and saw deep inside her thoughts. Somehow, the hotel had known.

Sam had said the longer she stayed, the more the hotel learned. Mabel had been a guest for less than a day. What would the hotel learn about her in a week? A month? How would it use her memories to please her? How would it use her secrets against her? If she was going to escape she needed to do it fast.

Mabel finished her breakfast in cold silence. She went through the motions of a hot bath she could not relax in and dressing in luxurious clothes she could not appreciate. The Grand was somehow watching it all. She straightened her pale blue dress, then selected the most expensive-looking watch, earrings, and bracelets from the many drawers of the mahogany jewelry box on her bedside table. Mabel reviewed herself in the floor-length mirror. The Canary gleamed around her neck, brighter than any other piece of jewelry she had donned herself with. She could only take so much with her, but what she had chosen would equal months of food and shelter once she was back out on the streets again.

Mabel made for the door and almost forgot about the letter waiting for her on the bed. What did it matter?

She broke the gold seal on the letter with her finger. Out fell a crisp white paper with the Grand Hotel's logo and letterhead, all black and gold like everything else.

Meet me for rehearsal on stage at 2 pm. Sharp.
I can't stand tardiness.

It was signed by Evelyn Greene.

Mabel flopped back on the bed with a groan and let the letter fall on her chest. Was Evelyn her director now? How could she stand to look Evelyn in the eye again, much less take direction from her, after feeling her hand pierce through her? After watching her devour that poor kid? If she had to listen to a word that horrible woman said, Mabel was going to have kittens.

Frank hadn't mentioned whose routine she was supposed to perform. Mabel had always written her own acts, apart from when she auditioned for Ziegfeld. He always tested his girls by having them learn the same choreography and number, bundling them together on stage like a school of fish. One wrong move and you could elbow a girl in the kidney, which Mabel had avoided with ease.

Mabel would much rather come up with her own themes, songs, and costumes. She didn't exactly know what it meant to be the star of the Grand's theater, or how much control she had over her own shows. From the spectacular display from the Van Doren's last night, she expected the bar for her show would be set even higher. A little help figuring out her show would be nice, but of all the people working at the hotel did that person have to be Evelyn Greene?

She couldn't afford to get worked up like this. Mabel was leaving. Right now. Today. The watch read 10:07. Plenty of time to make her escape without anyone knowing she had turned up missing. She assumed the Grand could watch and learn about her but didn't see how the hotel could stop her from physically leaving, no matter what Frank claimed.

Mabel left her bedroom and slipped out of the dressing room door. She would have to remember the twisting path Raymond had taken her, but her stomach lurched with the feeling of taking a misstep as soon as she exited her suite. When she found her footing again, the hallway was gone. The red damask wallpaper and star doors had vanished, replaced by a circular hall filled with a tropical display not unlike the dining hall. Her mind reeled as she stumbled through palm fronds, giant Monstera plants, and great succulents. Had her room moved? Or had the hotel shifted around her?

Mabel spun on her heel, desperate for a way out of the liminal space she found herself trapped in, but she was surrounded by identical black pathways set in the circular room. Beside each door was a room number engraved on a little gold plate, but Mabel didn't have a room number, and certainly no key. With no indication of a staircase or exit, Mabel was a little ball spinning in a roulette wheel, trying to land in the right spot. Maybe there was a way up and out instead? She looked up and immediately wished she hadn't.

The circular room's white columns traveled above Mabel for what seemed like forever. Floor by floor, the spiraling ornamentation continued like an intricate Alphonse Mucha painting, a famous painter who had a show at the Brooklyn Museum in 1921. Mabel hadn't been living in New York when the show was on exhibit, but she had seen his famous posters scattered throughout the city in bars. Each white and gold detail weaved in art deco floral patterns of glass and marble, with stained glass fixtures meeting at each floor's railing. She craned her neck, but she couldn't see past thirty floors, maybe forty floors. The ceiling faded away into a whiteout, and it gave her the feeling of falling upwards into a snowstorm. She had to look away or the vertigo would sweep her right off her feet.

There had to be a way out. Mabel stumbled through the warm jungle, sweat beading on her back. There was nothing, but somehow she had missed the large gold fountain at the center of the dais. Mabel headed toward the fountain, hoping there might be some indication of a way to move forward. It wasn't that she feared being trapped. She just did not want to be caught wandering the Grand by Frank, or worse, by Evelyn. Mabel shuddered to think of what might happen if that woman and all of her teeth found her alone. She wasn't sure how much protection Frank offered her by being his star, and Evelyn might be getting... hungry.

A gold statue of a woman with tiny demon horns on her forehead stood at the center of the trickling fountain, holding a black key in each hand. It reminded Mabel of a painting she had once seen of Venus, all flowing hair and shells. This statue was also naked save for strategically placed strands of long, wavy hair.

The golden demon opened her blank eyes at Mabel's approach.

"This is the Atrium, and I am the Navigator. I can take you anywhere in the hotel you wish to go. What do you seek, Mabel Rose Dixon?"

The mouth did not move, but the voice echoed upwards through the levels all the same.

Mabel faltered, unsure if she should tell the truth or a clever lie.

"I seek an exit."

The golden statue paused. "That way is blocked. You may travel anywhere within the bounds of the hotel."

Clever lie, it was. "I wish to visit the Lobby."

"Access denied."

Mabel thought about spitting in the fountain and resisted the urge. There had to be a way out without asking directly for the exit.

Lucky was pushing a cart filled with laundry out of one of the hotel room doors. She had on a sleek teal dress that revealed the skin from the nape of her neck all the way down her spine. Her brunette curls bounced under her peacock feathered headband, and her silver heels glittered across the black and white tile as she pushed the heavy cart.

"I can still tell it's you," Lucky called over to Mabel as she pushed the cart toward the fountain. "That jet black bob won't hide you. Glamors are useless on me now. I can see right through them."

"Where do you desire to go," asked the Navigator. "Louise Porter?"

"Louise?" Mabel said.

Lucky shrugged and her dress slipped off her shoulder. "Don't call me that. I hate that name."

She bristled.

"Mabel Rose Dixon." Lucky raised one perfect, penciled eyebrow as she regarded Mabel up and down again. A corner of Lucky's oxblood red lip pulled into a smirk. "How very Southern belle, you are. So, you're my replacement? Frank must have made an impulse purchase."

Mabel ran her tongue across her teeth. "And you're the one selling herself? In a hotel that can grant you anything you desire?"

Normally, Mabel didn't go for the jugular right away, but in a place like the Grand where the cast of characters could kill you on a whim, she figured it was better to be seen as a bearcat than a pussy cat.

Lucky laughed. It was a loud and hearty laugh, not really a fit for what Mabel pictured to be Frank's once glamorous star. "I'm not selling myself, but I have fallen out of the hotel's good graces. Still, that doesn't mean I can't have a good time. Besides, I did that whole Frank's star thing. One hundred souls by April 30th, right?"

Mabel crossed her arms a little too tight over her ribcage. "Did he give you the same deal?"

"Not exactly." Lucky yawned loudly and leaned an elbow on her cart. "I didn't have the assistance of your little trinket. I was expected to take souls without the Canary."

Mabel's eyes widened.

"I suggest you cut a new deal before your thirty days are up, or you might end up a little less human than you'd like to be."

"What do you mean?"

Lucky laughed and turned away to address the Navigator instead. "I need to make a delivery, same as always. Take me to Laundry."

"Access granted," the silvery voice of the Navigator responded.

The doors spun as the Navigator lifted the key. She pointed it and a new door expanded to become a set of white double doors with circular windows. Mabel's jaw went slack.

"Wait," Mabel said. "What happened last year? What is Frank trying to do with his stars?"

Lucky ignored her questions as she pushed the cart toward the doors, but she accidentally ran into one of the palm plants. Something fell out. Mabel saw the bloody fingers before Lucky could conceal the arm in the pile of sheets. There was a spot of brown-clotted red exposed on the sheets. Lucky used the sheets to cover it up.

Mabel froze. She hadn't wanted to think there was a dead body in that bin, but Mabel was starting to think that dead bodies and blood should be her base assumption for everything going forward.

"You killed them."

Lucky's laugh bounced off the Atrium walls, echoing upwards into the floors overhead like a distant peal of thunder. "Don't be such a puritan. You're going to see a lot more dead bodies than this one."

"Help me out of the deal then."

"I'm not helping you. Besides, it's done. You need to either roll with it and try to deliver what Frank wants or shake the dice and place a new bet on the table. Your choice."

"I didn't have a choice," Mabel shot back, but the fire of her words wasn't there. She was filled with too much sorrow to make her words cut like a sharp knife. "I was dying. They were going to eat me. I did what I had to."

Lucky paused. "They tried to eat me too. Frank... it doesn't matter what Frank did. The point is they tricked you. That's the thing they don't tell you. You had all the power before the deal. You don't learn that until they take everything away from you."

She wheeled the cart away again from the planter and pushed it over to the double doors.

"I don't care what you say." Mabel had to be the one to throw the last dagger, but it was strategic. "Just because you failed doesn't mean I'm going to."

Lucky considered for a beat. "You don't want to succeed. If you do, Frank will ascend, and it will be a whole lot worse for you, and for all of us."

"Ascend?" Mabel practically let out a yelp. "What do you mean?"

Lucky's jaw clacked shut as she realized she said too much. Mabel hated that dragging the truth out of Lucky was like trying to pull a stubborn mule back to the barn.

"If I were you," Lucky said, changing the subject. "I wouldn't find out. I would ask Frank to give up the starring role and become a regular demon while you have the chance. You might even get a spot in the speakeasy."

“The speakeasy?” Mabel was taken aback. Never, ever had she considered actually becoming a demon. She was a human, not some Satan-worshipping minion who was bent on doing dark and dirty work in his name. Mabel was a thief, not a bad person. “I will never be a demon. Frank promised I wouldn’t have to kill anyone.”

Lucky grinned a little too wide, bearing her pronounced canines. “And you trusted a demon to tell the truth? Besides, you already gave up your humanity when you cut the deal.”

Mabel’s resolve faltered. Could it be true? Did she become a demon when they took her soul? She still felt human. Lucky was just messing with her head. It was clear the girl hated Mabel the moment she walked in the front door. This was just a tactic to get Mabel to give up stardom and take it for herself.

“Try not to worry too much about it, Maby-baby,” Lucky said. “Besides, you’re the star at the best hotel in New York City. Why shouldn’t you have a little fun?” Lucky turned back to her cart and pushed it away into the laundry room. “You can try to fight it, try leaving. It won’t make a difference. You’re a part of Frank’s hotel now. The sooner you accept you’re never leaving, the better. All you can do now is pick your poison.”

The double doors of the laundry room swung closed, leaving Mabel standing alone beside the Navigator’s fountain, her thoughts rushing like a dark river out into a deeper sea.

She turned back to the Navigator, suddenly sure of where she wanted to go. “I want to see... the pool.”

The golden demon turned her head to the right. A lock turned over in one of the existing doors, as if someone had inserted an invisible key.

“Access granted.”

The onyx door swung open. Pale, blue light glittered across the black and white tiled floor. Mabel smiled at her own cleverness as she hurried over to the pool’s entrance. As she exited the Atrium and the door clicked shut gently behind her, Mabel laughed. Pools meant access to water. It had to lead somewhere outside, either by the patio or the maintenance door. Mabel was about to walk out with the diamond, right under Frank’s nose. She never should have doubted herself in the first place.

Sun streamed in through the glass ceiling of the greenhouse-like room. Several glass panes had been popped open in the ceiling to allow for airflow. Mabel had been swimming most of her life in the small lake behind her neighbor's barn, but the black and white photos in *Vogue* magazine failed to capture how clear the pool's water was. The urge to dive into the deep blue, despite the ruin it would make of her silk dress, was overwhelming.

Mabel's heels echoed off the enclosure as she walked around the pool, bringing her to the attention of the various people lounging by the water. She was well aware everyone had their eyes on her. Of course, they did. Mabel was the Grand Hotel's star. She held her head high as she strolled past the rubes.

She trotted by a couple sunbathing in their Jantzen suits. A child maybe seven or eight years old, splashed his mother in the shallow end, raining droplets of water on the hot cement. Mabel didn't like to think about when she was happy with her mother, years before her world was ruined by a hailstorm of rules and expectations based on her sex. It was all so very Victorian. Marry the right boy, bear the right children, keep wealth in land and family. Not modern at all. Not Mabel at all.

She hurried away from the child and all of those unnecessary memories of her own mother. Mabel would live in the present, even if it meant going without speaking to her family ever again.

She found what she was looking for on the opposite side of the pool. There was a door, somewhat hidden beside a towel cart. Someone had rolled the cart in front of the door. *Odd.*

Mabel snuck a peek over her shoulder at the poolside bourgeois. No one was looking at her anymore. She gave the cart a huge push as quietly as she could. The cart rolled across the pavement and freed the exit. Mabel expected some rush of air, some alarm to sound, but there was nothing. No one noticed anything at all.

She tentatively pushed the door open. There was a huge patio beyond, with a larger second pool on the roof. There were many more people there, but in the immediate glare of the sun, Mabel couldn't make out any of their faces.

Mabel took a step away from the glass enclosure out into the crowd. She had never seen a pool so crowded, or openly offering so much bootleg liquor in the middle of the day. Wouldn't someone from a neighboring building see them?

She took another step. Everything went blurry, like she couldn't see beyond a foot in front of her face. Her chest squeezed, like a giant hand had wrapped around her lungs. Mabel gasped and found she couldn't take a full breath in.

When she was eight, she had almost drowned when her older brother Avery had playfully held her down to see how long she could hold her breath. Mabel had managed to escape, but she never wanted to feel that burning sensation ever again. She knew what was happening. Mabel was drowning inside herself, even though she stood out in the open air of the rooftop deck.

Shapes swam in and out of her vision as she stumbled into a chair. With every step, her lungs squeezed harder. Mabel gave up sharp, stabbing coughs that sounded like barks. No matter how hard she tried, she couldn't take a full breath in. She didn't know exactly when she tripped over the chair she had been clinging to, but Mabel felt herself fall forward. She hit the cold water before she realized that she had fallen. Blue swirled around her as her lungs burned, desperate for air after having so little. If she didn't do something, Mabel was going to actually drown, but as she clawed for the surface, she found it harder and harder to exert energy. It was like she was having heart failure as punishment for trying to escape the hotel.

Hands clasped around her arms and shoulders. Mabel felt her body lift and was forcefully yanked out of the pool. She gulped in air, but it was shallow and rough, never enough. No matter how hard she tried, her breathing only got worse as she was laid down on the hot concrete. She lay shivering and numb. Worried voices clamored around her, but the sun bore down on their faces, obscuring them.

"I can't believe she tried to leave the hotel," a woman with a familiar voice said. "Didn't Frank warn her? What am I saying? Of course, he didn't warn her. He finds it much funnier to see what she'd do."

Strong hands lifted Mabel away from the ground and up into the sky as the woman shooed everyone away.

"Evie, darling," the man said. "She's quite heavy. Where should we take her?"

Evelyn scoffed loudly next to Mabel's ear. "Get her out of the sun and back inside the hotel. Take her to one of the lounge chairs. She's positively drenched. We'll need salts in order to revive her. I have some in my bag. Hopefully, it works. Frank will have kittens if she isn't ready for tonight."

Mabel hung like a broken doll in Martin's arms, vaguely aware of the argument passing between the demons who had tried to devour her last night.

"No." Mabel's voice slurred. "I'm not going."

Martin laughed as he carried her away from the sun and into the cool shade. Mabel swung hard to clock Martin right on the chin, but her arm moved in a weak circle. He swatted her fist away easily, as if her punch were no more than an errant butterfly.

"It's not like it's your fault, dear," Martin told his wife with mock sympathy. "The girl wandered out of the hotel on her own."

"If Frank's star isn't ready for tonight, it's not her he will blame, it's me." Her voice was even, but rage laced Evelyn's sultry words like a drop of arsenic in a gin martini. "I'm not losing this deal because of some headstrong girl Frank decided to take pity on."

It was worse than Mabel feared. Evelyn wasn't just directing Mabel—she was personally responsible for her.

"You worry too much," Martin said. "It's done. Frank agreed."

Evelyn snorted. "You forget Frank is a stallion. All he cares about is his personal freedom. We're going to treat him like a prized thoroughbred and ride Frank all the way to the finish line to get what we want."

Mabel winced away from being pressed against Martin's shirt, fearing the mouth that lay beneath. "Don't eat me."

He scoffed at Mabel. "You needn't worry, lamb. You're Frank's protégé now. We can't eat you."

Martin lay her gently on one of the empty lounge chairs beside the interior pool. Evelyn took some of her smelling salts and opened them under Mabel's nose. The effect was immediate. Mabel blinked into his brown eyes and wanted to run, but her body wouldn't let her. She turned away from Martin and Evelyn, but the people lounging by the pool were all staring back at her. Their eyes had changed. Everyone, even the child and its mother, shared the same white, pupil-less gaze.

They were all demons, every last one. They could go outside and enjoy the sun while the humans toiled down below.

Mabel hated her weakness. She was so human, so frail compared to the towering forms of Evelyn and Martin. She would do anything to not feel so small, but all she could do was lie there and feel every beat of her racing heart. At least her breath was returning. It was slow and steady, but it was coming back.

She had been mistaken. She was not the witty fox she claimed to be. They were. Mabel hated that Frank was right. She could not physically leave the hotel without going into some sort of heart failure. As soon as she recovered, Mabel would do the smart thing, find her soul coin, and then run as far and as fast as she could. She could play the part of a fox fleeing from their wolf teeth.

"Mabel, darling, really," Evelyn said, stroking Mabel's hair. "You needn't fear us. We will do what Frank says."

"You're lying." Mabel's voice was barely audible, but her words were steel. "The second we're alone, you'll eat me."

Evelyn sniffed at the insult. "It's not in our ranking to lie. That's for the basest creatures, fledgling demons. See these demons around the pool? Their white eyes? They're lower demons. A deal with a high demon is a done deal, and we are the highest there is. In the Grand, at least."

At Evelyn's touch, Mabel's head suddenly cleared. She leaned over the side and spat up a great deal of water, heaving onto the cement. Normally, she would be embarrassed, but Mabel was in front of two demons that had no problem ripping her apart.

Martin brought her several of the towels from the pool cart. Mabel took them, grateful but guarded. "Thank you. Both of you. For saving me."

Evelyn shrugged a delicate shoulder as she wrapped herself with the pretty navy-blue tasseled shawl that matched the blue and white striped bathing suit she was sporting. Mabel stared at her exposed collarbone and its smooth skin. She wondered where Evelyn's mouth had gone. "Don't sweat it, kid. You got bigger problems than me if you think you can walk out without your soul and survive. You got some kind of death wish?"

Mabel shook her head only once and instantly regretted it. A headache bloomed into a roaring fire at the back of her skull. "I was trying to find a way out." Again, she couldn't lie to them. "I didn't know that would happen."

Evelyn's laugh sounded like a chandelier twinkling. "Silly girl. The Grand is the only thing keeping you alive. Step one foot out its doors and your heart stops because your heart is not really beating without this place. Haven't you noticed?"

Mabel hadn't noticed. She hadn't thought to check. Her fingers shook as she placed a hand over her ribcage and pressed down hard into the skin. She waited several long moments, but her heartbeat was a slow, faint pulse that sounded like it was barely there at all. She didn't have a full heartbeat.

"Don't worry," Evelyn said. "You have nothing to fear so long as you stay inside the hotel. Besides, you won't be in this predicament long."

"What do you mean?" Mabel said.

Martin's smile was too eager on his stupid face. "You'll see."

Mabel pushed herself up to sit, irritated at their riddles. She decided to pocket that information for later. Mabel was surprised at how much better she was feeling now, but the fact that the hotel was the only thing keeping her alive made her want to throw up again. If she couldn't get her soul back, there was no out, and she had to have an out.

She had no choice. She had to get her soul back from Frank to walk free. Maybe these two could help her narrow down where he kept his soul coins.

"Where is Frank's office? I need to see him."

The Greene couple exchanged incredulous glances. "*You* do not make appointments with Frank," Evelyn said. "He makes appointments with *you*. There is nothing you need from him the hotel cannot provide. If you have questions about the terms of your deal, you can ask me."

"Why you?"

"I run the stage show," Evelyn said. "You could say the last stage director was... let go. You and I are going to be spending a lot of time together. I'm your director, and any question you have can go through me."

"There's nothing I want to ask you," Mabel said with a sniff. This was so much worse than she had anticipated. Now she had to try and steal her coin back under Evelyn's watchful eye.

Evelyn drew her circular sunglasses, which were perched on top of her bob like a headband, back down over her eyes. "She seems fine now. Come on, Martin. Let's get a little more sun before it's time to head down."

She came to stand and threaded her arm through his. "See you at rehearsal tonight."

Evelyn waved a little royal wave at Mabel before exiting out to the deck. Her arm flashed with a gold bracelet on her wrist, which Mabel hadn't seen before. It was a snake, wrapped around her wrist in two loops, eating its tail on the other end like the mythical Ouroboros. Its eyes flashed bright yellow at Mabel before the demon couple disappeared into the sun.

Mabel was positively soaked and the glamor the Grand had placed on her things was gone. She was still no closer to her goal of escaping than when she left her room that morning, but at least she had gained more knowledge than she had before. Oh, but how she hated Evelyn. If she was going to have to deal with her, Mabel could at least make the suffering worth her while. Walking out of the Grand with the Canary was fine, but the Canary and Evelyn's snake bracelet would make a smart set.

Ziegfeld doubly wouldn't be able to resist.

She stood up, smoothed the clinging silk of her dress, and kicked the lounge chair over. Mabel didn't care if the lower demons watched her as she stormed off. She hated how weak she had felt in the pool, how afraid she had been of Evelyn and Martin. She couldn't tolerate either emotion in herself, or she would never walk out of the Grand free again. When the time was right, she would find the exit. She was a fox, just like they called her when she was a girl. She was still a trickster. Even a fox could outsmart a wolf.

CHAPTER SIX

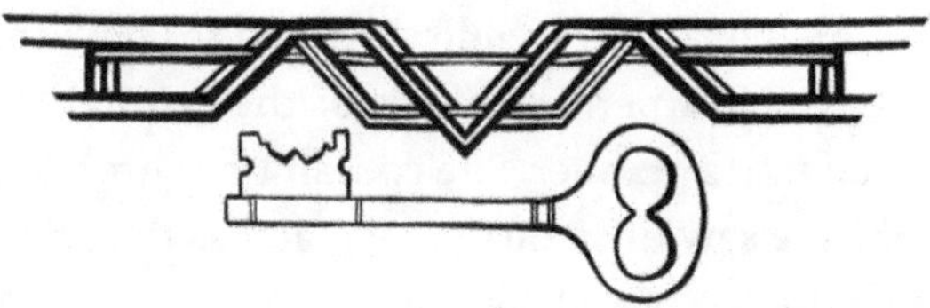

Hours later, Mabel paced behind the curtain of the Grand Hotel's theater. Her beaded dress swished and heels clacked across the wooden floor with her endless pacing. The Van Doren's were on stage with a little furry dog who had "stolen" one of their apples. Red-headed Gisela chased him in circles on a unicycle, followed by her brothers Karl and Stefan carrying full baskets of fruits and vegetables. Friedrich, the youngest, ran after them playing the ukulele as quickly as his little fingers would let him.

Mabel hardly ever got nervous anymore, but the Van Dorens' comedy act was a tough one to follow, especially when she didn't know what Evelyn had in mind for her. Her hair and makeup were lovely. The tap shoes were just her size. Her black and gold dress was perfect—simple yet elegant. Even so, pacing was all she could do to keep her knotted stomach from giving up her breakfast. Mabel didn't want to admit to herself what happened at the pool. She had never been so close to death before, and the idea that the Grand was the only thing keeping her alive was overwhelming. She had scrubbed herself down and soaked herself in a scorchingly hot bath for an hour, but still her chest ached from leaving the hotel hours later. When Mabel had tried to leave her hotel room, she had found the door locked. She had been unable to escape for hours, all the way up until rehearsal that evening.

"Mabel Rose Dixon! You're up!"

She was so lost in thought, she hadn't heard the music end. Her tap shoes echoed across the auditorium as Mabel trotted out into the center of the enormous stage. There were several box seats, and rows upon rows of balcony seats leading upward. Above her, a great crystal chandelier hung in massive splendor. Mabel had caught a glimpse of it the night before, but she was able to see better now that the stage lights were off. It was a perfect mirror of the celestial theme in her bedroom, but ten times grander. She couldn't be sure from a distance, but she thought she saw tiny stars strewn across the ceiling sparkling and wondered if they were real diamonds.

Evelyn lounged in the second row, flapping an overly large red feathered fan to cool herself. She was wearing a light gown made of crushed purple velvet and gold. The golden snake bracelet adorned her wrist again. Its two yellow diamond eyes glittered at Mabel in their twin settings, tempting her.

"You look smart," Evelyn said. "I wish I had chosen something as light. It is oppressively warm in here."

The theater *was* hot, and smelled horribly musty, like something had seeped into the carpet and never quite gotten out. She ignored the discomfort and stood tall, waiting for instruction. She was a professional, after all. She didn't know exactly what Frank saw in Evelyn to appoint her as the Grand's theatrical director, but she was determined to dazzle her anyway.

"I want to see your dance first," Evelyn said. "Whatever you use to audition. Go."

Mabel was going to have kittens. There was no music chosen. No direction from her supposed director. She had expected more instruction than that. Was this how Evelyn ran her shows?

Evelyn huffed at Mabel, impatient as always. "I don't have all day. If you're lost, tell Joshua the song, and I'll call out the moves. I want you to give me your best with no hesitation."

Mabel hadn't seen the man behind the piano. The boy was not much older than Mabel. She didn't understand why everyone doing the grunt work around the Grand seemed younger than twenty-five, but she had a feeling she wasn't going to like the answer if she asked.

She took a deep breath. There was no need to panic. Her memory for choreography was perfect. She could simply pair a quickstep dance number and combine it with some music from Ziegfeld's last audition, which had been quite good. Even Ziegfeld had said so. Mabel mentally flicked through the dances she had completed from her theaters back home in Atlanta to Ziegfeld's routines like mental notecards and picked the perfect song.

Mabel told the pianist to play "Sweet Georgia Brown" by Django Reinhardt. When the first piano keys twinkled out the upbeat melody, Mabel shook off her nerves and slipped into the luxurious silk feeling of her confidence.

"Give me your Charleston," Evelyn called out over the music.

As she tapped across the stage, the theater fell away. Mabel spun on all the right beats, making full use of the empty stage.

"Show me your Foxtrot."

Mabel responded quickly, slipping into the right steps. She wasn't performing in front of Evelyn. Mabel was out amongst the stars, as if the whole universe were there for her to tap across.

"Now, your Black Bottom. Your Varsity Drag. Your Lindy Hop!"

Mabel did as she was told, moving like the Devil had taken over her heels, whisked her away on the dance floor, and led her steps by the hand. The music ended and Mabel gave her grandest pose. She took her bow, smiling at the imagined crowd. Mabel didn't care what Evelyn thought. She had just given one of the best shows of her life, and her fear was gone. If she didn't like it, Evelyn could eat it.

Evelyn gave an appreciative frown. "Not bad for a human. Catch your breath because I need your final number. Let's hear you sing."

Mabel's heart pounded as she came to stand at center stage. She needed to calm down, but her hands were clammy and her shoes felt too snug and everything was going to go horribly wrong. The last time Mabel had sung was in front of Ziegfeld. The frown that had formed on his face was a permanent photograph in her mind. If she were honest, it wasn't just Ziegfeld's face she remembered. All her life she had been told she couldn't sing. Her sisters Daisy May and Maryanne had teased Mabel for her deep "boyish" voice. Her brother

Avery had told Mabel she was better off croaking in some lily pond for all her bullfrog boyfriends. No one thought she had any chance of being a star.

Mabel never understood what was so wrong with her deep voice. She could belt a sultry jazz tune that bordered on scandalous rather than croon a high, simpering tune. None of the other Ziegfeld girls could do that. Still, she wished she could change it. She wanted to land the starring role, not the chorus girl, and that meant being able to sing lead for the family-friendly floor show, and for the frolic after dark. She had to be able to sing both. Evelyn was going to kick her off stage for sure. She was going to tell Frank that he hadn't found his star, that Mabel had failed. And what would happen then? What if she failed? She doubted he would give her soul back, no harm, no foul. No, Frank had threatened to let Evelyn and Martin eat her if she failed. Her song test had to go well. It just had to.

She tried to convince herself that it would be all right. Frank *had* promised she would be able to sing, but she hadn't dared to test her voice since she gave up her soul. She didn't know what was going to happen when she opened her mouth.

A stagehand brought her a microphone stand and set it in front of her. As Joshua's fingers danced across the keys, Mabel drew up her courage and pushed her voice into song.

"Ready?" Evelyn said.

"Ab-so-tute-ly." But Mabel absolutely was not.

Her legs shook as she came to stand in front of the mic. She told the pianist to play a number she had auditioned with before. As the song began, Mabel thought she was going to toss her cookies the moment she opened her mouth to sing, but she parted her lips and belted the most beautiful song she had ever heard. Her voice—it was so different. She didn't recognize it. She sounded so beautiful, so wonderful. It was her own voice but pushed far beyond the notes she used to be able to barely hit.

As the song continued, Mabel let herself go. She felt more powerful with every wave of her hips and gesture of her hands. Mabel had never sung like this, but she had dreamed about her voice being as powerful as a mermaid luring sailors out to sea. Ziegfeld was a fool for casting her out. As she hit each note, something glowed inside of her, like a sun rising within her. The light enveloped her bones with its warmth.

Mabel held the last note as long as possible as the piano faded away. Something shined around her face, and she had to cup her hand to see the auditorium. It wasn't an errant spotlight. The light was emitting from her.

The Canary diamond glowed around her neck.

Evelyn's eyes went wide. She clacked the fan shut, snapping Mabel out of her revelry. The Canary light faded, retreating fingers of light back inside itself. Evelyn drew out her long cigarette and took her time striking the match and lighting the end. She took a drag, blew out the smoke and opened her mouth to say something, then shook her head. Mabel guessed she thought better of whatever cutting remark she had started to make. She watched Evelyn closely as she puffed a few times before settling back into her seat to gaze up at the starry ceiling.

"I'm surprised Ziegfeld passed on you," Evelyn said. "His loss. Our gain."

Mabel was taken aback by the compliment. "Thank you."

"I know what it's like. Both the theater and the pictures look for a certain type of girl. If you break that mold to make your own shape, you're not getting baked with the rest of the little cookies. You have something, Mabel, but it's not what people expect."

Mabel didn't know if that was good news or bad. She let go of the microphone, unaware she had clutched the stand so hard while she sang that her hands had turned sweaty. "So? Will it work for tonight?"

Evelyn batted her smoky eyes at Mabel, flashing a dangerous grin. "I think we can push you even farther."

THEY PRACTICED FOR HOURS, all the way up until dinner, which was wheeled up around 8 pm on little carts with silver trays. They dined in the center of the stage at tables with white linens and a set of chairs the bellhops brought out for them. Mabel didn't know what exactly Evelyn ate, but she was not surprised in the least when her trays were opened to reveal plates of various types of meat. Mabel devoured her chicken and vegetables with a side of cornbread and honey butter. She downed her fresh lemonade while Evelyn ate politely with a fork and knife, not using her second mouth at all. Mabel hadn't seen her second mouth since the night before, but she knew it was there, waiting and hungry under Evelyn's shawl. She wondered how often that second mouth needed to feed.

Evelyn sliced a delicate sliver of roast beef with her knife and placed a tiny bite in her mouth. "So, you came up here to New York six weeks ago, is that right?"

Mabel nodded. "And you just arrived from where exactly?"

"Tinseltown. I come from the land of the silver screen and silent pictures. Hollywood land. Martin and I are actors. I was a Ziegfeld girl, but then Hollywood plucked me up and I moved out west. You can say this trip is our grand homecoming."

So, Martin wasn't lying when he said he knew Ziegfeld, Mabel thought.

Mabel sucked down the last of her lemonade through her paper straw. "And you are here for the May's Eve Ball? Like you said?"

There was a strange pause before Evelyn answered. "Martin had to return to Los Angeles."

"Oh." Mabel knew that was not what had happened at all. "And you don't mind that he's gone?"

"Frank needed *my* help running his theater acts," Evelyn said, setting her knife and fork down on her plate with a clink. "So, *I* came. He was right to suggest you and I work together. You have potential here. There's no question. Between you and me, you wouldn't make it far in New York, kid. Frank is right. The stage is dying. You'd have better luck in pictures."

Mabel's shoulders stiffened at the insult. She had to remind herself to relax. There was nothing Evelyn could say she hadn't heard already. "Thanks for the advice, but I'm not accepting critique at this time."

Evelyn laughed into the back of her hand. "No, no, I'm not saying you do, but you left your home, even gave up your soul to pursue a dying art. A camera would be happier with you than a live audience. That's where the future is. The streets of New York are ruthless, and fresh competition is always rolling in by bus, train, and automobile. If you want to stay in New York, I think your deal at the Grand might be the best thing to ever happen to you. I can teach you to run things. Make this place your own."

Mabel didn't know how to respond. It was unexpectedly candid of Evelyn to offer career advice. While Mabel appreciated it, she hadn't forgotten that just twenty-four hours ago she was nothing more than a hot meal. She couldn't start to think of Evelyn as a friend.

"I believe that's it for this afternoon," Evelyn said. "We meet back here promptly at 9:30, no later. You'll need to select your outfits and prepare yourself before the 10 o'clock floor show."

She nodded as a reply. "Will Frank really be there?"

Evelyn raised one razor-thin eyebrow. "He wouldn't miss it."

"And how exactly am I going to collect souls for his diamond?"

Evelyn lit herself another cigarette. "That was always a mystery to me as well. When Frank asked me to get his diamond for him, I knew the legends, but not how they worked. Guess you'll have to find out. Focus on your performance. Shine like you did for me today. That's all that matters to get the diamond to work. Supposedly."

She was keeping the cards she wanted to play close to her chest. That was fine. Mabel had learned enough about Evelyn to form a plan. If Evelyn saw her as a prodigy she was here to train, what better fun than to make her think that's exactly what Mabel wanted too? She would cozy up to Evelyn, appeal to her need for flattery, and slip in a few questions about Frank. The more she knew about his habits, the more likely it was she could find out where he kept all the souls he collected.

"You will be going after the Van Doren's," Evelyn said, changing the subject. "The comedy act always opens. They warm up the crowd, get them riled up, and then it will be time for your dance number. Your song will close out the show. Are you ready?"

"Ab-so-tute-ly," Mabel said, though her nerves about performing live for the first time in New York were getting the better of her.

As Evelyn turned on her heel to leave for her dressing room, Mabel brushed past her and carefully slipped the bracelet off of her wrist without her noticing. When she was sure Evelyn was gone, Mabel exited quickly through the red curtains, and almost ran into the bellhop that kept attending her room and bringing her meals. They locked eyes for a moment as he pressed a note into her hand. As Mabel pocketed the note, she was certain she had seen the bellhop somewhere else tonight, but couldn't remember where. Perhaps he greeted her at the front door? The bellhop pushed the cart away before she could place his face.

Mabel hurried down the stairs, clutching both the note and bracelet, as she sprinted down the hall. She waited until she had returned to the safety of her dressing room before she opened the note.

I know how you can escape.
Meet me in the lobby after your performance. I'll explain everything.
Don't try to leave the hotel.

It was signed by someone named Will Donahue. Mabel turned the note over in her hand. There were no other instructions.

Mabel folded the note back up and tucked it between her breasts. She would not be doing something as foolish as meeting in the open lobby for anyone to see, thank you very much. Not that she'd had any luck getting back to the entrance. She didn't know who this Will Donahue was, but he sounded like another demon who wanted to slip her a fast one. A human couldn't possibly think meeting in the lobby was a good idea unless they were reckless, or worse, had a desire for Mabel to get caught in the act of trying to escape. She was no rube. Mabel would find another way out once she had her soul.

At least she still had the snake bracelet. Mabel slipped on the slender thing. It was so much lovelier up close. She was curious that it matched the Canary around her neck so perfectly. They really would make a smart set to present to Ziegfeld once she got her soul back and escaped.

She checked the little hands on her wristwatch. It was only 9:45. Plenty of time to powder her nose and select an outfit before returning to the stage. Choosing which outfit to wear turned out to be harder than Mabel thought. She hadn't looked closely at the outfits the night before, but the wardrobe had definitely changed in color and tone. It was packed to the gills with the finest clothing Mabel had ever seen, but there were now dresses for stage performances rather than everyday attire. There were silks and satin dresses cut so low there was no way she would be able to wear a band around her chest to achieve the boyish figure that was so very à la mode. Some were backless, others were draped in pearls and crystals. They were all so delicate, Mabel worried she would dance, and the fabric would rip, and the intricate beadwork would all go flying everywhere. She would have to be careful which outfit she selected for dancing and which for her final song number.

Mabel took out a little red backless number with dangling jewels just above her behind. Her mother would have died on the spot to see her daughter dressed so scantily clad, but she was a brave and daring Flapper, a girl who belonged to New York City and no one else. She would wear what she pleased.

She removed a pale white, floor-length gown with sequin accents and set it aside for her final song number when the door to her dressing room opened. A half dozen ladies in matching Grand black and gold tailcoats who had done her makeup earlier rushed into the room to dress her. They helped fasten her garters, slip on her red dress, and adjust the back beadwork. They sat her in front of the large golden vanity, painted kohl and eyeshadow on her eyes, freshened the rouge on her cheeks, and applied fresh red lipstick the color of oxblood. Mabel was surprised she had an entire team to attend her when a quick jaunt to the Augment would have sufficed, but she was not one to turn down a good pampering. She barely recognized herself in the mirror. Mabel was a vision in scarlet, her beauty far surpassing any stage darling Ziegfeld dared to claim was better than her. She didn't expect the color of her blood red lips to bring back the sudden memory of the poor elevator boy. As good as she looked, Mabel had to turn away. The memory of his screams and his blood on her shoes was still too severe.

The team brushed Mabel's hair and readjusted her headband and peacock feather. When they were done, Mabel removed her watch and laid it on the vanity. 15 minutes until curtain.

The attending ladies all filed out, leaving her alone in her dressing room once again. Mabel came to stand in front of a floor-length mirror, unable to stop herself from admiring her form again in her flapper dress, bobbed hair, and sultry makeup. This was a moment she had only ever dreamed of. She looked exactly like Louise Brooks, only better. It was exactly how she had always wanted to look, a modern girl, even if a small part missed her strawberry blond curls. Frank might have called her a star, but now she truly felt like one.

Mabel flung her shoulders back, took a deep breath, and exited her dressing room. She strutted down the hall and through the stage door like a vamp. Mabel was going to give Frank one hell of a performance; one he would never forget.

CHAPTER SEVEN

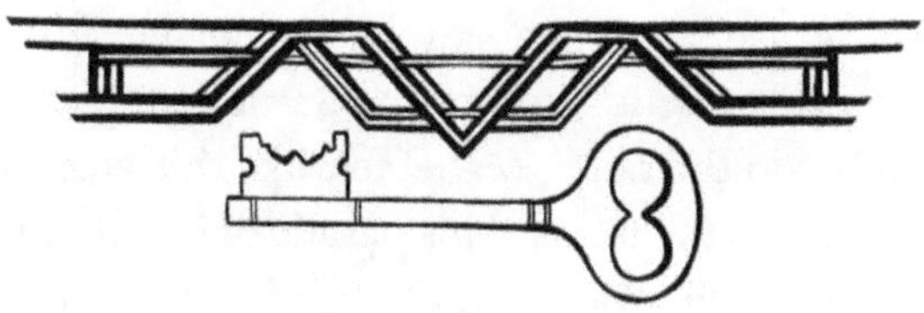

Mabel had never performed on stage in front of a live audience of this size before, but she had imagined this moment with such detail that her dreams felt like memories.

Her heels clacked across the hardwood floor, announcing her arrival. The crowd's roar was deafening, and the sound of their voices chanting her name reverberated in her chest like the steady beat of a drum. The illumination of the spotlight shone down on her like a beacon from an angel above.

Mabel had pictured this same hardwood stage floor every time she performed for her disinterested siblings. She had dreamed of lights so bright she could see the audience every time she closed her eyes to sleep. Mabel had visualized the live band so clearly in her mind. Until now, these mental pictures had been only photographs of some other life Mabel had longed for but never seen. Somehow, Frank had spun every straw-figure dream Mabel had ever had into pure gold.

The violin rang out the first note of her song, and Mabel tapped her heart out, getting every move perfect to the delight of her adoring fans. She leaped across the stage, spinning in a whirlwind of taps in beat with the jazzy rhythm. The cheers drowned out every tiny voice that had ever whispered doubt in her own ear, every moment she had ever wondered if she wasn't good enough for the stage. There was nothing left but the golden haze within her and without.

The music ended on a soft note. Mabel took her bow to the sounds of adoration she had always longed to hear. She wished they could see her now, all of the people who had ever doubted her or told her no. Her mother, her brother and two sisters, the stage manager of the local theater back home, Ziegfeld—they could never see her potential. They could never see what she saw inside herself, but now Mabel belonged to a world of light. She was the Grand's star, and for the first time since coming to the hotel, Mabel felt like this was a better place for her than Ziegfeld's theater and his parade of identical dolls. Maybe the Grand was where she was meant to be after all. If she could find a way to get rid of the demons.

Mabel blew a kiss, waltzing off stage in a sashay of feathers and sequins. Nothing could ruin this moment. Nothing could destroy her now, not even the loss of her soul.

She hurried back to her room as Gisela and the Van Doren's trotted past her in a haze of sequins and stockings onto the stage to do their second number. She had little time to change, check her makeup and hair, but Mabel was flying high above the moon. She doubted she would land on the ground ever again.

Mabel slipped out of the risqué red dress as soon as she entered the dressing room. She removed her feathered headband, suddenly concerned that no one had shown up to help her. Her mysterious entourage of attendants had gone missing. No matter. She was Mabel Rose Dixon, star of the Grand Hotel. She knew how to dress herself alone, as she always had done.

She took the silvery gown she had set aside and slipped it on carefully. It was strange to Mabel how quickly she had come to rely on the luxuries of the hotel, with people to dress her and bring her food, things that forty-eight hours ago she would have laughed at the thought of ever receiving. What would she do without the comforts of this place when and if she broke free? It was a thought that stuck with her as she unbuckled her silvery gray-green shoes, and as she puckered her lips and quickly reapplied her lipstick. She did like the benefits, and maybe being a part of the Grand was survivable enough that she could picture herself staying here. Maybe. The pull of the lights was strong, and if she didn't resist, Mabel would stay stuck here forever. After her moment in the spotlight, she wasn't sure she wanted to.

"You were a delight," a smoky voice said from behind her.

Evelyn Greene leaned against the wall of Mabel's dressing room. She wore a sleek red dress with black jewels sewn above the hem. Two giant feathers arched back from her forehead like ram horns. The crystalline-shaped black diamonds clacked as she turned toward Mabel on silvery heels. She looked like a chandelier dripping with blood.

"Can't wait for your next act," she cooed. "You're going to kill."

"Thank you." Mabel's body shook just standing in Evelyn's towering presence, but she tried like hell not to let it show. Did Evelyn notice the bracelet was gone? Is that why she was here? Mabel avoided looking where it lay hidden beneath her gloves.

She took a long drag on her cigarette and blew out the smoke into twisted shapes. "I've come to give the star a gift."

"Now?"

"Yes, now."

Evelyn's eyes were so heavily kohled that it was hard to read if her words were sincere. Up close, Mabel saw the most disturbing detail of her outfit. Two tiny red horns jutted out from her forehead. Not decoration, but part of Evelyn's skin, her true self fully revealed.

Mabel tensed, unsure why Evelyn wanted to talk now, of all moments. She knew Mabel only had a second to change costumes but had still chosen this short window of time to bombard her like this.

"Whatever it is, you could have told me earlier. Couldn't you have told me at rehearsal?"

Evelyn crossed her arms. "Not really."

She tried to ignore how closely Evelyn trailed her footsteps as she hurried to the privacy curtain to change. Mabel couldn't stop picturing the rows of teeth hidden beneath Evelyn's luxurious gown and was very aware that every moment spent alone with this towering demon could be her last. Mabel slipped behind her room divider where she had laid out her next outfit, relieved to be out of sight.

"First, I wanted to give you advice about your final song," Evelyn said. "One tip, straight from me to you. You should have worn red for the second number, not the first. There would be less to clean up that way."

"Less?" Mabel glanced down at her dress, which was a brilliant silvery white flounced ball gown. It didn't match her black gloves, but she didn't dare to take them off with Evelyn so close.

"Second, I wanted to ask you for a favor. It seems a bracelet of mine has gone missing. You wouldn't happen to know where it went?"

Evelyn's voice was poison in Mabel's veins. Her arms went stiff. Mabel reached for her shoes and found it hard to move, as if Evelyn's voice had seeped into her bloodstream and was attempting to pull her puppet strings.

"I'm sorry." Mabel's voice was so far away. "I don't know where it went."

"Don't you?"

Black claws stretched over the top of the room divider. Evelyn peered over to look at Mabel. Her eyes were not white like the demons by the pool. Her eyes were slick black, twin pools of car oil in her porcelain face. Mabel stepped backward, knocking into a small table, arrested by the absurd question of wondering why Evelyn's eyes were different than the other demons.

"Do you know what happens to humans who lose their souls *and* their bodies?" The skin along Evelyn's neckline rippled as her chest unzipped. "They're dragged down to hell."

Teeth unveiled across her breastbone, jutting out like broken piano keys in all directions. Mabel could not look away, not even when the long, pink tongue of Evelyn's second mouth gave her a rough lick across the cheek.

"I can smell it on you, Maby-baby," Evelyn's first mouth said. "Give me the bracelet back. I don't care what Frank says. I will devour you slowly, and I will make sure every bone snaps on the way down my throat as punishment for stealing from me. Last warning. Remove the bracelet."

"You can't take it from me," Mabel said, backing away from Evelyn as fast as possible around the room. "Like Frank said, I must give it to you as a gift. You need me alive."

Delight flashed across Evelyn's eyes. "That's only true for the Canary diamond, sweetheart."

Evelyn flung herself at Mabel, dagger nails outstretched. Mabel shrieked as she tried to leap away, but she tripped over one of the bistro chairs she had tried to hide herself behind. The table clattered over onto its side, taking the tea set down with them as Evelyn's nails tore through the chiffon of Mabel's gown and found the meat of her leg. Broken China scattered everywhere as a scream tore from Mabel's throat, more out of shock than pain.

Much like the first time Evelyn had skewered her, the cut was so deep that it didn't register at first. There was only the sensation that several slim knives were where they shouldn't be between her muscles. It wasn't until Evelyn yanked her nails out that the pain registered with all the force of a freight train. Mabel wailed as she tried to pry herself from Evelyn's grip, but the cupcake puff of her dress pinned her easily beneath the knife fingers of the onyx-eyed demon.

Evelyn reached for the bracelet, cooing at it as if the jewelry were her child. The skin around Mabel's wrist turned hot, but she barely noticed the heat compared to the fire that was in her leg. Warmth seeped out of the holes Evelyn had torn, staining Mabel's dress. She knew she was bleeding, that she should stop the blood, but Mabel was shaking too much to do anything about it. She was too stunned to do anything as the snake bracelet let its tail drop from its mouth and raised its cobra head to look Evelyn directly in the eye.

Evelyn's penciled brows drew together in a thin line of confusion. She opened her mouth to say "No," but the snake struck her in the cheek before she could finish. The beautiful demon wailed, falling back off of Mabel as she tried to yank the golden snake off of her face. Mabel fought through the pain to crawl away, dragging her bloody leg along with her. The pain was more manageable now, as if the worst were over, but Mabel knew if she didn't get a bandage around it soon, she would likely bleed out.

Mabel crawled over to one of the mahogany wardrobes and flung open the door. She scrambled through one of the drawers until she found a thick scarf. Mabel yanked up the poof of her dress and tied the knot tight, remembering everything her father ever taught her about knots.

Mabel staggered to her feet. Her head felt like a cloud, weightless and unable to form solid thoughts. Evelyn writhed across the carpet as she tried to pry the snake off of her face when Mabel turned around. Her cries were so loud, Mabel was surprised no one had come to see what was happening inside her room.

She needed to get on stage. Evelyn wouldn't dare follow her there. For all her talk, she would not risk angering Frank. There was no time to change or get rid of the blood on her dress.

Mabel stumbled out into the hallway, tripping on the torn chiffon. She used the wall as a crutch to keep herself from falling over as she fled, but her leg throbbed with a heartbeat of sharp pain with every step. She tried to push through it as Evelyn's screams followed her down the hallway, growing louder as if she were attempting to crawl after Mabel on hands and knees.

Mabel was so worried about Evelyn following her, she didn't know she was in front of the stage door until it swung open and almost hit her in the face. A dark-haired stagehand boy had flung it open, and he stared at her incredulously.

"We're starting," the stagehand said. "You're late."

Something cold and hard slithered down Mabel's arm and into her black glove. The snake wrapped itself back around her wrist, content.

His irritation evaporated when he saw Mabel's face. "Is everything all right?"

Mabel grinned, showing too much of her teeth. "Everything's jake. Just nerves."

The stagehand seemed to accept her lie out of the urgency to get the star on stage, but it was clear from his frown he was still skeptical if she was truly all right. Evelyn's screams were gone, and the hall behind Mabel was eerily quiet as she slipped inside the theater. Would Evelyn be there when she got back? She could worry about it later. That was a problem for future Mabel. She could only focus on keeping her balance and not toppling over as the stagehand dragged her into the curtain wings.

"And now, finally," Frank said to the full auditorium. "We have our last performance of the evening. She's always worth the wait, ladies and gentlemen. Please give a warm welcome back to the stage, Mabel Rose Dixon."

The orchestra swelled with the first chords of her music and Frank withdrew to the shadows without meeting Mabel's gaze. The stagehand gave her a push and Mabel gathered the bloody part of her skirt in her fist, hiding the stain as best as she could. She found her stage health in the bright roar of the crowd greeting her again and she practically floated over to the lonely microphone at its center. She wrapped her hand around it. The spotlight hit her dress, revealing her in all her glory, and Mabel sang as she never had before.

As she performed, Frank watched her from his box seat. The corners of his mouth were drawn up in an approving smile. He watched her with eyes that reflected back her starlight, a sharp reminder that there was nothing beneath his handsome face. He was a soulless thing, but was she really so different now that she didn't have a soul as well?

Mabel hit the chorus, flying through the notes, when a hand slapped the stage. She faltered when a man tried to crawl up into the spotlight with her.

"Mabel! Mabel! Look at me! I'm over here."

She had dealt with her fair share of hecklers and tomatoes. When she performed vaudeville for her theater back home, there were always plenty of men looking to pet, particularly during the burlesque acts. A girl could count on the bouncers to keep the audience from any hands that went astray.

With a theater as big as the Grand, surely Frank kept some protection on staff. Mabel was sure that any minute now, one of Frank's men would come. They would push the dreamy-eyed suitor away from her, but the starstruck man was almost all the way up on stage now. A moment more, and he would be up there with her.

Mabel picked up the mic stand and kicked the Johnny with her good leg. She clocked him right in the chin with her heel and her would-be suitor fell right back into the crowd where he belonged.

"Down, boy. If you're good, I might give you a biscuit later."

She played it off, smiling at the crowd as she resumed the song like it was all some big game. Weren't they having fun? Inside Mabel, every warning bell clanged that she should run. She was wide open on stage, unprotected. With her bum leg, she wouldn't get very far. The song was almost done. She could finish it. When it was over, where would she go?

She held a high note before the big finish, and a fervent hand reached for her dress. Mabel tugged her hem out of the steely grip of an elderly woman. She didn't want to hurt someone so old, but the look in the lady's eyes was desperate to get closer to Mabel, to touch her. There was a ripping sound as the old woman tore a souvenir from Mabel's dress and proudly announced she had claimed a piece of Frank's star.

Mabel finished the song to uproarious applause. The cries of so many people rushed over her like a tidal wave, nearly knocking her off her feet. She wanted this moment to feel like heaven, but instead found herself in hell as she glanced up at Frank's box. He was clapping, long and slow, for his star. Behind him, Evelyn stood with her arms folded, rage building behind her green eyes. There wasn't a scratch on her perfect face.

Something fell from the sky around Mabel, forcing her to look away from Evelyn. The pieces raining down were soft as snow, but as large as a silver dollar. Another fell on her dress, a violent pink shade. Mabel plucked it off her dress. Rose petals were falling across the stage like rain, showering her with velvety slips of pink, red, and white. Their colors were more vibrant than any roses Mabel had ever seen.

The curtain whispered shut and Mabel's world of light gave way to darkness. The audience cheered her name from the other side of those knockout curtains. She leaned down to pick up one of the red rose petals.

"Mabel? Where are you, Mabel dear?"

She froze, dropping the petal. It was the woman who had ripped her dress. She was peeking around the corner to see if she could come inside.

Mabel backed away. "You're not supposed to be back here, ma'am."

The old woman pulled back the curtain. "I just want a signature."

The woman's voice wavered with desperation as if Mabel held a loaf of bread in her hands and she was dying of hunger. "Perhaps a lock of hair?"

"You already got lucky, old woman," a male voice called. "I was here first."

Mabel spun on her heel. Two men—one blond, one brunette—emerged from the other side of the stage. The young blond wore his best suit and coattails with his hair slicked back, a new money type. The brunette was much older, but he had clearly come to the theater fresh off the docks from his cap and modest clothes. Mabel didn't understand what was happening. One minute she was taking her bow; the next these three fanatics were ganging up on her like a pack of wild dogs arguing over a bone. She searched the wings on either side, but she was alone. Where was everyone? The stagehands? The bellhops? The entourage that dressed her?

Where was Frank?

She knew she was meant to lure people backstage, but no one had explained exactly how she was supposed to take their souls. Mabel had assumed they would come to her, and she would relieve them of their souls like Raymond had relieved her of her own. Evelyn told her to just trust the Canary to take care of the rest, but these people were dangerous. If she couldn't figure out how to take their souls soon, she was going to have to defend herself.

"Please, just give me your souls," Mabel said. "I don't want to hurt anyone."

She held the Canary diamond toward them. It did nothing.

"I've come all this way," the dock worker said. "Gave my last dollars for the admission fee. All I want is a kiss. Just one little peck on the cheek. That's all I need. I'll be on my way."

There was something off about their eyes. Mabel had thought it was stage glare at first, but the closer they got, she knew it was no trick. Their eyes were filmed over with gold, and they wore their desperation like cheap cologne. She tried hitting the Canary diamond over and over. Maybe the damn thing just needed to wake up.

"I was here first." The old woman tapped her cane on the hardwood stage with a decided clap. "You two can get in line."

"Listen," Mabel said, desperate for an out until she could figure out how the diamond worked. "Just let me go back to my hotel room. I will get a pen and..."

The old woman grabbed Mabel by the hem of her white gown and reached into her bag. "I have a quill pen right here."

She stabbed Mabel with the point of the pen, right in the arm. Mabel shrieked as she tried to pry herself free from the woman's thin, steely fingers. The old bird refused to let go until she had gotten what she came for and the quill tore a long red ribbon in the back of her arm.

"You're not getting off that easy," the woman hissed in Mabel's face. "I want my money's worth. People will pay ten times over if your name is signed in blood."

"No!" Mabel yanked herself away, tearing her beautiful dress even more. She stumbled backward, only to fall into the arms of the blond and brunette men. Mabel begged for them to let her go, but they couldn't keep their hands off of her.

Mabel's wrist warmed where the snake bracelet lay hidden as she thrashed and twisted away from them. The metal grew unbearably hot, and she threw off her glove, hoping it would do exactly what it had done to Evelyn and save her.

Mabel looked into its yellow eyes. The bracelet was so heavy it felt like an anchor attached to her arm. "Please. Help me."

The snake let go of its tail slowly. It lifted its head to look at them.

"What is that?" the blond said.

The bracelet fanned out its cobra hood and tested the threat in the air with its tongue. The snake turned toward the old woman first, opened its small mouth, and hissed in warning, but the old woman did not let Mabel go.

"Make it stop," the old woman sneered. "I don't like it. This isn't the way it was supposed to go. This isn't what I imagined you would be like!"

Mabel used their surprise to her advantage and bolted. There was a tremendous tear as her gown lost all of its chiffon and Mabel hobbled away on her good leg. Blood seeped out of the scarf bandage and left a trail of droplets on the floor.

She only gained a few steps before the trio tackled her again. No matter how much Mabel begged, they continued to rip and tear at her clothes, her hair, her shoes, until they had grabbed every souvenir of the star they could get their hands on. Her palms started itching uncontrollably. The pain was white-hot, like she had touched metal that had laid out too long in the sun. The sensation made her wince, grit her teeth, and almost took her entire attention away from her assailants, but she couldn't let it stop her from escaping. The trio grabbed her hair, her arms, her dress. They ripped and tore, pushed and pulled at her body.

When Mabel finally let out a scream, the snake reared back its gold head, and struck.

CHAPTER EIGHT

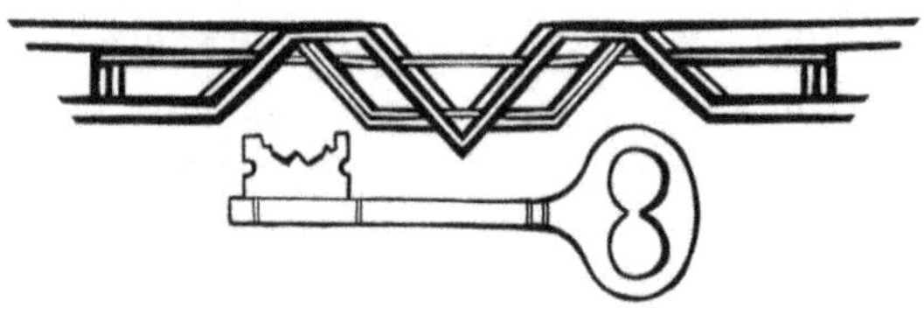

Mabel was covered in blood.

Her fingers were stiff with red matter. She didn't know what had happened, but somewhere between her final number and the curtain dropping, blood had splattered everywhere across the stage. She tried to remember the sequence of events, but her mind had turned the radio dial to an off-broadcast tone. She remembered singing, the curtain falling, and after that? There was nothing. The more she forced her brain to cooperate, the more it returned the favor with a scorching headache.

Her hands trembled so hard her knuckles hurt as she tried to wipe the red debris off her arms, her dress, her hair, but it was everywhere. The white gown was thick with red. The color clung to her skin and turned harder by the minute. Mabel took careful steps to keep herself from falling on the wet stage, but she slipped on something round, something both hard and soft.

She lifted her heel. The object was a large white marble with some red stringy material stuck to the end. It was a marble with an iris as blue as a cloudless sky, and a pupil as dark as a tunnel with no end.

Mabel screamed as she slipped across the stage to get away from the eyeball. She grabbed the microphone stand to keep from falling into the curtain.

"Mabel?"

The cheers were still carrying on from the other side of the curtain, so loud that Mabel could not be sure if the voice was the crowd still chanting her name, or someone else.

"Mabel, dear? Where are you...?"

The voice called her name in a singsong, so close she could have sworn they were standing right next to her. She covered her ears, worried she really was losing it, until fingers drew back the velvet curtain.

"There you are." Frank was looking smart in a black suit with gold embroidery woven into the swirling patterns of his shirt and coattails. She hated that he didn't seem the least bit concerned about the amount of blood and viscera everywhere across the stage while she was terrified out of her mind. If anything, his grin told her he was more pleased with her than ever as he strode over to her. "My, what a mess you have made."

"I don't know what happened. I—" She trailed off, her thoughts vanishing as the sharp memory of the old woman's face came rushing back.

She did remember what happened. It was so horrible; Mabel had gone into shock. Now that Frank had found her, what she had done was all coming back in messy fragments.

"You've gone beyond expectation, my dear." The intricate details of his suit swayed with every step. His suit, eyes, and face were so hypnotic that Mabel couldn't look away from him as Frank came to her side and lifted her chin.

"I knew you could do it." He sighed against her cheek.

"How dare you." She wanted to punch him right in his smug face, but her body and her senses weren't cooperating with her plans. Frank kissed the back of her hand and Mabel found herself wishing he had kissed her mouth. Her movements were thick, like she was trying to out swim a riptide back to shore. She didn't want to leave his eyes, or his arms. Not ever.

Mabel drew up her fist, but she moved so slowly, he was able to deter her easily.

"Not the face. A glamor this good is difficult to keep."

The Augment, Mabel thought. *Of course he would use it on himself*. It must have placed one hell of a spell on Frank. No matter how hard she tried to look away from him, the allure of his gray eyes was too strong.

He kissed up the back of her arm to her neck, not caring about the blood. Mabel found herself sighing in spite of herself. Frank's hand found her other hand, drawing her closer to him until their bodies were pressed together and Mabel could feel the bulge in his pants.

"What is this?" His grip tightened, squeezing her wrist as he turned her around to examine what was dangling there. He wiped blood away from the snake's face. "You clever little minx. You stole Evelyn's protection charm. She always favored vicious little spells."

Mabel glanced at the snake's diamond eyes. Did the snake do all this?

She had finished her song to a roaring crowd. When the curtain fell, she remembered three fans had climbed backstage to beg the famous Mabel Rose Dixon for a piece of her starlight. The old woman, dock worker, and young money had claimed they wanted just a signature, just a kiss, just attention—they had tried to claim so much more. Mabel had tried to defend herself, but the snake at her wrist was the one who had bit back. The bracelet had protected her, just like Mabel wanted, but she hadn't wanted to turn those people into snake chow just to save her own skin. She never should have stolen from Evelyn.

Mabel's lower lip trembled as she yanked the snake off and shoved it at Frank. "Tell Evelyn she can have the bracelet back. I don't want to kill anyone else."

Frank gently took the bracelet from Mabel. He chuckled as if she had just said the most amusing thing in the world. "You and I both know the bracelet didn't do all of this."

She took a step back from him, remembering. "No."

"I thought you had talent and true potential, but I underestimated how much," Frank said. "You've slaughtered everyone."

She closed her eyes, but it couldn't block out the memories. "I didn't. It wasn't me. It was the bracelet."

"Trust me," Frank said. "You need to face what you are, what you're becoming."

When the snake struck the old woman and her blood had hit Mabel's cheek, that was when a strange cramp had flared in the center of her palms. As the pain had reached fiery heights, her palms had bubbled up like a horrible burn. Mabel had watched helplessly as her skin unzipped, revealing twin mouths, one in the center of each hand. The rest of her memory was a buzz-saw blur of carnage and bloody arterial sprays, painting her in so many shades of red Mabel didn't know how many bodies her hands had devoured until the deed was done.

"How could you?" Mabel intended for her voice to be full of rage, but she sounded as fatigued as she felt. "What did you do to me?"

Frank pocketed the bracelet. "Nothing. I'm just as shocked as you are."

Mabel glared. "I highly doubt that."

Frank shrugged. "On my honor, I did not know this would happen to you. So quickly. In all the books I read, the legends described an object so powerful it could suck the soul right out of anyone who was drawn to its wearer. I came to witness the Canary's power for myself after the show, but I had no idea what *you* were truly capable of. None of the books said how the diamond would affect the caretaker."

Mabel grabbed him by the collar of his pressed suit, not caring how much blood she got on him or his precious attire. "You didn't know what the diamond does? And you put this thing around my neck?"

"I'll tell you what I know." His voice was so gentle. "But you have to let me go."

Mabel did as she was told, but she made sure to push Frank hard enough that it would hurt.

"The Canary diamond is much like its namesake. It helps people sing, but in a literal sense. It draws out your natural talents and makes them shine brighter. If you're pretty, it can make you beautiful. If you can sing, it can transform you into a diva. It brings out the best in people, for a price it would seem."

Mabel's brows drew together in a crease. "Is that why those fanatics were so desperate for anything I could give them?"

"Like I told you before, Mabel. People love a star. But humans become enraptured by fame. They become drunk with being in the presence of a celebrity. I'm sure you know all too well, Ziegfeld girl."

She did. Mabel was all too familiar with the desperate look in their eyes. When they attacked Mabel, it was more intense than she had ever seen, and she had seen plenty of eyes go wide at the sight of Ziegfeld and his dazzling beauties.

"The Canary makes them hungry for that kind of glory, willing to do anything for fame..."

"Even give up their souls," Mabel finished.

He smirked. "The Canary can enhance you, but I read it must be given something of equal value in exchange. My guess? When it helped you sing tonight, what it took was a chunk of your remaining humanity."

He looked her dead in the eyes and refused to leave her gaze. "You see, when a human sells their soul, the longer they're without it, the more demonic they become. The essence of their humanity cannot remain intact without their soul. It usually takes a few weeks, sometimes a month or two, for the change to occur to the body and your second mouths to grow. I've never seen a transformation like this, and certainly not this quickly. Your second mouths grew in twenty-four hours."

"You knew I was going to turn into a demon this whole time?" Mabel's voice was shrill again, but she didn't care.

Frank grinned that wicked, too wide grin again. "What did you expect would happen to you when you gave up your soul? You're the one who didn't ask questions about your deal. Let this be a lesson for you. Always read the fine print."

Her stomach tightened so hard Mabel feared she would vomit. She didn't know what to make of what he was saying. This couldn't be happening. She couldn't become a demon. That wasn't part of her escape plan. Is this how Evelyn and Martin got their second mouths? It didn't matter. The situation was even more dire than she thought.

She shook her head. "You lied to me, Frank. You told me I was only going to have to collect their souls, not kill everyone, and not turn into a demon. Deal's off. I want my soul back."

"I never lied." Frank's tone was surprisingly gentle. "I didn't know you would do this. None of the books said how the diamond would affect the wearer. And you can't take it back."

Mabel yanked and tugged at the diamond, but it wouldn't come loose. "Get this thing off me right now or I'll use my hands to eat through the necklace."

"The contract is binding," Frank said, voice rising. "You will lure adoring fans backstage so the Canary can take their willing souls. It feeds, you feed. Simple, clean. If anything, your transformation makes the process much easier."

He examined the Canary around her neck. The shine inside pulsed in a heartbeat rhythm, keeping time with the pounding of Mabel's heart against her ribcage. "How interesting. It seems the diamond ate their souls already. Or maybe it's no coincidence at all. But I am curious. When you ate them, did a ball of light emerge?"

She stopped trying to take off the necklace. It was no use. Mabel was so tired of this game and her part on the chessboard. "Yes. I remember now. Their souls all went into the diamond."

He nodded curtly. "Good. Then your duty is done. I'll need you to perform again tomorrow. Do what you did tonight and draw them in, then take their souls. Your second mouths will get hungry and need to feed again. They can clean up the remains. It seems you are more than capable of handling yourself perfectly fine on your own."

It was so quiet in the empty theater. The crowd's cheers were long gone, but she had only just noticed the deafening silence around them. The empty stage between Frank and Mabel seemed like they stood miles apart, even though he watched her face and waited for her reaction only a few feet away.

Mabel considered what he had told her, and what Lucky had said about his plans for an ascension. She doubted Frank would tell her his true endgame, why he had stolen a cursed necklace and flung it around her neck without knowing the result. Whatever the reason, Frank wanted to try collecting one hundred souls again with the Canary badly enough to effectively give her the necklace and see what would happen. Which meant the collection of one hundred souls had nothing to do with the diamond itself.

She was a grand experiment. Nothing more.

Mabel sighed with quiet resolve. "We're done here. I'm not collecting souls. Not anymore. Deal's off."

He scoffed. "Why? So, you can go back to having a mediocre shot as a part-time chorus girl for a dying business? Ziegfeld already has a hundred girls or more, and his attendance numbers have been dropping by the day. He's dead. Besides, you didn't come to New

York to be a Ziegfeld girl. You and I both know what your real dream is."

"We're through, you hear?" Mabel shouted. "The deal is over. I want my soul back. Where are you keeping it?"

His voice rose to dangerous levels. "Even if I told you, it wouldn't matter. I can't release you."

"Why not?" Mabel said. "I'm not your sacrificial lamb."

A red light flashed behind Frank's gray eyes. "Don't feign innocence. You wanted to live so you could have a chance at fame. You wanted it more than your own soul. Tonight, you became the object of everyone's desire, just like you always wanted."

"At what cost?" Mabel shouted, tears running down her hot face. "Why do you need a hundred souls? What can the Canary give you that you don't already have?"

Frank's expression darkened.

"When your deal is done," Frank continued lightly. "You will leave this place. You will go back to the streets and clamor for Ziegfeld's attention in a dying industry. You will starve in your quest for starlight. That, I can promise you. But here? The Grand will keep your dream alive, preserved forever. Is this really how you want to play your cards?"

"Don't con me," she snapped back. "You and I both know you want to make sure I never leave this place."

He said nothing and Mabel hated him. She hated him more than she had ever hated anyone, even more than her brother Avery, who loved nothing more than to tear Mabel's dreams down. She burned with her hatred of Frank's pretty words. She thought of Lucky, how she had failed Frank a year ago, and he hadn't sent her away from the Grand Hotel. He had cast her out. She wasn't going to be cast aside.

"This isn't about me getting what I wanted. This is about you using me to ascend. Lucky told me. What are you trying to do? What is your ascension?"

Frank turned away, ignoring her. "I want ten souls tomorrow night. No less. Three is a good start, but not nearly enough."

"And if I refuse?"

"Your mouths will feed regardless of whether they have a willing host or not. I hope for your sake, you're willing."

Frank left her standing alone in the middle of the blood-drenched stage, the remains of two men and one old woman in pieces around her ankles amidst the crushed roses. Mabel tried to slow her racing heart, but her rage at Frank, at the Canary, and even at herself was so powerful it threatened to burn her alive.

She had half a mind to follow Frank and let her new mouths eat him, but she was scared to feed again. She was too scared to even touch her palms, though the mouths hidden beneath her skin were clearly dormant now. Frank promised they would need to feed, and she got the strong impression it wasn't some big joke.

A floor show every night.

She would kill again. That much was certain. Her worry was acid in her stomach, but she forced herself to focus on the next logical step to keep herself from throwing up. She needed to keep a level head and think. Mabel inspected herself. She hadn't noticed with all the blood, but her wounds from Evelyn and the trio of starstruck patrons had healed completely. It seemed feeding her hands also healed her body. At least she had that information in her favor.

Mabel rubbed her temples to suppress her blooming headache. If the Canary had taken a piece of her humanity so she could sing, what would happen after a month of songs? There wouldn't be anything left to turn human again. The Canary wasn't coming off. It would never come off, not until the diamond was fed its hundred souls, but that was not what frightened her most. It was the loss of her humanity.

She took the stairs down, clinging to the railing to keep her shaking legs from completely giving out from under her. She would take off this dress, clean herself off, pull herself together. She was Mabel Rose Dixon, a great and terrible thief, a master of puzzles. She would and could figure this out, but not covered in all this blood.

She couldn't go back to her room, didn't want to risk facing Evelyn. From the enraged look on her face during her entire performance, Mabel would place good odds-on Evelyn returning to her dressing room right after the show. She would not care that her bracelet was now in Frank's possession. Evelyn sparing her life after stealing from her twice was about as likely as the two of them sitting down for a nice cup of tea. No, Mabel needed somewhere else to hide.

Lucky.

If anyone had more answers about Frank's plans for ascension, it was the girl who had once been Frank's star.

Mabel had to walk carefully across the bloody stage to keep from slipping, but she made it off the stage all the way back to the steps leading down to the stage door exit. There was blood everywhere, even spilling down the steps. Mabel clung to the railing as she slipped down them.

She reached the bottom and let out a sharp cry of relief. The blood seemed to stop at the foot of the steps. If Mabel saw even one drop of blood again, she would have what her mother referred to as "a conniption."

She pushed the heavy stage door, begging the hotel to open the door to the Atrium and not lead her back to the long, dead-end hallway where her rooms and Evelyn were waiting.

She pushed hard until the door swung wide. Familiar white light poured over Mabel's face, almost blinding her. She smiled, blinking into the whiteout.

Finally, something was going right.

CHAPTER NINE

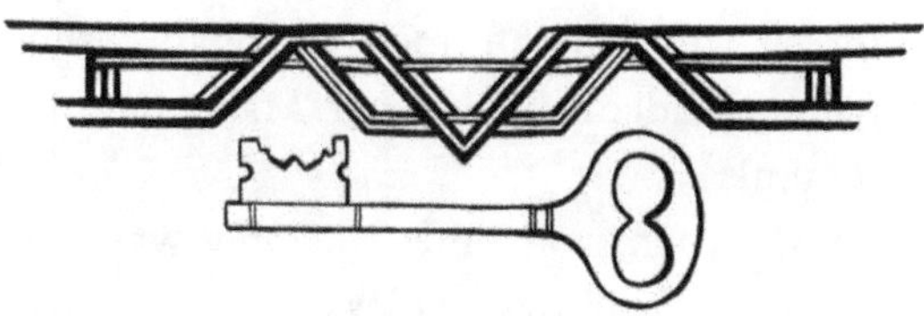

The empty Atrium echoed with the sound of Mabel's heels striding across the tile. The leaves of the palm fronds rustled as she passed, as if someone had left a window open and the night wind was blowing in from the floors above. Being alone in the vast halls at night, with nothing but the sound of her own movements, made her feel smaller than ever, like she was merely an ant in the vast clockwork of the hotel. As she glanced up into the bright lights of the many floors, she got the sense that she had only scratched the surface of exploring how enormous the Grand Hotel really was. There might be darker, lonelier rooms lying in wait to be discovered.

"Where do you desire to go?" the Navigator asked.

"I want to go to room 617," Mabel said. "I want to see Lucky."

The Atrium demon tilted its golden head, as if confused. "You do not have an appointment."

Mabel clasped her hands together. "I don't need an appointment. I need a friend."

The Navigator considered for a moment. "I will ask. Please wait one moment."

The Navigator's eyes glazed over. A glow emanated from her pupils as she tilted her head, listening to a voice Mabel could not hear.

When the light left her eyes, the Navigator turned her attention back to Mabel. Its silvery voice echoed up the empty floors. "Lucky agrees to meet with you. You have one hour."

The door behind Mabel flung open.

"Thank you," she told the Navigator.

So the hotel can speak directly to its guests. Mabel would be lying to herself if the idea of the hotel having a sort of will of its own didn't give her the willies. She fled toward the soft golden light of the pink room and stumbled through the open doorway without knocking. When the door shut decidedly behind her, Mabel found herself inside a kaleidoscope of pink.

Everything in the room was pink. Not only was the wallpaper a deep rose color, but the pillows, tables, and chairs were all heart-shaped. Romantic glass lamps with rose patterns sat on various white wicker tables. More lamps hung from the ceiling, creating a pretty haze throughout the room in various shades of fuchsia and purple hues. The rest of the room was filled with more flowers than a French garden, sporting tiny buds in every pastel hue Mabel could imagine.

Mabel had never seen a more romantic room, and she wondered what sort of job Lucky had been given after her run as Frank's star ended, but she could make a pretty educated guess.

"Mabel? Is that you?" Lucky said from the other side of a curtained room divider.

"Yes. How did you know?"

"Haven't you figured out yet that demons see more than humans can?" Lucky called back in her best mocking tone. "Present. Future. Who is in the room?"

Lucky stepped out wearing almost nothing at all. She was dressed in fine black lingerie made from delicate satin and accented with black floral lace on all of her curves, ending in a skirt that split above both knees with more black lace.

"In case you're wondering, I did not pick the color scheme. Given the choice, I much prefer black."

Mabel had seen the ladies of the Richardson Boardinghouse for Women in varying stages of undress. It was unavoidable in a house full of so many ladies you could hardly brush your teeth without elbowing someone, but Mabel had never seen any of the women there wearing very little of something so fine. She had seen an outfit like it once in *Vogue* magazine, but Mabel had only dared to linger on the page for a moment before blushing at her own attraction to the image and flipping it to something else. Seeing lingerie in real life was a whole other matter.

Lucky was a purposefully black stain on the spring pastel room, and she strutted toward Mabel in full awareness of that power to regard Mabel up and down.

"You're covered in blood."

"Sorry," Mabel said, shifting from one foot to the other. "About the mess. I kind of left in a hurry."

"Nothing to be sorry about, kid. Looks like your first show was a rip-roaring success. I'm not surprised. That glamor they gave you is one of the best I've seen."

Mabel's face turned so red it spread down her neck.

Lucky took a pink towel that hung over the back of a lounge chair and thrust it at Mabel. "You can clean up here. Just mind the carpet."

She led Mabel to the bathroom, which was all pink porcelain and soft gold French accents, from the damask wallpaper to the clawed feet on the bathtub. Lucky shut the door, leaving Mabel with her towel beside the welcoming bathtub. The room was not even a quarter of the size of the bathroom Mabel had up in her expansive suites. Those rooms probably used to belong to Lucky, but she hadn't thought about it until now. She imagined it must be strange, being Frank's star one minute and then replaced the next. Mabel guessed that was the future that awaited her if she was unsuccessful in delivering souls, and maybe even if she was. Lucky might not like her, but Mabel was grateful Lucky was at least helping her.

She peeled off her clothing, not sure where to put the remains of the stiff dress and opted for tossing the ruined chiffon in the empty hamper. The ballgown she had chosen for her debut night was unwearable now, and it was a shame that something so beautiful had been torn apart. Mabel's cheeks felt suddenly wet. She wiped her tears, unsure why she had started crying over some bloody, stiff fabric, but she found herself choking back a sob anyway. It was silly, being upset over how her big night that she had been dreaming of her whole life was suddenly ruined.

She should be happy she survived, but Mabel wasn't grateful, she couldn't be. Her dreams had been used against her, and she was going to have to not only free herself of the damned Canary, but somehow steal her soul back from Frank too. Every minute she spent without her soul was another minute Mabel slipped off the cliff's edge of her humanity. If she waited too long, she would plummet down below. She couldn't allow that to happen. So, Mabel would force herself through the motions, clean herself off, get dressed, find out Frank's true plan from Lucky, and then she was getting the hell out of the Grand Hotel.

It took some time, but eventually Mabel got everything clean, even her hair, which took some doing. There were many chunks that had hardened over the course of an hour. She didn't examine the pieces too closely. She would hate to recognize something. Mabel did her best to work with the beauty products in the bathroom on her own to fix her hair and makeup, and finally emerged wearing one of the day dresses that was a soft, petal pink. It was clearly meant for lunch outings, but Mabel imagined Lucky didn't get many chances to use it, if she had ever worn it at all.

"Much better."

Lucky was sitting at a little white bureau writing numbers in a ledger, but she shut it before Mabel could see what she jotted down.

"You're wondering what kind of work I do here," Lucky said. "It both is and isn't exactly what you think. I work for the speakeasy downstairs."

"I wasn't meaning to pry." Mabel took a seat at Lucky's little bistro table and folded her hands in her lap like she was back at school while Lucky mixed two cocktails over her golden bar cart. Mabel didn't know why she suddenly felt the urge to act so prim, like they were two Victorian ladies taking tea together and not two soulless women about to have a blunt heart-to-heart over gin. She had never been around someone as intimidating as Lucky. Mabel was relieved when Lucky handed her a glass.

"Bee's Knees?" Lucky offered flatly.

Mabel had never had the drink before, but it was more golden in color than the other gin drinks she had tried, with a lemon rind twisted on its side. "What's in it?"

"Honey. Lemon juice. I pegged you for a Bee's Knees girl. Though it would seem from how much bathtub gin you drink, you don't know what the finer version tastes like. The real thing, the top shelf gin, it has no comparison."

"So, why have you come to see me?" Lucky said. "I haven't got all night. I have a quota to fill, same as you. Also, take your pick of any of the dresses in the closet over there. I never wear any of them. Too pink. This color will suit your Southern belle life just fine."

"I want to ask what happened last year."

"Natural question. Frank wanted souls. I failed. What else is there to say? Maybe if I had the Canary, I would have had better luck. I had to kill everyone with only my charms to lure them in." Lucky settled into the bistro chair across from Mabel and crossed her legs, revealing the small knife she kept in her black lace garter. How dangerous a life Lucky must lead working the speakeasy to always carry a blade on her. How silly Mabel felt that she did not carry one already.

"Where did you get the knife?" Mabel said, hoping to warm Lucky up to her and get her talking.

"It's mine," Lucky took a sip of her drink. "Or it was in another life. My father used to take me hunting in the Midwest. Coyotes. Wolves. Anything with four legs, really. He thought a lady should never be without a knife, especially in a city as rough as New York. I miss him more than I can say."

"My father also taught me to kill," Mabel said. "Back home in Georgia, I was the one who beheaded chickens on the farm. Pa always said I had a way of steeling myself against death and violence, more than my siblings."

Lucky rolled her lemon twist around in her coupe glass. "Two farm girls in the big city. Your father was a wise man to teach you that. Gives you a stomach for blood. Speaking of, how was your first night? A real crowd pleaser, from the look of you when you first walked in."

Mabel buried her face in her cocktail and took a larger swallow than she intended. She grimaced. Gin always did funny things to her stomach on the way down. Maybe if she opened up, that icy exterior of Lucky's would crack, and she could get her to reveal more about Frank's plans. "The Canary diamond made me sing beautifully, and of course, it made me become so desirable they wanted a piece of that fame. Those fanatics thought I was the bee's knees and wanted to turn congratulations into some weird petting party. They tore my dress, tried to grab me."

"Did you kill them?" Lucky stared at Mabel with a hard sense of commiseration in her eyes. "He had me do it myself with my knife. Frank thought that scaring those poor souls seasoned them for his ascension ritual. It didn't work, of course."

"No," Mabel said simply, setting down her drink to show Lucky her hands. "Frank failed to mention that the Canary not only brings out the best in people, but the worst. I already gained my second mouths."

Mabel did what she was terrified to do and pressed her thumbs in the center of both palms. Her mouths responded immediately; tongues lolled open. She felt sick to her stomach, but it had to be done. Lucky had to see, had to know to tell Mabel more. Lucky's entire demeanor changed at the sight of Mabel's second mouths.

"Golly," Lucky said, her ice melting. "One day? I've never seen that happen before. Not to anyone. You're in serious trouble. If those already showed up, your humanity will be gone well before the month is out. The longer you go without it, the harder it is for your soul to return to your body. It will be lost, turned into a coin forever, and you will be a full demon. You won't remember what it felt like to be human."

Mabel waited with hands outstretched for Lucky to say something else, impart some wisdom on Mabel, but her demon companion only stared off into the middle distance.

Mabel clenched her hands tight until she was sure the mouths had gone away. Still, Lucky remained deep in thought, so Mabel cleared her throat to break the silence. "I need your help. I don't know what Frank is planning, but I need to get my soul back before I turn into a full demon. He won't cut me a new deal. I tried what you said, and he refused. I need to know where Frank keeps the soul coins he collects."

"You want to steal your soul back?" Lucky looked for a moment like she was so amused at Mabel's speech that she wanted to laugh at how ridiculous it sounded. She smiled into the back of her hand to stifle her laugh instead.

Mabel refused to let her hope deflate. "Yes."

"Interesting." Lucky set down her drink and lit herself a cigarette. She puffed out a big plume of smoke. "He keeps soul coins in a locked box up in his penthouse."

Mabel beamed, so happy she wanted to give Lucky a kiss on the cheek. She really thought prying the info out of Lucky was going to be a lot harder.

"Don't look so damned happy. It's a box with an unbreakable spell on it. Trust me. I already tried what you want to do. I even learned the symbols they use to turn all their instructions into secret code, but I couldn't figure it out. I got caught by Frank's secretary. The path to becoming a full demon? It's inevitable. You might want to try getting your soul back, but even if you do, Frank's hordes will find you and kill you before you even have a chance to get out the front door."

Mabel's fists balled on top of her knees. She couldn't believe how negative, condescending, and holier-than-thou Lucky was being. Just because she was a terribly incompetent thief and got caught didn't mean everyone else was going to fail in her wake. There was no convincing her, Mabel could already see. She would get what she needed from Lucky and get out. She had dealt with her fair share of critics from Ziegfeld to the various other theaters she had tried in her six weeks since coming to Manhattan. Mabel didn't need pessimists in her life if she was going to succeed.

She was going to keep going until she got what she wanted. That was show business.

Lucky puffed out another ball of smoke. "Do you know why Frank is throwing his little soirée?"

"No," Mabel said flatly.

"He needs a star to lure in crowds of people in exchange for his ascension. Frank wants to skip rank."

Mabel swallowed more gin, and it went down hard. "Skip rank? What does that mean?"

"Everyone in the Grand has a job to do and a quota to fill, even Frank. Demons are all about rank, but there's no way to ever quit or be promoted. When his parents disappeared, all the responsibility of fulfilling the soul quotas passed on to their prized son. He needs the amount of souls equal to the station he wants to claim—a prince of hell. Equivalent exchange to quit running the Grand Hotel."

Lucky's story sounded plausible, and exactly like the rules Frank had mentioned earlier, but Mabel couldn't believe it. Frank unhappy? When he ran a whole slew of hotels and was filthy rich? She couldn't imagine anyone with that much wealth could possibly be unhappy.

"That doesn't sound right." Mabel remembered the way Frank tilted her chin and her cheeks turned scarlet. "There seems to be something else going on. Something Frank wants. I don't know what, but I don't think he's doing this to quit his job."

"Why quit running the hotel?" Lucky said, her interest peaked. "All that privilege, that power, why give it away unless it was to move up?"

Mabel didn't know how to respond to that. "I don't know him. I don't like him, but my read on him was that his motives have something to do with his parents disappearing. When I confronted him, he told me he will never get back what he lost."

Lucky flicked the extra ash off the end of her cigarette into the ashtray. "What a pretty picture that would be if Frank was doing something for someone more than himself." She sighed. "I hate to say it, but even if you deliver enough souls for Frank to ascend, and miracle of miracles, he gifts you your soul back with a red ribbon, there will be nothing of you left to remember you were ever human at all. Demons of his rank don't lie but they twist the truth so hard they don't need to. Your soul will remain a coin. The hotel is never gonna let you go. It never lets anyone go."

Lucky blew out a plume of smoke and waited to see how Mabel would respond, but she wasn't sure she knew how. On one hand, she should be angry that Frank was using her hard work to become demonic royalty, but she knew what it was to live under parental expectations while also missing them more than she cared to admit. Maybe Frank wanted out of here, same as Mabel. Maybe he wanted to ascend to hell's royalty to resurrect his parents somehow. Whatever the case, she hated Frank for his methods and hated him even more for how she could relate.

She decided to appeal to something she sensed Lucky wanted more than anything.

"Come with me," Mabel said. "Help me find our soul coins, and we can be free. I'm good at cracking codes, picking locks, and sneaking into places. We can get out together. Maybe even swipe some choice items from Frank's office to fund our new lives."

She expected Lucky to be elated at this proposal, for her eyes to go bright and a smile to spread on her red lips, but Lucky's eyes darkened.

"I'm not coming with you."

"I don't understand. Don't you want to leave? Don't you want to shove everything Frank did to you in his face?"

Lucky smashed her cigarette in the tray, snuffing it out. "My soul won't be in Frank's box. Do I need to spell it out for you? I've been without my soul for too long. I'm not human, not anymore. I never will be again. My soul's been cashed in. Once your transformation is complete, you're a full demon and Frank sends the coins to hell. I've seen him do it. He showed me to prove a point, and boy did I get it. How do you think every other demon working in this place got trapped here? They were human once too."

The world dropped out from under Mabel. She had to grip the table to keep from keeling over. Mabel thought about everyone she had met. Raymond Black. Samuel Lewis. The bellhops. The doormen. The waitstaff. The ladies who applied her makeup. The Van Doren's. Were they all once people? Were they poor souls lured by their dreams into bad contracts, condemned to serving eternity in the Grand Hotel? Mabel thought of the Atrium, how it seemed to ascend up into infinity. How many demons populated those rooms?

Lucky shrugged it off, as if the truth didn't bother her at all. "When your soul is gone, it's gone, kid. That doesn't mean I'm not going to help you."

"But why help me?" Mabel laughed. "You hate me."

"I don't like you, no." Lucky couldn't look at her. "But I wish someone had helped me. You want to know how to open the box Frank keeps in his office? It has a circular spell on it. You need several stones to open it. Easy. You said you pick locks. Frank keeps the stones in a locked drawer beside his bed. If you can read the right combination to turn the stones, it will open. But you also have to make sure you know his schedule well enough to make sure he's out of the office. And then the hotel needs to not see you when you're doing it."

It was a hat trick, no doubt about it. No one said this was going to be easy, but if it was a choice between staying human or becoming a demon in less than a month, Mabel knew what she'd pick.

"Sounds tricky, but simple enough. What is Frank's schedule? When should I make my move?"

"Lunch. He never actually eats it. He uses it for appointments. Frank eats at a... darker hour."

Lucky got up from her seat, went to her writing table, opened a drawer, and retrieved an envelope stuffed with folded-up notes. She handed the bulky stack to Mabel.

"None of that is the hardest part," Lucky said.

Mabel took the envelope. "What is?"

"The hard part is you have to face your worst fear to find the box in the first place."

CHAPTER TEN

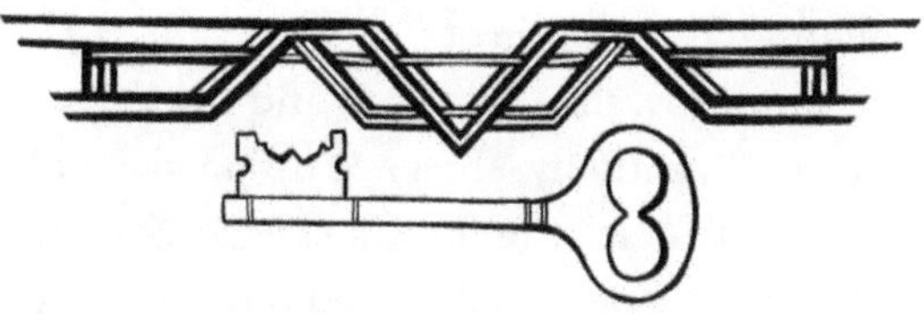

When her hour was up, the door to Lucky's room swung open. The Navigator's silvery voice carried over to where Mabel and Lucky were talking, bringing their conversation to a halt.

"Return to your room, Mabel Rose."

Mabel's momentary happiness blew out like a snuffed candle. She felt like just when she had started to form a relationship with Lucky, she had blinked, and their shared hour was over. With nowhere else to go, Mabel was forced to return to her room, but she left feeling better than she had since coming to the hotel. She had answers, she had a plan, and maybe, the start of a friendship with someone in the hotel. Lucky didn't like her, and she didn't really like Lucky either, but over the course of an hour, what Mabel knew was that she trusted what Lucky had told her.

Mabel hadn't made any friends since coming to New York. There hadn't been a time or an inclination to make any between trying to keep herself fed and the stiff competition at every audition. After Lucky, Mabel realized how desperately she missed having one. Lucky was the first person she had spoken to in the city who had any interest in Mabel at all. She only wished she could bring Lucky with her when she escaped. Maybe she could find a way to reattach Lucky's lost soul.

Mabel left Lucky's room and retreated back to the center of the Atrium as Lucky's words played over in her mind like a skipping record. She was going to have to face her worst fear, but what did that mean? The Navigator brought Mabel back to her empty suites, but she remained unconvinced she was alone for the better part of an hour. It wasn't until she caught sight of her bed that exhaustion overwhelmed her, and she collapsed into the sheets.

Mabel slept, but not well. She tossed and turned, worried Evelyn would come for her. Eventually, she gave up on sleep and decided to get out of bed and try to crack the code Lucky gave her instead.

Mabel sat at her little desk and played out Lucky's description of Frank's day over and over in her head, finding weaknesses in his routine while she pored over Lucky's notes. He wouldn't be in the penthouse where he kept the souls when he took lunch meetings, and he liked to swim every day at three pm. There were other spots Mabel could sneak into, but those two time periods were the most reliable. She wouldn't know the other options on a given day without knowing his full schedule, which she could only get from Frank's secretary. According to Lucky, there was nothing his secretary didn't see, so Mabel would have to sneak past her as well.

It was all so complicated, yet so very simple. The right timing, the right distraction, and she would break in no question. All that was left was the coded message, which Mabel found far more intimidating.

Mabel had returned to her room with Lucky's notes on the code, spread the papers across the dark blue desk in her bedroom, and made notes in the margins of Lucky's scrawling penmanship until she was too tired to lift her head. The symbols were various circles, stars, moons, triangles, and squares—simple shapes. Too simple. She hated codes like this, so easy on the surface but so difficult to crack. It took her hours, but the message crumbled and revealed itself to her like a spring flower opening its face to the sun.

When the sun turns its face to the moon
Cradle mahogany until the dark bleeds gold
Eight stones set four elements
While each star turns its face toward the door

Mabel had no idea what any of that meant, but she imagined she would figure it out when she broke into Frank's office at lunchtime tomorrow. She happily fell asleep with her head on the desk and remained there until a knock on the door woke her to a pounding headache.

She pushed her face off the hardwood and realized she was still in men's pajamas. She hurried to her wardrobe to look decent. The knock came again, harder and more rapid this time, as Mabel pulled the belt tight on a dressing robe and fled her bedroom to answer the door.

"Keep your pants on, Charlie. I just need a moment."

She opened the door to find the bellhop, who had slipped her a note, standing there with her breakfast cart. This was the guy who wanted to get her out.

"Morning miss," he said. "Where should I leave your breakfast?"

There was a distinct lilt to his voice, like he had arrived fresh off the boat from Ireland that morning.

Mabel gestured to the little bistro table beside one of the many dressing wardrobes. "Over there is fine."

The bellhop pushed her tray of breakfast silver dishes over to the bistro set. He uncovered her breakfast and sent a bloom of steam up into the room. It was another Southern breakfast with all the fixings. He set out her dishes of eggs and bacon, plates of biscuits and blackberry jam, a little coffee and saucer and creamer set, and paused very suddenly in his task.

"Did you get my note?"

Mabel blinked. Maybe she misheard him. She wasn't quite awake yet. "Note?"

"My name is Will Donahue. We met when you entered the Grand. Don't you remember? I slipped a note in your hand last night."

It took her a long moment to remember he was the doorman who had warned her to leave the Grand the night she followed

Evelyn inside the hotel. A flash of regret for not heeding his warning pierced her heart like an arrow, but she shook it off. No one would have listened to a message like that. It wasn't worth feeling guilty over.

"You're the doorman. The one I met on my first night here."

He grinned the same way he had the night she had brushed him off. Will wasn't terrible looking. In fact, he was terribly handsome. Mabel was about an inch or two taller than he was, but she imagined his good looks still turned heads wherever he went. He had a strong jawline, dark hair he kept slicked back with pomade, cheeks that looked perpetually windburned, and freckles that brought out his baby blues. Still, he was a wreck under his smart uniform.

Dark circles formed deep half-moons under his eyes, the skin so bruised it looked like he hadn't slept for weeks.

"That would be me. You never showed, so I came to you."

"I had other pressing matters to attend to." Mabel raised one thin eyebrow. "How did you make it down here?"

"I bartered with a waiter demon to trade shifts," Will said, as if it were obvious. "He wanted out, and I wanted in. Everything in the Grand is all about rank and position, but no one gets promoted ever. Instead, we trade. Everyone needs a break once in a while from their job, even demons. Also, giving him some of my blood helped."

He showed her the nasty slice in the center of his palm. She winced and had to look away.

"That's ab-so-tute-ly disgusting."

Will rolled the sleeve of his uniform back down, blushing. "I doubt it's your first sight of blood."

Mabel stiffened, and he took note, changing the subject immediately.

"Sorry for barging in on you like this, but I had to talk to you." He frowned. "You look different. Did you change your hair? It's darker."

Will *had* flirted with her at the door, and thanks to her deal with Frank and the glamor from the Augment, now he was looking for a petting party like everyone else.

"I did." She clucked her tongue and opened one of the silver trays. The dishes were filled with more fruit, bacon, and eggs than she could possibly eat. "The Augment mirror dolled me up. Let's get one thing straight, I'm not looking for a petting party, or anything else right now."

"No." Will's offended expression seemed sincere. "I didn't come here to pet. Actually, I need your help to escape."

Plenty of people had offered plenty of things since she arrived, especially her heart's desires, and there was nothing her heart wanted more. She rolled her eyes. She needed to shake this guy and get on with her day. Whatever his problems, Will could handle them. She had her soul to steal.

"My help?" She laughed. "Whatever for?"

"Because I need a thief."

She ran her hand over the bowl of fruit and selected an orange. Mabel wasn't very hungry, but she had to eat something. Who knew when she would get the chance again? "How did you know I was a thief? How does everyone know so much about me? Are you and Frank such swell pals that he told you my habits too?"

He had to laugh at that. "Demons are horrible gossips. You're all anyone has been able to talk about. The jewel thief turned star. If there was anyone that could help me free all the souls Frank keeps trapped in this place, it's you."

Mabel stopped in the middle of peeling her orange. She was planning on freeing her soul and stealing Frank's box anyway, but she couldn't guarantee everyone else along with her. Will didn't want to just get his own soul back, but every soul trapped in the Grand. Clearly, this bellhop had a death wish.

"What?" he said. "You think I'm crazy, don't you?"

"No." She returned to peeling back the orange, curious to hear his ludicrous sales pitch. "I want to know how exactly you intend on freeing everyone trapped inside the Grand."

"As the bellhop, I've had a front row seat to how the Grand lures people in through these doors, offering fame, specifically to artists. Ever since the people who run this place, Frank's parents, went missing."

"Artists?" Mabel's skepticism dissolved. "Is the Grand luring in a variety of artists?"

"Oh, yes. Actors, boxers, comedians, entertainers. I got to wondering, why? Why is the Grand luring all these people in? I overheard

Raymond tell Frank they have been behind schedule supplying not only artists, but also the subsequent patrons who come to their performances for months. Why does Frank need both artists to entertain and the people to see them? I snooped around. Turns out Raymond keeps track of every soul that checks into the Grand in his ledger."

"Yes." Mabel paused. A realization bloomed like a rose in her mind as the pieces connected. "Frank had Raymond record my soul in that book."

Will nodded. "I took a look at his ledgers in the front office. The deals date back to 1920. Every artist who checks into the Grand is offered the same deal. In each and every one, the artist offered up their talents as entertainers in exchange for a soul coin, and then the record states how many souls their talents lure in. The hotel is feasting on its patrons, body and soul. There was something weird about the numbers. It seems the charmed artist has as many shows as they want, until..."

Mabel's eyes widened. Her hand reached for the Canary diamond, but she was too scared to touch it. "Until what?"

Will's expression darkened. "Performing leads to killing. Always. Tabs in this place are paid in blood, but over time, as the performers, singers, and painters give the best show of their lives, they become a little more demonic every day. Their talent withers away, drawing less and less of a crowd. They lose the very thing that made their art in the first place—their humanity."

"When they turn full demon, they have no heart, and they don't even care about the art anymore. Only about themselves. They're demoted. They become staff."

Mabel didn't know what to say. She had lost so much more than she realized.

"Like you, right?" Her voice was so quiet. "You were an artist."

Will cleared his throat. "Boxer. I was a boxer. When I worked the boxing ring downstairs, I used to have plenty of people come to my fights. Over time, I noticed less and less. I started to feel not like myself anymore. I didn't know what was happening until it had already happened."

He pulled down his collar and showed Mabel a hint of his second mouth. She winced, but only a little.

"I failed. Now Frank put me on the worst job this place has—the doorman. Well, the worst job besides laundry. Now, Raymond hardly lets me sleep. I stand at the front door for all hours. I have to be there to greet the guests and guard the place. I think my humanity is almost gone. I checked the ledger. They haven't sent my soul coin down to hell yet. I still have time, but from the look of their accounting, not much time left. I want out of this place, but I don't want to be selfish. I want everyone to go free."

Mabel swallowed hard at the idea of freeing everyone in the hotel. It seemed too enormous a task. "How can we free everyone if most of them are demons already? Your heart is in the right place, but there are demons here who have had their soul coins already sent down to hell. It isn't possible."

"I have an idea, but first I need to know—are you in, or out?"

He said nothing else. Mabel silently ate her orange slices while she debated over what to do about Will. She had never worked a job in a team before. Like everyone else in this place, Will clearly had his secrets. It was possible he could be of help to her own quest. They both needed their soul coins back. However, if she were to choose a partner, Mabel would do so in the same manner she decided all things—as strategically and carefully as possible.

She could work with someone like Lucky, who had crucial information, but could be counted on to look out for themselves if things turned sour, but someone like Will? His white knight goal was too noble. He could risk everything trying to free everyone else. They would have to steal back both their own coins and the ones already sent down to hell. Impossible.

Either he really was that noble in his quest to save everyone, a rare and admirable trait, or he was keeping something from her. She could smell the secrets on him. Mabel didn't want to tell him what Lucky had shared just yet. She kept her cards played close to her chest. "Why not save who you can? We could easily steal more than just our soul coins if we find where Frank keeps the ones he hasn't sent downstairs yet."

Will sighed. "There is a portal at the bottom of the Grand Hotel, one that leads down to hell. According to Raymond's ledger, the portal closed once last year. It resulted in a catastrophic blockage of souls unable to be transferred down to hell. I think the door can be closed, for good. I want to stop the Grand from taking souls ever again."

Mabel peeled back the last of the orange rind, feeling the flesh against her thumb. "It's too risky. You'll get caught. I'm a good thief, but I know when the odds are impossible. I can help you find your soul coin. I want to get mine too, but I can't safely free us and everyone else. It won't work."

Will gaped at her. "But that would be wrong. I've seen so many people die trying to flee the hotel. They perish before they even reach the bottom of the front steps. There is nothing worse than watching someone die in front of you. I can't walk out of this hotel and do nothing to help anyone else. I'm not that selfish."

Mabel bristled at the implication. "There are too many people to save, too many humans who have already turned into demons. Not to mention, we don't know if they want to be human again at this point. Like you said, they may have completely forgotten their humanity. I'm not selfish. I'm realistic."

Mabel popped the last orange slice into her mouth and thought for a moment while she chewed. "I'm sorry, but I can't help you. Getting us out is one thing, but freeing everyone? Frank or any number of his staff would catch us for sure. You're welcome to do what you like, but I'm only interested in getting my soul back."

Will stuttered through trying to convince her, but Mabel ignored him. Let him play the part of the stand-up fella who wanted to be the hero and save the day, but Mabel knew characters like that always went down in flames in real life. She had seen it happen for herself when a girl at the Richardson Boardinghouse for Women wound up pregnant, her beau bailed, and little Mary turned thief overnight trying to support herself on her own. Mary got caught trying to take too much, too fast. Mabel had watched Mary get carted away out her room window by the police. Mabel knew the fate that awaited her if she failed would be much worse than Mary being carted off by the police.

"I'm sorry, but I've made up my mind. If you want me to steal back your soul coin while I'm stealing mine, fine, but that's where our arrangement ends."

Will's face fell. "Look, I haven't been entirely honest with you."

"They have my sister," Will said quietly. "She's somewhere in the basement levels of the Grand. We were starving on the streets. My parents died shortly after the boat dropped us off. Tuberculosis. We had nowhere to live, no money... the hotel lured her in with her dream of joining the circus. They took her soul and dragged her off down somewhere inside the Grand. I couldn't stop them. I checked for her name in the ledger. Her soul coin is already cashed in. If I don't at least try to save her, I would never forgive myself. She's only eleven years old."

His voice faltered at the memory. Will had to take a deep breath to collect himself. "I thought if there was anyone who could help free my sister, it was you, but it's clear you don't care about anyone else."

Mabel stiffened, cut deeply by his accusation. "That isn't fair. I do care. I didn't know all of this was about your sister. Saving everyone isn't reasonable, but getting one person out of hell? That might be doable."

She considered for a moment. They would have to first free their own souls from Frank's office and then make their way down to the bottom of the hotel where the portal was hidden and close it. They'd have to travel into hell and retrieve the soul coin, the specific soul coin that belonged to Will's sister. Mabel didn't know Will or his sister. She wasn't tied to him in a way where she should risk her life like this.

"My offer is this: I steal our soul coins, and you travel into hell to get your sister's soul coin back."

"I'd rather you go with me." Will shrugged. "There are a series of secret tunnels that run behind the hotel walls for maid travel, but they're always changing. Frank keeps maps of the hotel in the main office, but I wasn't able to grab one last time I snuck in. Raymond came in and interrupted my reading of the ledgers. That should lead us down to the portal in the basement."

Mabel rested a finger on her lip in thought. "Why not ask the Navigator to take you directly to the portal and skip all that? She could take you anywhere you wish to go if you ask."

"Yes," Will said. "But as you've learned by now, I'm sure, it does not take anyone everywhere they wish to go. I tried that and it blocked me. We need the map, which constantly updates with the new labyrinth configuration. That's the only way we find the way down."

Mabel sighed. "You keep saying we as if *we* are the ones going into hell. I'm not going down there."

Will matched her exasperated sigh. "Fine. I can't make you go down there with me, but I'm hoping you might change your mind. We aren't just freeing my sister, but every damned soul in this place. I agree to your terms. Help me steal my soul coin back. I can grab the map while you steal our coins." He held out a rough looking hand for her to accept. "Deal?"

She took his hand in hers. Something inside her warmed at the touch of his callouses, but Mabel didn't want to place the feeling of electricity in the air between them. Mabel shook his hand as hard as she could, as if the action could disperse any feelings passing between them like beating dust out of a rug.

"Deal," Mabel said. "I'll go up to Frank's office during his lunch break. Do you have a plan?"

Will retracted his hand, confusion written all over his face. "I was going to try and sneak back into the main office."

"And if you get caught? Seems like you almost got caught by Raymond last time."

Will adjusted his bellhop cap. "You're right. He almost got me in there. Luckily, he didn't check the closet where I was hiding. I don't know if I'll be that lucky a second time. If I mess up again, I will be sent where the worst of the worst offenders go—laundry. You'll never see me again. I'll be too busy scrubbing blood off the sheets."

"I have a plan. A way we can sneak into Frank's penthouse to retrieve the souls and into the main office to steal the map."

Will raised his eyebrows, eyes alight with possibilities. "What is it?"

Mabel smiled ever so coyly at him while she grabbed a piece of bacon. "Ever used the Augment before?"

CHAPTER ELEVEN

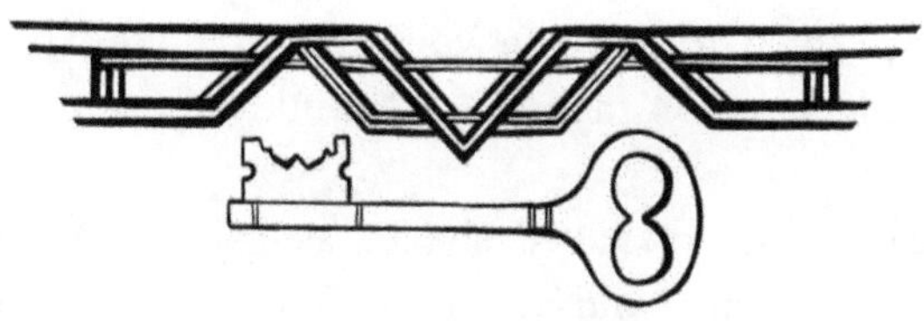

"Take me to the Augment."

She announced the request loudly to her room before placing her hand on the doorknob. She had never asked the hotel for something out loud before, but it felt odd silently begging the Grand to do what she wanted. She knew the hotel would give her things like biscuits and blackberry jam. The Navigator had even taken her to Lucky when she asked, but Mabel still doubted. She half expected to open the door and be led back to the Atrium, or simply open her door to a blank wall—the hotel's cheeky way of saying her access was decidedly not granted. Mabel whispered to the Navigator as if she were saying a prayer only to herself.

"Navigator, please take me where I want to go."

Mabel pushed the door open and revealed the familiar golden entrance leading to the Augment. It sat directly across from her at the end of the shortest hallway she had ever seen.

Mabel had asked, and the Grand had provided. Her wish had been granted so purposefully, there wasn't even a way to travel anywhere else.

"The hotel really does take you wherever you want to go," Will said. "Lucky."

"Something tells me luck has nothing to do with it," Mabel said.

"You know, it's funny. For most people, there is no way to know where a door in the Grand will lead you when you open it."

Mabel frowned at Will over her shoulder. "What do you mean?"

"The hotel always seems to know exactly where each of its staff should or shouldn't be at all times. It doesn't fulfill wishes. It doesn't do what it's told. It tells you where to go. I used to think it was Frank up there somewhere, watching all the little worker bees buzz around his hive. Raymond laughed when I told him that, as if it were the funniest joke in the world, but he wouldn't tell me the truth. At first, I thought this place ran on magic, but I think the truth is a whole lot darker than that."

Ever since Mabel had arrived, she felt as if she were trying to cross a desert of ever-shifting sands. Every grain could fall out from under her with a single step, but so far, it hadn't. Will was right. The hotel seemed to only grant Mabel's wishes. Will couldn't go wherever he wanted. Neither could Lucky. So why was Mabel so charmed? Was it because she was the Grand's star and carried the Canary diamond around her neck?

Everything costs something in the Grand, and Mabel wasn't sure when someone was going to come and collect her tab.

Mabel shook off the Navigator's creepy warning. At least whoever —or whatever—was watching behind the walls of the hotel was for Mabel, not against her. She could figure out why later. Mabel reached out and gave the cold door knob a hard twist. The door opened easily, and Will readily followed her inside the hexagon-shaped jewelry box of a room.

Mabel regarded her robe and men's pajamas in the mirror and her Louise Brooks bob. Her hair and style were how she had always pictured a modern girl would look and soon it would all be gone. Admittedly, she would miss her glamor when she fled the Grand today.

"I wish to look like one of the maids," she announced to the Mirror.

Mabel closed her eyes and pictured the Grand's maid uniform in her mind. When she opened her eyes, she sported one of the Grand's long black and gold maid's dresses, complete with a white apron, lace trim, sheer black stockings, smart little polished heels, and a white lace hat. Her dark bob was upgraded to a wavy redhead with bright blue eyes.

"That's better."

Will's face turned scarlet at the sight of her.

"Don't give me that look. Everyone thinks Frank's star has dark hair. This way, no one will recognize me."

"You look too glamorous," Will said. "You're going to blow our cover."

She simpered with her best lost lamb routine, showing Will clearly she could take any look and play the right part. "See? It's perfect. Don't tell me how to do my job. Besides, it's your turn. Just think of how you want to look in the mirror, and it should change you."

"I know," Will said quietly. "Frank brought me here before."

"What?"

Will sighed. "Frank dressed me up, put me in front of this mirror of his. Built up my muscles and got me ready for my first fight. During my first two days here, I put those muscles to good use. I was throwing hands at anyone who would come close. Frank loved it, of course. Kept me in the boxing ring, playing fights every night. Wouldn't let me leave, not even to sleep."

Mabel's eyes went wide. "What do you mean?"

He looked away from her. "I had to box for them every night. I should have thought to ask for how long. How many fights would satiate Frank's blood lust? The first night I boxed, I ended up with blood on my hands. By the second, I figured out that was exactly what Frank wanted. The longer it went on, the more I came to realize I was forgetting all about Saoirse. I started to fight back by throwing the matches. My fights got worse. Less bodies, but I was able to cling on to my memories a little better. It didn't keep this horrible mouth in my chest from forming. Frank was unhappy with my performance, and Raymond demoted me. Then you walked into the Grand Hotel and changed everything. They said Frank made you his star the moment you arrived. I knew if you could do that, maybe you could work a miracle for me."

She tucked her hair behind her ear. "I can't believe what they did to you."

He laughed. "If you can dream it, the Grand can make it yours. No one ever thinks to ask the price until it's too damn late."

"Why did you make a deal with Frank, anyway? Was it for your sister?"

"Yes. I was desperate to get her back, but I never should have taken that deal. That's the con. It offers you your hopes and dreams, but you forget who you are. I have very few memories of Saoirse now. I don't know if she will remember me anymore. I doubt she will, not with her soul in hell, but I can hope."

Mabel was not usually so bold, but she slipped her small hand into his. She wasn't sure why she did it. Maybe it was for comfort, for friendship, and maybe, selfishly, because it had been so long since she had felt the warmth of another person.

"You'll save her, Will. I know it. You're too stubborn not to."

He gripped her hand tight. "You're right. I am stubborn. A fat lot of good it did me."

Will pulled his shirt collar down until Mabel could see his mouth fully for the first time. The second mouth that had grown below his collarbone, like Evelyn.

"Is your mouth always there?" Mabel asked.

"Not at first. It used to vanish when it wasn't hungry. Now it's there all the time. And it wants to... eat. Every moment, I feel myself slipping. I'm fighting these dark thoughts about what I would do to Frank, without remorse. If I do make it down to Saoirse before I become a full demon, I don't know what will happen. I won't let it feed on anyone though."

Will had fought tirelessly for his little sister, worked hard to figure out how to help everyone escape, and still found the strength within himself to keep his second mouth from feeding. Meanwhile, Mabel had fine dresses, plates of food she had not thought to share with him, a fine bed, and even a bath. There was a cavernous gulf of privilege between them, and Mabel hadn't even noticed until now.

Will tried to read the sour look on her face. "What? Did my sob story get to you?"

Mabel didn't know how to explain, and every explanation she opened her mouth to tell him sounded like weakness. Her mouths had already tasted blood, and she could feel the impossible hunger for another meal growing inside of her. She couldn't do this to him. Not knowing all that she knew now. She couldn't leave him alone. It was like Will had said to her.

It wouldn't be right.

"I have something to show you." Mabel pressed her thumbs into both palms and waited for the horrible sensation of teeth blooming beneath her fingers. She raised her hands to Will. At the sight of her second mouths, Will stumbled backward into a mirror.

Mabel turned away from him, face flushed, like she had been caught doing something she shouldn't be, like heavy petting in a back alley. She gripped her hands tight until her second mouths disappeared and only the bare flesh in the center of her palms remained.

"They only appeared yesterday."

"Yesterday?" Will straightened his uniform to collect himself. "I'm sorry. I didn't mean to accuse you. It's just... I've never heard of that happening after just one day. Humans who make deals take a while to corrupt into demons after they lose their souls. They get the mouths first, then the horns. It's a process that takes weeks, months, not days."

"So, I've heard," Mabel said tartly. "Does everyone transform like this?"

Will frowned. "As far as I know. I've seen lots of people come through these doors and make a deal with Frank. Over their time working their debt off to the Grand, debtors form a second mouth, but they're still only half a demon. Even with the mouth, you're still aware of your humanity. If you let your second mouth feed enough times, you lose what remains of your humanity and gain your horns. Then your eyes change color. Then you lose everything that once made you human. You lose your talent and ability to lure in patrons."

"I know," Mabel said, desperate to change the topic. "I've seen the horns and eyes. It's fine. I'll help you."

"You'll what? Help me save Saoirse?" Will searched her face. "Why the sudden change of heart?"

"Don't make me regret saying yes." Mabel balled her hands into fists. "I'll help you free the souls, then go with you to find this portal and save your sister, but we need to be smart. I can help you get your sister out, but free the whole hotel? I hope you're right. I hope closing the portal even works."

"It will work," Will said. "When we're done, I'll meet you back in the kitchen. There's a break room for staff only, but it's always empty. Dining room staff don't get to take breaks during meals. If you can make it back down by 1 pm, we should be safe there during the lunch rush."

She checked her watch. 9:03. It was plenty of time, and yet, not enough time at all. Evelyn would be looking for Mabel at afternoon rehearsals. She had until then for everyone to learn she had gone missing. They needed to make it out of the kitchen and down to the lower levels well before then.

Mabel looked him up and down. Will was not only sleep deprived, he was made of skin and bones from a life lived on less than half of what he needed to survive. Maybe he could fight his way down to his sister in his prime, with decent rest and three-square meals. If he came across so much as one errant demon, Will was in no shape to fight, but Mabel couldn't be in two places at once.

"Are you sure you're going to be okay? You look like you haven't rested or eaten in a month."

"You'd be right," Will said. "I'm not allowed to eat good food anymore or sleep a full night's rest. I feel like I've been knocked out in just the first round, but don't worry. We're in the Augment. I'll have it patch me up."

He turned to the mirror and stared at his reflection. Mabel blinked and all of his fatigue had washed away. The circles under his eyes were gone, the sallow look to his face had melted away, the slight hunch in his posture from fatigue corrected and Will stood up straighter.

"That's better."

He was right. The shirt around his biceps and forearms was a little tighter. Will lifted his shirt. The second mouth on his chest was still there. Mabel couldn't look away from the horrible, cracked lips of that impossible maw, splitting the space between two ribs. Will's gaunt look seemed to come more from that second mouth not feeding than actual starvation. Mabel wondered if she didn't feed her second mouth, would her body shrivel as a result?

"I guess the Augment doesn't fix everything." He smoothed his shirt and straightened his bellhop cap. "We don't have time to waste on this nonsense."

"Don't get screwy on me now," Mabel said. "We'll get our souls back. Today. Come on. Let's dust out. We've wasted enough time already."

Mabel twisted the mirror doorknob and led Will out of the Augment, back down the short hallway to her bedroom. She checked her pocket on the way. The note with Lucky's deciphered code she had stuffed in her pocket earlier had now moved to the inside of her apron pocket. She was grateful the Augment didn't take it like it took her hip flask, only moved it. Mabel sighed a big breath of relief.

Back in her room, Will grabbed the cart as Mabel clicked her suite door shut behind her. She focused her mind on her request and opened the door again. She smiled to find the blinding lights of the Atrium waiting on the other side.

Will wheeled the cart of food toward the door, but Mabel inserted herself between him and the exit.

"All of that food is going to go to waste." She lifted the silver lid off one of the trays.

Will stared at the bacon.

"You should have something to eat."

His teeth ground together. "I'm fine."

Mabel plunged her hand into the cold bacon and shoved a handful at him. "You told me you were starving. The Augment fixes the outside, not the inside. Eat something right this moment, or I won't help you."

She glared at him. He stubbornly stared back.

"Sorry." Will took the bacon. "I'm not used to someone looking out for me."

When he had finished scarfing down the last of her bacon and eggs, Mabel moved out of his way with a curtsy that made Will laugh. "See? Don't you feel better?"

"Don't get smart," he said, but Mabel saw the hint of a smile play at the corner of his mouth.

She let Will lead her out into the Atrium, falling into character. She kept her head bowed and her face placid, even a little fearful.

Mabel didn't mind playing the docile maid accompanying a member of the kitchen staff. It was all part of the act. She would accompany Will up to the kitchen, return the food trays, lay the cart over with fresh alcohol for Frank's "afternoon tea," and Mabel would do her damnedest to find the soul box and crack the code before Frank showed up.

The plan was easy, apart from the first step. Mabel had outwitted the Atrium's golden demon before, and she could do it again.

"Where do you wish to go?" the Navigator asked. "Mabel Rose Dixon, and William Liam Donahue?"

Will stiffened, but Mabel strode up to the statue. "I wish to visit the dining hall. I'm tired of eating alone in my room. I will dine with company." She nodded at Will and looped her arm around his. "He's my date."

The Navigator's gold lips drew up in a knowing smile. "Proceed."

The walls around Mabel and Will spun in a circle fast enough that all of the doors became a blur. Distant clacking signaled the end of the cycle, a sound of great gears settling in behind the towering walls. The first level settled on a glass set of double doors with a tropical garden beyond. Great palm fronds and birds of paradise pressed against the glass, which was covered in steam.

Mabel smiled at her own brilliance. If the hotel would let her upstairs to dine, she would have access to the elevator on the first floor, and that was her ticket all the way up to Frank's penthouse.

"Thank you," Mabel told the Navigator and let go of Will's arm, but not without noting the bright flush on his face had spread down to his collar.

Will tapped the bar cart with his thumbs a little too rapidly as he pushed it toward the dining hall's double doors. Mabel placed her hand over his to quiet his nerves, but the color on his cheeks and neck deepened. She laughed.

"For heaven's sake," Mabel said. "At the mere mention of dating, you turn into a tomato."

Will's gaze snagged on someone on the other side of the glass. He stopped suddenly. All of the red from his face turned to ash. "You should get in the cart."

"Climb in the bar cart?" Mabel scoffed at his dour expression. "No one is going to recognize me."

"Raymond is floating around the dining hall to supervise," Will said. "We should take extra precautions."

"But demons can tell who is behind the curtain. What does it matter? They will know I'm in the bar cart."

"The dining hall is so busy, we can slip through without notice, but we don't want to attract attention. You're right. Demons can see through walls, curtains, bar carts—but only if you have their attention. If we move quickly with you in the bar cart, no one will think to look at your dirty dishes, but Raymond might notice a redheaded maid he's never seen before. He will see past your glamor."

It did make sense. She could either cross the hall and risk someone taking notice of her and looking past her glamor or hide in the bar cart and hope no one paid any attention to it. It was obvious which was the riskier option with Raymond on the prowl.

"Please. Do it for me. I'll feel better if you're hidden away while we try to cross the hall. I promise you can climb out once we reach the kitchen."

Mabel got the hint he wasn't suggesting, he was telling her. She hated him a little for being right about it. Evelyn and Lucky were both able to see through her glamor and realize it was Mabel.

"Fine, but only because you asked so nicely." Mabel grumbled at him under her breath as she climbed inside the white skirts of the cart and found herself well concealed, but enormously uncomfortable. Her knees were in her face, and her heels were two knives poking the meat of her calves, but otherwise, she was fine. It was better than being caught by Raymond.

Will pushed the cart forward as if it weighed nothing with her below. The wheels rattled hard beneath her, knocking her teeth together as they traveled over the tiled floor. She rocked back at the impact of the cart against the door and her head bumped up against the cart's hard metal ceiling. Mabel pursed her lips to keep from swearing.

They traveled through the dining hall, weaving between tables. Mabel couldn't see anything from behind the thick white table skirt, so she pried two fingers between the sheets to steal a peek.

The dining hall of the Grand was mostly empty, which made the room seem even more unnecessarily opulent than it did before. Waitstaff were busy bussing tables and cleaning stacks of plates, piled high with chicken bones and leftover potatoes, half-eaten ribs and crusts of bread. They passed a maid on her hands and knees furiously scrubbing something green out of the carpet, and another who was taking a brush to something red in the back of a chair.

As Will navigated her through a labyrinth of similar stains, their evidence buffed out by haggard staff with similar dark circles beneath their eyes. The truth struck Mabel square in the chest. The people in the Grand really were human once, all of them. Now they were cleaning up some sort of carnage that had happened in the dining room. Mabel didn't want to know what happened here, but from the evidence, she could guess. She wasn't the only one with a contract that came with a delivery of souls in its fine print. While Mabel had lured people to their deaths like a siren, someone had killed these people with food.

Mabel refused to look at anyone or anything too closely after that.

They passed enormous philodendrons, pink and yellow bromeliads, heart-shaped caladiums, and more Greek statues than Mabel cared to count, but she didn't see any sign of the towering scarecrow's shadow that was Raymond Black. Will's footsteps echoed off the tiled floor with a steady, nonchalant gate, as if he wasn't hiding the star of the Grand Hotel beneath his food trays. Mabel appreciated his discretion, although she could tell he was sweating like a sinner in church.

"William Donahue," a voice like dark chocolate cake floated over to the bar cart.

Mabel shrank back inside the cart.

Will stopped. "You must have me confused with someone else."

His American accent attempt barely covered up his Irish lilt, but it was something. Mabel couldn't see what was going on in the silence that stretched between Raymond and Will, but she didn't dare stick her head out to check.

"No mistake." There was a deadpan delivery to Raymond's every sentence, but Mabel could have sworn there was a drop of bemusement there too. "What are you doing with all of this... food?"

"I'm returning these trays."

"See that you do," Raymond said.

Will rushed forward and hit the double white doors of the kitchen with another rattle and a bump to Mabel's head. She poked her head out of the curtain, desperate for air and tired of being cramped.

"That was close," Will said. "I hope he doesn't follow us."

Mabel had to raise her voice to be heard. "He won't."

She had never seen a kitchen so massive, with so many prep stations, stoves, and sinks. The Grand's kitchen was the size of her dressing and bedroom combined, with stainless steel refrigerators and several stores of food for dried goods. Barrels of grain, barley, and rice lined the walls by the stores. Chefs in great white hats floated around, overseeing their assistants as they prepared another round of food, accompanying sauces, and side dishes. Steam rose off the sautéed Chicken Florentine, pasta steeped in creamy tomato wine sauce. French bread and cold cuts were piled high on a prep table to prepare sandwiches to grab and deliver to hungry customers.

"What are you doing? Raymond will see."

"Through those thick doors?" Mabel climbed out, but the kitchen staff did not so much as pause to notice. They were all too busy cooking. "Why does it smell so delicious?"

Before she knew what she was doing, Mabel grabbed one of the steaming hot plates of ravioli right off the prep station counter.

Will snatched the plate from her and returned it. "Don't. It's made to make you want it."

He guided her away from the kitchen.

"What about our cart?" Mabel protested, but really she just wanted another chance at that ravioli. "Don't we need that?"

"We'll get another one. There are plenty lying around in here."

Mabel saw one of the staff bus the cart away toward the dishwashing area and pouted at Will. "What is wrong with the food? Is there some kind of demon spell at work?"

Will steered her out of the kitchen and down a long hallway with the blandest, milk-and-toast white walls and absolutely no artwork at all. "Not all the food here is cursed. The dining hall serves an aphrodisiac. People here aren't dying from poison. They eat and lose themselves to the pleasure of it. They forget themselves and don't even realize the dining hall is eating them while they feast. The walls and floor sort of… absorb them. The mess we just walked through is all that remains."

Mabel had never heard of anything more disgusting. She shook off the allure of the food, grateful to Will for his gravity. "I don't think I will ever eat another bite here again."

"Eating meals in small doses won't make you sick with the pleasure of it. When I first found out the hotel was feasting on souls in a literal sense, I couldn't stop thinking about it for days. The Grand keeps some terrible secrets about how it makes its monthly quota."

Will entered a back room and Mabel followed. He was quick to shut the door and lock it behind them, even though he had told her no one would be taking a break now. She explored the horrible bare room. Compared to the garish decor throughout the Grand, the plain white walls and gray wooden lockers lined up like tin soldiers were insultingly indicative of what the Grand thought of its workers.

"Wait here," he said. "I'm going to back out and grab a cart of liquor for you. Don't worry. You'll be safe here. No one should come in."

"I'll be fine. I can wait five minutes."

She had expected him to look grim, maybe even a bit sad, but neither emotion was in his face. There was only hope in his eyes now, a kind of clear-headed vision that if they pulled off this heist, together, they just might walk out of here. Will looked at her in a way that Mabel could get behind. Maybe she had misjudged him before.

He was hardly gone for five minutes. Mabel felt like she blinked, and Will returned with more liquor than she had ever seen in her life.

"It's a good thing the coppers don't check the Grand. This amount of giggle water would get us busted until we lay in our graves."

"It should be enough for Frank's 'teatime,'" Will said, but when he saw Mabel's shocked expression, he added an addendum. "He's a full demon. I've heard he drinks an ungodly amount."

Mabel rolled her eyes. "Can you take care of yourself? If you get caught, we'll both be in a jam."

"I won't get caught," Will gave her an uncharacteristically roguish smile, and she liked it on him. "I have a plan."

"Good," Mabel said. "Let's blouse. I need to perform the starring role of sneaking into the penthouse, cracking the code, and releasing every soul in the Grand right out from under Frank's nose."

He laughed at her little flourished pose, genuinely delighted by her comedy. It brought back memories of when she first came to New York, ones she wanted to forget where she stood on a stage in an empty vaudeville theater, making the few people who were there laugh so hard they fell out of their seats.

Mabel didn't know how to part ways with him, so she held out her hand to Will. "See you soon, partner."

He took her hand and drew Mabel in, planting a kiss on her cheek. His lips were surprisingly warm against her face as his rough hands gripped hers tight, and just as natural. The blush on his cheeks was immediate beneath his freckles, but Will didn't seem the least bit embarrassed. "Thank you. I'd never be able to save Saoirse without you."

She waved him off, hating that her face was far redder than his. "You could do it on your own. I'm just in an obliging mood. Besides, what good is a thief if not to steal prized possessions?"

CHAPTER TWELVE

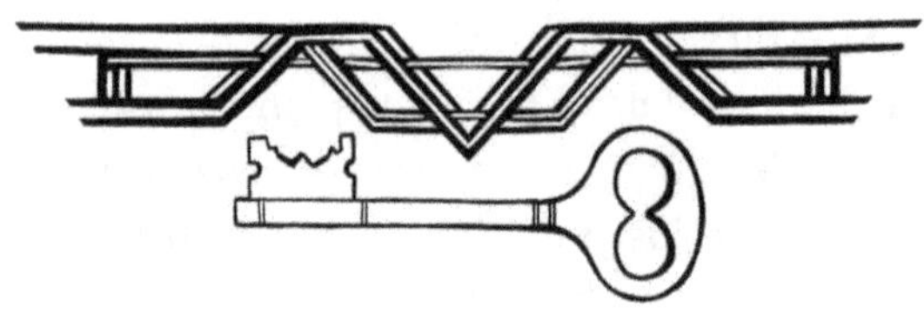

The bar cart rattled into the caged elevator as Mabel shoved the heavy liquor on board. The new bellhop—a tan boy with a wide grin full of teeth—asked Mabel which floor she was reporting to.

"All the way to the top, baby," she said.

The new bellhop pulled the lever to Frank's penthouse. It had been surprisingly easy to get upstairs once the cart was laid over in various bottles of bourbon, rye whiskey, gin, scotch, and little silver canisters of crackers and nuts. No one looked at Mabel twice with the glittering offerings of libations on her cart. Prohibition had made it impossible to cart booze around out in the open in most places, but normal rules of society did not seem to apply to the Grand.

She whistled as the elevator climbed the floors all the way up, more out of nerves than feeling cool about it. There weren't many female bellhops in the place, and she hoped that her new maid's outfit and changed features provided by the Augment were enough that the demons wouldn't look past her glamor. She was especially worried Frank employed more than just a secretary and employed staff who guarded his room when he wasn't around after Lucky mentioned not being able to get past her. All the way up, she pictured this woman to be a model of femininity like Evelyn. Mabel imagined

Frank's secretary would tower above Mabel in statuesque beauty, part Athena, part Venus in beauty and brains. She couldn't picture him employing anything less than a Sheba.

When the elevator finally dinged its arrival at the penthouse, a woman greeted Mabel. She was neither a sensuous beauty nor a battle axe—she was a small, elderly woman who could hardly see past her tiny glasses perched on the brim of her nose. Her skin didn't fit quite right over her bony hands and sunken eyes, which were so pale gold in color they were almost white. She wore a gray dress as frayed as her tattered hair, as if she had been buried twenty years ago and Frank had dug her up because he couldn't bear to live without her. Mabel wouldn't be surprised if that was exactly what had happened. Her name tag read: Gladys.

She squinted at Mabel. "Are you here with Frank's tea, dear?"

Mabel could hardly believe her luck. This little old granny could barely see a foot past her own face. She couldn't tell Mabel apart from any other hotel staff, much less the difference between a cart full of liquor and a tea set. Now she knew why everyone was calling it Frank's "tea."

This heist was going to be so easy.

"Yes, ma'am," Mabel said, pulling out her old Southern charm and her real accent to match. "I've brought all the *tea* he could possibly want."

"Oh good," Gladys said. "Frank hates when he runs out of tea after lunch. We wouldn't want *that.*" Gladys laid the emphatic need to please Frank on thick. The old bird really had no idea who Mabel was.

"No," Mabel said, winking. "We wouldn't." She followed Gladys into Frank's penthouse suite as the elevator cage rattled shut behind her.

Whatever Mabel had pictured Frank's office would look like, how it was actually decorated, she never would have guessed. Mabel followed the walking skeleton into Frank's penthouse and felt like she had gone back to chapel, though all the walls were painted black. There were matching dark file cabinets surrounding her, butted up against all four walls. There were no pews, but there was a wide, mahogany desk in front of triple arching windows to match the slimmer panes along the opposite wall. The stained-glass designs were almost like a church, but these windowpanes were not multicolored. They were all shades of red and gold wings, with multiple frames of a snake dying and being reborn across the panels to become a great dragon with gold for eyes and rubies for scales.

Mabel smiled to stifle a laugh behind her teeth. If Frank wanted to send a message about his desire for ascension, the mural alone could do the talking. It was so very gouache.

Mabel pushed the cart over next to the desk and had full intentions of leaving it there when Gladys tutt-tutted her. "Frank likes to take his tea in his bedroom. You should know that by now. Are you feeling well today, Mary?"

Finally, Mabel had a name for the part she was playing. "Everything's berries."

"Good to hear it." Gladys shuffled as quickly as her stiff bones could carry her into the next room, which was about the same speed as rolling her corpse up a gigantic hill. Mabel was relieved Gladys moved so slowly. The cart was surprisingly heavy with the amount of alcohol Will had put on it, and she was starting to sweat after pushing it all the way from downstairs.

They turned past the desk and entered a room that screamed Frank West. While the previous room had all of the flavor of a fiery sermon set to wallpaper, his bedroom was far more luxurious. It was a perfect recreation of the inside of Versailles, identical to the entrance hall downstairs with its Grecian statues, vases, broad-leafed tropical plants, and gold filigree in every inch of its decoration.

There was an enormous painting on the high vaulted ceiling Mabel wanted to examine closer, but her attention snagged on the one detail of the room that was not like the rest of the Grand. Two golden statues towered next to Frank's lavish four-post, kingly bed. They were not Greek gods, but statues of an elegantly dressed man and woman in modern attire. Their figures were significantly taller than every statue she had seen so far. One of their hands could crush her skull if it ever came to life. Mabel could only pray they were not animated like the Navigator.

Mabel vaguely recognized their sour faces, but she turned her attention back to heaving the cart over to Frank's blue marble bar.

"Slower, dear." Gladys winced. "These poor ears aren't what they used to be."

She pointed a feathery finger at the cart's wheels, which had clacked loudly across the floor. Mabel did as she was instructed and wheeled the cart even slower. Mabel was quite sure she would expire before delivering Frank's drinks, and a vicious part of her wondered if Gladys was simply stalling for time so Frank could walk in on them.

"You may set up the tea there," Gladys said. "I will be in the front office if you need anything."

Mabel waited for Gladys to shuffle back to Frank's office and shut the door behind her. She unloaded bottle after bottle, quietly, carefully. Each glass was set on the counter. Mabel could see that each area was labeled and properly organized, but she didn't have time to play the game "put Frank's things away." She set all of the booze on the bar and hurried around the room. Lucky said the box Frank kept the soul coins in should be hidden somewhere in the room near where Frank kept his liquor. The stones to open it were stored in a locked drawer right next to the box.

Mabel checked the China cabinet, the closets, behind the bar, and beneath the sofa set and checked under all the tables. The box was nowhere to be found. Lucky had mentioned having to sort through piles of junk as a test to find the box, but Mabel found nothing out of the ordinary. Like every other room in the Grand, Frank's penthouse likely shifted around, and that did correlate with something Lucky said that hadn't made sense at the time.

"I like things. It's my biggest weakness: valuables. I think the Grand knew that and made me overcome it to find where Frank hid the box. If I hadn't faced the darkest parts of myself and defeated them, I wouldn't have found it otherwise."

Mabel didn't want to think about her flaw.

"Your flaw has been and will always be your pride, Mabel Rose Dixon. You just have to be seen, don't you?"

Her mother's words were a splinter in Mabel's heart that she couldn't seem to pry loose. She had said those terrible things the day Mabel told her mother she was leaving home to be a star in New York City. Mabel still regretted the way she cursed her mother to her face, but she wasn't going to marry some poor farmer and bear his children. That wasn't the future she wanted for herself, and didn't what she wanted for herself matter?

She shouldn't feel guilty about the past. Mabel hated that this hotel, Frank, and the terrible deal she had made had now caused her to feel one second of regret. She was right to choose her life in New York over what awaited her back in Georgia. Mabel shook off the feeling that maybe her mother had been right about her. She took a deep breath and refocused. All she had to do was find something in this room that appealed to her greatest weakness—her pride.

With Gladys gone, Mabel could absorb the details of the penthouse. Frank's room was not unlike her starlit suite, only his bedroom and receiving area had all of the planets hand-painted across the ceiling in pastel hues. If Mabel reached up, she could hold the sun, the moon, and all the planets in the palm of her hand. She headed deeper into the penthouse. The walls surrounding Mabel were painted over in a mural of some kind, with scenes from the dawn of the world nearest the door. She traced her finger along the wide strokes of undulating water and tentacles of deep-sea creatures becoming long-legged animals and humans. She felt along paint ridges of plants growing out of the ashes of great volcanoes. On the opposite side of the painting lay terrible destruction. Towns and cities were laid to waste. People died of famine and disease, their tiny faces twisted in pain as they stared blankly back at Mabel.

Mabel pushed her gaze away from the writhing people and their horrible eyes. If she looked at those poor souls trapped in the painting any longer, despair would fill her bones, and her plan to find the box would evaporate like so much dust in the air. Mabel did not consider herself to be a student of biology, and hadn't read Darwin's book, but she knew of his theory called evolution from articles that long debated the topic of who was right, God or science. It seemed from Frank's mural that his beliefs on the subject were a blend of the two. Mabel had never been a god-fearing person. She had naturally gravitated toward any hint of modern ideas and ways of thinking, including scientific ones. Since coming to New York, Mabel hadn't given it much thought. Now that she was spending every day among demons, hell had become a literal place. There were no demons in the mural, no angels. Mabel wondered where their place in Darwinism would fall.

She circled the room. For all of the penthouse's ornate detail, the room was barely furnished. There was nothing of note besides furniture, clothing, and liquor. There was one place she hadn't explored yet, but she doubted it was where her weakness could be found.

Mabel entered the door she had found hidden in the worst imagery of the mural and found herself in a bathroom twice the size of hers. The splendor of his suites were matched in where Frank chose to bathe and dress himself. While her theme was Neptune, Frank's was Venus and her surrounding seas. Real barnacles had been inlaid with gold decor, even seashells and pearls. A towering statue of Venus stood beside a waterfall that ran down to an ostentatious bathtub the size of a circular pool. Her soft waves of thick hair cascaded past her shoulders and over a floor-length mirror she cradled in both golden arms. Venus's blank, white eyes gazed solemnly at the ever-trickling water, reminding Mabel of the demons lounging by the pool upstairs.

The mirror.

Mabel hurried over to it, taking care not to slip into the pool and take an unexpected bath of her own, and found nothing but herself in the mirror's reflection. She searched around the frame, behind Venus's bare feet, but there was no box-shaped anything. Maybe Mabel had this figured out all wrong. Maybe there was no rhyme or reason to where the souls were hidden.

She climbed down and found a vanity and tried searching each little wooden drawer instead.

"Is this what you're looking for?" a young, Southern female voice sweetly cooed from somewhere behind her.

There was no one else in the room with Mabel. Her eyes narrowed at the Venus statue, the only other figure in the room with her.

"Hello?"

"Silly," the voice said. "That's not me."

There was a dark shape in the center of the pool. Mabel came to kneel beside the undulating water and reached a cautious hand to sweep away some of the water's murkiness. It was only her reflection against the dark tiles of the bottom of the tub, but she could have sworn something was there. She had to put a hand over her chest to slow her racing heart.

"Not there," the voice laughed. "Over here."

"Where are you?"

"Listen closer to my voice. You know exactly who I am."

Mabel approached the mirror again. Her reflection grinned when Mabel's lips parted in a gasp. She reached for the mirror's glassy surface and her reflection did not move with her. It was her, but not her. They wore the same dress, same makeup, but Other Mabel's hair was like her old hair—honey curls, free and wild as the day she left home. There was something to her eyes, a sinister knowledge of what secrets Other Mabel held within, as if it might whisper. And there was a clear box cradled in Other Mabel's hands. Little white orbs, no larger than gold balls, floated around on the inside. Dozens of silver coins were gathered at the bottom.

"Maby-baby," she simpered. "Ain't we got fun?"

"Who are you?"

The Other Mabel shrugged her shoulder. "I'm the real you, the better you, the one who is willing to get her hands dirty to climb to the top."

Mabel ran a hand through her hair, flipping it with dramatic flair. "All I've heard in this place are lies on top of lies. You are not me, demon. Take a powder."

The mirror demon ignored her. "You've been talking to me more since you came to New York City. And I've liked that. We've had some fun times together. I like seeing this side of you, and your time at the Grand has only made you shine. This hotel has been good for you, baby, no doubt about it."

Mabel didn't like the sound of this. "I don't know what you're talking about."

Red flashed in the Other Mabel's eyes. "Of course you do. We talk damn near every day. Remember that time I convinced you to swipe that kid's purse? We were so hungry when we first came to New York. Starving, really. That rich kid in pigtails didn't need that bag full of toys. It was worth so much cheddar. We needed that money more."

"No. You're not me." Mabel's voice, once so full of bold sureness, wavered like a flag whipped by the wind. "You don't know anything about me."

"Or that time we swiped your friend Julie Gooding's dough out of her nightstand. We just borrowed the cash, really. We wrote a note that we'd pay her back. And we will. Eventually."

"You're not me. You're not my shadow." It couldn't be possible, but the longer she looked, the more noticeable the red horns became. They poked out of Other Mabel's forehead like tiny goat's horns, like Evelyn's.

"Swiping the dress from Ziegfeld was inspired. He should have picked you. You convinced yourself it was yours by right, so you took it, and would have given it back when he hired you. We both know the truth. You were keeping that dress for yourself, and you *are* worth it, baby. You're worth every dollar you've invested in yourself. All your wealthy patrons, all those jewels you stole, will be worth it now that you're the biggest star New York has ever seen. We're famous, baby. Famous!"

"Stop it!" Mabel covered her ears like a child, shrieking as if her cries could block out every horrible word spewed from the demon's mouth. "You're just a demon in a mirror! Give me the souls!'

"I brought you what you're looking for, but it will cost ya." The Other Mabel gave a playful wiggle like she was working over a crowd. "What will ya give me for it?"

She was going to have to outwit herself if she was going to win, but Mabel knew her own tricks. There was nothing Other Mabel didn't know, wouldn't try, wouldn't see right through.

"Oh sweetie," Other Mabel simpered. "Don't get all goofy on me. I'll make the deal real sweet for you. What's the one thing you would do if you ignored that little voice in your head that sounds like your mother? Admit the truth, and I'll give you the box."

Mabel paled. She was willing to do almost anything to be on stage, but there was one thing she refused to do in front of a crowd. "If you already know, why do I have to say it?"

Other Mabel grinned wider, baring her sharp canines. "Why are you so determined to show Ziegfeld what you're worth, huh?"

"You answered my question with a question," Mabel said. "If you're me, you already know."

Other Mabel gripped the box with both hands and crunched it. The metal bent so hard that some of the prongs snapped. The soul orbs inside flickered and winked out. "Souls are so fragile, like fine China. One wrong move and they just fall apart." Other Mabel squeezed again.

"Stop it! You'll break them!"

"Tell me the truth!" Other Mabel roared as her pupils rolled back in her head and her eyes turned pure red. "Why do you want to be a Ziegfeld girl?"

"Because I do, now give me the box!"

At her last audition, Mabel had stood with a long line of other girls, awaiting Ziegfeld's verdict. What Mabel had told Frank, Evelyn, Will, and everyone else wasn't exactly a lie. When Ziegfeld had first laid eyes on her, he *had* called her a Gibson Girl, too curvy to be a Ziegfeld star, but he hadn't said no.

When Ziegfeld called on Mabel, he asked her a question gently. Mabel had refused, to the shock of every girl standing on stage with her.

"You weren't exactly star material, were you?" Other Mabel said. "But you passed his tests on beauty, personal charm, magnetism, etiquette, grace, and poise. He asked you to join his chorus, didn't he?"

Mabel clenched her fists so tightly her nails bit into her palms. "Yes."

"But that wasn't all, was it?" Other Mabel crowed. "There was one requirement he asked of you, one that you turned down."

Mabel cringed, letting go of a long-held pain she had desperately held in. "He asked me if I was comfortable performing naked for him alone in his office."

Other Mabel paused. "Go on."

"He told me if I would take off my clothes and pose not only for his Follies act, but dance naked in his Midnight Frolic, I could be his chorus girl."

Other Mabel clucked her tongue. "Then what did Ziegfeld ask you to do?"

Mabel's tears threatened to fall, but she held them back until her eyes stung. "He wanted me to be comfortable and asked me to strip.

He knew I didn't want to. Ziegfeld told me I had a beautiful body, and it deserved to be shown. So, I took off my clothes. He made me do a test shoot with his photographer, but then he got on top of me. When Anna opened the door, interrupting what he was about to do, I ran out of the room. I couldn't pose naked in front of all of those men. The way they looked at me, that hunger. I'm a performer, not an object."

"Good, but not good enough." Other Mabel shook the box, threatening to crush it further.

"Will you stop?" Mabel yelled.

"Why are you doing all of this?" Other Mabel screamed back. "You don't want to be here. You didn't want to be his star, but you sold your soul for a chance to be Ziegfeld's leading girl. Why? What is it you really wanted when you fled your home, your mother, and that boy you were supposed to marry? Why did you leave everything you've ever known to come to New York?"

"I wanted to give people magic. I wanted to be a magician. The greatest female magician the world had ever seen."

Mabel stood alone in Frank's bathroom, hearing her truth echo off the empty walls like a sour note that ground the entire orchestra to a halt. Her clenched fists shook as hot tears drenched her face, tears that wouldn't stop coming.

"That's it," her other self said, triumph ringing in her soft voice. "That's the truth."

"Yes," Mabel said, her frustration and sadness all jumbling together into a ball of hot rage. "I came to New York to be a magician. No one wanted new vaudeville acts, especially not magic ones. Every theater I auditioned at turned me down. There weren't enough spaces for an act like mine. I wasn't unique enough, talented enough. Every door shut in my face, but then I found out Ziegfeld was holding auditions. I had to try something. I didn't want my dream of performing on stage to die.

"I told you your truths. Now give me the box."

Other Mabel only watched her, saying nothing, but not forking over the box either. Mabel chewed her lip. She had come all the way to New York not knowing Ziegfeld girls were not only expected to perform in the "family-friendly" Follies act, but they were also expected to appear upstairs at his Frolic nightclub after. And in bed with other men.

Her mother had warned her. She had told her what men in show business were like. She had never been so humiliated in her whole life.

Mabel huffed. "Even if I did say yes, Ziegfeld still refused to make me a lead. Even if I took those photos, performed naked in front of everyone, I still wouldn't be the lead. I thought maybe if I could buy my way into being the lead, I could decide what I wanted to do with my show and my body. I could choose because stars get a choice. I could turn my performance into a magic act and Ziegfeld could not refuse me."

"You want to be the best," Other Mabel said, voice mocking. "No shame in that. You had no other choice. You couldn't go back home, but your dream was dead. If you free these souls and you leave the Grand Hotel, you won't have a choice. Stars, chorus girls, they're all the same. You've been lying to yourself that things will be different for you if you flashed Ziegfeld enough cash. That's the real truth."

Mabel said nothing, but oh how she burned.

"You need a new dream, Mabel Rose. That's your truth whether you face it now, or later."

The Other Mabel pushed the clear box out of the mirror, whole and perfect without so much as one bend in the metal. The souls floated around like lazy summer fireflies, and their warm glow felt hot against Mabel's dress.

Mabel looked up to face herself again but found only her own reflection staring back at her, not a red-eyed, horned demon anymore. She clutched the clear box like it was a life raft that could keep her from drowning in an ocean of conflicted feelings. If she left the Grand, even if Ziegfeld made her a star, she would have to face the prospect of posing nude, dancing nude, strip teasing, sleeping with him, and everything else that came with being a star act. All Mabel wanted was to perform—to dance, sing, get them laughing, and to show them magic that would make people forget their lives for a while. She didn't want to have to give up her body for everyone to see.

It was her body, her choice.

Did she really want to get her soul back? Did she really want to leave the Grand Hotel? She had promised Will, Lucky, and herself that she would free these souls, but now that she was standing there, the debate inside her was greater than she expected. Will and his sister would go back to a life on the street. Mabel would also or be forced to dance naked for everyone in Ziegfeld's show. He wasn't the only gig in town, but the expectation would be there wherever she went in some form.

There was a rustling sound from somewhere behind her in Frank's bedroom. She didn't have time to debate. Gladys or Frank would likely return to the room soon, and she still needed the stones freed from Frank's drawer to open the box of souls.

Mabel peered out of Frank's bathroom and found his suite empty. She carried the enormous clear box, grateful that the carpeted floors didn't give away her movements. She set the soul box down on Frank's bed and reached for the decoded instructions in her pocket.

When the sun turns its face to the moon
Cradle mahogany until the dark bleeds gold
Eight stones set four elements
While each star turns its face toward the door

That part didn't make any sense, but she hoped it would when she pulled out the stones. Mabel found the bedside drawer locked and used a hairpin from her hair to crack it open. The door's lock gave easily, and Mabel opened the slim drawer to find a wide, mahogany jewelry box inside. Each side was delicately carved with the tiniest details. When Mabel brought the box to her face to study it, she gasped in delight. There were night predators on every side. Bats, wolves, foxes, bears, mountain lions, all with faces snarling and gold eyes. She unclasped the brass lock to reveal eight uncut stones in various shades of green, blue, red, and yellow nestled in lovely, crushed black velvet.

That explained the mahogany part of the puzzle, but Mabel was no alchemist that could transmute the box into gold. There had to be something else she was supposed to do, but the puzzle she had decoded was the answer. She only had to see the words from another angle.

Mabel took a closer look at the padlock on the front. There were eight stones divided into four settings. Obviously for the four elements, but when she stuffed the stones into their appropriate color settings, the clear box stayed stubbornly locked.

Cradle mahogany.

Mabel held the box close to her chest and waited. Nothing happened.

Bleeds gold.

How was she supposed to get wood to bleed gold? Or maybe it was the other way around. She examined the box; its grooves and shapes were perfect for putting something liquid in them. Everything in this place was run on blood. Why not try feeding some to the box as well?

Mabel raced back into the bathroom. She searched for something to create a small wound and found the solution in Frank's shaving set. She pressed the tip of his straight razor into the meat of her palm until a pearl of blood emerged. Mabel rinsed the blade off in the sink and placed it back in its home, cupping the pooling blood as she raced back to smear it across the box lid.

She held it against her chest again, cradling it like a newborn kitten. The box immediately warmed, and she felt something slick and hot form between her fingers. When she let go, all of the gold in each of the eyes came trickling out like water around the lid to form a solid pool in the center. It grew so hot that Mabel dropped the box on the carpet. A pentagram fell off the top of the box and rolled to a rest by Mabel's shoes.

The dark bleeds gold!

Mabel felt like a great mentalist conducting a moonlit seance as she set the pentagram around the stone formation in the clear box padlock. The setting had not been immediately obvious before, but now that the pentagram was in place, the missing piece was obvious. *While each star turns its face toward the door.*

She turned the star upside down. The tiny gears inside the padlock woke and clanked along their inner tracks. The silver coins slid around inside as there was a clicking sound, and the clear box door popped open just slightly. Mabel's heartbeat was as heavy as a raven's wings. She reached eagerly for the little door and popped open the box the rest of the way. The immediate rush of wind blew her hair back as hundreds of orbs flew out all at once.

Mabel cried out with joy as all of the human souls rushed out. They swarmed out like angry bees in a kicked hive, flitting around the room as the many silver coins evaporated into many fireflies of light. The orbs were so numerous it was like she stood inside a buzzing celestial formation. She couldn't help but laugh at the happiness their freedom brought her. People whose faces she had never seen would look up from cleaning, from cooking, from scrubbing floors and find their souls suddenly restored.

She wished Will could see this. Maybe he was right to want to free them all. Mabel hadn't thought it possible to save everyone, but she didn't mind being wrong. Once in a while.

An ungodly, ear-piercing shriek cried out from Frank's office, interrupting all of her good feelings. Mabel had forgotten all about Gladys. She needed to find her soul.

A single orb lingered by the hollow box.

Mabel held out her hand. Her soul beat steadily with a soft pulse of warm light in time with her own rapid heart. She had done it. Her soul was hers. Mabel brought the orb to her lips and ate it whole. She expected a sensation like eating food to follow, a literal swallowing of her own soul, but it was more akin to warm hope flooding her chest. A pins and needles kind of feeling she got sometimes while looking at something beautiful, like a sunset over an ocean.

The door swung open and crashed against the wall, damaging the mural.

"Thief," Gladys' voice was deeper now, more masculine. The skin on her enraged face hung off her bones more than before. "You freed the souls."

Mabel abandoned the box, inching her way across the wall, eyes desperately searching for another exit.

There was an enormous ripping sound as the flesh peeled off Gladys like wrapping paper off a birthday present. Mabel's horror became as sharp as a bloodied knife as six dark, sticky wings unfurled like spider's legs from the back of Gladys' ribcage. They unfolded from the rumpled remains of skin that had once belonged to Frank's secretary. Two wings stretched to their full length with white feathers sooted over in sticky ash. The enormous wings were joined by two more, and two more sets. There was no human shape about her anymore. The skin and bones of the corpse were a costume this creature had worn. The skeleton, no longer of use, crumbled away like rock fragments in a landslide tumbling off a mountaintop, revealing the horrible light of a volcano beneath.

"Mabel Rose Dixon." Gladys' voice boomed within Mabel's chest. *"Be not afraid."*

Gladys was all white-hot light, a sun burning at the peak of summer, with a dozen eyes blinking out of her broken center like wheeling fragments inside a crystal. Her six wings flapped each in turn to raise herself higher, and higher, until her wingspan brushed the elaborate ceiling. Gladys was as beautiful as she was terrifying, and Mabel had never felt such a mix of awe and terror before or been made aware of how small and fragile her bones were. If Mabel had listened to her instincts, she would have fallen to her knees in awe before what was clearly an angel. Thankfully, her desire to live was much greater.

Mabel had no weapon, but she had furniture. She grabbed the nearest lamp and yanked until the cord tore free from the wall. Mabel threw away the nonsensical lampshade and cracked the Edison glass bulb against her heel, breaking the filament. She pointed the sharp end at Gladys.

"Come on!"

Gladys leapt with a cry that sounded more like a sigh of ecstasy than a call to battle and was on Mabel in an instant. The world around Gladys became so bright that Mabel could not tell what was going on, but she kept her aim true on her target. There was a gust of wind and Mabel was flung back across the room, landing on something hard and sharp against her legs, and soft against her back.

Two thoughts flashed through Mabel's mind as she stared up at the four-post canopy of Frank's bed. First, she was sure the lamp's pointed glass had collided with something because a warm and hot liquid had burst onto her knee and was running down her leg. Second, she was sure something had struck her as well because there was a pointed spear shape pushing into her right breastbone.

Mabel spat up a great deal of blood.

Music swam in her mind, like a choir softly singing out a Sunday hymnal, calling her to worship. There was no pain in the light, only eyes. So many beautiful eyes stared at Mabel with golden lashes and pale pink irises as she lay flat against Frank's sheets. Gladys had struck her with razor-sharp feathers, piercing her in the chest, but Mabel had indeed sliced a wicked cut through Gladys' face. One of her eyes bled gold rivers down Mabel's leg.

So that was the warm liquid feeling.

Gladys screeched and beat her wings, blowing hot air into Mabel's face as she flew backward. Mabel was aware this was her chance. She needed to get up, run, defend herself, something, but as the sword-tipped feathers withdrew from her lungs, she found herself unable to do anything but ferociously cough up blood. She writhed, rolling over to one side, desperate to fill her lungs with air, but her right lung felt like a deflated hot water bottle.

Mabel hit the floor with a wet cough and clawed her way across the carpet, wheezing in trumpet bursts. She was not going to die in the middle of Frank's carpet because Gladys had decided it was a bad idea to free everyone from the Grand Hotel. It took everything in her to push the weight of her body up to her knees, and she shook the whole way. Gladys sputtered around the room, desperate wings scooping up her own blood in an attempt to heal herself as she made cooing noises like a distressed pigeon. She laughed at the winged creature, which only made Mabel wheeze in more knives of pain.

"I'm not dying." Mabel's hand wrapped around the lamp's gilded handle. "Today."

She crawled on hands and knees over to where Gladys writhed around the carpet and stabbed the broken lamp into Gladys' largest eye. Sparkling champagne-colored liquid burst hot all over Mabel's face, arms, and maid's dress. She spit the candy-taste out of her mouth.

Gladys collapsed, heavy against Mabel's lap as her many eyes lolled back in her orb-like form and dimmed to a flat gray shade. Mabel pushed off the ball of Gladys and her many sharp feathers and fell back, panting with cold relief. She pressed a hand against her chest, but Gladys' blood had smeared all over it. The cut was smaller now. With every breath in, the pain was a little less.

Strange. Mabel didn't know certain types of blood could also heal wounds in this place. She also didn't know there were angels in the Grand, but what were demons but fallen angels? At least, that's what church had taught her. But that wasn't true, was it? This hotel was full of demons who were once human.

Did her church get it wrong?

She would rest here a moment more, maybe a while. Mabel needed to find her strength again so she could make the long descent all the way back to the kitchen to meet Will. She could do that. It was only a short walk back to the elevator.

Mabel wasn't aware her eyes were fluttering shut, or that she had fallen backward onto the carpet until her face was smack up against the rug. She fought back at the drowsiness, but exhaustion hit her like a tidal wave and swept her out to a dreamless sleep.

CHAPTER THIRTEEN

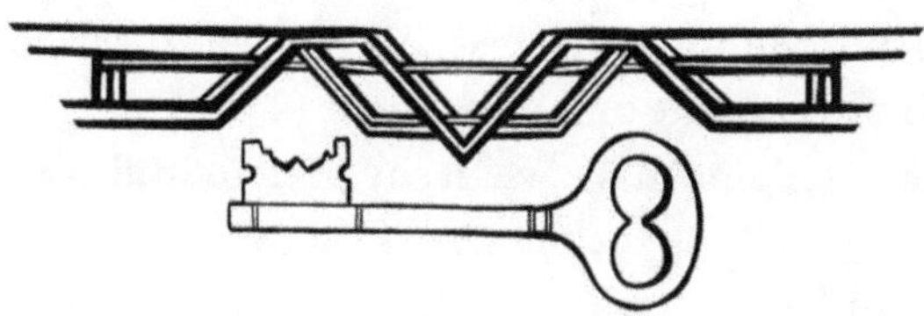

Mabel woke to a large boom somewhere below her. There was an unfamiliar ceiling above her, but it took Mabel a whole ten seconds to register that she was still lying on the rug of Frank's penthouse bedroom.

Will. She was supposed to meet Will.

Mabel rolled over to one side and coughed up something gold and sticky onto the carpet.

Gladys' body lay in a frumpled yet massive heap of feathers only a few feet away, all of her golden tones diminished to a dirty-rag gray in death. Her gold blood was everywhere, hardened into spiky clumps that would probably never come out.

Mabel felt sorry for killing such a beautiful creature but did not feel sorry for saving herself from a very certain death. Her emotions lately were full of strange complications. Whatever type of angel Gladys was, her blood was like a high-end cocktail mixed from top-shelf liquor. She could see why Frank picked Gladys as his "secretary."

There was another boom of distant thunder inside the hotel.

The shock of sudden vibration through the floor had Mabel scrambling to get up. She was surprised at her own vigor, and the ease with which she came to stand. Mabel should have felt like garbage warmed over, but her body felt like she had experienced a month-long vacation at a luxury resort. Now that her soul was back, she had never felt so well rested in her life.

The lights flickered as the overhead chandelier swung gently from the impact. Something downstairs had exploded, maybe electrical, maybe furniture, maybe the hotel itself. Whatever it was had collided with the framework and shuddered up the floors of the Grand like a hammer smashing through a spine.

Did releasing the souls do this? She needed to get downstairs as fast as possible in case the building collapsed.

Mabel's legs did not shake when she tried to walk, though she got a strong head-swimming feeling that if Gladys' blood had not healed her, the motion would have made her pass out. She headed for the door, leaving the destroyed angel, empty soul box, and stones all behind because she could not think of a reason to need any of them until she had entered Frank's office, and it dawned on her what a huge mistake that was.

Mabel pressed her hands into her palms, testing to see if returning her soul to her body had also returned her humanity. She pressed until her thumbnails had formed little half-moons in the meat of her palms. Her second mouths did not appear. She was fully human again, but also weaponless.

She doubled back and kneeled beside Gladys' broken, orb-shaped body. Mabel carefully removed one of her knife feathers from the closest wing and it came free with a wet tug.

Mabel didn't know what awaited her downstairs after releasing every soul Frank had locked up inside his soul cage. Better to leave with a weapon than empty-handed.

She held the knife-feather, which was the size and weight of a butcher's knife with a double blade, by the quill with care not to cut herself as she made for the elevator. Mabel pressed the call button and waited. Nothing happened. It dawned on her after a long moment that the bellhop working the elevator likely got his soul back and fled.

Mabel could try summoning the Navigator.

She closed Frank's office door, thought very hard about what she wanted and opened it. What waited for her on the other side was the same office, no golden demon, no Atrium. The Navigator wasn't coming, and neither was the elevator. Mabel was going to have to use the stairs.

The elevator clanked. Mabel wanted to cry with relief as the little arrow above the double doors chimed at each floor all the way to the top floor. Thankfully, someone was still operating the elevator and saved her from the long trek down many flights of stairs.

The doors opened and it was Will who greeted her. His face was deathly pale.

"What happened?"

"It's not good." He opened the cage for her, eyes unable to focus on anything for too long as he ushered her to quickly get inside. "When I realized you were trapped upstairs with no one to get you down, I came for you."

Mabel trotted inside with her feather, smiling, but Will was still stricken and paler than she had ever seen. She had done something good, for once. She had saved everyone. So why did Will look so panicked?

"What's wrong?"

He didn't answer her as he busied himself with shutting the cage and cranking the elevator's lever to send it back down to the terminal lobby floor. Will turned to answer her and suddenly realized Mabel looked like a candy apple that had melted in the hot sun. "What happened to you?"

Mabel glanced down at her candy crusty maid's uniform. "I had to kill Frank's secretary."

He raised an eyebrow, nodding vaguely as if he were only half listening, as if her outfit was not the strangest thing he had seen that day. "We need to get you new clothes before we descend. There are extras in the break room."

There was another earthquake and the elevator rattled on its cords. Mabel held onto the walls, suddenly made very aware of how far they had to fall.

"What's going on?" Mabel insisted.

A shudder went through Will. "Everyone got their souls back. The front office clerks, the lobby boys, the maids, they all got their souls back."

She frowned, elbowing him in the ribs. “So why do you look like you swallowed dirt? Buck up, kid. We should *celebrate*. We saved *everyone*.”

“I had no idea the event would turn into a light show. It got the attention of everyone in the Grand, and not just the humans. The staff figured out what was going on so quickly.” Will trailed off with a faraway look that usually belonged to war victims when they thought about memories of past battles.

Mabel didn’t like it.

“Will!” She grabbed his arm and shook him, hoping it would snap him back to reality. “Tell me what happened!”

It all came out at once. “I stole the map and then there was this rush of lights. Everyone started cheering. Then my soul found me. The light was so big, and I knew it had to be mine because it rushed inside my body. I had the map, my soul, and I thought I’d seen victory, but then I came back out into the lobby...”

Will raked his fingers through his hair like he wanted to pull every hair on his head right out of his scalp. “Frank thought of this. He and Raymond had plans for this. The staff started killing everyone with such... precision.”

Mabel’s happiness turned to cement in the bottom of her shoes. *“What?”*

Will looked Mabel dead in the eyes. “They’re gone. Everyone who tried to run out the front doors... they’re gone. Frank clearly didn’t want everyone fleeing out into New York City, so he called on the remaining demons. Those demons were waiting for the humans at the doors. They slaughtered everyone.”

Mabel swallowed hard as the weight of Will’s story humbled all of Mabel’s feelings into a complex knot she wasn’t sure she could ever untangle. On the one hand, she had helped everyone get their souls back, but on the other, every single one of those people had wound up dead.

All she had wanted was her freedom. She hadn’t considered for one second what would happen in the aftermath. Now, everyone who had tried to run was dead.

And it was all her fault.

Mabel buried her face in her hands and didn't bother to stop the tears from coming.

"Hey." Will grabbed her shoulder and shook her once, gently, but she wouldn't look him in the eye. He turned her chin and forced her blurry eyes to focus on his face. "Don't you feel bad for one second about what you did. Everyone's soul was trapped in this place. We had to save them. They went on to a better place because of you."

Mabel bit her lip so hard she tasted copper in her mouth. She was shaking with rage, with the enormity of the loss stretching out like a deep canyon before her, and she didn't know how to stop feeling the pain of every last person she had sentenced to death.

"These people died *with* their souls," Will continued. "They died *free*. You saved them."

His acceptance of necessary casualties for the greater good churned like spoiled food in her stomach. "No, Will. They died *because of me*. They died and I am the one who walked free."

The elevator continued to ding through the levels in the hard silence between Mabel and Will. She knew it wasn't true, but in that moment, she felt as soulless as Frank. There had to have been a better way, something between saving herself and saving everyone else, but Mabel couldn't see anything but her own hopelessness. She knew Will was right. Those people had met a better fate than a life as a demon, but her guilt was an empty well she had thrown a rock down into. Mabel kept waiting for a splash of hope to echo back up to her in the form of an answer, something to make her feel better, but nothing came.

Mabel could tell herself at least they reclaimed their souls, and avoided an eternity spent as a demon working for the Grand Hotel, but she couldn't not feel guilty. From the moment she had entered the Grand, she hadn't thought of anyone else. She had told herself it was for practical reasons, that she was just trying to survive, but that wasn't the truth. The worst was she hadn't cared about the effect of her actions on anyone else until now when everyone around her was dead.

Worst of all, Mabel was the one left standing with her soul, and she could walk out the front door now and leave all this bloody mess behind. But could she live with herself once she walked down the steps of the Grand Hotel?

Her face burned as she glared down at the floor through swollen eyes, hating Will, hating herself, hating everything. She clutched her knife-feather tight in her sweaty hand, debating the alternative routes they could have taken. She should never have tried to get her soul back. All of those people didn't have to die. But on the other hand, if Mabel had chosen to accept her life at the Grand, she could have lured a hundred souls to their death and damnation by month's end.

All of Mabel's choices resulted in death.

"I have to make this right," she said, voice faraway.

"You did make it right," Will said. "I'd rather be free and go on to meet my maker than a devil sitting pretty. Back in Ireland, the Black and Tans swept through everything. They pillaged our villages, kicked us out of our homes. We had to either comply, fight for our freedom, or run for it. My older brother died protecting us. My family fled their tyranny looking for freedom only to land on unfriendly shores. These people trapped here—they all deserve to be free. Freedom is worth fighting for, and it is worth dying for, even if it's only a chance. And you gave everyone in the Grand that chance today.

"Devils wear many faces," Will said. "They don't all have horns."

Mabel knew what it was to flee her home, but not for persecution, not like what Will had experienced. He was hard to the ways of the world, and the grim acceptance of death, in a way Mabel wasn't.

"I'm sorry," Mabel said. "I just feel so terrible. I wanted everyone to live. I didn't know."

"At least they've gone on to meet whatever god they believe in. When we close the portal, no one will ever have to be tempted into becoming a demon ever again. The suffering will end. I don't only want to save my sister. I want to free everyone."

She gave him a weak smile as she wiped her eyes. "Yes. You're right. We should close the portal. That way, we can make this right."

"More people might die," Will said. "But if we close the portal and free their souls, at least they will have a chance for heaven. Death is far better than remaining in hell."

The elevator door dinged, interrupting them with an announcement they had reached the bottom.

Will pulled out a thick, folded-up parchment from his jacket. "There's a maid's passage directly by the elevator to the kitchen. You can change your clothes there into something clean before we descend. Then we head to the door behind the bar in the dining hall. It leads down to the first basement level."

They could, but now they had the attention of every demon in the hotel. Frank would be desperate to find who had freed his humans, and all of the evidence would point directly to the one thief among his staff. He would hunt Mabel down and likely kill her for what she had done, and probably anyone who was with her. He couldn't take her soul again without her consent, but she didn't want to die. Not yet.

"Prepare yourself. There's quite a bit of blood. You coming?"

"Of course." Mabel had no fight left in her, only the crushing weight that she might cause another death tonight. "I promised you."

Will folded the map and slipped it back inside his uniform before reading the elevator cage to open.

"Whatever happens," Will said. "Thank you for freeing my soul."

Mabel didn't know what to say, so she was honest. "When Frank finds out I was the one who freed all of the souls and killed his secretary... You understand the risk you're putting yourself in by coming with me, right?"

Will shrugged. "Not if we suck him down to hell before he gets a chance."

His answer only made the worry inside Mabel thicken into a fog she couldn't see a way out of. Mabel had swiped a lot of purses and broken into a lot of doors, but figuring out how to reverse a portal to hell was a skill she did not have on her resume.

"You're sure closing the portal will work? The real demons, the fallen angels, will be gone, and the humans will get their souls back?"

"I saw the proof in the ledger," Will said defensively. "When the portal closed, the souls stopped going in. I found the spell to get them back out and I stole the map of the hotel. Not even Frank can find his way down without it. This plan will work."

Mabel nodded even though she still doubted Will's plan even more than she doubted herself. Still, she reminded herself if she wanted to free everyone, for real this time, this might be the one way to do it. There was no way to be sure. Mabel couldn't think of another way out. If she were to move forward, she would have to accept this plan came with that uncertain risk, but the hope of seeing Lucky, Saoirse, and every lost soul turn human again? That was worth everything.

Will placed a hand on the cage latch. "Ready?"

Mabel gripped her sharp feather tight. "Just open the door already."

Mabel

Will

Evelyn

Frank

Lucky

Raymond

CHAPTER
FOURTEEN

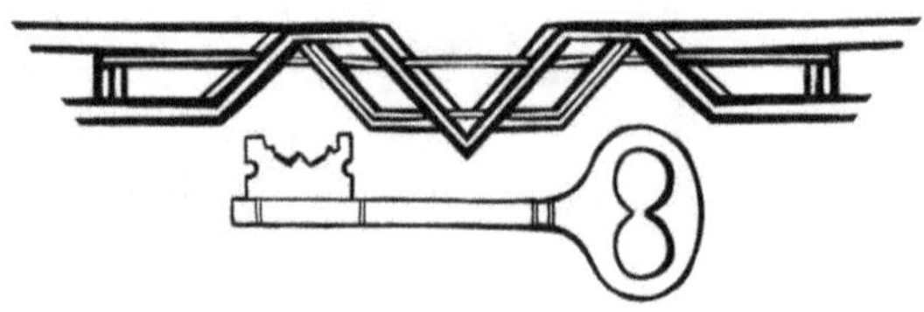

The cage opened to reveal a lobby painted in every shade of red. Brilliant wet splashes of crimson were strewn across the ceiling in arcs. Rivers pooled across the floor. Blood was smeared across the faces of the golden statues that regarded the lobby with indifferent faces to the carnage beneath their feet. Gore soaked the once glittering lobby and stained the marble floors of the Grand in wet pinks and dried in disgusting browns.

There were people moving around the carnage in the lobby. Maids and bellhops with blood staining their gold and black uniforms, turning their clothes many shades darker than they should be, carried mops, buckets, rags, and soap bars. Mabel didn't notice the clumps at first, but there were lumps of something carpeting the floor in every direction. What remained of the bodies was so numerous Mabel didn't know how they were going to walk without slipping on them. The staff did not look up at Mabel or Will as they exited the elevator. They kept their heads down and stepped around the labyrinth of carnage as they cleaned, every face grim with the hardness of their work.

"Be careful," Will said, urging her in a sharp whisper. "I wouldn't look for too long. It will only make you sick."

As she stepped out, Mabel got a clearer view of what was strewn across the lobby besides blood. Most of the bodies had been disposed of, but there were still pieces as far as Mabel could see in every direction. There were arms. Heads. Legs. Open sets of eyes staring back at her from slack-jawed faces.

Before coming to the Grand Mabel had seen a dead body only once in her whole life, when the neighbor's son had died of smallpox. His little body had been so rigid, so gray, but it had been whole. These bodies were diced apart like meat in a butcher's shop. She let out a little sound and covered her mouth to keep from vomiting. It was like opening night, the same aftermath of human remains strewn about like discarded puzzle pieces, but ten times over. Mabel could not shake Frank's words from ringing in her head.

"I want ten souls tomorrow night. No less."

"You looked, didn't you?" Will held out his arm to her. She accepted and didn't argue as he took the lead.

Her chest rose and fell so rapidly that she couldn't slow her breathing. She couldn't answer him. Her voice had left her body like steam off a hot road after a storm.

"Hold it together." Will pulled her close to him until his chest was pressed up against hers, and all she could see was his face and not the bloody room. "Keep your eyes on me."

Mabel steadied herself on his solid form to keep from keeling over, but her heels slipped, and she tripped over something big and solid. She couldn't help it. She looked down. Mabel had stepped over the partial remains of a woman. Her face was frozen in mid-scream and her costume lay in a billowy purple cloud around her head. Mabel's eyes went so wide they watered. It was Gisela Van Doren. Blood wept from what remained of her body like a filthy wound, staining the brown paper surrounding the space where her hand still twitched.

Mabel let out a sob she had been desperately holding in. The sob rose to a sharp, single-note, ear-shattering scream.

Will grabbed her face as gently as he could to stifle her panic. "Don't," he hissed. "Stay with me."

"It's my fault. My fault. My fault." She mumbled the words into his hand as her cry diminished into pathetic choke-sobs. *"Gisela is dead, they're all dead, and it's all my fault."*

When Mabel couldn't get out a full response between hyperventilated breaths, Will scooped up the trembling Mabel and carried her across the lobby into a carpeted side hall beside the main offices. She clung to him with desperate arms around his neck. As he wound through hallways and down narrow corridors they had never traveled before, Mabel closed her eyes. She wanted to shut everything out, her whole life out, but all she could see was Gisela's gray, rolled-over eyes. Mabel doubted she would close her eyes without picturing Gisela's dead face ever again.

"It's okay," Will breathed against her head. "We're out of the room. It's over."

Mabel heard the familiar sounds of clanking and scrubbing of dishes being washed. She lifted her head from the safety of Will's shoulder. They were back in the kitchen. The sounds and smells grounded Mabel a little as Will set her down in a chair inside the break room.

"Can I get you anything? Food? Water?"

She shook her head.

He left for a moment and reappeared with a cup of water in his hands. "Please. It will help."

She accepted the offering and downed it gladly.

Once she had taken a few hearty gulps and he was sure Mabel could sit upright by herself, Will shut and locked the door. Mabel slumped in her chair a bit as Will dove into one of the lockers to retrieve a spare Grand uniform.

"They always have extra uniforms stashed here," Will said, handing it to her with care to keep the pants from trailing on the floor. "Always fresh pressed. Try this on."

Mabel stared down at the folded jacket and pants in her lap, feeling like she did not deserve these clothes, or anything nice ever again. All of those people. They were someone's father, someone's sister, someone's mother, and now they were all dead.

Fresh tears fell, staining the white shirt in her lap.

"Come on. You don't want to be caught here by Raymond, or worse, Frank."

Mabel nodded vaguely, moving her arms to remove her soiled dress. When it became clear to Will that Mabel's motions were too slow, Will took the knife-feather from her, set it on the coffee table behind him, and proceeded to help her change quickly.

He slipped off the stiff fabric of the ruined maid's uniform and helped her noodle arms into the bellhop's uniform. Normally, she wouldn't want anyone to see her undress, but Will handled her with a doctor's bedside manner. He was both respectful in looking away from curves of Mabel he had not been invited to see and mechanical in motion, like an automaton helping her dress.

Will tucked all of her red curls under a little bellhop's cap and nodded approval. "This should work long enough to help us cross the dining hall to the bar. But you're going to have to walk on your own. Think you can do it?"

"Yes." Mabel was itchy and uncomfortable in this new attire, but the irritation brought her back to the present somewhat. The buttons puckered a bit over her chest, and it ballooned around her waist, but otherwise Mabel looked the part of a lobby boy. Her pants were too short, but Mabel had never been allowed to wear pants before. She would take stiff clothes over crusty, demon-blood ones any day of the week.

"Men's pajamas and men's pants," Mabel said with a little laugh. "If only my prohibition-loving mother could see me now."

Will clapped her on the arm. "That's the spirit."

She forced herself to give him a little smile she did not feel.

Will brought her uniform shoes to wear instead. Her toes were still a bit sticky, but she placed her feet into new socks and two spare Grand Oxfords anyway. As she got to her feet again, she took several breaths in and out until she felt ready to go again. If only her body would stop shaking.

"Ready?" Will said. "We're going to do the same thing again across the dining hall as before. You can push a cart this time if you want. You'll have something to lean on that way."

"Sounds Jake," Mabel said. "But won't we risk running into Raymond and Frank out there? What are you going to do?"

Will's blue eyes stared intensely into hers for a moment, spelling out for Mabel that which should have been obvious by now. He removed the map from his suit and handed the thick, leathery folded-up paper over to her. "If anything happens to me, I want you to free my sister."

Mabel bristled. His idiocy had washed away the cold dread of seeing so many dead bodies at once and replaced it with hot irritation.

"That's your plan?" Mabel said. "Charging straight through like bulls at a matador will only make everything worse. We have got to be smart about this, together, starting right now."

There was a little side table with coffee and tea set out that had obviously seen little use, and Mabel spread the map across the unused space beside the empty cups and full sugar canisters. She had not had much experience with ancient maps, or any maps at all, but this was unlike any she had ever seen in books or museums.

This map *moved.*

Every level of the Grand Hotel had been drawn in doll house detail, like the artist had opened one side of the building and could look down into the walls and floors of each level. There was the penthouse, Evelyn and Martin's honeymoon suite, the stage, and even Mabel's room listed on the Grand's map. At the center leading up from the bottom was the Navigator. Her central Atrium and long tunnel traveled up the Grand like a throat on a human anatomy illustration.

The strokes of quill ink fluttered across the page as the Navigator summoned a floor from far above her down to the bottom Atrium level. It was strange to see such a massive enclosure in miniature, but the sight delighted Mabel to no end. She could spend days staring at the inner clockwork, but she shook off her rapture like a dog with a wet pelt when she saw what lay beneath the splendor.

The towering shape of the Grand Hotel, which stood high above the rest of the city, was inverted past the main floor. As the floors descended downward, the rooms got narrower and narrower, leading to a pointed pen-tip shape at the very bottom. The map was a perfect mirror above and below. There was a hotel for everyone to see above, all glittering and perfect, and one down below, crafted from every purple-green shade found in infected skin.

Mabel surveyed the living illustration until she located the dining hall and kitchens. Something glittered around the edges of the walls, and when Mabel leaned in to give a closer inspection, the walls shifted to reveal the passageways behind them. They were slim, no bigger than two shoulder widths apart. There was just enough space for a maid to clean up the room and cart the laundry downstairs to the basement levels.

"Those are the maid travel tunnels I was telling you about."

Mabel pointed at the wall behind the sink in the next room over. "There seems to be a door hidden here. Which would make sense. They need to wash the table linens."

Will blinked at her. "I hadn't thought of that."

"We can enter through the door behind the sink." She traced her finger downward along the path to the next floor, which was labeled: *Horse track.*

"The Grand really does have whatever you want," Mabel said.

"Place your bets," Will said. "On whatever you want."

He was right. On the floors immediately following, there were continuing markings for races, gambling, multiple boxing rings, and even animal fights. Mabel marveled at the kaleidoscopic display of pleasures and had to force herself to refocus on the path to the bottom.

"We take the tunnel past the horse track through the boxing ring, down several floors past dog fights, down to... a carnival? We'll have to cross it to reach the door behind the carnival games."

From there, it seemed much less complicated. Mabel traced her finger across the speakeasy level. She did not have to stretch her imagination far to assume what went on there. Then, the dreaded Laundry level she had heard so much about was located right before the final floors.

"Right," Will said, tapping a finger near the bottom of the hotel map. "This is the one part I don't understand. Once we get past Laundry, everything reverses."

He was, again, right. The floors after the speakeasy faded into strange shapes, as if the map had been smeared by a careless thumb, but when Mabel looked closer, the rooms appeared to be upside down versions of the honeymoon and penthouse suites. The staircases between them also looked to be upside down.

The three bottom floors were simply labeled: "the Below."

"Well," Mabel said. "Looks like we've put a finger on the path down. There seems to be no other clue about how to free everyone once we get down there."

"Actually, I learned a little something during my heist." Will removed another piece of paper from the inner pocket of his jacket. It was torn on one side, indicating Will had definitely ripped it out of a book. He unfolded the heavy brown paper with care to reveal a circular spell with triangles and symbols weaving in and out of each other like stars across the heavens. Its spell was surrounded with words in a language Mabel did not understand. At the center stood two people, one clearly the silhouette of a human man, and the other a very tall horned black smudge that was clearly not human at all. The only part in English read the name of the original signature: Henry West, Frank's father.

"How did you find this?"

"I hope you don't mind, but I borrowed your act. I brought in a bar cart full of liquor into the front offices. The front staff is full of boozy Sheiks and Shebas paying off their debt by keeping track of who checks in. Everyone clamored for the cart, allowing me to slip out the back and into the archives. I grabbed the map and searched the catalog, hoping to find some kind of spell book or instruction manual to return all the souls up from down below. There was a book labeled 'The Grand Hotel Agreements' that was full of the first contracts to ever be written. This was the first one listed, the original Grand Hotel deal."

Mabel hadn't considered there would be one deal that started it all, but it made sense that the hotel had to start collecting souls somewhere.

"So, you're saying there was an original deal, and we can somehow reverse it and then what? Everything's berries?"

Will pointed to one of the words. "It's written in Demonaic. The only words I can read is '*Reverse to Return in Offering.*'"

"Okay, so we reverse the original deal and what happens? How is it supposed to work? Can you try and read the rest?"

Will shook his head. "I only speak a little. We might need to find someone who is a full demon to read it. It has something to do with how the hotel was founded. I might know just the guy to ask, but he's down below. Marty keeps the books for all the bets. We could get him to read it."

For the first time, Will had stumbled on an answer Mabel felt might have winning odds. This was the spellwork for the original contract, something concrete that could possibly be undone. They could place money on that.

"You're a true grifter now, William Donahue," Mabel said, genuinely proud of her influence on him. "Let's hope your friend can tell us how the spell works."

When he saw the appreciative way Mabel was looking at him, a shade of rose pink spread from Will's freckled cheeks down his neck. "You asked me earlier how could I be sure closing the portal would restore all the souls Frank took, even the ones in hell. You were right. I decided to be sure. The Grand keeps records of spells in the main office. I never would have thought to rifle through those books until you questioned me."

"I dub thee Sir Thief." She pretended to knight him with the tip of her finger half-heartedly.

Will made a show of it, bowing deep until his cap almost fell off, trying to get her to crack a smile. "I learned from the best."

Mabel rolled up the map in a hurry. For all their revelry, she couldn't laugh at Will. She still felt poisoned from what they had done. The pain and guilt were like a dull headache in her heart as she grabbed Gladys' feather and turned back to Will. "We have a map, a spell, and a plan. All we have left is to promise no one else dies because of us."

Will's happy expression melted like ice in the sun. "We didn't know what would happen. You shouldn't blame yourself for their deaths. I'm the one who told you about the soul cage, about the plan. If it's anyone's fault, it's mine."

Mabel stuffed the map carefully inside her slim jacket the way she had seen Will tuck it away. "We should have been more careful. We don't entirely know now that this spell you stole won't kill more people trying to save them. If we get down there and find out it's the wrong spell or it will kill people, I'm calling it. I won't let what happened happen again."

"Whatever the cost of this spell is, I will pay it," Will said. "Just get me down there and help me crack it like you did with the soul cage. You don't need anything else on your conscience."

She chewed the inside of her cheek. Mabel didn't want him to pay any cost. She would help him, but what he didn't know was Mabel had resolved to lead Will through this, not the other way around. She still wasn't sure closing the portal was a good idea, even with Will's spell. If she had to be the one to save Will from himself, she would do it.

"We've wasted enough time," she said. "Let's find that portal."

Will led Mabel out of the break room, off to the left, and down into the deeper rooms behind the main kitchen. Her worried thoughts raged in dark storm cloud formations as they weaved through several rows of sinks where dozens of people were cleaning up after the lunch rush. The staff worked so tirelessly scrubbing the filth from the plates and glasses and were so dedicated to their tasks that they moved as efficiently in unison as any ballet dancer performing Swan Lake. No one looked up as Will and Mabel hurried past.

"There," Mabel said, pointing to a bit of wall that was out of place behind two workers hunched over dirty platters filling a deep, stainless-steel sink. "That's the opening."

"Could you step aside?" Will grabbed one of them on the shoulder.

The dishwasher turned to moan at Will. There was a bandage over his eyes, stained brown in the spots where his eyes should be. There was another old bandage over his mouth where his tongue had been cut and the blood had dried long ago. Mabel's gaze traveled down to the dishwasher's hands. They were also bandaged over at the wrists. Where his hands should be there were scrubbing utensils instead. They were part of his body now. They were his hands now.

Will cried as he stumbled back, colliding with Mabel. She had tried her very best not to scream and failed the second Will knocked into her. Both dishwashers had the same horrible wounds, and they moaned as if begging for help. Mabel wanted to do something, anything to help them, but her terror kept her from moving. These people had done something to warrant life-altering disfigurement in Frank's eyes. She knew he was horrible, manipulative, and cruel, but he was so much worse than she had assumed.

Frank was a monster.

"Mabel. Rose. Dixon."

The familiar boom of Frank West's voice should have sent Mabel shivering in her too-big Oxfords, but it did the opposite. It jolted her out of her terror and sent her immediately on the defense. She wheeled on him, ready to fight for both herself and Will, with Gladys' sharp feather in her tight grip.

Frank stood in the doorway wearing a dark blue suit and silver-gray tie, but his fine clothes had hardened with old blood. His swept back hair had fallen into his wild eyes, and it was clumped together by red matter. Behind him stood Raymond, his ever-present shadow looming over them all. He lingered in the doorway, coolly detached, as if he were just as interested in what Frank was about to do to them as he was what Will and Mabel might stoop to in order to defend themselves.

"You caught me, Frank. What do you want?"

Frank clucked his tongue. "You, *darling girl*, are more trouble than you're worth."

"You should have cut a new deal with me," Mabel said, twisting the knife of his words back at him. "You would have saved us both a big, bloody mess."

Frank huffed as if Mabel had mortally wounded him. "You've murdered my Throne angel. Do you know how difficult it was to find Gladys? How hard it was to procure a fallen angel of that status? All the paperwork that must be now filed to replace her?"

Mabel laughed at him and there was nothing Frank hated more.

"You released the souls," Frank said. "What a mess to clean up, all over the return of one soul. And you do have yours back, Mabel. Why are you still here, running around with this fool?"

"Because you still have his sister," Mabel said. "Let Saoirse go, and we'll leave you and this hotel alone."

Will grabbed her arm, face twisted with pain, as if Mabel had just struck him. "What are you doing? What about everyone else?"

Mabel stared back hard at him. She had a plan but couldn't relay that to Will with just her eyes. "Trust me, Will."

Frank saw the discord between them, and a little smile crept up into the corner of his mouth. "I'll make you both a new deal. Agree, and Saoirse goes free."

Mabel crossed her arms, careful not to nick herself with the feather. "Go on."

"Give me the Canary," Frank said. "And you can have her. Mind you, she won't want to leave with you. Saoirse is a demon now."

Mabel was getting Frank where she wanted. If she played him right, she could get the information she wanted too. "So, when you turn people into full demons, they can come and go from the hotel as they please without their souls? They're free?"

"Some are free by rank." Frank waved his hand. "Evelyn may come and go as she pleases, but as you can see with her, they always seem to find their way back home. It's all very Greek, as if the Fates themselves cut the puppet strings of the soul and down it goes to be counted in hell. They lose their soul one way or another, stay on as demons, become my responsibility to employ. No one appreciates what a trial it is, how many of them must feed, how many of them must be given work."

"Do you... not want to do this job?" Mabel said coyly.

Frank glanced back at Raymond, who remained placid. "Why are you asking?"

"I heard a rumor." Mabel walked toward Frank, slowly and carefully, like a deer venturing out into an empty field. "You could stop all of this. You could shut down the operation, leave, do something else instead."

Frank's face flushed. "Who told you this?"

Mabel locked eyes with Raymond. His face was stone, but his eyes were alive with a deep bemusement. They both knew who it was spreading the rumors that Frank was unhappy at his job, and yet he was saying nothing, and was all the more powerful for it.

"That's the thing about rumors," Mabel said. "They come from everywhere and nowhere. Is it true?"

"I have my own deal to fulfill, and you are making it so much harder to do it. You're stalling for time. Give me the Canary."

Why did he want her necklace so bad?

She placed her hand over the yellow gem and its pearls. "No."

Frank dove for the necklace, but it was so quick, Mabel did not catch the moment his nails elongated to form a fan of knives.

"No, Mabel!"

Will pulled Mabel, yanking her by the meat of her bicep away from Frank's blow. Warm blood splattered across Mabel's arm. Mabel had sliced her feather across Frank and the quill had shattered in her hands. She had struck Frank, yes, but she did not expect the gush of hissing, green blood to come spilling out of the ribbon cut she had opened down Frank's chest when he collapsed.

Frank instantly dropped like a wet sack of meat onto the soapy floor.

Mabel prepared herself for Raymond to attack next, but Raymond had dissolved like mist back into the ether, abandoning his boss. Verdant blood pooled out of the wound as Frank wheezed.

"I will take your soul again, Mabel Rose Dixon. When I do, I will devour it in pieces as I rip every inch of your flesh apart." He stared up at Mabel, rejected, hurt. "I gave you everything. You asked me for your dreams and I gave them to you. I could have left you for dead."

Mabel's fists clenched and green squished between her fingers. "You gave me lies. And death. You gave me damnation. Not my dreams. Not my real ones."

"You're the one who didn't ask for your real dream." Frank coughed up green down his button shirt and grinned sharp teeth at her. "All I want is to be free of this place and its damned demons. I don't want the future my parents wanted for me, just like you."

Mabel's resolve faltered. "We are nothing alike."

"Aren't we?"

Mabel did not have to answer him. A smirk crept up the corner of her mouth and threatened to become a full smile. "Everything you want is about to come true. No more responsibility, no more Grand Hotel, no more you."

Mabel turned her back on Frank to trot over to where Will waited near the opening in the wall. Will stood there, agog at the way she spoke to Frank West. She inspected his wound, which Will had already bandaged over with some fresh, thin rags he had found near the dishwashers.

Frank laughed. He laughed louder, and louder, and louder. "I am the Grand," Frank sputtered. His groan and coughing fit came out sickly wet as he doubled over. She was not going to be baited into giving her plan away. "There is nowhere you can hide. I will find you."

Mabel stomped back to his bloody green body and kicked Frank hard in his wound. She did not care about the horrible animal sound he made, or that his frothing, green blood had gotten all over her shoes and hands.

She scoffed and tossed her curls. "I'm counting on it."

Mabel gently steered Will into the hole in the wall, pushed him inside the narrow slat first, and blew Frank a big kiss as she entered the walls of the Grand Hotel.

CHAPTER FIFTEEN

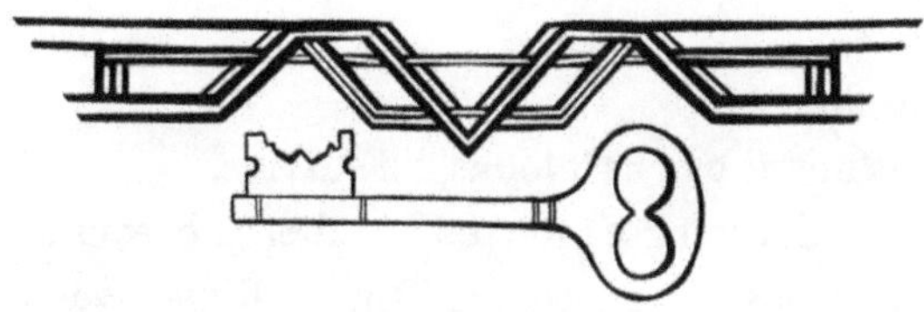

The map had absolutely lied.

Everything below the Grand Hotel was a labyrinth. The map had barely scratched the surface of showing Mabel and Will the sheer number of passages available to them. There were at least a dozen carpeted hallways extending out from every wall, like ant tunnels, only these were kept neat and clean and dust-free by... someone. Their decorations and wallpaper were identical to the back halls she had traveled down on her first night. Mabel was part of the whole circus below, the top of the wedding cake of delights the Grand had to offer, but that reminder was only as sharp as a paper cut now. Sharp, stinging, yes—but not deep. Now all Mabel felt was the cold, sober responsibility of what that position meant to the people depending on her.

Gas-powered lanterns hung against the green wallpaper every ten feet or so, but the dim hallways were as welcoming as a dusty tomb. Mabel led Will with the unfolded map stretched out in front of her, not wanting to admit she already felt lost. She had always had the best sense of direction of her family members, but an inherent sense of north and south was useless when the walls and corridors kept shifting right in front of her. She hoped Will, with his time spent boxing in the bowels of the hotel, would prove to be a better navigator of the strange, liminal spaces than she was.

She glanced back to where Will followed close behind her, still nursing the slice Frank had given him.

"Does it sting?" Mabel said. "I hope he didn't cut too deep."

"No, he didn't," Will said. "I've been cut by demons before, and this one wasn't laced with poison. If we stop on the fighting levels for some healing balm, that should patch me right up. I can hang on until then."

Mabel gave him a look.

"This cut is not as bad as it looks. I'll survive."

"So long as it doesn't get infected," Mabel said, eyes alighting over the parchment to observe another shifting hall they were supposed to have taken. She sighed. "It moved again."

"We should have turned back there." Will nodded at a corridor that looked identical to all the other corridors in this place. It did slope a bit in a general downward direction.

Mabel frowned at him. "I don't know how you read this thing."

Will gently grabbed the edge and tilted it until Mabel let out a small "ah."

"It's several images laid on top of each other," he said. "You only have to tilt it in the right light to see what you're looking for. Hold it up to the lamp and tilt the map until the light falls across it. You'll see all the illusions, every time."

Mabel did as he instructed and indeed the map gave a rainbow shimmer and gave up its multiple secrets when tilted. They did indeed miss their turn. "Thank you for showing me."

"You were more than capable of figuring it out," Will said. "I just helped with a shortcut that I found by happy accident."

They turned down the gentle slope of the correct hallway and followed the trail of lights.

"The demons patched you up after your fights?" Mabel said, making conversation because the silence was getting to be too much in this claustrophobic place.

Will snorted. "No. Demons don't care. The people fighting down there look out for each other. Blokes in the fighting ring figured out how to magic ourselves a healing balm out of beeswax, menthol, roses, and other basic kitchen ingredients. We had a good trade with the kitchen staff going."

Mabel raised an eyebrow at him. "Thrifty."

They took a sharp corner, where the floor's angle became so sharp, Mabel nearly tripped down the carpeted ramp. Will had to let go of his wound to stop her from falling.

"Easy, there," Will said. "The walls aren't the only things that move. The floors have a mind of their own too."

Will held Mabel's hand tight to keep her from tumbling down the ramp. She placed a hand on his chest to move gently away and stopped when she saw his blue eyes. His hands were bruised and cracked from so many hours standing out in the cold, from boxing to save his sister's soul.

Before she thought better of it, Mabel found herself placing a hand over the rag on his arm. When he grabbed her, it had started bleeding again. Mabel clutched his arm a little tighter to stop the fresh round of blood from seeping up between her fingers.

"It looks painful," she said.

"It's not so bad."

His chest rose and fell more rapidly as Mabel re-tied the rag. She hated that Will was in so much pain and hoped he would survive tonight. For all her rage at Will and at herself, she was glad she did not have to face finding the way out of the Grand alone. She didn't want to lose him.

"I should never have freed those souls." Mabel finished the knot and pressed her hand down to stop the bleeding. "I should have stayed Frank's star. None of this would have happened."

Will put his hand over hers. "Was that what you really wanted? To be his star? Is that what you sold your soul for?"

Mabel couldn't look away from his blue eyes. "No. I came to New York... to show people magic. No one wanted magic acts anymore, and I wasn't a Ziegfeld girl. I was starving and then I was stealing. This was supposed to be my last job so I could buy my way into the Follies. I didn't really want to be a Follie. I wanted to be a magician."

She wanted to mock herself at how ridiculous it all sounded, but Will wasn't laughing. He was smiling a goofy, little boy grin at her that Mabel lapped up like a kitten with milk.

"For what it's worth, I think you would make a great star magician."

A distant peal of thunder hurdled toward them from the other side of the wallpaper. The stampede came and went abruptly, ripping through the moment like scissors through a sheet of paper. Mabel's breath caught in her throat as she pushed herself away. The thunder receded as rapidly as it came.

"Sorry," Mabel said, face and chest flushed. "What was that sound?"

"Horse track," Will stuttered. "We're close. If you put your ear against the wall, you'll hear hoof beats and neighing on the other side."

Mabel pressed her ear against the wall and heard exactly what Will had described, but there was also the sound of far-off cheering. Placing your bets on anything you want seemed impossible, but that was the Grand for you.

"Where to next?" Mabel said, leaving the wall. "Do we go through, over, or around?"

Will frowned. "Let me see the map."

Mabel held it up to the light, tilting it until the doorways revealed. "Looks like we are about to meet a box of some sort. There's an entrance into the horse race beyond."

Will's face scrunched up as if he had just bitten into a very old lemon. "That's what I thought."

"What is it?"

"Follow me close. Don't make any bets. If you don't mind, I'll do the talking, or we will be here all night. He loves to suck people in."

Mabel followed Will as he strode down the hall toward the box on the map with an irritation she did not understand until they rounded the corner. The box betting room came into view, fully lit from within, and filled with stacks and stacks of file cabinets in a library behind a single man. He was thin with long fingers and very bored eyes behind oval glasses. The tall man was an accountant type with floppy brown hair and a green visor. He shifted a cigarette from one side of his mouth to the other as he quickly jotted down numbers on a score sheet. There was a gate next to his box with a padlock.

Will swore under his breath.

"Marty," Will said, striding over to lean his elbow on the edge of the wooden box frame as if they were the dearest of friends. "It's been too long."

Marty looked up at Will, bored already. "Hello, William. You're getting blood on my booth again."

Will stepped back. "Sorry about that."

"What will it be today?" Marty said, turning back to his numbers as if they were far more interesting than people. He didn't even acknowledge Mabel's presence. "Odds are good on Moonshine, and better than even odds on By Golly. Cleopatra has been having a bit of a winning streak though. My money's on Martie Flynn, who is a bit of a dark horse, but if you feed him some liqueur, he's quicker before the race, if you know what I mean."

"I'm not betting today, Marty. I just want to get by and visit my pal, Red. I need a patch up." Will showed Marty his bloody arm.

Marty sniffed at the gaping wound and shifted the cigarette in his mouth from one side to the other. "No need. I have balm here. Will clear that wound right up."

Marty pulled out a little silver tin the size and shape of a hair pomade tin and tossed it to Will. "I don't have a lot of that, so just give it back when you're done. Can I interest you two in anything? What is your pleasure?"

As Will smoothed the clear balm over where Frank had stabbed him, he kept his face hard. "We're not betting today, but balm or no balm, we still need to get down below."

Marty sighed. "Heh. Bleeding or not, fat chance Frank will allow that little day trip. I'm not letting you through."

"Frank is lying in a pool of his own juices upstairs," Mabel said. "Let us through."

Marty's sleepy boredom vanished. "Did you all have something to do with the soul breakout earlier?"

Mabel's breath hitched a little too loudly. Will shot Mabel an angry, hammer-on-nail look, which told her to zip it. Will turned back to Marty. "If you could take a look at this spell, I can explain..."

Marty glanced from Will's pleading face to Mabel's smug one and frowned, then he squinted at the spell and blanched. He nearly dropped the cigarette out of his mouth. "My answer is no. I don't want any part of it. You did not talk to me. You did not see me. I did not help you with this spell."

Marty reached up to grab the metal shutter to close off the box office, but Will grabbed the shutter before it closed. "Just tell me what the spell is for, Marty," Will said. "You don't have to do anything. Just help me read it."

"No," Marty said. "You don't understand. If you do that spell, this whole place will fall apart."

"Explain." Will reached over the ledge and grabbed Marty by the wrist and twisted until Marty's arm was behind his back in a wrestling hold. Marty tried to thrash away from Will, but it was like a worm trying to free itself from the talons of a hawk. "You've seen what my hands can do, and I just got all my strength back. I'd rather not do that to all your tender parts, especially things you'll miss. Like your fingers."

"Okay, okay!" Marty said. "You better have left Frank for dead, or we'll all be much worse off than this when he gets down here and finds what you've got."

Will let him go with a push that sent the bookie cartwheeling back into the desk behind him. A stack of betting ballots slid off and hit the floor, scattering everywhere.

"Fine. I'll tell you what I know." Marty straightened his shirt and smoothed his hair back with a hand. He nursed his arm and glared at Will and Mabel. "You two did have something to do with the soul breakout earlier."

"Yes," she said. "We were trying to set everyone free. I released the souls from Frank's box. It all went wrong."

She expected Marty to look angry or irritated even, but he looked stricken by a sobering truth, as if Mabel had just delivered the terrible news that Marty's mother was dying and there was nothing anyone could do.

"You did?" Marty wiped his mouth. "Then why didn't I get my soul back?"

Mabel paused, seeing the sad bookie behind his lonely counter in a new light. Marty seemed so very small now. She and Will exchanged a look, both at a loss at how to comfort him.

"Are you a full demon?" Mabel said.

"What does that mean? Full demon? Ain't everybody demons in this joint?" Marty snort-laughed at his own joke.

Will rolled his eyes. "Do you have a second mouth? Is any part of you still human?"

"I'm not sure." Marty lifted his shirt to reveal the second mouth in his stomach. It was so wide it almost wrapped around his entire lower half. The tongue licked his second pair of lips. Mabel winced. She had never seen a mouth as wide as his.

When Marty saw the look on her face, he hurried to put his shirt back down. "I still feel like myself apart from the intense hunger, but I take care of that with the spare steaks they keep for the dog fights."

Mabel's nose wrinkled, both at the treatment of the dogs and at Marty's solution for feeding his second mouth. "How long have you been down here?"

Marty shrugged. "No idea. Henry West hired me the second the ink dried on the Prohibition law. I've been down here ever since. Why? What month is it?"

Mabel softened. "That was January 1920. It's April 1925," she said as gently as possible.

Marty wiped a hand over his mouth, eyes watering as he let out a sad little laugh. "Five years. I thought it was five months. I guess I became a 'full demon' a long time ago, huh?"

Mabel's heart turned to putty inside her chest. She had resolved to save everyone in the Grand, even Marty. She could stand to be a little kinder to him. "I'm not sure when one becomes a full demon, or how, once their soul is gone. What I know is we want to help everyone."

That broke Marty out of his internal debate. "What? What do you mean help everyone?"

"We're going down there to free the rest of the souls, including yours. We're closing the portal and setting everyone free."

"Down to the Below? Closing the portal?" He laughed, and Mabel didn't like his mocking tone. "Do you know what this spell does?"

"Let me see it."

She opened her mouth to argue maybe they should not let Marty see the spell after all, but Will handed it over before she could protest. Marty snatched it out of Will's hands and spread it across the counter.

"Did you know this was about the original deal?" Marty didn't wait for them to answer. He turned away from them and the spell, chewing on the butt of his cigarette as if it were a pen cap he needed to gnaw on in order to think. "Going back on the original deal? I guess you technically could undo it all, but the cost? Too steep. No one would pay that. No one in their right mind."

Marty suddenly wheeled back at them. "Which one of you is it going to be, huh? Which one of you? Because if you don't choose, it's not possible."

Will's hackles raised like an animal whose territory had just been threatened. "It *is* possible. That's a reversal spell, isn't it? We cast it and the Grand *will* return back to what it was. All of the real demons will be gone, like it never happened. Every person who ever sold their soul will get theirs back again. We're pulling the Grand up by the infected root."

Marty stopped pacing and leaned over his white counter. "Not exactly. Did you read the fine print?"

Will crossed his arms with a frown. Mabel rolled her eyes. "No, he did not read the fine print. We can't read Demonaic. He stole the spell out of some book. Is it the right one? Will it undo everyone's deals and give them their souls back?"

Marty sighed. "Yes, theoretically, if you break off the original contract with the Grand Hotel and the first demon, that will set off a chain that would rip apart every contract ever written here. That's only if you manage to make it all the way down and survive long enough to use this spell on the portal; it will break the original contract on the Grand Hotel. Before you do this, do you know what happened here? Why the Grand is the way it is? What you would be undoing?"

Will and Mabel drew a little closer.

Marty scoffed at the pair of them as if it were the most obvious thing in the world. "Of course, you two chowder heads don't know. The Grand used to be normal before Prohibition, but it was a dying hotel. Times were tough after the war. The Grand was a well that had run dry. They were so empty they offered up their rooms to war victims as a temporary hospital."

"Then one day, Rockefeller comes around, flashing all of this cash. Rockefeller's company was sweeping up as many properties as they could in the city. I worked for Henry West, keeping his ledgers, so I knew how in the red he was. He was going to have to give up the hotel and his legacy which he wanted to pass down to his son, Frank. So, he comes to me and he says, 'Marty, I'm about to sell the last thing I have left to give. When it all goes down, will you stay on here with me?' And I did much to my regret."

Marty's face fell into a dark memory. "Henry sold his soul to make the Grand what it is. They found a demon, but the price was steeper than they thought. When the papers said they were murdered by the mob, I thought something wasn't right here. They were demons. How could they be murdered?"

It was something Mabel had not thought about at all, but Marty was right. How could someone murder a demon? Send it back down to hell, injure them, sure, but murder? Something funny *had* happened to Frank's parents, but there was no way of uncovering that truth any time soon. Right now, they had bigger problems ahead.

"I remember that period," Marty said, frowning. "It was chaos when Henry and Lillian were banished and left the Grand to him."

"I thought they died," Mabel said.

"No," Marty said. "When I thought something was fishy about their disappearance, I looked into it. Rumor around the betting tables is it wasn't the mob that offed them. The rumor is someone wanted the Grand Hotel. They wanted it bad enough they cast a ritual forcing Frank's parents to be trapped in hell. Frank was a kid caught up in his parents' bad deal. He was human once too."

"What?" Will said. "Frank was, *is*, human? That's not possible. The things he's done... he's not human."

The little white stub of a cigarette switched from one side of Marty's mouth to the other, like a desperate player in a speed dating circle. "Everyone in the Grand was human before they were demon, no matter how far they've fallen. That's the whole point of this place. Tempt artists to come perform, collect souls with their talent, increase their offerings of suffering through the arts to the city down below."

"City down below?" Mabel said.

"This hell you speak of?" Marty scoffed. "It's a literal city, and it thrives on artistic suffering. It thrives on fame—all its tears, all its cost, all its longing. What better source of misery than the artist who can't feed themselves?"

"If I were you," Marty said. "I would leave well enough alone and just get yourselves out. Or you can go barreling down there, reverse the deal Henry made, and 'free everyone.' Choosing that path will take something I don't think either one of you wants to give away. You won't even get what you really want in return—freedom for everyone."

Will folded up the spell and pocketed both the paper and the healing balm. "Don't listen to him, Mabel. He's so far gone he doesn't remember what it is to be human anymore. His loyalty is to Frank and this place. Trust me. I've seen him turn in many a deserter who tried to flee. We're wasting our time."

"Listen, if you do this, I support you," Marty insisted. "Don't get me wrong. I want to be human again as much as the next guy. I didn't like turning those people in, but Frank was going to eat my skin if I didn't. Look, your spell will work on the portal, yes. But all I'm saying is there's a cost you're overlooking. You have to balance the books."

Mabel's stomach gave a little flip. "What do you mean?"

"It's basic alchemy," Marty said. "And basic accounting. Every transaction must be counted, both coming and going. Get something, give something. As above, so below. You want to break the original contract and pull all of those souls out? What is going back in to replace the deal?"

When the pair stared at him, pale as ghosts, Marty tapped a finger on the spell Will had found. "It says so right here: *Reverse to Return in One Offering.* A reversal costs one soul paid up front to the city Below. To get what you want, someone has to give up their soul. Of course, it's written in Demonaic. It now occurs to me why you didn't get the fine print. You two got your souls back, didn't you?"

Will nodded. "That's why we're here. I need to find my sister. She didn't get hers either. We want to help those of you that didn't get yours. If one of us has to pay the price we have to pay, so be it."

"You still want to give your life away?" Marty said. "After you just got your soul back?"

Mabel brought a hand to the Canary diamond around her neck, the weight of which she had gotten so used to she had forgotten it was there. She had exchanged her soul for her stardom and had not thought about how the deal physically worked beyond that transaction. Mabel thought of the map to the Grand Hotel, the same above as it was below, both giving and receiving. The Grand had given her the ultimate desirability but had taken her humanity in exchange. When she got her soul back, Mabel had returned to the same human she was before and lost her demonic powers in the process, but what about everyone else?

When she first came to the Grand, all Mabel had cared about was getting out alive with her jewels, her talent, and her newfound fame. Now all that mattered was getting everyone out.

"If we paid the price, would reversing it return every human to simply what they were before?" Mabel asked.

Marty's nod was as grave as a locked tomb. "Yes, but you will be running a thankless grift. Many of them won't want to return to being nameless, jobless artists. I wanted to be a painter, had big dreams of painting murals, but everyone in the art world rejected me. I was always good with numbers. The West family gave me a job, a good one, and a home where I could work on my murals. I painted every mural in the Grand. I can see people hating you for turning them human again. Not to mention, this is a fool's errand. Do you know what stands between you and the portal? You'll be dead before you make it down there."

"I understand," Mabel said.

Mabel stared at the damask flooring, feeling like a little boat pushed off a dock with no paddle. Unmoored. Directionless. There was no easy answer. Did all of the artists remaining in the Grand actually want to be saved? Mabel searched Will's face, but he remained as stubborn in his convictions as ever. She knew what Will felt, and how far he would go for what he believed in. They might be descending to their deaths.

Silence hung like lead in the air between them. The cost of this place had come to collect, and Mabel wasn't sure she could pay the tab with her life. She had thought reversing the spell would suck Frank, Evelyn, and all their little cronies back down to hell. If everyone in this place was human, they were fighting shadows all this time.

Even Frank, the worst of the lot, was going to be saved. Even Frank was once human.

"There might be another way," Marty said.

"What do you mean?" Mabel said.

"Spells can be used in more than one way," Marty said, lapping up Mabel's attention like a cat with a bowl of cream. He turned the spell upside down. "Not a reversal, but an invocation. You could call on the original demon, the one who made the deal with Henry, once you get to the portal and then..."

He turned and opened one of his file cabinets, removing an envelope with something very thin, very long, and strangely dense concealed inside. Marty nodded for her to open it.

She puckered open the envelope to find a long hairpin made of heavy silver. It was in the shape of a stake with diamonds on its tip in flower formations. There was a woman's face among the silvery flowers.

"Lots of things end up here. People place all kinds of down payments to make a bet. I've been holding onto this one for a long time. It's Persephone's hairpin. Queen of the Underworld, able to walk among the mortals. It's said to turn any full demon back into a human with the prick of its tip. You summon him down there, prick him with this, and kill him."

"Will that free everyone?" Mabel asked.

Marty licked his lips. "The way I see it, you have two options. One is to undo Henry West's deal, which would turn the hotel and everyone in it back to the original state they were all in before the demons came, but costs the unpaid balance of one soul. One of you two chuckleheads would have to die. Or you can summon the original demon, turn him mortal, and kill him. The second is a riskier option, but more likely both of you will survive than by risking your lives closing the portal. However, no one has ever tried this before and survived to say. You would have to be the first."

"That sounds like a much better idea," Mabel said. "How do we summon him?"

Marty looked down the bridge of his glasses at her. "Reading it backward, of course."

He handed her a pocket-sized book on Demonaic. It was leather-bound with lots of ribbons to mark particular entries. The pages were as soft as rabbit ears in Mabel's hands from frequent use. Marty showed her how to read the alphabet and had her practice the annunciation while Will watched them both. When Marty got her laughing, Will cleared his throat.

"Thanks for the information, Marty," Will said, every syllable an icicle. "We'll keep that option in mind. We need to get going before Frank finds us."

Marty, who had a moment ago looked so sure he was helping, so sure he was included, retreated like a spare tire out of their circle. "Yeah, sure. I'll just get back to the books, then. Got that after dinner rush coming up. Here's the door for you."

He pushed the button beneath the counter. The wall directly beside Will and Mabel, which had been a dead end before, shifted backward and slid to the right. There was a long tunnel on the other side, and the cheering was much louder now without the walls to pad the uproar.

Will stormed off down the next passage, not waiting to see if Mabel followed. She grabbed the pin and shoved it in her hair. Mabel tried to keep up in her showgirl heels, but it was more difficult when Will refused to slow down.

"What is wrong with you?" Mabel said. "Why are you being so cruel?"

Will did not stop walking as he turned the corner and looked back at her, but he did slow enough to check if she was following.

"I know Marty," Will said when they were well out of earshot. "He's Frank's puppet. He's playing us for fools trying to save his boss. Every time someone in my boxing ring couldn't hack it, he would report it to Frank. He's a weasel, and he's being a weasel now."

"And you're being too stubborn to see the choice you're making," Mabel said, returning his vigor right in his face as if they were in a boxing match with words. "If we take this spell down there, we can kill the one, real, honest-to-God demon in this place. Don't you get it? This gets you exactly what you want without sacrificing anyone. You want what you want, to save everyone, damn it all, even yourself, don't you? Why aren't you listening to anyone but you?"

Fire flashed in Will's eyes. "I know people had it rough before this place, believe me. You, Frank's *star*, had a warm bed and a place to stay before the Grand, and an even warmer bed when you got here. My sister and I were on the streets. I know what we're going back to, but on the streets I have a chance for a future. If we banish the only demon here, we don't know, besides Marty's word, that it might turn everyone human. It's less risk to us only. There's no certain outcome that it will free every one of the Grand's deals with hell. No. There's only one way, and that's reversing everything."

Mabel's stomach dropped around the word "star," and she continued to feel sicker and sicker with every word Will spat at her. So, this was what Will actually thought of her. Now she knew. She chewed her lip to keep from crying as she looked down at her shoes.

"You know this spell costs one soul to enact," Mabel said. "You're going to damn yourself?"

"If it's what saves Saoirse, I will do what needs to be done."

She grabbed him by the wrist. "Will..."

"Maybe it's like you said before," Will said, his face becoming stone, without feeling, shutting the door in Mabel's face. "You go your way, and I go mine. I'm undoing the contract. I'm closing the portal. You're welcome to do what you like. Be free of this place."

Will pulled himself gently from her grip and it was like watching him fall in slow motion as he descended the sloping passageway. Mabel trailed him down the wider hallway past the entrance to the horse track like a lost stray, unsure if she should leave and return to the wilds of New York City or join Will in the bowels of hell.

She could leave. She had thought about it many times. Could she do it and not regret her actions, killing all of those people and then abandoning Will for the rest of her life? It would certainly be the safer option to save her own skin, and it was what she had always done. Mabel had always looked out for number one. That's the way it was in show business.

And Frank. His parents had trapped him in this deal too. His motives, which had always been mercurial, now were clearing like fog retreating out to sea. He wanted to ascend, but why? He didn't want the deal his parents had given him, the curse of running this place, of his legacy. He wanted out too, so why not use the pin Marty gave her and turn Frank and all the rest human too?

It was strange to care about Frank, or even picture him as an innocent human. As if humans were all that innocent to begin with.

As they wound around the corner, the horse racetrack was so much bigger than she pictured could fit underneath a hotel. Mabel didn't understand how the Grand built all of these things, and Will didn't slow long enough for her to care. He stormed past the track and the seats filled to standing room with clamoring patrons like an angry storm cloud passing by the sun.

Mabel was struck by how these people's glossy-eyed faces were filled with the same desperate need her audience had when they looked at her after a performance. She didn't like seeing what performances in the Grand looked like from the opposite side, and she especially didn't like being made to feel like a racehorse in one of the Grand's many arenas. She was more than a show pony. She was a whole human being.

Will forked right down another passage that seemingly appeared out of nowhere in the middle of the damask wallpaper as Mabel struggled to keep up and follow him. She barely made it inside before the wall shifted and shut behind them.

"You're going to hurt me," Mabel said. "Slow down. I'm following you whether you like it or not, so we might as well be a team."

Will stopped in the narrow, dimly lit hall that was no wider than their shoulders. "Why are you coming? You don't believe in this. You still want to save yourself. You got your soul back. So, leave."

"No," Mabel said. "I'm not leaving. I will feel guilty about slaughtering everyone to save my own skin for the rest of my life if I do. I got my soul back, but Marty was right. We should summon the real demon instead and kill him."

Will scoffed, but he said nothing. He was listening for a change, and it was a start.

"We could use this pin, turn the original demon human, get rid of him. Don't sacrifice yourself when there's another way. Can't we at least try?"

"Fine." He shook his head at her wet eyes. "But if that doesn't work, we do things my way. We undo the original deal. You need to accept that some eggs are going to break if we're going to pull out the demon infestation by its root."

When tears filled Mabel's eyes, Will snorted.

"Go. You have your soul. Then you won't have to worry about any more deaths hanging over your head. I'm happy to make the hard choice on my own."

Will's tone was angry, but his face was so forlorn, as if he knew the fate that awaited him was his own. It was obvious to Mabel that the knowledge that someone had to exchange their soul to undo the original deal was hanging over them both like a distant storm they both did not want to sail into. If he continued down this path, the string of Will's life was about to be cut, and both of them knew it.

Her fists clenched. "I'm not leaving you."

Will flustered, then his defense softened. "Fine. I won't stop you."

She wasn't going to let Will die, but Mabel did not say that out loud. He would only get defensive, close himself off, and not listen. She was going to have to find a way to summon the original demon and kill him without facing the alternative—closing the portal and undoing the original deal, ending with Will sacrificing himself for everyone else in exchange.

Mabel knew what she had to do, and she was full of more terror than she had ever felt in all her life. She was going to have to save Will from himself.

CHAPTER SIXTEEN

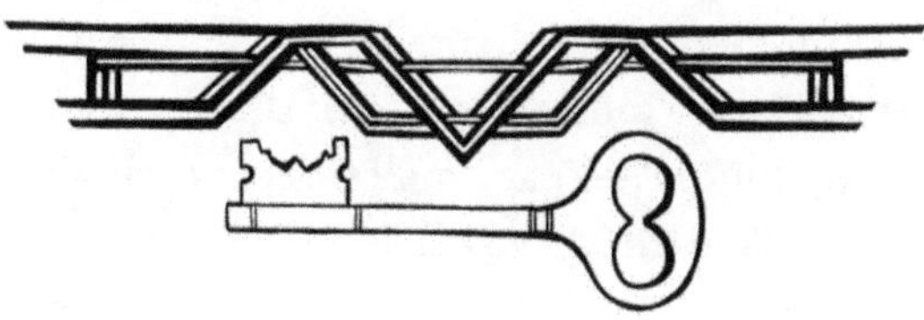

They traveled on, descending to another level. Mabel and Will passed a dog fighting ring where she lingered briefly. It was a smaller room than the horse track, but still large enough to house five or six fighting rings and stands for food and liquor. A knife twisted in her heart at every yelp that came from the other side of the jeering crowds.

"Can we help them? The dogs?" Mabel said.

"When we save the Grand, we will save the dogs too."

She followed Will, who seemed to know where he was going without the help of Mabel's map. She hadn't thought about the fact he would know this area well after being a fighter down here to start. His face remained in a permanent scowl as they hurried past without another word. He was clearly as upset about the poor animals as she was. He had been a prized dog in a fighting ring, while Mabel felt like a prized racehorse. They were both merely animals to the Grand, meant for show, meant for entertainment, meant ultimately for food, and nothing more.

"Keep walking," Will said, muttering so low Mabel could barely hear him. "Don't stop for anyone. They'll try to get you betting."

Mabel opened her map again to check where they were, and it was labeled: Boxing rings. *Great.* Will was going to have kittens. She hoped he would keep himself in check and it wouldn't slow them down too much on the off chance some of the boxers or betters recognized him.

The hall ahead of them swelled with the sound of yelling voices, arguments had over payments, and which money belonged to whom. Will took Mabel by the wrist and pulled her close behind him so that his form would mostly block her from view. It was the first instance of Will showing care for her since their fight, and Mabel wanted nothing more than for them to get back on the same page together as a team. Her gut told her neither one of them was going to get out of this grift alive, but their odds were infinitely better if they worked together.

"Don't say anything. They can smell someone who hasn't placed a bet before. If you talk at all, they will know. They will do anything to pull you in."

She did as he advised, but her eyes and ears were wide open.

"Place your bets," a familiar voice called above the ruckus of desperate men. "Next bought is Gulliver 'Gutter' Duval against Hank 'Heavy Hands' McGill. Odds are double on McGill."

Mabel squinted, unsure if she was seeing a mirage. The barker looked just like Marty with the same foppish hair and bookish spectacles. He even made the same facial expressions as the roughnecks and dock workers all flashed wads of green at him. Marty's cigarette hung out of his mouth as he took bets and wrote them up in chalk on a blackboard behind him, then placed the cash in enormous barrels behind his wide stand. She had never seen so many people betting in one place before, and the crowd of men all had the same vacant, glazed-over look in their eyes. Their eyes were almost white, like all the other demons in this place except for Frank and Evelyn.

Mabel shadowed Will past the crowd, who barely seemed to notice they were there. Nobody wanted to bother with two silent bellhops when there were fresh fights happening again in ten minutes. Their timing couldn't have been more perfect in the distraction regard, but Mabel walked away with a greater understanding of the horror of what Will's life must have been. He had lost his brother to the Black and Tan mobs, then his sister to the temptations of the Grand, then been placed as the doorman working without end just in view of the freedom he could no longer enjoy. Will had lived down here on this dank and dusty wood-chipped floor that smelled of too much man sweat, a mix of spoiled bacon and hair grease. Mabel held in her gag until they were well clear of it.

"How did Marty get down there so fast?" Mabel hissed at Will, still unsure whether the men should hear her or not.

"It's Marty. He does that. He takes the bets on every level. Marty always seems to be everywhere at once."

"I had no idea the history of this place," Mabel said. "Did you?"

"This place is full of sad stories," Will said. "Marty is merely one of them."

"And you're one of them. We both are now."

Will sighed long and deep. "Saoirse is worth it. She loved flowers, rabbits, and painting. She told me she had always wanted to be a professional painter when she grew up. I didn't know the circus life was the real dream she kept hidden away inside her heart."

His expression became cold and vacant again, but his thoughts were about as obvious as a hammer.

She touched the crook of his elbow. "We're going to find her, Will."

He didn't answer her, but he didn't push her away either. The relief brought on by Mabel's confidence was all over his face.

"We should keep moving. Frank may make good on his word and follow us down here. If he catches us... I don't want to know what would happen. I've never been past this level. You should lead with the map. I don't know the way forward from here."

"Will?" Mabel let him go. "What happens if we don't succeed?"

She trailed off down a tunnel of dark thoughts. Everything she wanted to say to him sat on the tip of her tongue but refused to come out of her mouth.

"Don't worry about that now," Will said. "We're going to get out of this alive."

Will followed Mabel into another sloping, lantern-lit passageway. Every hallway they traveled grew dimmer and dimmer as they descended. By the time they had passed through three more long hallways, Mabel had to squint in the low light to see her own feet. Every floor they traveled had a dank, wet fur and filth smell of kept animals that had received little care, a smell Mabel remembered all too well from the time they lost their entire chicken coop to a particularly hot summer.

"Do they have a zoo here?" Mabel said. "It smells like they do."

"Dogs, chickens, snakes, mongooses. You name a fight, the Grand's got it."

They turned a corner and the stinging animal waste smells retreated back and were replaced by something far more delicious. The sudden shift jarred Mabel's senses as they stood in a wider, well-lit hallway. The green wallpaper had vanished, replaced by twin walls of thick, red curtains, and there was a buttery popcorn scent in the air. Lights shown down from above, bright as spotlights, every three yards or so. The hall alone reminded her of entering a movie theater, but the smell of distant popcorn and cotton candy only added to what Mabel was sure was an illusion. She had only been to a theater once or twice to take in a film, but the place was clearly made to make Mabel feel as though she had bought tickets to a matinée and was now rushing to get in before the show started. The question was, what lay on the other side of the red curtain? Between the sounds of games and laughter, it sounded more like a carnival.

Mabel checked her map again. "Carnival level" was written in spidery handwriting.

"I didn't think it was possible," she said. "That one hotel could hold everything you desire. If Marty is right, and equivalent exchange is how one can broker deals, Henry West must have offered up a lot to get this kind of deal with the devil."

Will nodded in agreement, but there was something more going on with Will. His face was permanently pensive, and his posture was more hunched and apprehensive, as if worried over something. She was worried about plenty herself, but Mabel didn't think what was bothering Will was their probable impending doom. She guessed he was likely worried that, for all their efforts, they would not be able to save his eleven-year-old sister. He had a look in his eye that said he was ready to offer himself to close the portal.

It didn't matter what Will was going to do about the sacrifice. She wasn't going to let him go through with it. Marty said they had two choices, and Mabel was determined to summon the original demon and use the hairpin to turn him human and kill him.

"I don't know which tent she could be in," she offered, and Will's eyes widened as if she had read his thoughts. "But we should search both the tents and the carnival games. She could be a stage act or working one of the booths."

"Yes." His voice was much softer than before. "That's what I was thinking, too."

Voices echoed down the hall, jovial and carrying on, followed by a peal of female laughter.

"Have you seen them? Two staff members—one dark-haired man, one redhead girl?"

Mabel and Will quieted at the sound of Frank's voice.

"No, Frank baby. We would have told you if we had seen them," a voice with a thick Jersey accent said.

"If you're looking for a good time, I can give you company." The second woman added.

"Not now. If you see them, send me a flyer up the Navigator."

"Bye, Frank!" The girls chimed in unison like schoolgirls.

Heavy footsteps approached Will and Mabel. She yanked Will into the red curtains with her, grateful to find they were as surprisingly deep as she suspected. Will closed the curtain in front of them and they huddled together, pressed against each other in the dark as the footsteps stormed quickly past.

They waited in the quiet, unsure if they should move or not. Both of Mabel's hands were against Will's chest. His arms were around her, pressing her to him out of a need to make both of their forms smaller.

More laughter echoed down the hall.

"I think it's safe," Mabel whispered.

"Not yet. I can still hear the women. Let's wait until they leave."

"Okay," Mabel said. "Or is it you just want to stay close to me?"

Will hesitated so close to her face, debate written all over his face. He licked his lips as if he wanted to say more, and finally answered her in a hot whisper. "I appreciate you coming with me. I truly assumed all you cared about was yourself. I was wrong."

Mabel shushed him, but her face flushed with pleasant embarrassment. She was glad the darkness could hide it. The laughter moved farther away. The gaggle of demons were leaving, but Mabel and Will still lingered. When he stayed, Mabel found herself staying too, despite the urge to move on.

"You're welcome. I don't want anything to happen to you."

Will's eyes wouldn't leave her face. "You... don't want me to get hurt?"

"No."

His bright eyes and wild dark hair were the kind of danger she could afford to give herself, a risk of her heart and her head that thrilled her in a way that only the stage had been able to before. He had challenged her. He had, even at times, pushed her farther than she had wanted to go, but his fire for what he believed in matched her own.

"I knew," Will said, his breath hot and heavy against her face. "From the moment you entered the Grand. I knew I was waiting for a door to open, and you were the key."

Mabel whispered against his mouth. "I don't want you to die."

"I don't want to either."

His lips drew closer to hers, but he was still holding back, still forming a question with his mouth if it really was all right to kiss her now. Mabel leaned forward with her answer, and they fell out of the curtain in a tangle of red velvet and gold ropes and landed into blinding light and happy noise. Mabel had difficulty keeping her footing as they tumbled out together, and nearly face-planted on the ground had it not been for Will catching her.

The amount of light was disorienting, like stepping out onto a white sandy beach in the noonday sun. Every shape and color shimmered like a mirage until Mabel's eyes adjusted to the bright carnival booth sign advertising "Knock 'Em Down." She blinked until the people throwing balls at smiling clown figures made of cloth became clear. A party of three women and two men in their best evening attire laughed uproariously as they paid another twenty-five cents for a lucky throw. From the vacant delight on the well-dressed patrons' faces and the white glaze forming in their eyes, these people might have been down here for days without knowing. They were already becoming demons.

Mabel spun around on her heel. There were thick crowds of people playing at dozens of booths in every direction. Tents formed a sea of white curtains beyond where the lights of a carousel spun by a Ferris wheel, and three circus tents beyond that. Mabel had seen so much in the Grand Hotel. She had seen things beyond imagination, large and small. She should not have been surprised that one of the floors was dedicated to housing the largest carnival possible, but all she could feel standing in the largest state fair was utter shock. It was the first time a small part of her whispered its delight since her first night.

She had always loved the fair. She loved the rush of people, the smell of salted popcorn and cotton candy, the tents filled with every kind of marvel you could think of. Mabel had only been to the Georgia State Fair once—the one time Avery took her to an audition—but the Grand's carnival was easily ten times bigger.

She pulled out the map, but there were no pathways listed on the carnival level. It was all one big white space, but Mabel did see the tunnels on the other side of its borders. There was one in the southern direction where a door was supposedly hidden.

"I think if we go past the big top, we'll find the way out." Mabel had to shout to be heard over the crowd.

Will nodded. "The map seems useless here. We'll have to fight the crowds to get over there."

Mabel stuffed the map in her Grand bellhop's uniform and took Will by the hand. "The crowd is thick. Let's stick together."

He was only too happy to oblige.

The Grand's carnival was something out of a dream. Lights flashed across the ceiling, spotlights waving back and forth, illuminating great neon signs listing the next shows. Every step Mabel took felt like she was stepping right up onto a stage. The floor beneath her was all red carpet, not wood chips, or dirty lawn. Will and Mabel forked away from the carnival games and found themselves under an aisle marked with a great red sign advertising:

"Wonders of the World and Rare Curiosities."

Will and Mabel entered with a fresh crowd of people, all cramming to get into a tent that offered its viewer a look at conjoined twins and men with two heads, bearded ladies, and other curios. They passed jars filled with eyeballs and human hands, half-chicken half-human fetuses in jars, and pickled heads of wolves. There were peddlers selling bones and raw gemstones their tenders swore contained magical properties.

Mabel put her hand to the Canary diamond at the sight of dozens of citrine uncut gems lying across the tables in great hunks. All of this was in the Grand Hotel, and yet the Canary looked like it came from one of these booths. Where exactly did the Canary come from? Mabel didn't have an answer, but Evelyn knew, and she had apparently gone a long way to get it.

Mabel and Will turned away from the aisles of curiosities toward food stalls filled with cake, cotton candy, alcoholic beverages, hot dogs, and candy apples. Mabel licked her lips. Will drew out several quarters from his pockets to buy them both a bag of hot peanuts.

"Where did you get that?"

He raised an eyebrow. "You're not the only thief."

Will returned with two steaming paper bags and handed one to Mabel. It was slick and sticky, but she didn't care. They could spare a moment to happily devour their bags and refuel for the journey ahead.

"Thank you," Mabel said. "I was going to have kittens if I didn't eat something soon. This food smells too good to resist. Won't it affect us more now that we're human again?"

"I hope not," Will downed several more peanuts. "Right now, I'm too tired and hungry and thirsty to care. Want a drink?"

She nodded with a mouth full of peanuts. He brought her back two cups filled with something fizzy and pink. Mabel didn't care what it was after those salty peanuts. She downed her whole cup in two gulps, and it tasted like strawberries and buzzed in the back of her throat like hard liquor.

"I've been to a sideshow and seen the rides over on Coney Island," Will said. "But never a freak show, never the circus. We never had the cash to afford a ticket," Will said, his voice as wistful as an old man recalling a golden past. "I do remember Saoirse's favorite thing was to go stare at the rides. She might be down here. Frank typically gives you a job related to the thing you long to be, but I don't know what Saoirse's job would be."

Nearby, a carnival barker yelled to step right up and take a gander at a real-life mermaid. Another yelled for all to come and see the world's strongest man. A distant woman called for the crowd to come witness the greatest magic act since Harry Houdini.

Mabel paused. Frank had said her dreams of the stage were dead, that both vaudeville and Ziegfeld were a thing of the past. As Mabel gazed at all of the other acts in this place, the thread tying them all together became so obvious she didn't know how she could not have recognized it before. The Carnival level was full of shows that had fallen out of popular style or were in desperate need of funding after the Great War. It was a floor full of forgotten sideshows, of entertainment acts that had been popular a decade ago or more but had fallen to ruin in favor of vaudeville, then in favor of great theater productions, then motion pictures.

Entertainment was a field forever turning its great wheel, leaving its artists behind unless they were lucky enough or skilled enough to change with the times. These performers had all sold their souls to keep performing just like her. As she passed the various acts, Mabel lamented this tremendous loss, the performances lost to time, and the ever-fickle audience needs.

"This carnival," Mabel said. "These acts and performances, they all found refuge here."

"What?" Will said, but when he looked around, it was clear from the confusion in his eyes that he could not understand. "Refuge? What do you mean?"

"Look around, Will. I was lured here because I wanted to be a magician who couldn't hack it as a Ziegfeld girl. What I wanted to do, perform live for a theater audience, is a dying art. That's what this place is. They are no longer the focus of everyone's attention. They have all found a home here in the Grand Hotel, a shelter from the changing times, safety from being forgotten. If we do this, they will all be homeless, and these art forms will shrivel up and die."

As she searched for the dawning realization in Will's eyes, Mabel anticipated that he would remind her of their mission, that leaving the Grand open would only mean more carnage.

"I wanted to play the fiddle," Will said.

Her brows drew together in a crease. "What?"

He winced, as if explaining more caused him great pain. "I used to play for everyone, back in Ireland, back before the raids. I would play in the pubs. I was quite good. Got the crowd really going. I was funny, too. Before my brother died, I dreamed of coming to America and making it big. My dream was to play the fiddle, but what did it matter when my parents died. I sold my fiddle to buy us food."

He turned back to his bag, picking at the last of his peanuts, struggling with what to say next. Mabel quietly waited, eating the remnants of her bag while Will watched the crowd pass them by.

"Maybe," Will said. "When we get out of here, I'll play again."

Mabel considered for a moment. "When we get out of here, I want to try a new magic act. Maybe add song and dance. Who knows? Maybe it could work."

Will smiled at her in a way that brought color to her cheeks. "This land was supposed to be a city of dreams. You reminded me, Mabel. I forgot what it was like to dream."

"Have you seen these two?" Frank's voice carried over the cacophony. "One dark-haired boy, Will. One red-haired girl, Mabel. Disguised as two bellhops. Does anyone recognize them?"

He was several yards away, but close enough to see that he was carrying pictures of their faces. No, not black and white pictures—he was holding two full color portraits. The sight of Frank carrying a painted picture of her face brought a chill that penetrated Mabel down to her bones. He had their likeness done up who knew when by who knew which painter, but he was storming through the crowd with them, announcing his desperation to find them.

At the sight of Frank, Will grabbed Mabel's hand to pull her away from the food stalls into the colorful noise of the crowd. The moment they ran, Mabel heard Frank's voice boom after them.

"There," Frank said. "Bring them to me."

Mabel checked back over her shoulder. Frank was indeed pointing at them as she and Will pushed through the throng of people. Frank's voice carried over the happy patrons, so loud that all of the music, the noise, and the revelry came skidding to a halt.

The entire Carnival level went quiet. The Ferris wheel shuddered to a stop. Mabel and Will stopped running. Everyone had stopped what they were doing. They dropped their drinks. Their food fell out of their hands to the ground. Every well-dressed patron had their eyes on Will and Mabel, and they surrounded them like a pack of snarling, white-eyed wolves.

"Bring them to me!" Frank thundered and the crowd rushed Will and Mabel all at once.

Their hands were on her arms, her bellhop's jacket, her legs. Her bellhop cap fell off her head and tumbled somewhere into the sea of glittering bodies all struggling to grab her at once. Will punched a man's face, freeing Mabel enough she could twist out of a flapper's grip. She bolted toward the magician's aisle and turned back to call Will's name, but his form was quickly disappearing into the bodies.

"I'll meet you at the exit," Will yelled. "Run."

She didn't question him or linger to see if he was okay. Mabel had to trust Will to take care of himself, and if only one of them could make it downstairs, Mabel knew it had to be her. As she ran into a darkened aisle filled with mirrors and black smoke, she found her heart was pounding out of fear more for Will than for herself. She had to break free of this level and somehow make it back down into the lower levels. That was the best way she could help Will now. She needed to find the portal and free them all of this place.

But she didn't want to do it without Will.

Mabel ran past ventriloquist dummies lined up in rows. She turned down a short alley of cages filled with white doves and rabbits. Mabel found herself beside an act where a magician lay a beautiful woman in a box while sawing her in half with a massive saw. She passed magicians performing card tricks, metal ring illusions, giant boxes with elephants appearing and disappearing, the assistant levitation illusion, and all the while her thoughts raced with how many talents the Grand had lured in here. How many actors, actresses, vaudevillians, musicians, prized fighters, curiosities, and wondrous people the Grand had sucked in and turned their dreams into something darker. For what? What was it all for? Why were these people and their acts all here in this hotel?

Whatever Henry West had offered in exchange to change the Grand Hotel, the fact that the entire entertainment industry had somehow wound up within these walls had something to do with that original deal. If Mabel found a way to break the original spell when she reached the portal, she could figure out what it was all for.

Mabel continued running past tanks filled with water and people chained up inside them. The crowds that had gathered to see them all turned toward Mabel, and their eyes glazed over white. She ran faster, stumbling through a maze of mirrors, happy to be out of view. She panted inside the reflected world, unsure of how much longer she could keep this pace up. Mabel spun around, suddenly lost in her own image reflected back at her. She remembered an old trick of how to escape one of these rooms from her brother Avery, who told her to look at the floor instead of at herself in the reflection to find the way out. Mabel followed the red carpet, darted right, and left, avoiding the confusion of the reflection's lies until she found herself out of the mirrors and inside a pitch-black tent.

The lights flickered on right in her face, showing a spiraling, kaleidoscopic illusion floral-shaped graphic behind her on a screen. She had fallen inside a magic lantern show, a stage comedy act that required the use of a conductor operating the lantern in tandem with several actors. Mabel had heard of such shows from the 1890s when she had studied theater books in the public library after arriving in New York, but she had only seen old photos of them.

Mabel raced away from the crowd sitting in folding chairs and their white eyes. She careened out of the tent, back into the crowd, and did not slow. There were throngs of people lined up for an electric light show claiming to harness Tesla's power. Great sparks blew from enormous coils down on a cheering crowd as Mabel slipped away toward the circus tents.

She had kept her eye on the Ferris wheel as her landmark and it had not steered her wrong. She found herself at the entrance to the circus. Glamorous patrons pushed through the red and white curtains to enter the big top, but many of them were starting to stare. She had to get out of this uniform, and what better place to find a quick change than a circus?

Mabel darted quick as a sparrow through the caravan of wagons outside the massive trio of tents and found what she was looking for. All stage players were much the same, and they kept their costumes in similar stations. She found an open door with no one inside; the best luck Mabel had had all day. She dove into rows of dresses and leotards, tutus, and clown uniforms, and did not stop until she found an outfit practical enough for the rest of her journey yet showy enough to blend in.

She had found a pink and pearl burlesque outfit.

Mabel hesitated to put it on. It was the exact sort of outfit Ziegfeld had wanted his girls to wear, with a sequined bustier and feathered ruffles draping from the corset, but the crowd was looking for a redhead in a bellhop's costume. She was going to have to give them something else.

She changed into the outfit as quickly as she could, but the process was arduous and lacing the corset on her own was even trickier. When she was done, she admired her outfit in the floor-length mirror and selected a harlequin mask and feathers to cover up most of her red curls. The only thing left to cover was the Canary diamond, which she hid expertly with a feathered choker. She was perfectly disguised now and absolutely uncomfortable with how she looked. Mabel would just have to lean into it and selected a role in her mental cards of a burlesque star who had longed to return to the stage. She could play that part.

Mabel strutted out of the wagon in her feathers and pearls and little kitten heels. She sashayed over to the tent, and even had a few Johnny's give her a whistle which she played back with a flirtatious wave.

She stiffened at the sight of Frank and a gaggle of girls that followed close on his heels desperate to help him. Mabel told herself to relax, that if she acted the part, Frank wouldn't notice. She wasn't one of his demons anymore.

He paused at Mabel. "Have you seen a redheaded girl in a bellhop's uniform?"

Mabel used her most convincing British accent. "No, love. I ain't seen anyone by that description. I'll keep an eye out."

Frank's eyes narrowed as he looked at her, but she pretended to be too busy examining a missing sequin on her dress. "Say, could you be a love and let the seamstresses know my best dress has gone to waste? Thanks, doll."

Frank straightened his suit. "That's not my department."

He stormed off with the woman giggling behind him. Mabel relaxed, sweat now lightly soaking the back of her corset from the effort of holding it together. At least her disguise was convincing. Now all she had to do was find Will and pray his was just as good.

She parted the curtains and entered another world of light. There were high wires overhead with people flying across the ceiling, barely catching each other on the other side as they flung themselves in the air. Mabel marveled at the center rings with a trio of animal and clown acts, all juggling or spinning fire or chasing little dogs. It looked like not every performance had ground to a halt at Frank's command. The big top performances were still going on.

At the center of the middle ring was an eleven-year-old girl.

"Saoirse!"

It was Will. Mabel craned her neck. Mabel wouldn't have known the girl was Saoirse had Will not called out her name. Saoirse wore a skin-tight, sparkling uniform and had her face done over in clown makeup with a red nose. Saoirse was spinning fire as she balanced on top of a ball. Her dark curly hair was wound up in a tight ballerina's bun. She balanced on top of a ball as she rolled it around fire eaters and hoop spinners.

The dapper crowd was busily taking their seats, obscuring most of Will from view. All Mabel could make out was that he was standing in a neighboring entrance. His cheeks were ruddy, panting hard, his bellhop hat was long gone, and his hair was a firecracker exploding in every direction. He had made it after all. She wanted to throw herself around him in relief, but he was standing dozens of feet away. The crowd was too preoccupied by the show and the lights to have heard Will, but some of them did. They stopped eating their popcorn, their boiled peanuts, and turned to look at Will with white eyes.

Mabel had to warn him.

"Saoirse! It's me! It's Will."

Will bolted for his little sister like an arrow shot from a bow. Saoirse paused on top of her ball. Saoirse cocked her head like an inquisitive predatory animal that had spotted fresh prey in the thicket. His little sister pressed her thumbs in the inside of her palms just like Mabel had done. Two second mouths appeared. Twin pink tongues rolled with hunger as Saoirse's eyes faded to the color of curdled milk.

"Will, stop!" Mabel called to him, but her voice was drowned out by a trumpeting elephant.

Mabel clawed to make her escape from the middle of the pushing and pulling crowd, desperate to find her way out of the bog of people that had somehow thickened around her to prevent her escape.

Will skidded across the sand. Mabel could barely see him, but the sight of Saoirse's new demon form must have sent him into shock. She pushed up someone's shoulder to see that Will wasn't moving. Will wasn't running toward his sister or away. He was only able to stare as Saoirse ran the length of the circus tent and pounced on top of her brother.

"Will! Run!"

A well-dressed man in a dark blue suit and a woman with layers of pearls tried to exit the tent. Mabel shoved between them and finally escaped the throng of patrons who wanted both in and out of the big top. She shoved the man over to run for Will. Mabel didn't care that he fell. She ran, feathers flying everywhere from the base of her glittering bustier, heart pounding with fear that she was already too late.

Mabel made it to the first ring by the time Saoirse had pounced on her brother. He was screaming something awful, like a pig that knew it was about to be slaughtered and helpless to fight back. Will would never hurt her, would never stop her from hurting him. Mabel didn't know what she was going to do to intervene, but she ran like hell across the circus rings anyway. She ducked past the fire-eaters, the trio of clowns juggling fruits, and the man on the unicycle with the handlebar mustache.

Blood spread across the sand where Mabel stopped beside Saoirse and got all over Mabel's shoes as she yanked Saoirse off of Will. He was bleeding from the several bite marks Saoirse's second hands had taken, little rings of fire the size of oranges with teeth punctures that had seeped through his uniform. She giggled uncontrollably as the rest of the circus carried on around them, never slowing. The manic musical only grew louder until Saoirse was in a laughing fit that forced her to double over.

There was so much blood on her mouth that Mabel had to keep her eyes locked on Will's to not panic, but his eyes were unable to focus. He kept looking everywhere and at everything with a very discerning wonder and vacant joy.

“I found her, Mabel,” he said, so delirious Mabel worried he might expire on the spot. “I found her. We can turn her human again. We can get her soul back. We can. We must—”

Will’s face went slack, but his lips kept trembling, and they were rapidly losing color.

She slapped his face enough to get him to focus on her. “Don’t. I’m not losing you too.”

Saoirse stopped laughing so abruptly that Mabel turned back to her. The little girl’s happy white eyes danced as she wiped the blood from her mouth.

“That was fun.” Her voice was a kind of demented music Mabel never wanted to hear again. “But I have just one question for you toys—who are you?”

CHAPTER SEVENTEEN

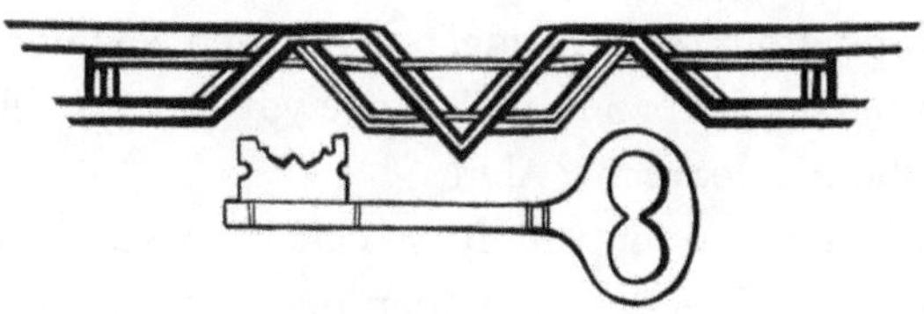

"Who am I?" The sound of Saoirse's voice roused Will. He was covered in so much of his own blood, lying broken in the middle of the circus ring, yet the most shattered part of him was his voice as he stumbled through begging his sister to remember him.

"I'm your brother, Saoirse. Try and remember."

Saoirse cocked her head at him, a predator who had tasted blood and was not sure why her prey had the audacity to speak to her.

"Remember the little house on the hill by the cliffside? Our garden where I taught you to plant all the good things, green and growing. I would play the fiddle to help you fall asleep."

Will began to whistle a tune Mabel did not recognize, but his little sister's ears perked at the long, drawn-out notes of an Irish song. Saoirse's eyes alighted with a sudden memory that gave Mabel hope. When Saoirse grinned at her brother, her gums were pink with blood. She licked some of it away.

"I know your face. You're the flesh and blood who abandoned me." Her voice was not that of a child, but something ancient, as if the sands of time had scratched the back of her throat and turned her insides into an old woman. She rasped every word as if it were a curse she was spitting back in her brother's face. "You play the part of the heroic older brother, here to save his little sister, but we both know that's not what happened at all."

Will's face fell.

The little girl didn't stop. Her sorrow was a steam valve Saoirse sighed to release, her every word laced with delicious guilt. "Frank saw your fights in the back alleys. He led you to his hotel with his charm and his offer. He told you he would make you the Grand's biggest boxing star, the best boxer New York had ever seen. I told you to stop, that something was wrong, but you were so hungry for fame. You signed the contract, and Frank made you pay the tab with your soul. Where did that leave me? Alone."

Will had lied so monumentally, so catastrophically, that Mabel's entire world shifted out from under her like the floor she was standing on had just exploded. She had pegged Will as noble, as someone who was trying to look out for everyone. Will had been lying the whole time.

"No, Saoirse. It's okay. I'm here now. I can take you away from all this. I'm going to make everything right. I've come to pay for my mistakes."

"You wanted to be famous," Saoirse cooed joyfully over Will's blood-splattered body. "Don't lie. When Frank took you away, Raymond took care of me. He brought me to the one place I always wanted to go. Frank has given me everything I've ever wanted."

Will crawled toward his sister, begging her to forgive him, but Saoirse only laughed. Mabel's thoughts reeled like a tilt-a-whirl. All this time, Will had stubbornly refused to even consider any other option. He had ignored Mabel's doubts and Marty's advice and insisted that undoing the contract and turning everyone human was the only way. He *wanted* to be punished for what he had done, and it was why he was so willing to give himself up as a sacrifice.

Mabel had never seen someone so broken in all her life. Will had gone through hell boxing unending fights in the basement of the Grand, then weeks of working as the doorman without rest, and finally all of it made sense. He was trying to undo what he had done to Saoirse in a moment of weakness. Now the only family he had left didn't want him anymore. Mabel was angry at her brother and sisters when she fled her home, but she didn't know what she would do if her siblings hated her back. He had always been looking to put a bandage on his guilt, and Saoirse was refusing to let him heal their wound.

Saoirse crushed her brother's head under her ballet slipper. "I don't want a life on the streets with you anymore. You have no idea how to take care of me. I'm not leaving with you. Not now. Not ever. I'm finally home."

"Please, Saoirse. You don't want to be a demon."

"Better than starving with you."

Saoirse pounced on Will, second mouths outstretched and wet with hunger. Mabel didn't have time to think. She snatched one of the clubs as a nearby clown was juggling mid-air, wrapped her hand around the club like a baseball bat, and knocked Saoirse across her face out into left field. The eleven-year-old went careening backward into a tall clown who was juggling on top of a massive red ball. The clown toppled down on top of Saoirse in a pile of polka-dot fabric and red ruffles.

Mabel could feel like a garbage can in human form for hitting a little girl later. She hoisted Will up by the scruff of his neck like a lost puppy and forced him to his feet. Will's blood smeared over the feathers of her dress and down her arm, but Mabel didn't care so long as she managed to get a very shaky Will to his feet. She did get him up, but he fought her the whole way, wrestling to get to his little sister.

"Will, we need to go."

"But Saoirse—"

"You can't help her here."

She tried to yank him by the arm, but Will was extraordinarily dense, like hoisting a boat anchor. Mabel buckled under his weight, as she pulled him away from the center ring. When she led him back into the cheering crowd, Will began to perk up and walk on his own, filling her with relief. People applauded them as they passed, as if Will's bleeding was all part of the act, part of the amusing game the big top had to offer.

Mabel and Will fled the biggest circus tent and raced through the crowds back to the main entrance. There was no sign of Frank or their earlier, white-eyed pursuers so they proceeded to the smallest of the three circus tents that stood in the back near the far wall. The towering red and white tent's curtains were drawn back to beckon in a crowd, but there was no one lingering around its opening like the other two larger big tops. As Mabel and Will stumbled past, the lighting within was so dim she could barely make out the silhouette of the ringmaster at its center. He was dressed in the Grand's velvet black and with the palest gold accents, so dark he blended into the night backdrop behind him. The only feature that Mabel could set apart from the shadows was his top hat, which was as red as a field of roses. The ringmaster stood beside a box, or something covered in a curtain as reflective as an engine oil slick. Mabel did not want to linger for the big reveal, but her timing was serendipitous. The ringmaster drew back the gossamer curtain to reveal a single figure hidden within.

It was a young woman not much older than Mabel herself. She was paler than ivory linen sheets in a fluttering dress as iridescent as fairy wings. Her face was so taut that Mabel could see every bone in her fragile face beneath her translucent skin. The bars of the cage that held the wisp of a woman glowed a soft blue, as if the iron bars were lit from within by some phantom lantern. It was the most otherworldly sight Mabel had ever seen, and fear crept into her bones like spiders to look at the young woman.

"Witness with your own eyes, a visitation from beyond the grave," the ringmaster boomed at the crowd. "A ghost, captured right here in this very hotel. See how she cries to be returned to the land of the living."

The female ghostly face was the picture of a dazed, serene young woman who might be gazing out her bedroom window rather than at a crowd in a darkened circus. Someone let out a sharp gasp, breaking the ghostly woman's placidity. Her dark eyes and mouth contorted into sharp angles as her grin stretched far too wide to be real, revealing row upon row of needle-thin teeth. The ghost let out a sharp, unearthly wail like distant whales at sea. Mabel shuddered against Will as she tried to keep him from falling over, too terrified to move.

The ringmaster slammed his boot against the cage and the ghost finally quieted. "See how her soul cannot rest. This woman sold her soul, fleeing an unwanted marriage, but the price was too steep to pay. She met her untimely end by jumping from one of the upper Atrium stories and the soul she had used to buy her freedom became trapped within these walls..."

Mabel fled before she could hear the rest. She didn't want or need to hear anything else. She was furious at these people and their carelessness. They didn't care about the ghost of the dead woman in the cage. So long as they were entertained, the show would go on, and their deals offered to the Grand Hotel would carry on, even in death. Mabel carried Will onward around the third tent, grinding her teeth together so hard her jaw ached as they approached the long, red curtained wall.

An unwanted marriage. Trying to get out of a bad deal. One misstep and that could have been her in that cage. The similarity was enough to make Mabel want to throw up, but the ringmaster had said that the girl's body died without its soul. Her soul had been presumably taken by a Frank West deal. If Mabel had died hours ago before she got her soul back, that would have been her.

How many ghosts were floating in these halls?

"Did you see that?" Will coughed and it sounded too wet.

"I wish I didn't."

"If we die in this hotel, are we stuck here forever?" Will said, echoing her thoughts.

She didn't answer him as they ducked inside the red curtain wall. She didn't want to think about it. Mabel had her soul back. That ghostly future was probably never going to happen to her, but it might to Saoirse or Lucky. If she kept her focus rather than losing herself to fear of what might happen to her, she just might be successful in her quest. She swallowed her worry that one day she might be the ghost in that cage and led Will far away from that horrible place.

"What are you thinking?"

Will's face was pale as they pushed forward through the red velvet trying to find the other side. It made Mabel's heart clench.

"I think that's what will happen if we don't get everyone else's souls back," Mabel said. "Anyone who dies without their soul is trapped here. Forever."

Mabel pressed forward until she found the familiar damask wallpaper of the lower hotel floors. She patted her way across the wall until her hand caught in a slim, hidden groove that the map had revealed. She pushed it back until the wall caved. This passage was darker than the ones before, so Mabel helped Will stagger inside the opening and leaned him up against the green wallpaper so he could catch his breath and she could check the map.

"It's all right," he said. "You need to go on without me. I can take care of myself." His eyes were watering and spilling over as he panted his way back to his breath.

They were free, but Mabel's head thumped with too much adrenaline to feel triumph for having made it out alive. She rested her head against the wall beside him and tried to rip pieces of her outfit off to give something to Will to stop the bleeding. He put his shaking hand over hers.

She squeezed his hand back. "I'm not leaving you behind. What if Frank finds you?"

He turned away from her gaze. "I just got my soul back, but I feel like my soul is already gone."

Will turned away from her. All that loss, all that hopelessness. It was too much for one person to bear alone, so she took his hand in hers and stayed by his side. Mabel bore the pain with him. No matter how much she was there for him, this was still a personal lament, and she knew this moment of weakness was hard for him to give in front of someone else. He had made a terrible choice and was not everything Mabel had made him out to be, but in a hotel full of sinners, Will was hardly the worst of the lot. Mabel had done far worse. She had stolen from the young and old alike, lied, and cheated. Now she saw Will's nobility came from a desperate guilt to not only right the wrongs he had done, but out of sheer fire to stop all of this from happening to anyone ever again; Mabel found that she trusted him more than ever. She had to stop him from sacrificing himself. Mabel would save him, save everyone, even if she had to risk everything that ever mattered to her to do it.

"We'll get her back, Will."

He let out a shuddering breath. "How could Frank do that to her? She's just a kid. Saoirse shouldn't have to suffer because of me. Now he has twisted her into someone—something—I don't even recognize."

"It doesn't mean we can't remind her that she's human," Mabel said. "We'll go down to the portal, free all the souls Frank sent down there, and she'll be her old self again."

"And what if we fail?" Will whispered back. "What if we go down there and our plan doesn't work? What if we close the portal and it's all for nothing?"

She had never had to convince Will before, yet here he was, echoing all of the doubts Mabel had had since the very beginning.

Mabel squeezed his hand. "We freed all of those souls, didn't we? Admittedly with terrible results. But they didn't die soulless and trapped."

Will frowned at her like she wasn't helping.

"There's always been a very good chance we would fail," she continued. "That was before we learned everything in the Grand Hotel goes back to one, original deal. Every other person in this place was human once, and it's possible they could be again. We should undo the deal Henry West had struck by taking out the real demon."

"You." Will's voice was so quiet Mabel could barely hear. "You need to undo the original deal."

"What are you talking about?" she said. "Aren't you going with me?"

"I'm serious. I'm weak from the wounds. I will slow you down. You're the one who broke the code on the soul cage. What do you need me for?"

She ignored him. "Let me see your bites."

He showed her one of his arms. The flesh around where Saoirse had bit him had turned a deep black-green that had seeped into his blood. The putrid color was running up his arms and turning his veins the same strange shade of deep, night green. Mabel's stomach became a knot she could never hope to untangle as she held his wrist. He looked like he had been poisoned by some kind of plant or snake, not bitten by an eleven-year-old girl.

"Is that poison?" Mabel asked.

"I don't know," Will said. "I don't have much experience with demon bites."

Mabel dug into his pockets and reached around until she fished out the little tin of healing balm Will had taken from Marty earlier. She didn't know if it would work on poison, but she had to try. The clear balm was cold and semitransparent, like the inside of a shell. When she rubbed it on Will's wounds, it seemed to soothe him, because he leaned into her hand with a sigh.

"You lied to me, you know," Mabel said. "You said you were going to be fine."

Will gave her a look. "This is about what Saoirse said, isn't it? You feel I lied to you."

Mabel said nothing for a moment. "Turns out you were looking for the same thing I was—fame."

Will turned to look her in the eye. "I was. Saoirse didn't understand. I did it for her, but I would be lying if I said I didn't want the fame too."

"Is that how Frank lured you in?"

"Yes. Fame is the only way to make any real money, the only way I could truly keep her off the streets. Being famous is the only way to get anyone to ever pay you what you're actually worth."

In the silence of the narrow passage, Mabel replaced the tin lid on the balm and stuck it back inside Will's pocket. His wounds were healing, but the poison was there in his veins still faint gray in color. The balm, no matter how much magic was in its foundation, was not working on this particular wound.

"I'm sorry I said you were selfish," he told her. "I was just angry you wouldn't help me."

It stung, but this time Mabel wouldn't push it aside. "You shouldn't have said those things to me. I'm not Frank's star. I was just trying to survive."

She tore a great strip of fabric from the tail of her gown and wrapped the pieces around his bite wounds. The silk fabric wasn't much, but it held back the blood, and Will had a little color return to his face. It was enough.

"Can you walk?" Mabel said. "I don't know that I can carry you in a corset, but if I must, I must."

Will raised both eyebrows, as if he had just realized what she was wearing. "Where did you get that?"

"Frank would be looking for a bellhop, not a performer. I swiped it from one of the wagons. He even walked right past and talked to me without recognizing me."

He frowned appreciatively. "Not a bad idea. I might want to find something else to wear in the next level. I've never been down there, but—" He winced, cutting off his next thought.

"Let's move," Mabel said. "The sooner we get down there, the sooner we can fix you up for real."

They fled inside the walls, down the sloping narrow passages. Mabel had expected the next level to come up quickly like all the rest. She kept stopping to remove the map and check where they were, but the tunnels were nothing but damask wallpaper and lanterns ahead without openings.

They hit a dead end, and Mabel's breath came on hard and fast. She checked the map. Will leaned against the wallpaper and closed his eyes, panting hard while Mabel studied the parchment. They were interrupted by a low rumble. Behind where they kneeled, the wall shifted and formed an opening on the opposite wall.

"Can you move?"

Will gave her a smile, but it was a phantom of the one he used to give. "I have to."

"Are you sure we can access this level?" Her voice came out more frantic than she wanted it to. "There was a passage up ahead and it just disappeared."

The map was now telling her that they were trapped in some sort of pocket between floors, presumably until everything shifted again. Mabel could have sworn there was a route here before the last time she checked the map, but now it was gone. The Navigator was always moving people to where they needed to go in the hotel. It was bound to happen that one of those shifts would create a dead end, but she hadn't thought of it logically until that moment. The way they came was still open, and Frank was still pursuing them. If he found them here, Frank would have them.

"Where are we?" Will said. "Why are we in this room?"

"We're not in a room. We're in the maid tunnels. Remember?"

She didn't like the sound of his voice, like he wasn't sure where he was or if he was even awake right now. Will was getting paler and more disoriented by the minute.

Mabel removed the map and checked its ever-shifting notes. "The speakeasy is the last stop before the final below. It says there is a way down behind the dressing rooms."

One of his bandages slipped down his arm.

Mabel choked. "Will..."

He gaped when he saw how the flesh had healed over. Blackish green veins ran along his arms like snakes spreading up from the bite wounds toward his heart.

"It doesn't look good, does it?" he said.

"It looks better on the outside at least." Mabel tried not to let her voice shake. "What can we do?"

"I'm fine," Will covered his arms with the remains of his sleeves. "I feel a lot better now that I'm not bleeding all over the place. We should keep moving. Besides, I think you're going to like this level."

She helped Will tighten his bandages back up as best as she could, trying not to gag at the smell coming off of them. Mabel didn't want to make Will feel more worried than he already did.

The opposite wall thundered like a rock rolling over a cavern, slowly closing their opening. Getting him to his feet was easier than she expected, but as soon as he was back up, he staggered into the damask. Mabel pulled Will inside before the hotel moved and shut the way out. A lone trumpet blared an opening note to a song. Lights spilled across the wallpaper and danced in an array of pinks and blues. Everything smelled hot and floral, a mix of bright roses and the smoky bite of strong whiskey.

"Will, I think we found the speakeasy."

CHAPTER EIGHTEEN

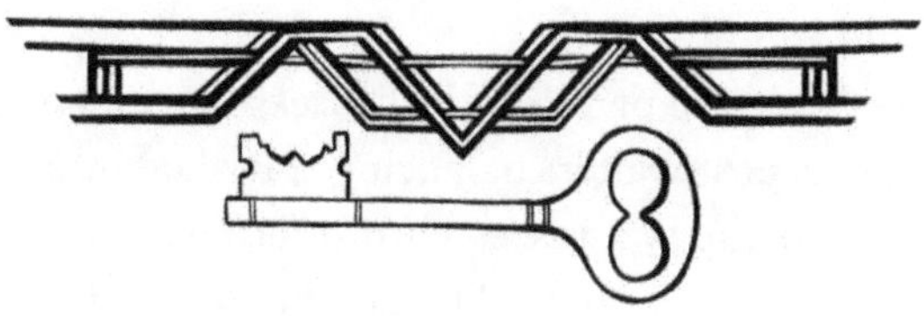

Mabel and Will stepped out from the darkened hallway and into the inside of a diamond. The speakeasy was gold and softly glittering from floor to ceiling, accented with draping canopies of pink fabric and half a dozen twinkling chandeliers overhead. The stage was lined with round fluorescent light bulbs and a runway that came down the middle where many beautiful dames were catwalking up and down in their corsets, diamond-crusted bustiers, and great billowing dresses. The jazz band blared hot at the crowd, who were liquored up plenty and sloshing against each other like bubbles in a champagne flute.

Mabel grabbed Will's arm to tell him they should search for the door that led down below when a familiar face on stage caught her eye. Lucky strutted in front of a parade of other girls, more naked than Mabel had ever seen her. A large feather fan covered up the top half of Lucky's clearly naked body as she trailed a vibrant blue and turquoise tail made of thick feathers behind her. She twirled playfully, suggesting a peek at her topless form beneath. Each of the other girls were dressed as flamingos, toucans, and scarlet macaws and danced in perfect synchronized formation to support Lucky's starring role.

Watching Lucky beaming center stage reminded Mabel so much

of Ziegfeld, so much of "the audition" she had refused to give, that she flushed unpleasantly like a child who had walked in on something she shouldn't have seen. How she longed to be up there. Mabel shook it off. They had a job to do.

"Come on, Will." She had to yell to be heard over the music as she looped her arm through his and pulled him away, but she couldn't help but notice the faint smile on his face at her demeanor.

"Don't you like the show? I thought this would be the kind of thing you would adore."

They wove through a parade of well-dressed flappers cutting it up on the dance floor, past waiters balancing trays laid over with shining coupe glasses, past the waitresses with offerings of cigars and cigarettes. If there was one thing Mabel had learned about picking pockets in New York City, it was to always act like you belonged. People could smell uncertainty from a mile away, and there was nothing worse than being picked out as a tourist when you were trying to make a clean steal.

It was all so glamorous, a world Mabel had been in only a handful of times before. She would drown herself in speakeasies to burn away the pain of rejection. They were the one place she could feel seen when she otherwise felt invisible. Something about being here felt wrong, like a poison hadn't only gotten into Will. It had seeped into the air and was souring everyone and everything in it, and Mabel felt like the only canary that could smell the poison in the coal mine.

"Not really." Mabel shook her head. "That's not what I mean. I do like the show. Something's wrong? Can't you feel it?"

Will stopped abruptly and pulled her into his arms. He searched her face, but his expression had become all doughy, as if the air itself had made him drunk. "You need to... lighten up." All his words came out in a slur. "You should have... a drink."

Mabel shook his arm. "Will?"

He staggered away from her to whisk one of the coupe glasses full of pale yellow liquid and downed it in a flash. "Golly. This is... strong stuff. A real... crackerjack."

Mabel took another look around the room. Every person was so drunk they could hardly stand. They were possessed by a frenzy that made them all want to dance, drink, and party until they dropped, and some of them already had. She hadn't noticed the people on the floor, the bodies scattered here and there to be stomped on by the rest. Mabel hadn't noticed the blood on her heels.

There had to be a way out of this party, but so far, all Mabel could see were four heavily draped walls and too many people in all directions. She had never been one to feel anything but ease in a crowd, but even Mabel was starting to feel there were too many people in this small room. The flashing lights, colorful dresses, and heavy perfume smell in the air were all pressing in on her head as if she had sunk to the bottom of a lake. Mabel had to swim across the room to find her way back to where they had come in. When she and Will reached the stairs they descended into the speakeasy. But the wall at the top of the stairs had shifted, concealing the exit.

They were trapped.

She patted Will on the cheek hard, trying to sober him up. "The exit is gone. We need to get out of here."

He giggled. "But why would we ever want to leave? We're having such a good time."

She grabbed Will by his torn bellhop collar. "We have to get out of here. Come on?"

"Where you going, baby? Ain't we having fun?"

He had never spoken to her like that, but she had heard plenty of folks catcall her before, especially after a bottle of wine or two, but Will sounded like he had downed the whole barrel. He only had one glass. It had to be the room, the air, something making everyone this drunk. Mabel seemed to be the only one immune to the speakeasy's charms, and she guessed it had something to do with the Canary diamond she still wore around her neck interacting with her newly acquired humanity.

"Sure, we are, honey." She yanked Will out of the crowd toward the back just as the number ended and he happily followed her like a lovesick puppy.

There were a number of little round bar tables she had to weave through, which were thankfully mostly empty. Most of the crowd was up on their feet cutting it up around the dance floor, but Mabel passed more than one drunken fool sitting with their mouth wrapped around a bottle in their suits and sparkling dresses. She locked eyes with a gaunt man and woman. Their hands were joined under the table as their heads lay in a large pool of blood that covered the table like a tablecloth. The sight nearly brought Mabel to tears.

Parties weren't supposed to kill anybody. They were supposed to be a relief from whatever tormented them in their daily lives. It was strange to see a place that brought her comfort all twisted in this way, like a bad poster painted by prohibitionists touting the sins of liquor.

Behind the main bar and its offering of every liquor and wine bottle known to man, Mabel had difficulty finding an opening to get to the dressing rooms. It was all one big wall of alcohol with no openings. She had to drag Will to get her to follow him as she searched. He was so distracted by everyone and anything that the slightest shine on a garment would have him clamoring to join the crowd.

"Don't you wanna..." Will hiccupped. "Dance baby?"

"We need to sober you up." Mabel patted her hand on the bar counter to get the bartender to come over. "You got anything to absorb some of this liquor?"

The bartender's short gray hair was slicked back like a man. Her dark slacks were paired with a purple vest, and the sleeves of her gray shirt were rolled all the way up past her pretty impressive forearms. "Why would anyone want to do that? You should join in the fun."

"I can't," Mabel said, licking her lips. She had to admit she was sorely tempted. "I'm tied up at the moment."

"I can make your favorite. Bee's Knees, right?" The bartender began to mix Mabel's favorite drink despite her protests. She slid the shining coupe glass down to Mabel. "Trust me. It will taste like a dream."

Mabel had never seen a more delectable drink in all her life. The liquid shimmered pink and gold inside, like the rest of the room. She drew closer until her lips were near the edge of the coupe glass. It was just one sip. What harm could one little taste do?

Mabel took the smallest possible sip and the explosion in her mouth was immediate, like she had drunk a soda and its carbonation had run fizzy all the way down her throat. It filled her mouth with sunshine and her head with stardust, and suddenly everything in the world seemed right.

"Bottom's up, baby," Will slurred.

She turned back to Will, forgetting everything, remembering everything. His face was so handsome, and she had forgotten to kiss it. Mabel drew the bellhop who had warned her to run, the noble boy who held a dark secret, and brought his mouth to hers until the buzz wasn't only from the drink but from drinking him down.

She drew away from him to come up for air.

"Wow." Will breathed into her neck. "That was something else."

"What were we doing?" Mabel sighed the words against his neck.

"I can't remember anymore."

Mabel stumbled out with Will back into the crowd, drawing him by his collar into the party. She had been so worried about everything that she hadn't stopped to have any fun. Mabel danced with Will while the band wailed on the trumpet. They synchronized perfectly with the crowd to the Varsity Drag, cutting and wheeling between the snapper dressers and their flourished steps. It was like being on stage again, but she was with Will, and everything was light and fun, and Mabel was finally feeling like herself again. Why had she worried so much about everyone's souls? They were all smiling at her with their too big grins and their white eyes. They were all fine, Mabel could see. They didn't need her to save them. Everything was perfect and Mabel was finally home.

The song ended with an eruption of applause. Mabel's stomach dropped as Raymond came out into the center of the stage and placed a hand on the microphone. He looked directly at her.

"For our next act, please welcome to the stage, the one and only star of the Grand Hotel, Mabel Rose Dixon!"

A giant champagne bottle burst down onto the crowd in a shower of confetti and sparkles as a spotlight came on where Mabel and Will stood. Will brought Mabel's mouth to his as every color rained down on them. She disappeared into his kiss, falling so deep she never wanted to come up for air. Mabel stumbled through vague shapes of people. Their faces smeared as she passed like wet charcoal. She had heard her name but didn't know what she was supposed to be doing or where she was supposed to be. Mabel's hand was in Will's, but she could have sworn when she looked back to check, it was Frank's hand she was holding.

A hand yanked her hard by the arm. "Mabel?" Lucky's face floated up to center stage out of the kaleidoscope. "What are you doing here?"

There was another eruption of applause as the crowd chanted Mabel's name over and over again.

"Come on." Lucky suddenly appeared by her side and threaded her arm through Mabel's. "We gotta get you in tap shoes."

Mabel drunkenly stumbled after Lucky toward the velvet curtains. Her hand left Will's and his form disappeared almost immediately from sight, blending into waves of faces that bobbed up and down like sea foam. Mabel called Will's name, tried to pry herself free of this disastrous girl who was ruining her good time, but Lucky refused to release her from her inhuman grip.

The backstage behind the speakeasy stage was filled with so many performers that Mabel blended into the crowd like one of the showgirls. No one looked twice at Lucky or the bloody pink starlet she dragged behind her through the hallways of dark curtains out into a huge open room. The dressing room was bigger than the speakeasy itself, housing endless stations filled with costumes, accessories, makeup vanities, and fitting rooms lined up in curtained rows like at department stores. Everything was theatrical from the red curtains to the gold tassels, with no Greek god statues or bathing fountains to be seen. The walls were frosted with beautiful impressionist paintings of ballet dancers and folies bergère advertisements. The details swam in and out of Mabel's view like impressionist paintings, all color, and smeared shapes.

Lucky dragged Mabel down into a row filled with every color of burlesque dress and Mabel nearly stumbled into a dress rack.

Lucky left Mabel's foggy view and disappeared somewhere. Mabel wished Will was there, and even in her haze she worried about where he had gone and how she could sneak out of Lucky's room to go back to him. She didn't want him dancing without her.

Lucky's face floated back out of the ether. "Smell this."

Mabel found a red bottle in front of her face and took a big whiff of the gray smoke emanating out of the lid. The second the smoke hit her nostrils, Mabel's whole face contorted as her brain crash-landed back to reality and the mist in her vision finally cleared. Her head throbbed so hard she worried she might throw up. Lucky anticipated this and brought a small trash can so Mabel could relieve herself of her stomach contents and all the liquid therein.

When Mabel had finished, Lucky removed the putrid-smelling trashcan away from her and struck a match, then dropped it inside the metal can. Something writhed and shrieked within as if it were alive.

"What in all the holy ghosts was that?" Mabel said.

"It's what they put in the liquor, a kind of chemical demon," Lucky said. "It possesses you from the inside out. They use it to steal your soul. If you vomit it up, the damn thing starts to grow into a shape of its own. You have to burn it, or it will grow to consume everything."

Mabel's head felt like someone had taken a sledgehammer to her temple. "Wait, so that thing was inside me?"

"Yes," Lucky said.

A cold sweat ran slick down Mabel's spine. Will was still out there. She had to get the demon out of him. She tried to stand and immediately her body refused to cooperate. Mabel's legs gave and she found herself planted right back where she started.

"Slow down," Lucky said. "You need to rest. That poppy inhalant is going to need a minute to run through and clean out your system."

"But Will?" Mabel's words came out all gummy and she had to chew on every syllable. "He's still out there."

Lucky's eyes widened. "I didn't see him. We can go back for him, but I need to talk to you first. Quick, change into these." Lucky thrust a pair of tap shoes at her. "They will add a little something to your magic act."

Mabel stared at the shoes. "I can't. I couldn't possibly go out there, looking like this, and dance." Her every defensive word sloshed out of her mouth.

"Yes, you can," Lucky said, placing her hands on Mabel's shoulders. "You said you've been held back all your life by your mother, by Ziegfeld, by your own self-doubt, by everyone who couldn't see what you were worth. You've been holding back all this time."

Mabel's head swam with too much liquor, even though she had only downed one glass. Lucky spun Mabel around to look out on the world behind the speakeasy, the land of entertainers. "Forget Frank. Forget saving this place. We don't need saving, and neither do you. Remember your dream. You wanted to be the biggest star, and now you are. Become who you were made to be. Be our magic act."

Surrounded by all of these girls as they applied their makeup and changed into new outfits, Mabel's head rang with a knife of recognition. She knew some of their faces. They were just like her, the ones deemed not "the Ziegfeld type." They were too tall, too short, too fat, too busty, too pear-shaped, too brown, too black, too pale, too old, too masculine, or too plain. They were American beauties, but no one fit the Anna Held model that Florenz Ziegfeld held higher than the rest. All these girls had gravitated toward the Grand, all the ones who hadn't made the auditions, and they had been offered the same thing Mabel had—a second chance to be a star.

Mabel flushed as she hugged the fabric to her skin. She closed her eyes as she imagined giving into the star she had always held back from being. She pictured herself on stage finally comfortable with her body, with herself, with her curves, with taking up space. Why had she always been uncomfortable in her own skin, so unwilling to show the barest hint?

"All right." Mabel let slip a long, held in sigh. "I'll do it. But only if you tell me the way out of here"

Mabel withdrew the map from the front of her corset and handed it to Lucky. "I have to find the portal."

Lucky yanked Mabel around by the arm. "You want to what? Go down below? No. No one goes there. No one should ever go there. You'll wind up worse than dead in that place."

"I have to make things right," Mabel said. "All those people whose souls I let go? They... they died. It's my fault. I have to undo the original deal and kill the demon who started all this."

Lucky's eyes held a dangerous light. "You know how to undo the original deal?"

Mabel shifted in Lucky's uncomfortable grip. "Yes... but I need your help. All I need is to find the door somewhere on this level."

Lucky clucked her tongue. "When you first came, I thought you were a self-obsessed, starstruck-in-love dope. Now I see you do not have a self-preserving thought in that head of yours. Of course, I want to be free of this place." Lucky loosened her grip on Mabel's arm. "I will help you find the door."

Mabel's heart raced. "Thank you."

"They're expecting you out there." Lucky flicked her wrist, somehow producing Mabel's tap shoes. "You tap and distract them. I will find the door down to the portal."

"What about Will?"

"Find him in the crowd," Lucky said. "We'll grab him after your number."

Mabel grinned wide. "Ab-so-tute-ly. We can do this."

"We can."

She positively glowed as Lucky led her back to the stage. Every head turned as she passed. Mabel reached a hand for the Persephone pin, re-securing it in her hair for the dance ahead. With Lucky's help, they would find the door. They would grab Will. Everything was about to end, or maybe begin, and as Mabel strode with fierce taps up to the stage curtain, she had never been surer that she was about to take this whole place down. She could do it. She could turn every person who had become a demon into a human again, and that was worth fighting for. It was worth dying for.

Mabel's tap shoes let out decided clacks across the hardwood as Mabel strutted out into the center of the T-shaped stage. The audience waited, giggling and chirping to each other that the star had arrived. The music swelled, a trumpet blared, and in her fine gown that barely covered her body, Mabel danced her heart out. She didn't care about getting every move perfect. She spun across the stage like a dust devil in beat with the rhythm inside her. Even when she had performed before, she had never felt so good to be on stage, so carefree while she tapped. Her doubts were shedding off her like an old snakeskin, and Mabel liked this new version of herself.

The music stopped so abruptly, Mabel nearly spun off the end of the catwalk trying to stop.

"Well, if it isn't my favorite starlet. How did you wander all the way down here, mouse?"

Cold sweat ran down Mabel's back at the sound of the one voice she never wanted to hear again, but there Evelyn stood like an uninvited house guest in the middle of the dressing room. The white, sheer, lacy piece she donned clung to every curve of her narrow waist and long torso. Tiny white pearls wove around her neck and shoulders, concealing her second mouth. The snake bracelet was wound around her wrist, returned to its rightful owner.

"Mabel Rose Dixon," Evelyn Greene said. "We have so much to talk about."

CHAPTER NINETEEN

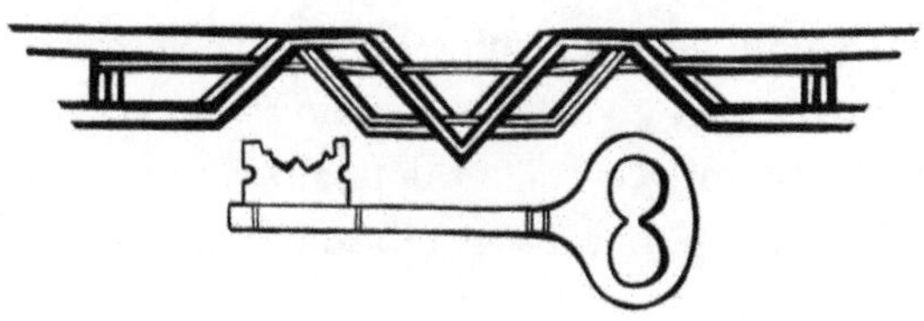

Mabel stood at the end of the catwalk, facing Evelyn where she had emerged from between the red curtains. They stared each other down with hard, heavily kohled eyes, each waiting to see who would make the first move. The speakeasy had gone unsettlingly quiet. Even the band waited with bated breath to see what the women were about to do to each other. At least she had a weapon. Her hand itched to check that the Persephone pin was in place, still lodged somewhere in her curls. She had to wait for the opportune moment.

Evelyn strode across the stage as if she were the star of the Grand Hotel and not Mabel. "You caused quite a scene."

"If you're going to eat me, just get it over with," Mabel said, hand reaching toward her hair.

Evelyn swayed across the catwalk, her black sheer ensemble fluttering with all her power. She towered above Mabel like a queen, her second mouth unraveling across her skin, tongue licking her collarbone. "Mabel Rose Dixon, you've been destroying everything you touch. How about we put an end to your crusade before you wreck my hotel further?"

Mabel's brow creased. "*Your* hotel?"

Evelyn smiled into the back of her hand as if Mabel had just told a fine joke. "You really have no idea what is going on, do you? Who did you think was taking over things after Frank has his little ascension party at the May's Eve Ball?"

So many pieces fell into place, Mabel's head swam. "Is that why you brought Frank the Canary? You want his job?"

Evelyn inspected her nails as if Mabel's revelation was so very dull. "Your job was to deliver Frank souls. My job was to make you the star of the Grand, teach you how to collect souls, and feed them to the Canary. Then I would get everything I wanted. Where did it all go so wrong, Mabel? Didn't we give you everything you ever wanted?"

Mabel was desperate to make the final reach for the Persephone pin Matty had given her, but it was too soon. She needed more information. "No. You didn't."

A smile spread up to Evelyn's dimples and her eyes danced, clearly bemused. "Ah, yes, your little soul. So precious once it's gone, but was all the carnage to get it back worth it?"

Evelyn wanted Mabel to go back to being the rabbit caught in the wolf's jaws. Human. Defenseless. She had no idea how much bite Mabel now possessed.

"No one should have to die for their art," Mabel insisted, egging Evelyn on. She just needed her to draw a little closer. "And no one should have to kill to ensure their artist career is secure."

"No artist should have to die of hunger, either," Evelyn snapped back. "I climbed my way onto the silent screen, never reaching stardom unless I was willing to get into more than a few heavy petting sessions. I played their game, got scraps in return, and was told to be grateful. Wasn't I lucky to be living the dream?"

Mabel's rage simmered. That's exactly what had happened to her, exactly what she had never told anyone about that day she was alone in Ziegfeld's office. She had denied him and had paid the price. Mabel knew what it was for beauty, attractiveness, and compliance to go hand-in-hand with needing to present a plethora of talents all stacked like cards in a poker deal. You could win everything you ever wanted or lose it all. That was entertainment. That was being an artist trying to survive a world where the people with money and the competition shared the same knife. It was death by a thousand cuts.

"We're safe here, can't you see that?" Evelyn said. "I would gladly give my soul again to have what the Grand offers. Forget Frank. Forget what he's doing. In a few weeks, he will be gone, and the hotel will be mine. If you go forward with your plan and undo the original deal, we'll all be out on the street again."

"Did the Grand really save you, though?" Mabel asked. "Or was it just another man with a deal that was too good to be true that cost you everything?"

Irritation flashed in Evelyn's eyes. "The golden age of theater, silent pictures, and vaudeville will fade. Here in the Grand, dreams can last forever. With Frank gone, I can help other outcast girls like you achieve their dreams, free of being preyed upon. Free of having to give their bodies to a man to prove their worth, free from the passage of time. Isn't that what you want, Mabel? Why take that all away?"

"All for the cost of their souls," Mabel said, gesturing back at the crowded speakeasy. "This paradise is fed with blood. It doesn't deserve to stand."

"Four years from now," Evelyn said. "In 1929, silent pictures will fade. Ziegfeld's theater will shut its doors. Talking pictures will take their places. Tomorrow, talkies. Years later, pictures in color. On and on it will go until people won't even go to the theaters anymore. Entertainment will fragment into so many disconnected parts. An endless cycle of evolving or dying, but here we can stop time. No one will be left behind. A little blood is merely a patron, and you and I both know you have paid your own way with a parade of patrons."

"I stole," Mabel hissed. "I didn't kill anyone. You can't know the future. You can't know everything will come crashing down. This can't be the only way to save artists."

"That's the thing about being a demon." Evelyn's dress fluttered like bat wings around her ankles as she wrapped her hand around Mabel's throat. "The longer you live without your soul, the more you see what's coming. If you had stayed one, you would have seen the future too."

"You have two choices, Mabel," Evelyn squeezed Mabel's esophagus gently as she caressed Mabel's yellow diamond with one finger that slowly elongated into a claw. "You can finish what you started. Feed the diamond. Be a star. Belong to no one but yourself. With Frank gone, you can finally be free."

Mabel shook with hatred at what they wanted her to do, what they were asking of her. They wanted her to lay waste on the theater floor, paint it red with sacrifice. They wanted her to complete the one hundred souls and preserve artistic paradise, free of rejection, free of being forgotten by the passage of time.

One hundred souls. Was paradise worth it?

"So, what will it be? Feed the diamond? Or death?" The skin from shoulder to shoulder beneath Evelyn's clavicle unzipped slowly to reveal its hidden set of teeth.

Mabel reached for the pin and sliced it across Evelyn's face. "Not my death. Yours."

Evelyn's cheek hissed as she screeched like a dying crow. Her face hissed steam as the many teeth within her mouth tumbled out of her breastplate like a smashed jar of candy, scattering everywhere across the stage.

The speakeasy erupted into a panic. If there had been any hope of finding Will's face in the crowd, Mabel had lost it as every patron scrambled to find an exit that was not there. Mabel stumbled back along the catwalk, choking, trying to catch her breath again, gripping the Persephone pin as if her life depended on it. She wiped the tip on the end of her black dress, cleaning the blood as Evelyn writhed and all her demonic life force bled across the stage in seeping black bile that bubbled. Mabel placed the Persephone pin back inside her curls.

She had done it. She had turned a demon into a human. As she watched Evelyn's eyes return to a soft green color and her hair become less perfect and more matted and her towering form shrink down, Mabel knew she could do what had to be done. She could find the courage to descend and summon the original deal-making demon. She could turn him human. She could kill him.

There came the soft ringing of a bell downstage, so crisp and clear that it could be heard over the uproar. Raymond stood at the back of the stage, holding his very small bell in one gloved hand.

Mabel's toes curled inside her heels as Raymond silenced the bell in his palm. "You could have just used my bell, you know," Raymond said. "I promised to bring you anything you desired, Mabel, but like most humans, you chose the hard route."

Raymond turned to face the curtain and waved his long fingers in front of them. The red velvet curtains rippled in on themselves in a wave like a stone tossed in a lake. In the percussive aftershock, the curtains reformed to stack into a gray stone archway and a heavy wooden door with an iron knocker in the shape of a demon's mouth holding a heavy ring. There was no doorknob. Only the intricate demon's face laughing at them.

No wonder Mabel could not find it, which is why it was so difficult to read the location on the map. The door leading down to the portal was the literal back of the stage, but it could only be opened with the snap of demon fingers, and Mabel was no longer a demon.

"Mabel!" Lucky screamed to be heard over the panicked Speakeasy. She climbed up onto the stage and lunged for Raymond, second mouths outstretched to defend Mabel. "Don't go with him. It's a trick! He's the—"

Raymond's leap across the stage was so fast, his form blurred in front of Mabel in a stream of dark color. His nails elongated in a red arc and sliced across Lucky's neck. A ribbon of green blood bubbled out of her wound as she clutched the skin, trying to stop the bleeding.

"No!" Mabel rushed to her side as Lucky fell in a thud to the floor. "No. No. No." She clung to the word like a life preserver as Lucky's blood kept spilling down the front of her dress. Mabel scooped up Lucky, not caring if the blood got on her, not caring about anything except trying to save her friend. She pressed her hands down on the wound as Lucky shook in her arms. Lucky choked out a small wheeze and her eyes went white.

Mabel sobbed, shaking Lucky to try and wake her up again. She couldn't see one more person die, couldn't lose one more friend. She had helped Mabel get her soul back, had given her crucial help, and had fought to defend her at the expense of her own life. All this time, she had been helping Will save his sister, but Lucky was the person Mabel had been thinking of. Lucky was the one person Mabel had wanted to turn human. Now she was gone.

She couldn't look at Raymond to ask the question. Her voice was shattered glass. "Why? Why kill her?"

Footsteps fell across the stage. Raymond stood over Mabel, regarded Lucky, and leaned over and whispered in Mabel's ear.

"Leave her." There was a hint of bemusement in his answer. "She's not important."

Mabel burned with rage as she looked up to watch Raymond stride across the stage. "She is important." Mabel blinked back angry tears. "I'm not going with you."

"If you want to do what you came to do," Raymond said coolly. "Then we must descend."

A shudder ran along Mabel's skin like distant thunder. She knew who Raymond was. She had always known who Raymond was.

"You're the first demon, the one who made the deal with Henry West."

Raymond ignored her. He stepped over Evelyn, walked up to the door with a clipped step, and gripped the knocker. He sounded it three times. The door swung open on creaky hinges to reveal granite steps leading down into black. In the darkened doorway stood Will, slumped like an empty sock puppet. The black veins were in his face now and spreading a sick green across his cheeks. He stared vacantly down at the hardwood.

"Will!" Mabel ran to him and reached for his face. His skin was cold to the touch. "Come on, Will. We need to get that liquor out of you."

Raymond snapped his fingers and the lights along the cobblestone walls turned on, each in succession, leading down into nothing.

"Come," Raymond said. "I will guide you both down below. Don't worry. He will walk on his own."

Mabel wrapped her arm around Will and helped him to his feet. He was so much lighter than before. At least she would be able to save Will—at least that.

Mabel led Will toward the dark opening with Raymond following behind. She had needed to find the demon that made the deal with Henry West, but now that Raymond was with them, Mabel thought traveling with him was an extraordinarily bad idea. But she had made her choice. She hadn't left with her soul when she had the chance. As she stepped down into the darkened corridor led by the original demon of the Grand Hotel, Mabel wondered how much longer she would get to keep it.

CHAPTER TWENTY

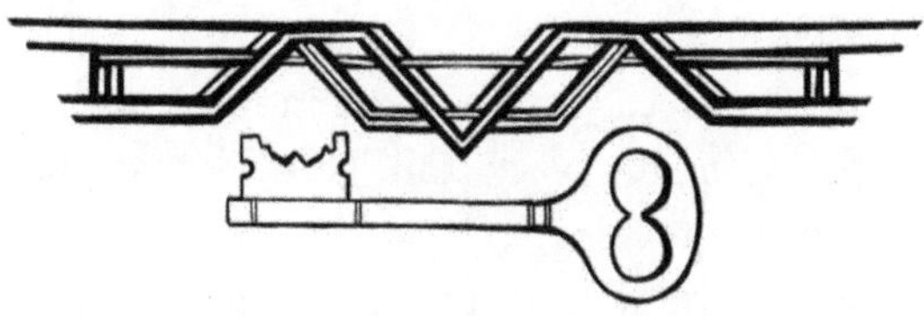

Will and Mabel followed Raymond out of the bright speakeasy and into the Below. The steps went down forever, repeating on into darkness without end. Black metal sconces, more at home in a Gothic novel than a luxurious hotel, only lit the staircase below a few short steps. The moment they descended the temperature dropped significantly and Mabel shivered in her thin dress. The surety that Mabel was doing the right thing and had chosen the right path was leaking out of her rapidly, like steam out of a tea kettle. When Raymond snapped his fingers again and the door shut decidedly behind them, Mabel's hope nearly extinguished.

"Come on, Will," Mabel whispered. She didn't dare raise her voice. "Keep it together." She was unsure if she meant that more for him or for herself. He said nothing, but his face seemed even greener in the candlelight. Mabel swallowed hard.

The walls pulsed faintly beside them. Mabel froze as a bit of wall stood out from the others. She blinked and the dimple in the wallpaper was gone, but if she had to place money on it, she could have sworn she saw a bit of cheek, an eye, and part of an ear emerge and then fade back into the damask.

"Don't be afraid," Raymond said. "It's not far. I assure you. The steps are quite safe."

Mabel took three steps down and the stone hallway shimmered in flat grays. She wasn't sure if that moaning sound was the wind, or human voices coming from the walls around them. Will lifelessly took each step down beside her as a distant rumbling echoed off the lower walls. They were coming to a landing, with several lights spilling out of windows up ahead.

"It's not much further," Raymond said as if he were merely directing them to a restroom and not the pits of hell. "If you like, I may take the lead from here."

Mabel nodded and let Raymond pass in front of them. He strode down the steps with his very tall gait like a praying mantis descending a stem, all grace.

Mabel led Will by the wrist out onto the landing and past the big, darkened windows. She had to squint to see within but knew immediately what level they had come to. There were machine washing drums fading out into the distance, with more people than Mabel could count standing over them scrubbing clothes. She had picked up a rock and found an ant hill hidden beneath dozens of times, and Mabel felt like she had picked up the rock of the Grand Hotel and uncovered its terrible underbelly. There were so many people who had been sent down to Laundry, and they were scrubbing blood and viscera from the sheets only to have it carted back upstairs, freshly pressed for the new batch of victims. At the sight of the endless washers, Mabel's stomach threatened to give up whatever was left.

"You needn't linger in the Laundry level," Raymond said. "It can be quite upsetting to see what happens to the ungrateful."

He snapped his fingers. A yellow light grew all around them until it was so bright Mabel had to close her eyes. When she blinked them open again, she found she and Will stood in a room spun out of gold.

The vaulted ceiling went on and up above their heads into darkness, the exact opposite of the Atrium's many floors. High above their heads, the hotel's central, golden clockwork churned like a storm made of metal. Every floor was attached to the glittering spiral axis and its gears. Mabel stood, mouth slightly open, as the base spun to let one of the floors turn and lift upward toward where the Navigator demon waited. Mabel felt sure she was looking up into a watchmaker's heaven. There were so many gears clanking and sputtering away so the Grand Hotel could turn on a dime. Mabel was filled with more wonder and horror mixed together than she had ever known. They were tiny bugs in a doll house, two human souls trapped miles down below, hoping to stop a building from eating them alive.

Mabel spun around, but the strange stairwell and the washers were gone. There was only Raymond behind them, his long fingers woven in on themselves like folded spiders.

"I will lead the rest of the way," he said coolly. "If you still wish to follow. I understand this is a lot to process. Why don't I help rouse your companion a little?"

He snapped his fingers and Will's eyes lightened, as if he were just coming out of a drunken stupor.

"Where are we?" Will said.

"Below." Mabel said the word with a hitch of fear in her breath. "Raymond is taking us to the portal. He's the first demon. The original deal maker."

Will glanced back at the concierge and dropped his voice as he leaned against Mabel's ear. "Forget me. Go. Get out of here."

Raymond cleared his throat. "We need to press on. It isn't much farther. This way."

They descended the metal stairs like hell itself was on their heels. Raymond wasted no time making sure Will and Mabel were keeping up. At least Mabel didn't need the map anymore. There was only one path, and it was downward. Will panted behind her, sweat beading on his neck and temples, face flushed. He still didn't look right, as if the poison from Saoirse's bites were still affecting him in both body and soul.

Minutes passed, or hours, but Raymond stopped so abruptly that Mabel almost hit him in the back.

"There is a test you both must pass," Raymond said. "Steel your minds if you can. The worst will haunt you here. Survive, and earn passage to the other side."

Mabel wanted to punch him in his smug face. "Why are you leading us down here? You know what we're here to do."

Raymond only smiled. Over his shoulder, she finally got a clear view of what had stopped him. The stairs, which had descended straight down a moment ago, were now swooping in an impossible arc to lead back up again, this time out into total darkness. No walls. No floors. There was only the path sloping upward before them. To move forward they would have to ascend upside down.

"There's no way we can do this." Will's voice was an echo in an empty house, so far away and lifeless. "How do we go down? Do we go... up?"

"If you wish to complete your journey," Raymond said. "The only way out is up. Don't worry. You won't fall if you stay on the path."

Mabel didn't like how cryptic Raymond was being, or what Will had implied, as they approached the upward stairs. How long had Raymond been here? She had heard nearly everyone's story but his.

"Why are you doing this?" She spun around to ask him, but found that Raymond had vanished.

"Where did he go?"

Will shrugged. "I guess we have no choice. We move forward."

She edged down the gentle slope, holding Will's hand as he fumbled to follow her. She didn't like the way his legs were shaking with every step, or how icy his fingertips were. She had to find a way to help him, but there was nothing she could think to do for him here. Mabel took a step upward and found the experience not unlike walking upstairs, though her body was flipping upside down. She couldn't put another step in front of her.

Mabel felt a hand on her shoulder. For a moment, she could have sworn the hand had claws. "Keep moving," Raymond's voice hissed urgently in her ear.

She couldn't see him, but when he let Mabel go, it was like a graveyard wind had whistled against her skin. Her heart flipped up into her throat as she teetered to keep her balance on the sloping path. Will grabbed her by the wrist as her world spun on its axis. The sensation of nearly falling off the edge reminded her of the moment before she had once jumped off a rock face to take a leap into a waterfall.

"I've got you."

He pulled her fully back onto the path and kept them moving forward step by step until they were fully upside down. Mabel's hair was in her face.

"I think I'm going to be sick," she said.

"You and me both, kid."

They ascended upside down to walk on the ceiling, her hair still fluttering around her face and into her eyes as if she were weightless. Something was keeping her feet planted firmly on the ground. She adjusted the Persephone pin and dug it deeper into her hair, desperate not to lose it before she could confront Raymond over the portal.

Mabel moved forward deeper into the room, toward the hanging chandelier in the middle. Several paintings hung on the wall opposite, all impressionistic paintings in shades of red and gold of screaming faces, every one of them hung upside down. She walked around the ceiling, ran a hand along the twinkling chandelier and enjoyed the icy feel of the crystals between her fingers. It was oddly soothing in such a horrible place.

In the opening archway beyond, there were more rooms of a suite, each more decadent than the last. It took several moments before Mabel realized. She was right back where she started, right back to the very beginning.

"Where are we?" Will said.

"It's the honeymoon suite," Mabel said. "We're upside down in the honeymoon suite."

"Are you okay?" Will said, but he was the one who was trembling from his face down to his arms.

She shivered. "Don't you worry about me, doll. Everything's jake." Her Southern accent slipped through again, a sure sign she was losing her cool. She collected herself. "You look a little green in the gills over there," Mabel said. "Come on. We still have a ways to go."

"Not if I throw up first," Will said.

There was a popping sound, like a pinprick in a large bubble, followed by a chirrup not unlike a bird.

"Did you hear that?" Mabel said.

Will clutched his stomach. "I think there is something wrong with me."

Another popping sound went off, followed by more in rapid succession, until the room sounded like they were standing beside the popcorn stand at the carnival.

The damask was moving. An eye blinked open between the dark

pattern, and when it saw Mabel was looking back, it shut and melted into the wallpaper like candle wax.

"Will," Mabel said. "The wallpaper just looked at me."

There was a thud behind her.

"Will?"

She had spun around too slowly. Will had already hit the floor on his knees, and he was moaning like an animal with its arm caught in a trap while he clawed at his stomach.

"It's inside me. Get it out!"

Mabel rushed to his side to help, but there was nothing she could do for internal wounds. Lucky had helped remove the liquor from her stomach, but she didn't know how to do what Lucky did without demonic powers. She was a human. Helpless. Without Raymond to beg for help, the liquid demon inside Will's stomach was threatening to claw its way out. Either that or the poison in his veins had finally worked its way deeper.

Another set of eyes blinked at Mabel and Will in the wall, but this time, they didn't close.

"Will, I'm sorry, honey. We need to move."

"I can't," he said between gasps. "It burns."

Black pupils peered at them both a moment before deciding to push out of the wall, along with a very distinct, very long face. It pressed farther and farther until a long, black horse skull tore out of the wallpaper with its shiny, black, flat teeth. Sharp fingernails tore back the paper, ripping it apart so the rest of the fleshy body and horse ribcage could poke through. Long, black hair matted around its bony face as the humanoid body stumbled into the room on two legs. Maggots writhed out of what flesh was left on its half-eaten bones.

The horse was something out of Mabel's nightmares. As a young girl, she had stumbled on a dead horse in the middle of her family's field. She had not know where the horse came from, or why it had died on their land, but maggots had made its dead flesh come alive. Mabel had run away screaming at the sight of it. Now this demon wore the same face, and Mabel was slick with terror at the sight of her nightmare made real.

"Will, we have to move. *Now*."

"Okay," he managed to gasp, but he wasn't moving at all.

"I'm not leaving you," Mabel yanked him upward, but there was no paleness left in Will's skin, only green.

Another set of eyes in the wall pushed another face through. A pig snout followed with human hair and hands made of writhing snakes and its ribs jellied over with sliced organs that had long since been excavated. She had seen their faces in her nightmares living on the farm, all of that animal carnage. The hotel had conjured up her dreams, and now it was feeding her nightmares.

Mabel yanked Will up by the arm so hard he was forced to stand as the horse demon and pig demon stalked closer, leaving a trail of inky, maggoty blood in their wake.

Will staggered after Mabel as they fled the upside-down honeymoon suite. Mabel ran down the same hallway she had at the beginning, the same length she had taken when Evelyn was on her heels and dying to make her a meal. It was a mirror world, showing her worst fears. She knew when she found the elevator open, waiting for her like a welcome mat at the end of the hall, that it would only take her down deeper.

Raymond said this was a test, she told herself. She only had to pass it. He said it was a test. She didn't know if she would mentally survive.

Mabel pulled Will inside the elevator and slammed the cage door shut behind them.

The horse whinnied as it tried to press its meaty face through the bars to bite them. The pig squealed, pushing its half-eaten flesh between the golden bars. Maggots dropped from its face onto the elevator carpet. It took all her strength to keep Will from falling over into their waiting claws.

"Stay with me, Will," she begged, but his heavy, boxer frame slumped against her small form. She heaved him in the other direction to the floor of the elevator, where he collapsed, unresponsive. Mabel punched the elevator button hard and fast to head downward. When the elevator descended, leaving the nightmares behind, tears welled in her eyes.

"He will survive," Raymond's voice said from everywhere and nowhere. "Come down and see, Mabel Rose. I have been waiting for you."

The elevator flew down level after level, so far Mabel didn't know when it would end. She closed her eyes, praying to any god and every entity that would listen to keep them safe. The elevator cage hit the bottom floor with a great clang, shuddering the metal around them.

"We're here, Will."

He didn't respond.

She peered out past the elevator cage without opening the door. It felt safer with it closed. The room they had entered was the coldest room of all. Mabel had to rub her hands frequently along her arms to keep from shivering. The floor ahead was flat slate, as were the walls and ceiling. They were in some sort of cave. A distant wind whistled from some opening in the darkness beyond.

Evelyn was wrong. This place wasn't saving people. It was hell. She had never been more certain of anything in her life.

"Will, you have to walk."

His eyes fluttered open. They were totally green now. "I can't."

"You have to." She tried to hide the terror from her voice.

"You just can't let me go can you?" He coughed, ragged and deep.

"Come on." Mabel shook him, refusing to cry. Crying meant conceding. Crying meant giving up. Crying meant admitting what she didn't want to admit. "No, Will. You're going to be fine. I'll go to Frank, to Raymond. I'll make a deal. I'll do anything. Please."

"That's exactly what I wanted to hear."

Raymond appeared on the other side of the cage. He slid the door open with a gentle clang. "Come, Mabel. I have something to show you."

Will reached into his bellhop's jacket and pulled out the spell, making sure Raymond didn't see as he stuffed it in Mabel's hand. "Give him hell."

"I will." She cupped Will's face in her hands and kissed his very green cheek. "I'll save you, Will."

Mabel left Will in the elevator. She took Raymond's outstretched hand. She knew it was always going to come to some moment like this, from the second she had entered the Grand Hotel on the Upper West Side and Evelyn's second mouth had unzipped for the first time. She knew it the moment she had struck the deal with Frank West and every moment after. Everything Mabel had done, every pocket she had picked, had led her here. She didn't know what she was supposed to do with the spell Will had given her, or if she could really kill Raymond, but she trusted she had to be the one to try. She was the thief, the sleight of hand, the magician—it always had to be her.

Raymond led her past granite walls into a bleak abyss, down stone steps that echoed with empty footfalls. The walls pulsed as if sensing that they were there, breathing in and out in sighs at the presence of life. Mabel turned to see a face in the stone looking back at her and it was so lifelike that she let out a small cry.

Raymond turned at the noise. "What do you think the walls of this place were built from? Here, people dream, and it all feeds back into building more levels of this hotel. The more bodies, the more delights the Grand offers. Dreams are baked in the literal fabric of its foundation. Every dream and every person becomes a part of the Grand Hotel in the end."

Raymond's voice was sadder than she could ever picture him actually feeling, and she wondered if he was trying to elicit a response from her. As she took each cold, windy step further down, Mabel felt nothing but a detached resolve of what must be done.

When they reached the bottom of the rocky staircase, their footsteps echoed across a wide stone cavern. There was a hole like a well in the floor, all unfeeling gray stone, and whispering that Mabel could not be sure was the wind or hundreds of voices. That was the whistling sound she had heard before, but up close it was so much more than just one note. It was everyone, every voice softly begging to be heard, every lost soul that had been swallowed by the pit.

"Don't get too close," Raymond cautioned.

"I'm not." Mabel was not sure what she expected to find, peering down. The city beneath filled the cavern endlessly in every direction with dots of red light. The city's buildings, its towers, were crystals growing up from the darkness beneath. There was a distant boom that came up from the cavern and the floor shook so hard the errant rocks vibrated around Mabel's feet.

"Is that what I think it is?" Mabel said, but her throat was like sandpaper. There was no water in this place, only emptiness, and she could hardly wet her throat to ask another question.

"Yes," Raymond said. "The city wants you down there. It wants us all down there."

Mabel clutched the spell tight in her fist as she backed away from the opening. "Why did you want to show me this?"

Raymond placed his hands decidedly behind his back. "This is not the only hotel, you know. There are many ways down, many hotels, many deals. We're merely one of them." Raymond nodded at the pit below. "As you've seen, the only true way out is to join us, offer your talents to us, but you've managed to skirt all of that process. You were the first to get your soul back, and yet you did not leave this place for the cold world above. You've succeeded, Mabel. I congratulate you most heartedly."

She bristled at his compliment, unsure what game he was playing at.

"Still, I must ask, and you must forgive my rudeness if the question is too personal. If you have your soul, why stay?"

A thought occurred to Mabel, a plan, but she had to maneuver quickly, carefully. "I stayed to make a new deal."

But Raymond was gone. Mabel was left standing alone beside the pit, which somehow seemed even higher up with Raymond gone. She didn't know demons could just disappear like that, but it itched at the back of her neck that she knew exactly who Raymond was, and maybe had always known who he really was. She unfolded the spell and read the parchment again.

Reverse to Return in One Offering.

The heavy brown paper held a circular spell with triangles and symbols weaving in and out of each other, but Mabel couldn't read Demonaic. She stared at the two people, one clearly Henry West, and the other clearly Raymond Black. One soul. One exchange.

"The way I see it, you have two options. One is to undo Henry West's deal, which would turn the hotel and everyone in it back to the original state they were all in before the demons came, but costs the unpaid balance of one soul. Or you can summon the original demon, turn him human, and kill him."

As Mabel remembered what Marty had told her, she slowly removed the Persephone pin from her hair.

Footsteps fell on the cold stone behind them. Raymond descended, cradling Will's ashen body in his arms. He was all skin and bones now, so frail that his body might have been made of paper.

"Get out of here, Mabel." Will's voice was as thin as his body.

She could have. She knew that, but still, Mabel lingered. She unfolded the spell in her hands. The drawing of Henry West was shaking the hand of someone tall and nondescript, someone with long fingers and cold eyes.

"You require one soul," Raymond said. He laid Will gently down on the rocks beside Mabel's feet. "And the original demon for that spell to work. Both are accounted for."

A part of Mabel had always known. There had always been something about Raymond. He had always been a walking shadow, somehow different than the rest. His face shifted into paler features until he had no eyebrows, no nose, only large eyes the same black as a hole in the ground, and two sets of horns: one that hooked around his ears like a ram's and up above his head another like a stag's crown.

So why was he standing here so willingly?

"Raymond," Mabel said, tossing aside the spell. "I've come to make a deal."

"It's as I've always told you, Mabel." Raymond's voice was as rich as dark chocolate cake, and his words melted in the air. "You need only ask."

A fresh wind howled up from the city Below. She had to be patient. She needed him closer.

"What do you desire?" he asked. Again, Raymond's voice came not just from him, but from everywhere around him.

"I want to undo the deal Henry West has done. I want you to return everyone's souls to them."

Raymond waved a long, clawed finger back and forth. "An exchange must be paid in equal value."

"Very well," she said. "I offer myself."

Raymond wagged his finger at her as if she had been a naughty girl. "You offer me one eternal soul, Mabel Rose Dixon. Henry West made a deal with his soul to remake his hotel into a safe haven for artists, but now it is filled with souls who offered themselves in exchange for their precious dreams. To undo the effects of Henry's deal and all the souls thereafter, you need to offer far more than one. However, I am willing to make a deal for what you really want. One soul for a soul. Saoirse for one of yours. Do you still offer yours in exchange for hers?"

Mabel swallowed hard. She thought of Will, who wanted to become a star to feed his little sister. She thought of Saoirse, who didn't want a life on the streets. She thought of Lucky, the burlesque star lured in by Frank to help him ascend, who had found her home here, and died so that Mabel could have this chance to undo it all. She had to succeed and make him think she was here to cut a deal and not turn him human to kill him. If only she could lure him closer.

He snapped his fingers and there Saoirse stood by his side in her clown outfit. Her eyes were flat white, and her teeth were longer and more pointed than before. There was green around her mouth and a feral look in her eyes. Mabel's heart clenched. This wasn't in the plan.

Saoirse made a lunge for Will's body and Raymond grabbed her by the arm.

"Will you offer Will's soul in exchange for Saoirse? Or yours? Choose, and I will call her soul coin up from the pit. The little girl will get her soul back again. She will leave this hotel, free as a bird."

All her life, Mabel had looked out for herself because no one had truly looked out for her. She looked at Saoirse's small, snarling animal face, and her heart broke. Mabel had the Persephone pin. So long as she had that, it didn't matter if she lost her soul. She could turn human again. She could defeat Raymond. It was the only way to get close enough to him.

"Who will it be, Mabel Rose Dixon? Make your choice."

It wouldn't be right.

"Mine," Mabel said. "I offer my soul in exchange for Saoirse. All I ask is that you heal Will. Let them both go, and I will give you my soul."

"Done." Raymond flicked a long finger and a small light ascended out of the pit and into the mouth of the little girl. She swallowed the light down and collapsed next to her brother. Raymond waved his hand and Will turned over on his side and spat up the same sticky bile Mabel had thrown up earlier. The wounds on his arms disappeared. Color returned to his face. He slumped back down next to his sister and slept. They dreamt soft dreams and Mabel's heart swelled at the sight of them reunited again.

Raymond strode over to Mabel. He was even more frightening up close, but Mabel refused to tremble. She clutched the pin tight, concealing the tip behind her arm.

He opened his mouth wider than Mabel thought possible, his face opening like a flower. The light inside Mabel, the one she had worked so hard to return to her body, left like a butterfly out of her throat and floated down into Raymond's stomach. His face peeled back together, stitching to weave into something more human-shaped, and that was when Mabel struck.

She lanced Raymond's chest with the Persephone pin. He let out an unholy scream as his body fell back. Black wings beat against the ground, ones that Mabel had not seen before. They hurtled wind against the flat stone as Mabel glimpsed the hell beast's leathery true form, more decaying animal than man, writhing with a silver pin in its chest. The percussive wind stirred up by the wing beats blew Mabel back, all the way toward the opening.

Mabel's body fell.

She had only ever jumped off of a cliff's edge once before. There was a waterfall in north Georgia her brother Avery had dared her to jump off once, and the fall was much too far down, but Mabel did it anyway. She didn't want to be seen as less than the boys, didn't want to be called "weaker" because she was a girl.

There had never been anything weak about Mabel, and she had never felt true weakness until now when the city Below was rising up with dark arms to catch her small body on its many rocks below. High above her, the hole she had fallen through drifted farther and farther away as the ceiling opened two huge, cat-like eyes. The stone ceiling bared its teeth, and Mabel finally saw the true face of the real demon of the hotel. She had fallen through its mouth, had lived inside of its walls. She had been digested by its stomach. The hotel itself was the demon, and its walls were made from the souls it had swallowed.

A crack split across the ceiling forming the demon's mouth as the enormous face boomed each word down to her.

"Be not afraid, Mabel. Our city welcomes you. All are welcome in the Below."

All this time, she had been living inside the demon she had been searching for, the original deal maker. The Grand Hotel itself was the demon—was Raymond—it had been him all along watching her every move and granting her heart's desire.

Mabel wanted to close her eyes to the truth, but she couldn't. She refused to shut out her own death, so Mabel fell, opened arms, into the night city with all her fear raging inside her turning into a light-headed calm. Screams rushed up to greet her. The city Below and its dark lights grew brighter as the wind whipped her face and her hair scratched her eyes. Mabel's stomach clenched and she had to remind herself to take a breath in.

Mabel had done what she came here to do. The first time Mabel had given up her soul, it had been for herself. The second time, it had been for Will. She was glad it was for him. Did demons die from falls of this height? Or would Mabel black out before her body was crushed? Her mind was already beginning to swim with the euphoria of dropping from such a height.

At least Will and Saoirse were safe.

Something whipped around her stomach and snagged her with a sudden pull. Her knees were tugged in her face and her wrists clacked against her heels like a rag doll.

Mabel was aware of what had happened very slowly. First, she processed that she was not falling any longer. Second, she registered how very high up she now dangled above the porcupine quills of the city. Third, someone had caught her with a rope around her waist.

"Don't move," Frank called down. "I'll pull you up."

She craned her neck skyward up to confirm, but it really was Frank West standing at the opening in the ceiling clutching a rope that held her by the waist. Mabel closed her eyes. Of all the people that could have caught her, the last person she expected in all of heaven and hell was Frank god-damned West.

The rope pulled her up foot by foot, back up toward the long well she had entered. Somehow, it was even more terrifying to be pulled up above the city than to be dropped down into it. Mabel found herself clinging to the rope more out of instinct than actual will to survive. Were it not for the rope cutting off her lungs from shouting, she would have yelled for him to stop, to just let her fall, but she didn't really want to die? Then again, she didn't want to live as a demon again either.

Frank pulled her up and over the edge. Mabel collapsed and lay there, trembling and panting. As she caught her breath, she searched for Raymond, for Saoirse, for Will. It was just her and Frank sitting on the cold stone floor, listening to the voices cry in the distant wind.

"They're not here," Frank said gently. "Raymond took them."

"I thought," Mabel said. "I thought I killed him."

"I tried to tell you. You fought the same battle against Raymond I did. I tried undoing the original spell and lost. I wanted to undo what my parents had done, cast out the original deal. I tried the spell and failed."

"The spell required one soul," Mabel said. "You didn't have one to pay it."

Frank nodded. "You tried the Persephone pin too. It doesn't turn Raymond human. The hotel is Raymond. That form he takes as the concierge is a mirage. The hotel itself is a demon. All the lower levels are his body and his claws are dug into the upper levels. He grants your deepest desire or your worst nightmare. There is no fighting him, not unless you're more powerful than he is."

"Your ascension." Mabel's body felt so far away.

He nodded. "Yes. I want to ascend to defeat him."

"Why didn't you tell me the truth?"

He frowned. "When you came here, you only cared about being the star. If I told you, you wouldn't have believed me that I was doing this for the good of everyone."

She swallowed, but it did little to wet her froggy throat. "We need to find Saoirse and Will."

Frank's expression turned sorrowful. "Likely Raymond took them to the Laundry level."

She lay there shivering on the floor, unsure what to do with all this information, considering the possibility she had never entertained before. Had all she done been for nothing? Could she wrap her head around helping Frank West? She had burned with hatred for him more than anyone. If she had known then what she knew now, would she have believed him? Helped him? He was right. She wouldn't have.

Frank offered a hand to her. "Can you walk? I'll bring you back to your room."

Her eyes filled with so many tears she couldn't see his face anymore. "Yes. I think so."

"Come with me." Frank pulled her up to her feet. "Help me, Mabel. Help me ascend. Help me beat Raymond. It's the only way to free this place from my parents' mistake."

She swallowed hard. "Isn't he hearing our conversation? If he is the hotel, doesn't he know what we're planning now?"

Frank considered a moment. "He knows. He thinks I won't succeed in such a complicated spell as ascension. He thinks you're too stubborn and self-involved to willingly feed souls to the Canary diamond. He thinks we won't be able to stop him, especially not as a team. He knows how much you resent me."

Mabel held the hand of the person she despised most. "If I help you and you succeed in killing Raymond, do you promise to let everyone go free?"

"Yes," Frank said. "I promise. Feed the Canary diamond. Finish collecting souls with your performance. At the May's Eve Ball, I will cast the ascension spell. I will be above him. I will be stronger than him. Then, we can finally kill him."

"Okay." Mabel let Frank lead her toward the stone steps. "I will help you ascend. I will help you beat Raymond."

CHAPTER TWENTY-ONE

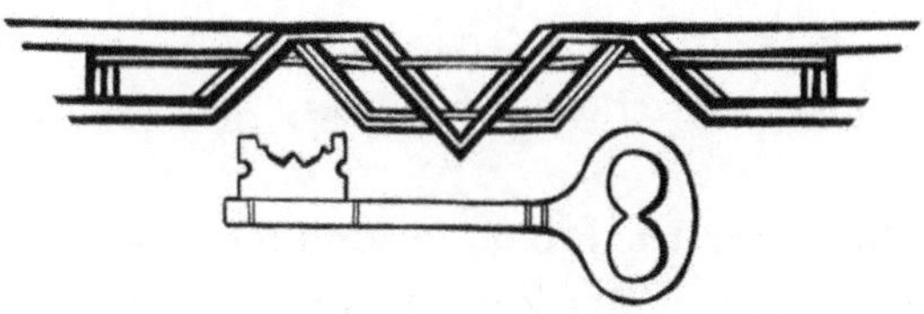

When Mabel returned upstairs with Frank West, she decided to fully invest herself in the promise she had made. She woke every morning, ate the breakfast the bell-hops brought her, attended rehearsals with Frank, ate a light lunch, attended more rehearsals, and ate a quick dinner alone. She moved through her routine with no sign of Raymond, or Evelyn for that matter. Frank proved to be quite the coach in her acts, pushing and challenging her to the limits of what she could achieve. He praised her when she exceeded his expectations and gave her thorough notes when she missed her mark. Apart from her performances, Frank was the only person she spoke more than a few words to each day, and the loneliness hit her like a knife every time the curtains dropped and her performance was done.

Her evenings were once again filled with blood. More and more people came to see her until the auditorium was filled to standing room only, and even when the amount of people swelled out into the hallways, Mabel had never felt more alone. Without Will, without Lucky, even without Evelyn, the days passed on together as one long red river before her, never-ending, or beginning, just always rushing toward the inevitability of the night of the May's Eve Ball.

The first week passed in a flurry of silk and blood. Still, Mabel gave every performance her all. She performed her magic acts, tapped until her body wanted to collapse under the heat of the stage lights, sang her heart out, and each night, her second mouths returned. Every night, the mouths in the palms of her hands fed. Every feeding, she grew a little less satiated. As the numbers climbed higher, Mabel got used to the feeling of blood on her skin. Every time she left the drenched auditorium, the sensation of the warm, coppery liquid bothered her a little bit less, until the feeling of blood on her skin was as natural as makeup. The Canary diamond, her one constant companion, glowed brighter with every patron they devoured together.

At first, Mabel had tried to go looking for Will and Saoirse. The hotel had always known. She knew this was because Raymond was always watching her. Still, she would try her best to change her appearance, cloak herself, and sneak out of her room after dark to try to find the Atrium. Every attempt sent her wandering long hallways only to be led straight back to her room.

On the seventh night after her journey into the bowels of the Grand Hotel, Mabel sat in her room and stared at the wall of her bedroom, where she knew Raymond watched her. She directly asked the starry night sky of her suite if he knew what she was doing. She asked the wallpaper if he knew she was going to find some way to free Will, but the hotel and Raymond gave no reply. Still, Mabel knew Raymond was there in the foundation, watching her, listening. She knew this bedroom and all its finery was merely an organ inside a greater beast. She was simply a speck of dust inside his mighty frame.

Raymond was wrong to not fear her, to ignore her.

She and Frank would be the ones to bring this whole beast down. Mabel was a talented enough thief to steal souls from Frank's penthouse. She was clever enough to fight her way down to the pit, to turn her friends and herself human, and to face down the original demon and nearly defeat him. Mabel would free Will and Saoirse, even if it took all that was left of her humanity to do it.

She and Frank had their plan. While Frank ascended and fought Raymond at the ball, he would be distracted. Mabel could travel down to the Laundry below and save Will and Saoirse, along with anyone else she managed free along the way. She had made her way to the

Laundry before. She could go there again, though she wasn't sure how. Mabel had lost the map somewhere in the Speakeasy while she was drunk, but it did not matter. She could find her way down again. She could ask Marty to show her the way if she had to. All she had to do was put her head down and do her job until the May's Eve Ball.

At first, Mabel counted the days, but after that first week, she gave up marking time. What she did mark was the count of the bodies.

7. 26. 31. 43. 51. 76. 81. 95.

As the kills mounted, she did not have Will to talk to, no icy Evelyn to spar with, and no Lucky to confide in. Maybe that was for the best. Maybe it was better Mabel couldn't ruin any more lives than she already had. Maybe it was better she was alone.

Each day, a little more of her humanity withered away. Where once she was numb to the mechanical motion of it all, putting her head down and waiting for it to be over while she drowned in isolation, despair became an emotion Mabel had come to forget. There was only the light of her fame, the never satiated emptiness of her hunger, the warmth of her nighttime feedings. She almost entirely lost the focus her task of tricking the hotel so she could find Will and Saoirse again.

After her 95th kill was devoured, Frank approached her backstage.

"I need to go away for a bit. To prepare for the ascension. Can you perform these last five kills on your own?"

"Everything's jake," Mabel cooed. "I got this handled."

For a few days, Mabel saw no sign of Frank West. She did not see him in his box seats or backstage after her performance to tally the bodies. The night the final body dropped, the day before the May's Eve Ball, Frank finally returned.

Mabel stood drenched in blood and the afterglow of completion. She tapped her heel impatiently in the center of the stage for the final man's soul to be sucked inside the Canary. Mabel clenched her fists until her second mouths pleasantly retracted, a sensation which used to bother her, but now felt like zipping up a plush velvet purse. As the hundredth soul shined inside the Canary, the yellowish tint changed to a sunset-warm gold.

She closed her eyes. She had done it. Mabel had collected one hundred souls for the Canary diamond. With the Canary fed, Frank could complete his ritual, and he could ascend and finally defeat Raymond. Mabel expected to feel relief, but all she felt was satisfaction. Being a demon felt so gorgeous, and her newfound confidence was infectious. From the back of her mind came an errant butterfly of a thought that she could free Will and Saoirse, and get her soul back, but part of her didn't want to change back, and that feeling was growing stronger and stronger by the hour.

Mabel left the bodies on the empty stage. It was not her job to clean them up. She knew the hotel—that Raymond—would absorb what remained of their flesh and bones, that the carnage would be used to make more levels down below.

She descended the stairs and her long beaded train trailed blood like comet stardust in her wake. Mabel strode down the hall, thinking of perhaps asking the Navigator to let her up to the bar a little later, where she might have gin and a *snack* to go with it. She had started trying that approach the past few days that Frank had gone away. Raymond would allow her small excursions with the Navigator upstairs to the bar, but never down. The small taste of freedom and downing of spirits had contributed to feeling less and less inclined to do the work of freeing everyone and getting their souls back. She was always so hungry. Her stage performances were starting to not be enough to fill the sharp hunger of her second mouths, which had begun to feel more like the hunger pains in her own stomach than an ache down her arms.

Before hitting the bar, Mabel would need to change into something glamorous first, something that made her look like honey to all the bees in the beehive.

Mabel glided into her suite. She peeled off her stiff clothing, tossed them in a laundry bin, and dove into the hot bath that was already waiting for her. As she scrubbed the debris off her body, she was not bothered anymore by the blood and viscera that coated her form. Mabel thought instead about what shoes would best match the green gown she had thought of trying on later tonight.

It was all so silly to her now, her resistance. If she had just played along, no one would have died. Well, some people would have, but they were her patrons. They should donate to the arts. There was no worthier cause than that.

She took her time scrubbing herself clean, unsure of how the water stayed clear when she was so drenched in red. Truly, it did not matter. Some of the hotel's secrets, it could keep. Mabel was sure she could stay for years and never learn how Raymond did all that he could do running the hotel and keeping track of everyone in it. He had started a steaming bath for her, and that was all that mattered in that moment. He was giving her exactly what she had desired, just so long as she paid back her stay in pounds of flesh for Raymond to build more levels, bigger attractions, and more temptations.

Mabel stood in the center of the wide bath and climbed out of the bubbly waters. She should be feeling like Botticelli's Venus emerging from the sea foam, fresh and newly made, but her thoughts were more akin to a Bosch painting of hell. Everything from that night merged together and broke apart in strange shapes, attaching and reattaching as if each image were made of clay, but she was strangely... happy about it.

Mabel shook away her happiness. She truly was losing her humanity. She tried to picture what still made her human.

Will's face. Finding Saoirse. Her pain at seeing Will collapse as he turned green. Him saving her from falling off the upside-down staircase. The teeming black pit filled with red eyes. The horse and pig in the walls. The entire cavernous world that seemed to stretch into a whole other sky beneath her feet. Teaming up with Frank West.

And Will.

God, she hoped he and Saoirse were all right. Mabel had to admit how much she had lost all but an inch of her humanity, and that inch was her feelings of guilt over not saving Will and her feelings for him. On this last day of her partnership with Frank and the arduous task of collecting one hundred souls for the Canary accomplished, Mabel did not wonder if she would ever be human again. If she even wanted to be. Instead, a small voice whispered the truth. She would do her part to save Will and his little sister, but she didn't want to be human anymore.

Mabel dried off with a fluffy white towel, desperate to drown out what had happened in the pit, and the pure job of being a demon seeped back into her bones.

There were several more sets of men's silk pajamas waiting for her in the drawers when she exited the bath, and she relished them all. Of course, Raymond had provided for her. She was his star after all. Since returning up above, the Grand had tried to offer little trinkets, gifts large and small. A box of chocolates on a bedside here, a bouquet of fresh flowers there, her mother's home-cooked meals every night, but none of it could satiate her hunger for more.

She slipped on a white and mint striped pajama set, dried her hair, and brushed it thoroughly before slipping on a pair of matching silk slippers. The luxuries did not register to her the same way anymore. At first, the nice gifts brought no comfort to the loneliness that had seeped into her like poison, sapping her will to fight her fate a little more each day, but now they somehow felt so good and cool against her skin. Did she not deserve this from working so hard? Did she not need a little comfort after sacrificing so much of her sanity to this game between Frank and his concierge?

When she went to get dressed in her evening gown, Mabel found a tray of high-end gin, vodka, and whiskey options waiting for her back in her dressing rooms, with clear coupe glasses. It was Raymond's way of saying there would be no going upstairs. She was to stay in tonight. Again.

She huffed as she poured herself a glass of gin. Mabel had never drunk as much as some of the other girls at the Richardson Boardinghouse for Women, and didn't really need any liquid courage to perform, but she had accepted a sip from a flask of bathtub gin when it was offered. Mabel took a sip of the better stuff, not bothering with any ice, and its smooth bite was just enough to calm her racing thoughts.

There was a knock at her door, interrupting her irritated thoughts.

Mabel set down her coupe glass. It was a late hour for visitors or room service, but she had started to receive presents at all hours, day or night, since her return. She did not bother to put on a robe to open the door.

Frank stood in the middle of the hall with a bouquet of a dozen red roses. "I've come to congratulate the star on her final performance."

Frank's gray eyes were so pale now, they were almost white. He wore a dark suit of deepest blue, which made his fine features seem that much fairer, but he had always been so handsome. His hair was slicked back tight against his scalp as if he were doing a test run for the ball.

"Come in," Mabel said.

Mabel shut the door behind them and followed Frank over to the patio set and bar cart. She slid into her chair, her instincts pricking that something about this was a trap. He laid the roses on the table in a rustle of velvet flowers.

"You were sublime, my dear," Frank said. "I could not have asked for a better host to the diamond."

Mabel played with one of the rose petals between her thumb and forefinger. "I have done what you asked. The Canary has eaten one hundred souls."

Even if she hadn't been robbed of her soul again, Mabel was not the plucky, headstrong girl she had been when she first entered the Grand Hotel a month ago. After her descent with Raymond and her loss of Will, she was now like rock cooled after a volcanic eruption, heat still teeming below the surface, all instinct to defend herself hidden beneath cool detachment. In the slow loss of her humanity, Mabel had evolved into something and someone even she no longer recognized, something entirely more fearsome.

"You are the epitome of the American dream." Frank smirked and started mixing something up for himself with Mabel's many liquor options. "You reached for the stars and found them. Then again, the American dream has a way of bringing out the worst in all of us in our climb to the top. In you, it brought out your best. You are now a truly fearsome creature."

Mabel tapped the tip of her finger to her lower lip, pondering. "Much as I love the company and the flattery, why the visit? Have you simply come to collect the diamond, or is it something else?"

Mabel pondered this as Frank shook the golden mixer in both hands and poured golden liquid out of the mixer into a coupe glass.

"Some for you?"

"Yes, thank you."

Frank smiled as he poured another glass for her. He cradled the pair of golden, frothy drinks over to Mabel and handed her the fuller one. "Lemon drop. It's so good, you can hardly drink just one. I learned to mix my own drinks after learning how many demons thought they could run the hotel better than me."

Mabel took a sip. It went down surprisingly smooth. "You learned from Evelyn."

Frank slid into the seat opposite her. "Yes, Evelyn. She wanted to take over the hotel for me, you know. It was the only way she would agree to find the Canary diamond and bring it to me. I don't know why she didn't understand that once I ascend and put an end to Raymond, that will be the end of the Grand Hotel as well. Oh well. She will eventually figure it out. All that is done with now that you've succeeded."

"Not surprising," Mabel had no emotions left to sound shocked. "However, are you sure Evelyn will just let the hotel go without a fight?"

Frank frowned at his drink. "She's abandoned her cause."

Mabel raised an eyebrow. "Oh?"

"By the time I followed you and Will down into the speakeasy, Evelyn was gone. After you stabbed her with the Persephone pin, I heard rumors she apparently begged Raymond to turn her back into a demon and fled."

"Should we worry?"

"That Evelyn will affect the ascension? No. I should think not. I will be too powerful for her to stop me if she does return to reclaim what she thinks is rightfully hers, demon or not." Frank's eyes narrowed as he tried to read her placid face. "What is the one thing that could help you in your position right now?"

Mabel had given a lot of thought to what she would do once the Canary was fed, and Frank ascended, and she was free to go. She had fought so hard for so long to save Will and Saoirse, but now that Mabel was almost a full demon herself the entire endeavor seemed so pointless.

Where would she go when Will was returned to her? Back to begging Ziegfeld for a job? She could see Frank's future stretched out ahead of him. How he would open his own theater only to be unable to fill the seats. She saw how he would die in ruin. Evelyn was right all along. She had come to New York to be a star, had to abandon her dream due to over-saturation, only to shift again into a career that was about to die. Was this the life cycle of the artist? Forever doomed to evolve or be crushed by the wheel of capitalism?

The Grand had offered a reprieve to all of that, a safe bubble away from the passage and destruction of time. All it had cost was a little blood, and now it was about to be gone forever.

Was that what Mabel really wanted now?

"What could you do now that could possibly help me?" Mabel's nose wrinkled at the sound of her own voice. She realized how her voice sounded so much like Evelyn now. Detached, worldly, and oh so bored by everything. "You promised to let everyone go. That's all I ask."

"I know." Frank downed his entire drink with one tasteful gulp and reached into his breast pocket. He removed a very long, silver hat pin with a woman's face at the end. "But that's out of my control until after tomorrow night. You know that. I can, however, give you back your humanity."

"The Persephone pin?" she said.

Mabel should be gob-smacked at all of this, but not a drop of emotion registered on her face. Her feelings had all been replaced by the general ennui of becoming a demon over the past month. Mabel should feel relieved that the return of her soul was in sight, or rage that he had not first offered the return of her friends. There should have been tears streaming down Mabel's face at all he had done to her, but all Mabel felt were vague shadows of her old human emotions passing like distant clouds on the horizon. How Mabel wished she could cry.

Mabel took the pin from Frank and could only stare down at it, unsure how the pin could be back here in her hands. Last she saw the pin, she had stabbed Raymond with it. "Where did you get this?"

"A deal is a deal," Frank said, resting his hands on his lap decidedly. "I've come to return your humanity."

Mabel chewed her lip for a moment, debating. "You mean I can prick myself with this and... just walk away?"

"Yes. Tonight, if you wish. Now that I have the Canary, I will return Will to you. Turn yourself human. There is no need for you to stay." Frank sighed. "When I lost my soul in my parents' deal, Marty gave me that pin to free myself, but I waited. It was tempting to become human again, I won't lie to you, but I waited. I had hoped to turn Raymond human, kill him for taking my parents. I tried the pin on Raymond and banishing spells, but nothing worked. He is the hotel itself, a poison with roots too deep in the Grand to be expelled. I soon discovered the only way to purge the poison would be to kill him, but one would need to outrank him. I don't know what will happen at the ball when I complete the ritual, or even if I will ever be human again once it is complete, but you've truly saved us all, Mabel. Without you, I'd never have been able to stop him. I can't thank you enough for what you have done."

"Frank." Mabel waited for a beat, feeling nothing. "I don't want to be human anymore."

The silence that followed between them was so thick, Frank shifted uncomfortably in his seat. "Is this not what you wanted? Could it be that the famous Mabel Rose Dixon has finally become... a demon?"

She said nothing.

Frank considered Mabel. "It's your choice. I leave it entirely in your hands. Do you wish to attend the ball instead? You've earned a celebration after all, and your revenge. You could help me take him down. If you choose to become human now, I promise to deliver Will and Saoirse to you, unharmed."

Mabel stared down at the floor, processing. "To remain a demon is what I want. I want to make sure he pays. Will, Saoirse... I still want to spare them. They are the last of my humanity. I'm not sure I want to be human again."

Frank set down his coupe glass gently on the table. "If you help me, I will doubly make sure I extract them in time before this place comes tumbling down. They will go free."

Silence filled the room again, less palpable this time. "Thank you, Frank."

Frank got to his feet. A debate played across his face as he chose his next words carefully. "You're welcome."

He strode over to stand beside her. Frank was so close she could smell his cologne. It was musky and heavy, like clean forest air. "May I?" He indicated if he was allowed to help her remove the Canary diamond.

She moved her hair to the side so Frank could remove the necklace. When it unclasped, she sighed that the heavy weight of the Canary Diamond was gone, but the moment Frank removed it, Mabel immediately missed its absence. It was like she had just had a limb removed.

Frank pocketed the Canary. "I know you. You will not stay a demon forever. At the sight of your loved ones returned to you, you will prick your skin with the Persephone pin and become human again. You still have your heart. Don't forget."

Mabel turned around and stared deep into his cool gray eyes. "And what of you?"

"I will be too far gone to ever resemble anything human again. I'm sorry I didn't tell you before. I always knew what this would cost me."

She reached a hand for his. He took her offering and treated her hand like it was the most precious thing on earth. Frank gave a deep bow and kissed the back of her hand like a knight.

"It will all be worth it to avenge my parents, to see you human again. Don't remain a demon. Your heart and passion were what made you shine, Mabel. Don't ever dim that light or let it go out. That's the light of artistic inspiration, and my parents valued that ingenuity and talent above all else."

Mabel's heart swelled with another emotion, something like her hatred turning over into a newfound warmth. She wasn't sure if she liked it, if she loved him or burned with hatred for him stealing her soul in the first place. For the first time, she saw Frank as the young man caught in his parents' deal and unable to escape its expectations, not unlike every old money family she had ever met.

"When you kill Raymond at the ball," Mabel whispered. "After you're done, come find me. I could use the Persephone pin on both of us. We could walk away from all of this human, together."

Frank's handsome smile faltered, and he let go of her hand. "I will come find you, but... I make no promises. Besides, you're not even sure you want to be human anymore." He gave her the warmest smile she had ever seen. "I may not survive this fight, and I need you to accept that now, or we will never win against him."

Her breath hitched at the thought of watching Frank die, but she couldn't find the words to tell him.

"See you at the ball tomorrow night, Mabel Rose. If you'll have me as your date."

"Yes." She managed to choke out the word with great difficulty.

When he turned to go, Mabel's eyes were so full of tears she could not see him leave, and she hated him for it.

CHAPTER TWENTY-TWO

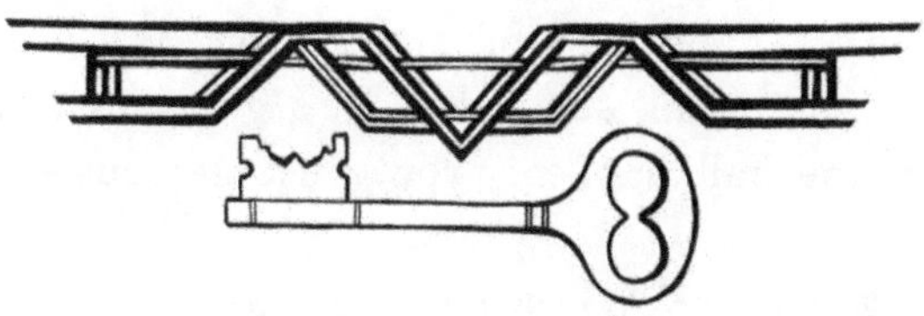

The night before the May's Eve Ball, Mabel no longer dreamed human dreams. When she slept, she saw pictures that felt more like memories playing out on a film reel across a silver screen in black and white. The night of the ball, Mabel wandered the halls of the Grand in her sleep. She knew every moment in her dream was somehow real; the ability for her spirit to leave her body while asleep was one of her new demonic abilities. She could walk through the liminal spaces of the Grand and pass among its patrons like a ghost. Mabel's spirit moved through the quiet Atrium, wandered the empty dining hall, passed unseen through the betting circles and the merry carnival, but no one saw or heard her. Mabel did not worry or pay any mind. This new ability felt as natural to her as her second mouths feeding, but instead of satisfying her lust for flesh, she was satisfying a new and more curious need for information.

This must be how demons watch and prey upon the living, she thought to herself as she traveled downward on to the speakeasy where the party was still swept into an endless golden roar. Mabel sank through the stage floor and her feet softly landed on the cold stone of the Laundry level.

She treaded carefully through the rows of washing drums, careful not to step on the bodies of the many sleeping workers who were given only a cot and blanket to rest their heads on. Mabel wandered for what seemed like ages until she found Will sleeping near the back of the massive room. His face was tense as he slept on a cot beside Saoirse. His hair was matted, hers was in two messy braids, and their hands were raw and bleeding from scrubbing.

In her dream, Mabel leaned to kiss his cheek, but Will woke with a start.

"Mabel?" he whispered.

"When the ball happens, run." Mabel's voice was a faint whisper in a lonely wind. "Frank succeeded. He's going to take Raymond down. When the ball happens, you must get out of here. Take Saoirse."

"What do you mean?" Will swallowed hard, eyes wide with fright.

"When the ball happens, the whole hotel will come crumbling down. You need to escape this place before tomorrow night."

Will nodded slowly, processing. "They're asking for volunteers to work the ball tomorrow. I'll volunteer us to help, but..." He took his time before asking his next question. "Are you a ghost? Did you die?"

Mabel shook her head. "I'm not dead. I think this is a new ability."

"That makes sense." Will's brow furrowed. "You have horns now."

Her hand went up to her forehead. Her finger ran over the curve of the tiny points that had emerged on either side of her scalp. She gasped.

Mabel woke with a start to the smell of fresh flowers. There were new arrangements on every table in her bedroom and balloons with silvery streamers hanging from the ceiling. It was lovely, but she couldn't suppress the way her body shook as she climbed out of bed. What time was it? There were naturally no windows on her basement level of the Grand, no real way to tell time by the fall of light, but Mabel had the sense from the way her body was slick with sweat and her movements were groggy that she had slept through the whole day.

Mabel ventured into the dressing room, stretching. She helped herself to the French-style breakfast of fruit, brie cheese, and warm croissants that waited for her on the little cart beside the bistro table with more jam and butter selections than she could possibly ever eat. She wasted no time devouring what she could. Mabel wanted to find what new dresses and shoes had been laid out for her to peruse. As Mabel entered the dressing room, she faltered, and her hand went over her mouth in shock. In the center of the starlit room was a mannequin dressed in the most gorgeous gown Mabel had ever seen.

The dress was beyond any magazine clipping or advertisement in *Vogue*, or any dress she could conjure from her daydreams. The mannequin donned a gown fashioned from the shades of sunset, with a delicate rose at the bottom melting upward into a dark blue velvet sky. The layers draped off the mannequin in navy velvet and flounced pink tulle, with deco arch patterns woven from sequins, pearls, and sparkles that Mabel could have sworn were diamonds. There was a satin cape with starbursts around the collar, and a great moon in a feathered and beaded accompanying headpiece resting on the mannequin's forehead. It was Georges Méliès' *A Trip to the Moon* in dress form.

Mabel was beside herself at the stunning gift. She ran her hand along the fabric in utter disbelief that such a dress could exist, and she was meant to wear it. Mabel thumbed the delicate beadwork, both afraid to touch it and unable to stop. This could be the dress she turned back into a human and escaped in, or the one she remained a full demon in. It was a dress of fate, and Mabel could only hope she would be brave enough to face whichever path lay ahead of her.

There was a note tucked in the front breast of the dress. Mabel already knew who it was from without having to read it.

We have had quite the journey together.
I hope you find it in your heart to forgive me for all my shortcomings.
Will you dance with me tonight before the end of it all?
- F

She folded up the letter but did not throw it away. She left the note on her vanity table where it slowly unfurled beside a brand-new selection of makeup and perfumes to choose from, all spread across the glass countertop.

Mabel slipped into fresh undergarments and stockings before trying on the luxurious dress. It was a dream against her skin, lighter than air despite the heavy detail work, and Mabel suspected Frank had the staff seamstresses weave in some sort of magic that made it so light. She stared in wonder at her reflection as her dressing team entered the room and did her makeup, selected pearls and diamonds for her wrists and ears, and chose for her a set of buttery satin heels encrusted with more diamonds. When it was time for the reveal in the floor-length mirror, Mabel could not help but gasp. She had never looked more expensive in her whole life. Mabel did not recognize what she saw in the mirror.

She would dance with Frank. It would be a fine way to wish him luck before he faced Raymond.

As she regarded herself in the mirror, the dress was so beautiful, it took her a full minute to notice Will was right. There had indeed been a change to her face while she slept. She ran her index finger over the smooth surface of the tiniest red demon horns jutting out of her forehead. They were so small, no bigger than a thimble each, but they were impossibly huge in Mabel's mind. Her blue eyes were gone. Now, they were pure blood red.

"Has it happened?" Mabel asked the hotel, her tone calm, merely questioning. "Am I a full demon now?"

Raymond did not answer, and it was only then Mabel noticed that each of her attending ladies had pure white eyes and small white demon horns of their own. At the sight of them, what she had lost pierced her heart. Mabel Rose Dixon, the dreamer from down south, the spunky girl who had come to New York with big dreams and swift fingers, was gone. She only felt the tiniest twinge of regret and knew that was the last whisper of her humanity.

"Yes." Frank's voice drifted coolly from her open door. "But don't worry. They're only a sign that the transformation is complete, not that you can't come back from it. If you do end up choosing to leave the underworld."

At the sight of Frank, all of her doubts and regrets of losing her humanity evaporated like steam. Mabel gaped at the sight of him. He was devastatingly handsome in his black coattails and slicked back hair. Frank shooed the team away, and they retreated out into the hallway in a flurry of maid skirts, leaving the two of them alone.

"Are you still my willing escort for this evening?" She struck a seductive pose in her dazzling gown. Mabel had no desire to resist the temptation of him anymore. That part of her humanity was also gone.

He grinned. "Of course. Will you accompany me this evening, Mabel Rose Dixon?"

"I will indeed."

He held out a hand to escort her. "It would be my honor."

As she accepted his warm hand in hers, the silver Persephone pin caught her eye. The pin was so pretty with its woman's face and gentle pomegranates. It might yet come in handy.

"Wait just a moment. I forgot the Persephone pin."

As Mabel picked it up and slid it into her feathered headband, Mabel had to remind herself over and over again she could become human again with one prick.

"So you've made your decision?" Frank's voice was like being laid down in silk sheets. "When the night is done, I hope you'll choose to be human again somewhere far away from here."

"I haven't made my decision yet," she teased. "And what of you? After you become a prince of hell, what will you choose?"

"This hotel will be rid of the poison," Frank said. "That's what ultimately matters. The levels that are Raymond's body and blood, erased. Only the old building will remain, in theory. I want to return the hotel to the grandeur of what it once was before my parents made their deal—a shabby, rundown excuse for a hotel, but a haven for the arts just like they wanted."

"And you?" Mabel asked quietly.

He did not answer her as they left the suites and departed for the Atrium at their leisure.

Mabel was given no formal invitation, so she was not sure where this big party was supposedly taking place. As Frank led her toward the golden Navigator, Mabel wondered if Frank didn't want to answer because this transformation meant no turning back. She wondered if he would be more powerful than Raymond by the end of it, and the Persephone pin would do nothing to turn him human again. If he would even want to be human.

"We wish to join the ball," Frank said to the Navigator.

The Navigator turned her golden face to smile down on both of them.

"Access granted."

The gears behind the walls clinked and spun as the circular Atrium turned on its central axis. Now that Mabel had seen the great below and how it all worked, she had a better understanding of the floors enveloping each other, shuffling and stacking like mechanical cards. The Atrium's gears slowed and finally settled on a long hallway with great, creamy columns. Angels held up vast curtains of delicate pale pink and bright gold. Frank wrapped his arm around Mabel's and paraded her down the hall as if they were an item, as if their relationship was the talk of the town. He escorted her over to the massive double-door arching entrance that looked like the gates of heaven.

The doors parted before them as they approached. Frank and Mabel glided into the ballroom like two dark birds flying across a golden cloud and entered the most massive, decadent room Mabel had ever seen. Above their heads, there was a stunning painting of angels sweeping across the heavens, leaping beside a winged Pegasus and Apollo's chariot. More columns towered around the room with different Greek gods holding up each pillar. In the center was the mighty bearded Zeus sitting atop his throne of clouds in Olympus.

Despite its grandeur, Mabel did not feel as small or uncomfortable as she might have before. With her humanity gone, she was in her element in every situation. Powerful, peerless. Becoming a demon had taken every doubt away and replaced it with a juicy confidence that flowed in her veins like fine liquor. As Mabel let Frank lead her, she glided across the room in all her dark splendor. She was drunk with the feeling of power being a full demon gave her. She and Frank turned every head they passed, human and demon alike.

The demons were easy to distinguish from the common humans. In the ballroom, they did not bother with concealing their horns anymore, or the shade of their eyes. The humans were all of New York's finest elite, each of them amused and clearly thinking they were attending the most exclusive costume party of the year. Scattered throughout the ballroom were various performers Mabel recognized from the circus downstairs. They performed fire swallowing and acrobatics, just like the Van Doren's troupe used to do nightly before her acts, but Mabel did not feel the pain of their death anymore.

Mabel passed conversations of wealth inheritance and stock market deals, all of which involved more money than she could conceptualize or ever possess. They were her patrons, all of them, and her mouths were hungry to taste their flesh, though she didn't need to feed the diamond any longer, only herself. Now, her only desire was to feed her insatiable hunger and give the rest to the city Below. All of the blood must flow to the city Below.

The ballroom's double doors opened with a great bang. Evelyn entered the ballroom like an eclipse in the most magnificent peacock gown. The lights in the room all lowered in her presence, though not a single lamp had dimmed.

Evelyn floated straight to where Frank and Mabel had stopped dancing. Her eyes didn't leave Mabel as she tapped on Frank's shoulder. "May I have this dance?"

Frank hesitated. "Play nice, Evelyn."

"I'm always nice," Evelyn simpered. "Until I'm hungry. Besides, I have no stomach for demon flesh. Your star is safe with me."

Frank released Mabel into Evelyn's care. She swept up a confused Mabel into her arms. An energetic jazzy number filled the ballroom, but it was more subdued than the speakeasy's vibrant melodies. Evelyn twirled Mabel around so that the full sunset of her dress spun across the opalescent floor, then brought her straight back into her arms. Mabel's cheeks grew hot as Evelyn drew so close their breasts touched.

"You got your horns." Evelyn dripped every delicious word from her mouth like they were precious diamonds. "About time. I grew tired of dealing with your silly human tantrums."

She was a vision in forest green silks. The accents on her flounced gown were similar to Mabel's, but the blue and gold sequins with mother-of-pearl beads formed a peacock that stretched from her chest down to her knees. The delicate triple layers of pearl rows in her headpiece lay against her dark bangs and ended with a peacock feather that framed her sharp chin. Her horns were also back again, and they were twice Mabel's horn size over each brow.

Normally, Mabel would have been terrified to see Evelyn back in her full demonic glory. Now that Mabel was a full demon, nothing surprised or really even scared her anymore. She could easily take Evelyn in a fight if she had to. *When* she had to.

"How wondrous a demon you are." Evelyn said. "You really should have always been this way. Being a demon suits you."

"What do you want?"

Evelyn pressed her cheek against Mabel's. "Why, revenge of course."

"How predictable." Mabel sighed every delicious word into Evelyn's ear. "Back to your demon form and still as ugly and unoriginal as ever."

A beat passed between them as the women stared daggers with their eyes at each other. Mabel's gown fell like water over her curves as she turned her head to fully lock eyes with Evelyn.

Mabel straightened. "Are you here to eat me? Or are we to become bosom friends?"

"Little mouse," Evelyn replied, "I do not forget. I do not forgive. However, I did not return for you. When tonight is done, this hotel will be mine, and when it happens I suggest you run. Because if you stay in *my* hotel, demon or not, I will finally feast on your flesh."

Mabel noted that her usual fear of standing so close to the demon who had tried to eat her on multiple occasions was absolutely gone. Lucky was right. There were some perks to becoming a demon, including losing her human nature to constantly act like a prey animal instead of a predator when threatened. She thought for the briefest impulsive moment to let her second mouths devour Evelyn, but Mabel did not want to risk stopping Frank's Ascension.

"Not if I devour you first," Mabel said with a cutting smirk.

Evelyn giggled as she spun out of Mabel's embrace. "We shall see who devours who by the end of tonight, won't we? You and your beau might have big plans but trust me when I say they're all for nothing."

"What do you mean?"

Evelyn chuckled that terrible laugh of hers and cupped her hand behind Mabel's back. "Raymond knows everything."

Mabel's eyes went wide as Evelyn dipped her and planted a kiss solidly on Mabel's waiting lips. When she pulled away, Evelyn's eyes danced with triumph.

"Raymond also doesn't forget. And he also doesn't forgive."

Evelyn spun Mabel around but found herself back in Frank's arms. "I thought that would be the right moment to cut back in."

Frank led her across the dance floor, confidence radiating with every step. He was a man who knew his power, knew how to show his gratitude for those who supported him. Mabel was grateful to be back in his arms, even with her newfound confidence.

"Frank," Mabel whispered. "Raymond knows you're trying to ascend tonight. Evelyn told me. He will try and stop you."

Frank smiled at her statement and seemed to ignore the information. "It surprises me, your choice. You're still a demon, and still here. I thought you would have at the very least turned yourself human once you saw your horns."

"Are you listening to me? Raymond knows. He's going to stop you from ascending!"

Frank took a deep breath in. "I know, Mabel. I already made the first move."

"How?" Mabel said.

Mabel did not fight the way Frank led her across the dance floor. Strangely, she enjoyed the feel of his hand in hers, the shape of his broad chest pressed against hers. Mabel had always found him handsome, just like the rest of New York, but he was even more beautiful up close. She was sorely tempted to never leave his arms again.

"I placed the Canary diamond there." Frank nodded to Zeus. "This entire floor has been painted with a summoning circle. All the proper runes and rituals."

Mabel eyed the floor a little closer. It was indeed painted with strokes that were a different shimmer from the rest of the pearl. It sparkled light gold.

"How?" Mabel said. "Raymond has never let me do anything or go anywhere he didn't approve of. How did you manage to hide the Canary diamond and paint the floor in an enormous summoning circle?"

"Angel dust," Frank said. "Gladys painted the sigil weeks ago with her heavenly wings. Raymond can't erase it."

Mabel cringed, remembering she had been the one to defeat his guardian angel. "I'm sorry about her by the way."

Frank shrugged. "All in the past. She was dear to me, but not all things are meant to last."

"What happens now?" Mabel said.

Frank leaned against her ear and breathed his words against the skin of her neck. "In a few moments, I will ascend. I need to ask you for a favor, and will understand if you say no."

"Will it cost me my soul?" Mabel said, breathless.

He leaned in so close his lips brushed against her collarbone. "When the ascension happens, there is a risk I will forget who I am. I may forget your face or forget what I'm meant to do."

Mabel could smell whiskey on his breath, and smoke in his clothes, and something earthy underneath that reminded Mabel of long weekend visits to the mountains when she was young. The old Mabel might have wanted other things, but that Mabel was gone. She wanted to know what Frank tasted like, what living for what she wanted in the moment tasted like.

He moved away from her neck to look into her eyes. "I need you to help me take Raymond down. Remind me of what I'm here to do. Can you do that? Can you face me at my worst? Will you promise me?"

Mabel faltered. "How?"

"Find a way."

She nodded and he kissed her cheek. "Thank you, Mabel."

"I could prick you when it's all done," Mabel said, leaning in until her mouth was almost against his. "The Persephone pin could turn you human again. You could leave. You could finally be free of this place."

Frank's smile was grim against her mouth. "Persephone was a goddess of the human world and the underworld. When I ascend, I will have traveled too deep for even her light to reach me and bring me back to the surface. There will be no saving me. Just as the pin didn't work on Raymond, it won't work on me."

"Frank... why did it have to be at a ball? With all of these people? Why did the ascension have to happen here?"

Frank closed his eyes for a moment. He let out a sigh when he opened them again. "You know why."

Equivalent exchange. A soul for a soul.

"You need a hundred souls in exchange for one's ascent to a throne of hell," Mabel said. "But you might need more to defeat him."

The smile he returned was wistful, almost sad. "Exactly."

Mabel twirled in her chiffon gown at the end of Frank's steady hand. "You don't need to ascend. You don't need to become a prince of hell. Let the hotel go. Let everyone go. You can walk away too. We can leave all of this. I can't let you sacrifice yourself."

Frank kissed Mabel's wrist and kept kissing up along her arm, not stopping until he found her neck. A small moan escaped her lips when he bit down lightly on the flesh just above her collarbone.

"It's already begun," he said.

Beneath them the floor lit up with a golden glow. Frank grimaced and Mabel didn't hesitate. She pressed her lips to his and was immediately surprised by his tenderness. Mabel's world tilted off balance as she found her match in his embrace. He was powerful, with strong arms that caught her up in them, and each kiss explored deeper parts of Mabel than she had ever dared to tread.

She had never been kissed so tenderly, so intimately. Frank knew exactly what she wanted, which made him even more dangerous. A dark part of her desired Frank, and there was no longer any part of her doubting or regretting. There was only demonic want, only need, and right now, she needed to feel Frank.

Just when she thought he was going to kiss her again, Frank pulled away. He was glowing too.

"You, my dear, are a marvel. Never forget it. Besides, you have someone else who needs saving."

Frank let her go and nodded toward the buffet table. Mabel spotted Saoirse, not in clown makeup, but dressed in a small maid's uniform. She turned her back to Mabel while holding a tray of tiny cakes and cookies, which she was offering to the many guests. Mabel scooped up her gown and raced over to her.

"Saoirse?" She placed a hand gently on Saoirse's shoulder.

"Yes, miss." When she turned around, Saoirse's eyes were white. There were tiny white horns jutting out of her forehead.

Saoirse squinted at Mabel. "Do you require refreshment?"

Mabel shook her by the shoulder. "Don't you recognize me?"

Saoirse's face remained placid. "If you would like something else, I can go to the kitchen for it."

Mabel let Saoirse go. "Where is your brother?"

Saoirse pointed over to the bar behind them where Will Donahue was mixing drinks. He was crafting cocktail after cocktail, fully in the rhythm of his work despite the absolute chaos of so many guests surrounding him. Mabel had to elbow two demons out of her way to get his attention.

She waved a hand to flag him down, but he ignored her. Will had the same set of white eyes, the same white horns as his sister, and his face was devoid of all the fiery emotion that had made Will a formidable threat to the Grand Hotel. Now, he had been placated, turned into a demon slinging drinks that got people possessed and poisoned with the liquid demonic. Despite offering herself to Raymond, he had gone back on their deal. Mabel had been the one to suggest they try to get into the ball, but now both Will and Saoirse had lost their souls. Before, she would have been consumed with guilt and self-hatred over ever suggesting they escape the Laundry level. Now, the fact they were demons again merely felt like an obstacle. She had the Persephone pin. She could turn them human again at any time. First, she had to make him remember who she was and why he was here.

Mabel scurried around behind the bar and grabbed Will by the sleeve. He spun around; his fury awakened in her direction.

"Customers aren't allowed back here. Wait your turn like everyone else."

"Will, it's me. It's Mabel." She had to start somewhere.

Will grunted. "I don't know what you're talking about. I don't know any Mabel."

Despite her icy demon emotions, that one statement pierced right through her heart. "I gave my soul for you and your sister."

A small light of memory flashed across Will's face. "Oh yeah. Right. You're the doll that was with us in the pit. You sent us down the wash. Thanks a lot kid, but I got my own problems. You have a nice night now."

"Will," Mabel insisted. "We don't have time for this. You and your sister have to get out of here before Frank's ascension."

But Will was gone. He traded positions with another bartender and moved further down the line away from her. The second bartender, the woman she had seen before down in the basement speakeasy, shut the gate decidedly between them.

"Beat it, kid," the bartender hissed, and went back to slinging drinks.

Mabel burned with fury, but she couldn't do this now. She'd have to come back for them. She raced back into the crowds, desperate to find Frank. The ascension would be starting soon and she needed to be wherever Frank was.

There was a shattering of glass and a cry of pain.

Oh no, Mabel thought. *I'm too late.*

He doubled over and fell to the floor on his hands and knees. He cried out as he curled up in the middle of the party, writhing on the floor. Mabel rushed to his side.

"Frank," she pleaded. "What can I do? Tell me."

He didn't answer her. Frank roared with pain and convulsed on his side. His mouth went slack and the shade of his skin, once warm with life, had turned a sickly shade of gray like ash left in a dead campfire.

A loud crack interrupted the glowing party and its marvelous revelry, and turned Mabel's attention away from Frank. A split had formed in the Zeus statue, emanating from the lightning bolt that was climbing down the statue's arm toward the god's serene face. The statue fractured with the violent yellow color of the Canary diamond and threatened to burst from so much power inside the bolt.

Mabel turned back to Frank and tried to help him sit up. He had gone as cold as a winter lake in her arms. His gray eyes flooded with a poison yellow as he shoved her back. Four slender, black horns twisted gently up and out of Frank's forehead. One set twisted and curved upwards like an antelope in a nature magazine, and the other thick set curved down and around his ears like a ram. Smoke billowed out of his mouth and he coughed against the floor. Thick, black smog poured out of him as his entire body stepped into shadow until all of Frank was made of smoke.

"Frank?" Mabel said.

His black leathery bat wings ripped through the cut of his fine suit and stretched up to fill his corner of the ballroom. That was when Mabel finally registered that the guests were all screaming. She had been so mesmerized by the horror of his transformation that her brain had quieted everything else, but now the actual sound around her had risen to a crescendo of terror.

Everyone was rushing for the doors, clamoring all at once to exit through the pearly gate. The doors remained shut despite their cries, none of them ready to accept their fate. They were now trapped in a gilded ballroom cage. Mabel stood her ground against the tidal wave of their pressing bodies of stitched sequins and glittering gowns, determined to stay by Frank's side.

There came a high whistle sound from inside Zeus's lightning bolt. A woman grabbed Mabel's arm and begged for her help, but the woman's eyes quickly filled with yellow smoke. The human woman dissolved into a demon, her eyes a sick shade of yellow as her own set of horns sprouting from beneath her beaded headband.

The Canary was spreading, turning not just Frank, but every human attending the ball into a demon. Mabel stood helplessly as more humans formed second mouths on different places in their bodies and grew new sets of horns of all colors and shapes. Mabel had not anticipated this at all, and she was sure Frank likely didn't know what would happen either once the ascension spell was enacted.

"Frank!" Mabel called. She had to crawl across several people in order to get closer to him. There were so many people running away.

He spun to look at her. Frank had grown at least seven feet tall. He was now a towering cloud of dark smoke sporting a black suit with four dark horns and enormous wings. His two yellow eyes were blazing as bright as the Canary.

"Remember why you're here. Remember Raymond!"

"Francis West," a voice Mabel knew all too well carried over the panicked roar to the enormous prince of hell that now filled the ballroom. "You should have listened to me. Now everyone is a demon, and I grow more powerful from them all."

Raymond parted the crowd, knocking back the bodies of partygoers as if they were merely streamers in his way. Mabel didn't hesitate, even if she was about to witness a demonic fight of biblical proportions.

"Kill Raymond!" Mabel screamed at Frank, pointing in Raymond's direction. "Do it now!"

Frank turned his massive head toward Raymond, who had already begun to shift into his towering demon form.

"As if you could kill me," Raymond said.

Fresh shrieks erupted from the crowd at the sight of two towering demons. Raymond and Frank didn't hesitate to launch themselves at each other, but at their massive sizes, every claw swipe and tailspin sent more of the party flying backward. They were at each other's throats to win control of the Grand Hotel, and at this rate, there wouldn't be anyone left alive to rule.

Frank knocked a human woman out of his way, trying to hit Raymond, and ended up pushing her directly into Raymond's path. Raymond sliced her out of his way and she flew back into the wall. The human woman collapsed with a thud. Yellow light flooded her veins. Horns sprouted out of her forehead. Second mouths formed in her palms as she screamed, then she burst into a cloud of blood and viscera all over Mabel.

She cried out, wiping the blood from her eyes. She wasn't sure what had just happened, if that woman had been affected by Frank's ascension spell, or if it was Raymond's claws that had caused her to burst. Either way, she had to get Will and Saoirse out of there before they were crushed to death by the two titans who were using the crowded ballroom as their personal wrestling ring.

Mabel raced back to the bar, heart pounding in her chest, worried she wouldn't find them in time. She did not fear them becoming demons, but watching that woman burst put the fear in her that one strike from either titan might cause Will and Saoirse to meet a similar fate. She nearly gasped in relief when she spotted Saoirse cowering with her brother behind the counter. Bottles of alcohol shook and shattered once they hit the ground, littering the small space between the bar and wall with sticky shards. Mabel did her best to dance through the debris and reach the siblings. She removed the Persephone pin from her hair.

Mabel grabbed Saoirse by the wrist first and pierced her palm. The little girl shrieked as the white left her eyes, returning them to a normal, human color. Her demon horns shrank back inside her scalp, retreating as if they were never there.

"Get off her!" Will countered by throwing an uppercut straight at Mabel's gut. All of the wind escaped her, and she collapsed face down onto the broken glass. Her hands instinctively went up to protect her face. She was only vaguely aware of the blood filling her palms where the shards had sliced her flesh. The pain from Will's boxer punch was so intense.

Saoirse's lower lip trembled as she shifted her focus from Mabel to the towering demons fighting across the ballroom. "What is happening?"

Raymond's hand crashed through the counter, splitting apart the bar and everything within, sending all three of them flying across the ballroom.

Mabel hit the ground rolling and only stopped when she collided with one of the columns. She lay there panting, unsure of what had happened. She was in so much pain she couldn't move for a moment, but that pain was quickly subsiding. *More perks of being a demon.* She took a big breath and coughed air until her lungs could breathe normally again. She still gripped the Persephone pin tight in her right hand, despite all the cuts from the glass, which were also healing very quickly.

She pushed herself up to sit and slid the pin back in her hair. Mabel didn't know where Will and Saoirse had been flung, but she hoped the blow hadn't killed them. She needed to do something. They were too matched for power. Neither Frank nor Raymond seemed to be winning, and from the growing amount of blood coating the floor, it seemed more and more demons were bursting around them.

Mabel glanced up at Zeus, where the golden Canary diamond glittered in the lightning bolt grew brighter and brighter. It had turned Frank. Maybe it could turn more than one person. She took a deep breath before she thought better of it. She gathered all of her courage for what she had to do next, but first, she needed to climb.

Mabel skirted around the room, past the broken bodies and debris, and raced as fast as she could manage over to Zeus. Her dress was covered in blood, torn in places that caused her to trip on her hem. She took a gob of fabric and ripped pieces away until her legs were free to move and she could run faster. Mabel ran through the carnage, ignoring it all save for the wrestling forms of Frank in his smoke-cloud glory and Raymond in his towering, terrible presence that Mabel could not look at for too long for fear of losing her nerve.

She started to ascend the crumbled form of Zeus. If he hadn't been in pieces, he would have been impossible to scale. She ascended the impossible heap of the massive statue, groping for the hand that held the lightning bolt. The bolt where the Canary was stored was even larger than Mabel thought. It was the size of a Model T, and it glowed with the horrible sickly light of the Canary at its center. She tried to reach in and grab the diamond, but it was so hot inside the lightning bolt, she recoiled. She would have to use her second mouths to withstand the heat.

Mabel removed the Persephone pin from her hair.

Mabel Rose Dixon. You don't want to interfere in our little discussion, do you?

She heard Raymond's horrible voice tempting her, and it was as sweet as sugar in her mind. Mabel took the Persephone pin from her hair and held it fast in her hands. She unleashed her second mouths and gripped the pin in her right hand's teeth.

Don't make me angry.

Mabel struck the tip of the Persephone pin down hard into the space where the Canary diamond met the lightning bolt and pulled until there was a popping sound.

The diamond flew out of its socket and Mabel caught it swiftly with her second mouth in her left hand.

Power swelled inside of Mabel, pushing light through every pore. Everything inside her unleashed with a pulsing brilliance that she could no more contain than a flood of sunlight. Her hands turned to claws and her second mouths grew so large they split her arms apart, but she felt no pain. She didn't feel anything at all. It felt... good. So good she didn't want the transformation to stop. The flesh unzipped between each finger, splitting each of her limbs into tentacles like an octopus with jagged teeth rippling down each tendril. Her arms were two throats. Her arms were two mouths. Mabel herself was towering now over all. She grew until she was high above the other pathetic little squabbling demons below.

Frank and Raymond paused their fight at the sight of her, but not for long. Raymond launched himself at her, but Mabel's arms instantly went to her defense, wrapping sets of tentacles around Raymond's neck. She squeezed his flesh and found it easy to puncture. It was oh so easy to cave in his neck, to squeeze until his eyes went wide. He wriggled out of her grasp and used his claws to tear his way down the floors of the hotel, burrowing away from them.

She had injured him enough to send him running, but she had seen Raymond's real face and knew it was the levels down below her feet.

Mabel and Frank followed him downward, tearing apart the hotel as they descended each floor in Raymond's wake. Each blow they struck, the more the walls of the building—and Raymond—howled in pain. They fell on and on, downward level after level, bringing all of the hotel with them until Mabel and Frank came to rest at hell's opening.

Now diminished, the broken shadow that was once Raymond lay beside the howling maw—the same entrance to hell that he had crawled through all those years ago to make a deal with the West family. His form was much smaller now. It was like a shadow had been given a body. He was flat, slippery, and made of claws and horns. There were no discernible features on his face. Only his orange eyes shone brightly in the dark. Above them, the hotel floors were crumbling, and errand wood and brick and glass kept falling toward them. Mabel didn't feel any of it when the debris collided with her.

"I can give you anything," the Raymond shadow pleaded. His voice was so much weaker now. *"Just name it."*

Mabel wrapped a tentacle around Raymond's throat. Frank leapt up in the air to gather momentum on his great wings and dove down into Raymond, and he shattered like glass.

There was a pressure drop that came so hard and fast, the world muted. Reality bent and stretched around her, sucking inward toward the opening to hell. Mabel went wheeling backward as all the air surrounding her sucked inward.

She had only been near a tornado once. It had sounded like a freight train rushing in a tunnel made of wind, coming closer and closer to her family farm. The portal to hell closing sounded like she was standing not in a tornado, but in a full-on hurricane. The walls pulled inward toward the spot where Raymond had shattered. The lower floors of the Grand Hotel pulled toward the city Below, which was now sucking everything back inside.

Mabel held onto the floor with all the strength her second hands could muster as bodies flew past her into the black hole of oblivion. Demons shrieked as they sailed by her hand like cars screaming down the road, there and then gone. Everyone in the party, every demon, was being sucked back down into the city Below.

Mabel felt her fingers slipping. There was nothing to grab onto but cold slate rock all around her, too smooth to grip. She tried to find her hold again, but her tendrils were growing tired of holding onto the floor against the powerful wind.

Maybe it was for the best.

Maybe this was all how it was supposed to end. Mabel was a high-ranking demon now, just like Frank. There was no way to be human again. Was that what she wanted? Did she want to live as a monster, looking like this, forever?

She could just let go, end it all, let the oblivion of the city Below welcome her with dark arms.

Something grabbed her by the neck and lifted her up, higher and higher, fighting the current of the ballroom. Mabel looked up into the smoky face of Frank's demon form. He carried her up and up into the golden light of the Atrium, on through the broken dome of the ballroom. How he was able to fight the pull of hell, Mabel would never know.

As she passed the heaven mural on the ceiling, Mabel could have sworn she was ascending into heaven itself. Mabel's last sight was of the black hole beneath her devouring everything Raymond had built. Every level was sucked back inside that dark dimension that had been broken by destroying Raymond. It was all falling to the city beneath.

The city wants you down there. It wants us all down there.

Mabel wanted to be in its dark light forever, but Frank was carrying her upward on great wings. As he carried her away, the debris finally snuffled out the red lights of the city Below and closed the entrance to hell for good or a dark part of Mabel's soul almost wished he hadn't saved her.

CHAPTER
TWENTY-THREE

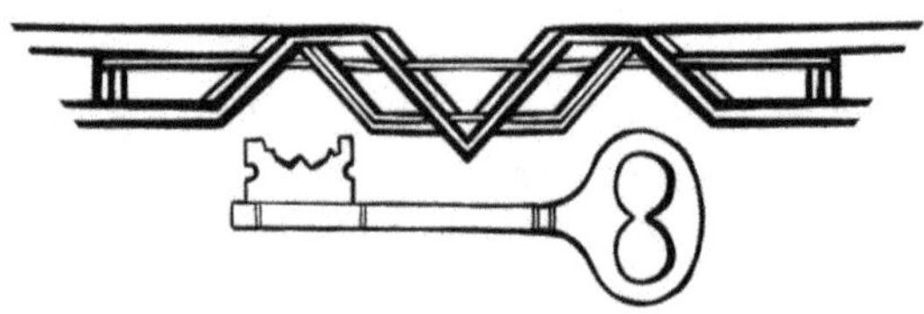

Dawn broke over New York City. Golden morning light streamed through the main floor of the Grand Hotel on the Upper West Side, across its empty floors and broken tiles. Light fell on its liminal hallways. Torn curtains flapped in the morning breeze.

Mabel woke with her face on the cold tile, every bone filled with memory of the torment she had put them through the night before. Her body hummed with the horrible song of pain, and all she wanted to do was lose consciousness again. The Persephone pin lay on its side only a few feet away. She must have held onto it all this time. She reached out for it and tucked it back into her hair.

Was she alive? Was she dead? Did it matter?

She blinked into the morning light to see Will lying beside her. His eyes were closed, his long eyelashes against his cheeks as if he was asleep. At least their chests were rising and falling.

Mabel forced herself up to her elbows with great effort and wheezed in a breath that reached the bottom of her lungs with a sharpness that made her shudder all over again. She crawled on her elbows to draw closer to Will, to touch his arm and try and shake him awake. Mabel hesitated to touch him, expecting to find her second mouths split into tentacles still. They had thankfully retreated down into her normal, human-shaped arms.

She shook his shoulder and called his name until he opened his eyes. Mabel found herself instantly drawn to tears. "I thought you were dead."

He coughed and a great huff of dust blew across the tile. "So did I."

"How did you escape?" Mabel said.

"Frank brought us up here. Saoirse too. I don't know where she is."

"Where is Frank?" Mabel said.

Mabel took in the broken, abandoned hotel. It was now the shape it was before the demon deal. Everything and everyone was gone. So much for saving them all.

Will came up to sit and rubbed the back of his neck. "What happened?"

"I ascended to stop Raymond," Mabel said. "Frank and I killed him together. I may have accidentally closed the portal to hell in the process."

"Well," Will's laugh turned into a happy coughing fit. "That sounds like something you would do."

"Will?" Saoirse was climbing through the rubble coming from the direction of where the dining hall used to stand.

He got up to his hands and knees in time for his sister to hit him with a wallop of a hug. Saoirse cried into his shoulder for a good minute before they parted.

There was still no sign of Frank, but there was a distant wail of fire trucks coming up the street. The building was still smoking as all of the west side came to stare. Mabel sighed as she looked out on the glittering cityscape and the many ogglers that had come to take in the broken-down building that had collapsed overnight. Boy, were the papers going to have something to write about after this mess. She was tired. So tired that she might pass out on the spot.

"Do you have anywhere to stay, miss?"

She turned around to find Frank West standing there, his smoky prince of hell form noticeably absent. He did look a little different. Now he wore a gray sports coat that looked even more refined than before. It matched the color of his eyes. Something else was different about him, but she couldn't quite put her finger on it.

"I can offer you accommodation."

Mabel threw her arms around Frank's neck. "I thought you'd died."

"Hardly," he said into her hair. He squeezed her real tight.

Mabel let him go. "I'm not sure you can offer me accommodation."

They both took in the broken hotel and the smoking hole in the side of the building that exposed several of the upper floors. The firefighters had arrived and were currently trying to douse the many flames.

"Not every room is a smoking cinder," Frank offered. "Besides, between the two of us, I'd say there was enough demon power to patch things up quickly. What do you say? Will you help me patch up the Grand Hotel?"

She held out her hand. "An amusing offering, Mr. West. I accept."

"You're staying a demon?" Will said. Saoirse cowered behind him.

Mabel removed the Persephone pin and handed it to Will. "Yes. I ascended. A prick won't turn me human anymore. But you don't need to stay a demon like me."

Will hesitated but accepted the pin with gratitude in his eyes. He pricked the tip of his finger and sighed as the horns retreated into his scalp and his vision cleared.

Saoirse squealed in delight as she wrapped her hands around her brother's neck. Mabel watched them and supposed she should feel a hint of sadness, maybe even nostalgia at the fact the siblings would now be on their way, but such emotions were human.

"Want to get out of here?" Will asked his sister.

Will and Saoirse clasped hands. "More than ever," she replied.

Will turned to Mabel with watery eyes. "Thank you for all you did and for saving Saoirse. For the sacrifice you made, I'm in your debt."

Mabel crossed her arms. "Don't start your new life in debt to a demon. Go be what you always wanted to be, Will. That's thanks enough for me."

Will gave her his warmest smile as he led his kid sister away from the Grand Hotel one last time. Frank put his arm around Mabel's shoulder.

"I imagine that was hard for you."

Mabel sighed. "Now that I'm a demon, it's not as hard anymore."

Saoirse gave a backward glance toward Frank and Mabel. She waved before Will and Saoirse strode out into the warm dawn of New York City.

"Want to run my new nightly show when the hotel is rebuilt? Promise it will be blood-free this time."

Mabel laughed at Frank and threw her arms around him. "We're demons. You know you can't promise that."

As Will and Saoirse strode down the street, Frank and Mabel drew in for a kiss. They did not see the woman in green who moved like a scarecrow's shadow rise quietly from the rubble. They did not hear Evelyn's footsteps as she retreated from the hotel and scurried down a dark alley. After all, the pair were now in charge of the hotel of dreams with so much left to rebuild, and there was so much more ahead of them to dream about.

ACKNOWLEDGMENTS

Sam Gafford is the reason this book exists, and he passed away thinking his work did not matter and that no one would know his name. When Sam died, I thought a lot about how writers, artists, dancers, actors, musicians, filmmakers, and more produce work never knowing the outcome. I wanted to write about how the entertainment industry is full of dreamers who may never see their dreams come true.

I wanted to dedicate this book to all the artists I've met during my time working in broadcasting, publishing, video game development, and also write about my experience working as an artist in a variety of industries. Most of the people I met as a graphic designer turned animator turned game developer were artists, all of them with big dreams. Most of them wanted to create art partly for themselves for the love of the craft, and partly for others with the secret hopes of making it big in some way someday.

I got my start in publishing back in 2013 and I spent the next decade trying to break in. I was much like Mabel, a starry-eyed former bookseller from the south who was looking to New York publishing to publish my work so I could sit alongside my heroes. What I quickly came to realize after years of rejection was I did the work of writing for the love of it, but I stayed in this industry not for the promise of fame, but because of the people I met along the way. The fellow artists I met–writers, game developers, artists, filmmakers, editors, and more —they became as close as family. I felt like their dreams were mine too. We were all just trying to break in together. I wanted to write a book about them—*for* them. I hope this book speaks to you in some way, and that you don't give up on your dreams.

Particular thanks go to my fiancé, my family, and my two children. Thank you for supporting me during the writing of this novel and all the countless hours I wrote and rewrote Mabel's story. Huge thanks go to my former agent Miriam Kriss for suggesting this short story needed to be a full novel and worked with me until it really shined. Enormous thanks goes to Christoph, Leza, Kaitlyn, Theo, Joel, Angela, and Matthew and the whole team at CLASH for helping me make this dream of a book a real, tangible story I can hold in my hands. Huge thank you to my agent Jolene Haley for working with me on this project and helping me get it over the finish line and out into the world. You're a gem and I'm so lucky we are working together! You all made my dream of becoming an author come true.

Special thanks go to my author friends who listened to me ramble about the book endlessly and offered critical feedback that helped this book become something truly special: Gina Loveless, Erica Waters, Ann Fraistat, Ian Rogers, Lyndsay Ely, Ash Van Otterloo, Briana Morgan, Cayla Fay, Shaun Hamill, Jason LeBlanc, and Lorien Lawrence. This book wouldn't be half as good without your thoughts and wisdom. And a special shoutout goes to Jose Canas, who was the first to be as excited about the idea as I was. This book probably wouldn't have come to be without your enthusiasm to read it.

About the Author

Cat Scully writes and illustrates scary stories for all ages. She is the author-illustrator of YA horror series, *Jennifer Strange*. As an illustrator, she's best known for her world maps and her first picture book, *The Mayor of Halloween is Missing*, by Emily S. Sullivan. When she's not writing and illustrating books, Cat works in video game development and lives just outside of Salem, MA.

ALSO BY CLASH BOOKS

THE PINK AGAVE MOTEL

V. Castro

CATHERINE THE GHOST

Kathe Koja

SELENE SHADE: RESURRECTIONIST FOR HIRE

Victoria Dalpe

INVAGINIES

Joe Koch

EVERYTHING THE DARKNESS EATS

Eric LaRocca

THE BLACK TREE ATOP THE HILL

Karla Yvette

I DIED TOO, BUT THEY HAVEN'T BURIED ME YET

Ross Jeffery

CHARCOAL

Garrett Cook

HELENA

Claire Smith

FLOWERS FROM THE VOID

Gianni Washington

VIOLENT FACULTIES

Charlene Elsby

www.ingramcontent.com/pod-product-compliance
Lightning Source LLC
Jackson TN
JSHW080307110425
82399JS00001B/1

* 9 7 8 1 9 6 0 9 8 8 5 8 4 *